FIERCE AS FIRE

EARTH STONES TRILOGY BOOK THREE

FIERCE AS FIRE

LISA CRAM

THUNDER ROAD PUBLISHING

For my readers
What am I without you?

N
Sea
of
Meura
Winterlands
(Arctakai)
City of Ice
Desertlands
(Seakai)
Forestlands
(Terrakai)
Inception
Great
Ocean

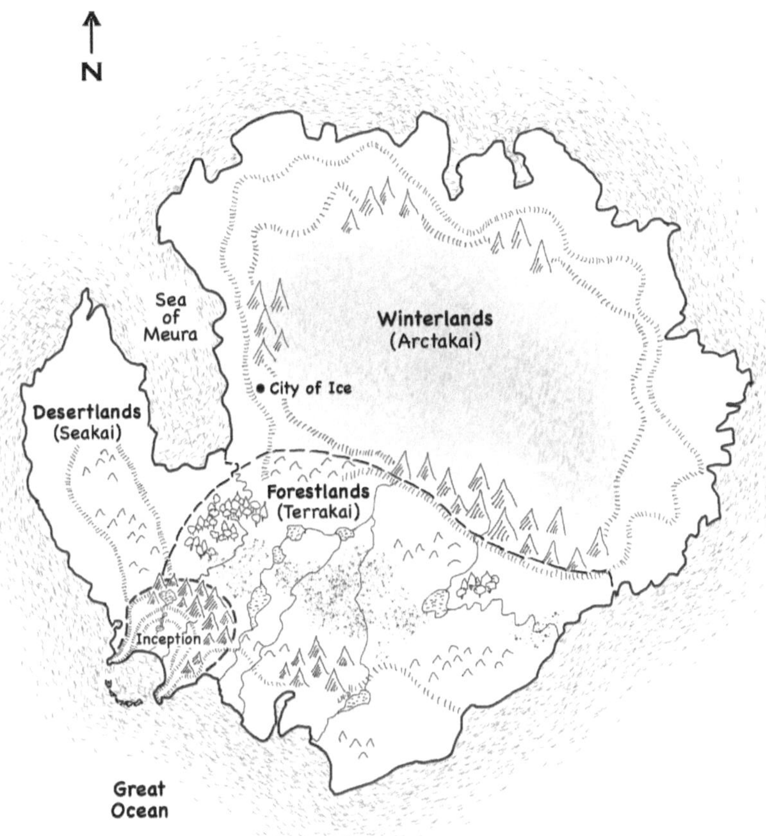

MERLUMA

N
The Ruins
Black Mountains
Deep Lake
Labyrinth
Great Ocean

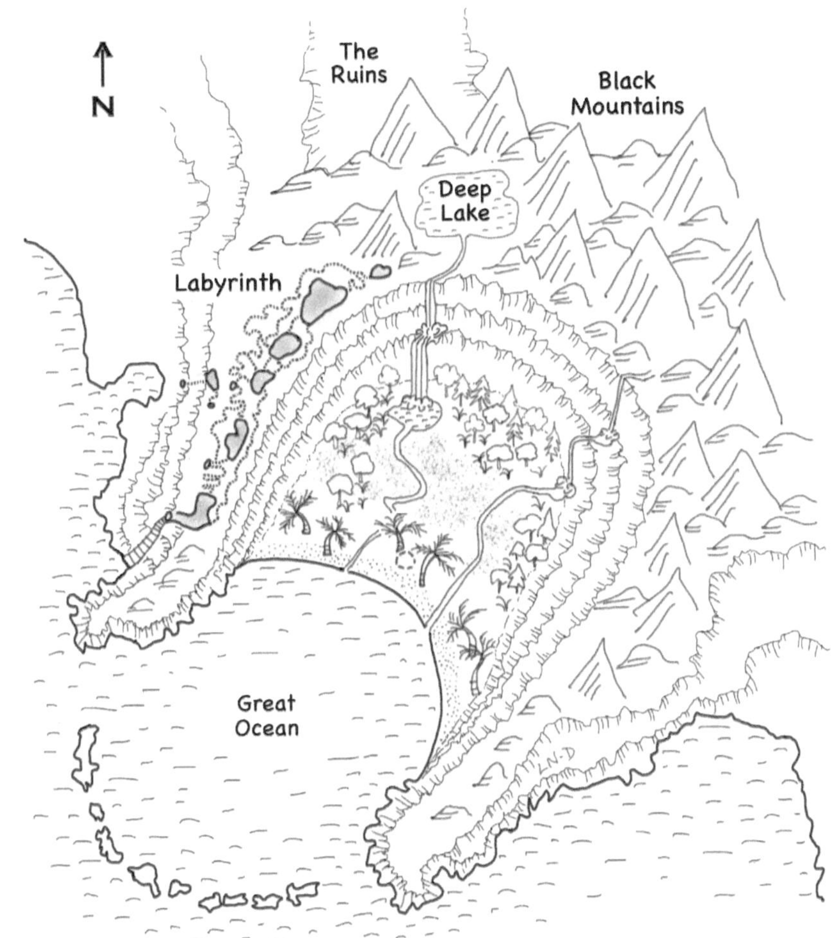

INCEPTION

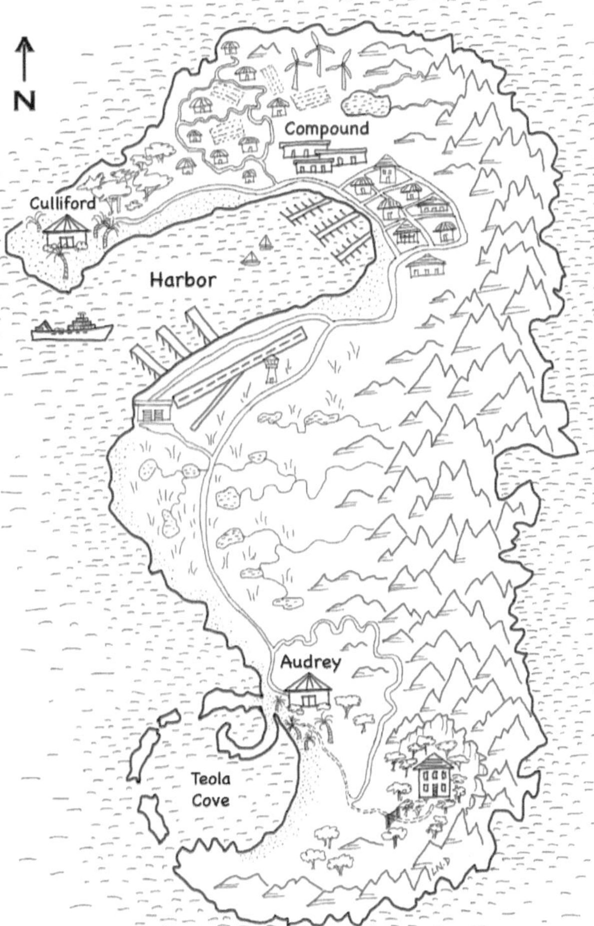

ISLA SALVACIÓN

PART ONE

1

Francesca

THE FIRST TIME AUDREY Culliford met Francesca, she felt as if a warrior goddess had entered the room. The power of her presence elicited the subconscious urge to drop to one's knee and kiss her knuckles—a ridiculous reaction for someone born in the twenty-first century where such an act upon meeting someone was rare and unusual. Yet it felt as if the mere presence of this woman silently demanded that level of respect.

Francesca stood half a head taller than Audrey—who was pretty damn tall herself at five feet, ten inches—and carried an air of infallible confidence. Thick cords of muscle stood out boldly beneath her smooth umber skin, marred only by occasional faint scars from injuries long past. Her eyes—wide-set and planted firmly above high, solid cheekbones—were dark as night and gleamed with high intelligence. She kept her hair short, tightly curling around her skull like a night-watch cap.

Francesca was born in the seventeen-hundreds, a time when she would have been valued for her physique—thick-boned and strong as an ox, commanding the highest bid as a slave. But she dodged that fate by pure cunning and brute force.

Francesca fit in perfectly with Audrey's father's original pirate crew of misfits who founded the Larkian Nation on Isla Salvación in the eighteenth century. She was one of the six remaining crew members who had lived for over three hundred years because of a timely encounter with the Merahvu queen from Earth's conjoined sister planet, Merluma. Queen Ianthe gifted them the secret of a life-extending elixir in exchange for their friendship and knowledge of the Sapien world—Earth.

While she'd previously come to know the rest of her father's original crew, Audrey had finally met Francesca a couple of weeks ago, and it confounded Audrey that the woman standing before her was hundreds of years old. Francesca didn't look a day over thirty-five.

"My name is Francesca "Fixit" La Roche," she proudly announced when they first met.

It was hard to pin down Francesca's exact origins. A Spanish first name and French surname might imply she was from the European continent, but she would be the first to tell you that doesn't mean shit. She was who she was.

When Audrey asked where she was from, she simply declared, "Where else? Earth. I have no tail or means to shock you. I am certainly not from the *other* place."

That other place was Merluma, home of the Merahvu, who did indeed have tails and the ability to generate enough of an electrical shock to kill you twice over.

Audrey quickly learned how she earned the "Fixit" part of her name, which Francesca was most proud of. Because if something needed to be fixed, broken, invented, or reinvented, Francesca was the one who made that happen—like the development of the high-tech suits they both wore and were getting ready to test.

Francesca tugged and poked at Audrey's suit, testing its customized fit. She secured the overlapping seam running from groin to neck but left the hood down for the moment. The suit hugged every inch of Audrey's body, fingers and toes included.

At just over an eighth-inch thick and super flexible, she could move freely and easily manipulate her fingers. It was like wearing a second skin that mimicked a Merahvu's, but with bonus high-tech features, thanks to Francesca.

The suit's material was embedded with minute silicone LED modules and a sophisticated sensory system. Sensors picked up immediate surroundings and the LEDs instantaneously reflected it back on command, rendering the wearer fully camouflaged and nearly invisible to the naked eye in any possible setting. It reminded Audrey of a sci-fi movie where an alien hunter seamlessly blended into the jungle.

The inner mesh layer vented heat and moisture when overly warm and generated warmth when temperatures dropped, maintaining one's internal temperature of ninety-eight-point-six degrees at all times. The suit's self-contained battery was powered by a flexible layer of gold filament and ion nodes embedded in an organic gel. Highly durable, it held a charge for forty-eight-plus hours before requiring a charge by solar exposure or electrical transfer simply by touching an electrified object. That meant the suit could withstand a high-voltage shock, protecting both the suit's sophisticated technology and the person wearing it, and in turn feed that electrical charge back into its battery reserves.

It wasn't exactly like the skin of a Merahvu, but pretty damn close. Added to that were thin layers of graphene to protect the wearer against penetration from sharp objects, even at velocity. Hidden pockets along ankle, thigh, and forearm were conveniently placed for stashing knives or nutrition sticks. A matching pack of the same material was attached to the back for carrying and camouflaging larger items—water bladder, miscellaneous survival gadgets, or even a compact weapon like a mini-cross bow with extra ammo.

The suit was a technological wonder Francesca had every right to be proud of.

Francesca looked down at Audrey. "Are you claustrophobic?" When Francesca asked you a question, you answered it, truthfully.

"Er, I didn't use to be." Being trapped in a powerless submarine sinking to the depths of the Pacific had a way of introducing newfound fears. Ever since the event that nearly took her life, as well as her father and the submarine's captain, Stokes, she struggled not to panic in total darkness and in tight confined spaces.

"Ah, right, I can imagine. That was a lucky thing to survive. Don't tell your father I said anything, but him getting bonked on the head was the best thing that could have happened to him."

Audrey smiled. "I would have to agree, at least once he realized I was not my mother, and after regaining his more positive memories. Accepting the truth about her death and rekindling his relationship with Ianthe has resurrected the man he once was, maybe even better than he once was."

Though she puzzled over the paradox. Her father's initial encounter with Ianthe three hundred years ago planted the seed for all the troubles to come. Before the submarine incident, her father had been hellbent on revenge against Ianthe, with whom he had a passionate affair hundreds of years ago. He believed Ianthe ordered the murder of Audrey's mother out of spite and jealousy. But it turned out it was her jealous mate, Ramasis, not Ianthe, who killed her mother. And now Ramasis had joined the Orankai tribe, their shared archenemy.

"Breathe naturally and be patient while I download the programming for the goggles. You won't be able to see anything for a moment."

Francesca held up a pair of sleek feather-weight goggles that fit perfectly across the bridge of her nose and snuggly sealed to Audrey's face. Stretchy bands held them secure to her head. As warned, the world went utterly black. Audrey gasped when Francesca pulled the hood over Audrey's head and secured it around her neck. She imagined this was what it felt like to have your head bagged right before a hangman affixed a noose around your neck.

"Breathe," Francesca said. "Nothing's gonna happen to you." She gave Audrey's hand a gentle squeeze. "Give me a moment to download the program."

Audrey could hear Francesca's fingers tapping on a keyboard.

Regardless of Francesca's reassurances, Audrey's heart raced, and she felt that sinking dread. She shut her eyes and practiced the breathing technique Dr. Wickman taught her for moments like this. She had worked hard to overcome this newfound fear but still struggled to overcome the sudden onset of panic attacks. Dr. Wickman warned her it could take years, maybe never, to fully recover, and as long as she understood why it happened, she could accept the reaction and manage it.

But... Knowing that didn't make it any easier.

"Okay, the goggles should react to your voice commands now," Francesca said. "Open your eyes. What do you see?"

"I see a white room, and you and me, starkly contrasted in black."

Francesca chuckled. "Sorry there's not much to see here."

Everything in her modestly sized lab was white—floor, counters, ceiling, and walls—and exceptionally tidy. The counters were clear of clutter. Whatever equipment she needed was secured in cupboards, with tools and other implements tucked into stark white drawers. Her computer was fully integrated as part of the lab. An image of a keyboard was rendered in gray on the counter next to where they stood, and the computer screen was projected onto the wall. With this system she could move about the lab as needed or put it away altogether by a simple voice command.

"Try to expand your world view beyond the lab."

Audrey said, "Oh, right, a test, sorry..." She cleared a frog suddenly lodged in her throat. "I want to see my location."

A map replaced the image of the lab, showing the seahorse shape of Isla Salvación in the middle of the Pacific, west of the

Hawaiian archipelago. A red flag marked the ship where they were currently located, docked in the harbor.

Audrey prompted, "Zoom in on *Masquerade Ball*."

The goggles reacted, dialing up one of many Larkian satellites recording details on Earth in real time. The image zoomed in on the deck of the ship with vivid detail.

Masquerade Ball was one of several floating labs where most of the Larkian technological magic happened. The exterior looked like a well-used research ship you might find anywhere in the world and in need of restoration. That look was on purpose. The Larkians, and Francesca particularly, didn't like unwanted attention. Especially from certain governments who would kill to steal the Larkian technology if given the opportunity.

Fake funnels and other extraneous equipment and randomly placed containers littered the deck, hiding the many antennas, dish receivers, cameras, and sensors installed all over the ship. The design of the ship was a technological wonder in and of itself. But the real magic happened below decks. Clean, modern, and uncluttered—a hundred-eighty-degree contrast to the outside. Even the ship's name was a play on this fact.

"What else?" Francesca asked.

"Find team members." A schematic of the ship's interior popped up with three blue dots. One each for Francesca and herself, standing in the lab, and someone waiting outside the door.

"Who's outside the door?"

"You'll see soon enough. Ask about your vitals."

"Report vitals." It took a few seconds, then her goggles displayed her heart rate, body temperature, and blood oxygen level along with a thumbs-up emoji.

Audrey looked around the stark white room. "What else can they do?"

"See in the dark, zoom in and out, render three-hundred-sixty-degree vision, and look up whatever information you request—from the Internet or our internal servers—to name a few. You'll have a chance to play with those features once we begin the tests, but there is one more element to cover before we begin."

Audrey paused, then said. "The neurolink." She noted her heart rate rising through the goggles. The neurolink, referred to simply as nLink, was a nano-neurobot that once injected into the bloodstream adhered to one's brain. "So we can communicate silently, like the Merahvu."

"That, and more. With the nLink you can control the goggles and features of the suit with a simple thought. Like switching on or off camouflage mode or zooming in on a distant object. But yes, most importantly, you can silently communicate with other team members, which is vitally important in sticky situations."

Francesca opened a drawer and withdrew a syringe. Audrey's stomach dropped ever so slightly when she placed it on the counter with a soft *clink*.

She fixed Audrey with her dark gaze. "Are you ready?"

2

Neurolink

AUDREY GAZED DOWN AT the syringe Francesca had laid on the counter. Within the clear liquid was the nLink that Francesca was preparing to inject into Audrey's bloodstream.

"Is this really necessary?"

"Mm-hmm. Only way to fully activate the technology is to link it to your mind. It's the real meat to this wonder suit."

"Where, uh… where do you, stick it?"

Francesca's short hair glistened like steel wool beneath the harsh light of her pristine laboratory. She pinned Audrey with an intense dark gaze and tapped Audrey on the neck where her jugular pulsed with rising panic. "Here."

"And this is okay with everyone?" Audrey knew of course that originally it was not. The first design concept—a nano-neurobot designed to embed itself in the brain, *permanently*—was flat-out rejected by the crew. Tucker, the Larkians' top weapons tech, was quite adamant about where he stood on the topic, sharing his feelings with a diatribe of colorful language including every foul word Audrey had ever heard in her twenty-one years of life plus more.

Francesca clarified. "The first, no. But this version, yes."

"Tucker agreed as well?"

Francesca's gaze wandered for a beat, then she smiled. "Yes. Tucker agreed."

The first version was developed before the Larkians joined forces with the Merahvu, and it had more problems than just being permanent—the communication piece was limited to a short list of words and was not much more advanced than Morse code. So nLink 1.0 was scrapped before it was employed.

Once the Larkians joined forces with the Merahvu, Francesca started working with Wantemo, an Arctakai Healer and Sinto's childhood mentor, to come up with a different solution.

The Merahvu communicated telepathically, using what they referred to as mind-speak or "sharing." Sharing allowed full conversations, privately and silently, within groups or between individuals—and not just with each other. The Merahvu could communicate with other species within the natural world by pushing sensation, emotion, imagery, and intent without the use of words or language. While communicating with other species was much more complicated, Wantemo claimed it should be possible to teach the Larkians the rudimentary basics for communicating with another human. The trick was to find this neurological "mind muscle," then learn how to use it.

Naturally, Francesca tapped Wantemo to teach the Larkians how to find and use this mind muscle. Unfortunately, although Sinto and Wantemo tried repeatedly, they failed miserably with much frustration on all sides. Though they did successfully teach the Larkians how to sense when one's mind was being manipulated and how to ignore it. That was a skill Sapiens, like Audrey, naturally lacked, and it nearly got her best friend, Ryan, killed, so not all was lost with their effort.

With great disappointment, that plan was scrapped. So Francesca suggested they pick up where they left off with the nLink and address the limitations and other concerns voiced so colorfully by Tucker. With Wantemo's help, Francesca came up with nLink 2.0.

NLink 2.0 allowed a simplistic form of mind-speak by plugging into that neuro "mind muscle" directly. Connected hosts could converse in common language and share images and memories.

While this was a great breakthrough, there was a bit of fine-tuning required on the part of the host. A certain level of control was required, or else one might accidentally let slip thoughts best kept to themselves.

Audrey was aware of this possibility. She had discovered this mind muscle with Sinto's help. Why she was able was anyone's guess, but it may have had something to do with the rare connection Audrey and Sinto shared through the Mark embedded in their forearms. She also learned that her father had learned this skill from Ianthe long ago. So it was possible, just not easy, for the Larkians to master.

Thus nLink 2.0 was refined, successfully tested, and accepted.

Having the ability to communicate efficiently and silently in sticky situations was paramount to the safety of the entire team. And if Audrey wanted to participate, she would have to agree to injecting this latest nano-neurobot technology into her body, where it would embed itself into her brain.

Francesca tapped the syringe. "Wantemo guarantees this version should not interfere with normal brain function and will naturally dissolve after a preprogrammed period of time based on the duration of a given mission or the failsafe maximum of seventy-two hours. The one here is programmed to last four hours, which is plenty of time for us to run our initial tests."

Her fingers grazed the side of Audrey's neck and traced their way up her jugular past her ear to the base of her skull. "Injecting the nLink directly into the jugular provides direct access to the basilar artery." She tapped the back of Audrey's head. "We found doing so led to near one-hundred percent success of the nLink finding and embedding itself properly here in the middle brain." She dropped her hand. "In addition to the communication advantage, the nLink is essential for controlling your goggles and suit with your mind. Think of these objects as extensions of your body: enhanced vision and a second layer of skin for added protection, to give you stealth, and to ward off a powerful shock."

"Am I the first?"

"Oh no, no. Don't you fret. My team tests all of our technology on ourselves before sharing with others." She patted her chest. "See, I'm wearing the same suit as you." She tapped her head with a finger. "I implanted my own nLink for our test before you arrived. My team believes in eating our own dog food."

"Dog food?"

"You know, we use it on ourselves, extensively, to make sure it works as designed with no unintended side effects before releasing it to others. And that includes me."

Heart pounding, Audrey looked around the modest-sized uncluttered lab located in the bowels of the research ship where Francesca's team did most of their work. "Sure, let's do it."

"Alright, but it works best with more than just the two of us." She paused and her gaze grew distant again, then she chuckled and shook her head. The door to her private lab opened and another body fully clad in the same type of black suit entered, hood up and indistinguishable. "I believe you know Tucker. He made it quite clear he intends to win back his hat."

"Just now, he told you this, through nLink?"

She tapped her head. "Yes."

The hat Tucker referred to was the prized *badass* hat Audrey won fair and square from him in a regulated UFC-like challenge while killing time crossing the Pacific to investigate a pair of missing research vessels last month.

"So how does it work?"

"How do you talk to your friend Sinto?"

"I just..."

"Think it?"

"Not just. I think what I want him to hear, otherwise..." She felt her cheeks flame. "Something I'm not ready to share with him might accidentally slip through."

Francesca smiled knowingly. "I see. Remember Wantemo was key in our development of the nLink, especially the communications piece, so every aspect of what you have experienced with Sinto should be close to, if not exactly, as you expect. So, are you ready?"

Audrey cringed at the thought of something violating her brain. Maybe it was because it had happened before.

Sinto was the first. Like most relationships there were rough patches between friendship and fevered passion and gaining trust. When they were recently reunited as adults, Sinto had manipulated her memories to hide the fact he had kidnapped her friend, Blake, for his mother, Ianthe. The second time was when Audrey met Ianthe and she rifled Audrey's mind. Both had done so without asking Audrey's permission, an act deemed unforgivable by the Merahvu. Though she ultimately forgave them both, she vowed never to let it happen again and demanded Sinto teach her how to protect her mind from future violations.

"Does the nLink allow you to do more than just communicate?"

"Like what exactly?"

"The ability to poke around where one shouldn't be poking."

"Ah," pause, "you mean can you be manipulated by another member in the nLink network."

"Yes."

"Your father was insistent that feature not be implemented. The rest of us agreed."

"But you could?"

"No one should be able to manipulate your mind using the nLink but one thing I have learned in this world is anything is possible with enough courage, resources, and time."

Audrey had no doubt what Francesca said was from firsthand experience. She had done a little research into Francesca's past before meeting her. Surprisingly, it was Ianthe who told Audrey about Francesca's story.

Francesca went by the more masculine name of Francis when it suited her or the situation. No one ever questioned the gender of the deadly warrior who fought with stealth and by any means. She had harbored resentment for being born a woman in the early part of her life, when she had been taken advantage of and violated at a tender age. When Audrey's father invited Francesca to join his pirate crew after capturing her ship in the Caribbean, he believed she was a man as she often pretended to be in those days. When she finally revealed her true gender, it took his crew a while to adjust to that new fact and Francesca had to work hard to gain their respect. Luckily no one was killed in the process. But once respect was won, they embraced her fully for who and what she was.

"Shall we begin?" Francesca smiled again, using that smile Audrey was beginning to figure out she had perfected over the years: disarming and trust-gaining and very difficult to refuse when coupled with a request, which at this moment meant letting Francesca inject a biologically programmed nano-neurobot inside her brain.

Audrey looked over at Tucker, a statue in his black wonder suit observing her exchange with Francesca. She wondered if a second, private conversation was occurring between them.

Audrey felt the back of her neck prickle.

Most certainly.

The black statue came to life and Tucker said, "Oy! Try it! This thing is awesome. You could harass your opponent non-stop while tumbling on the mat or, better yet, pass subtle wishes to a lady friend without having to stop what I'm doin' to her with my mouth and—"

Audrey held up a hand. "Stop. I get it, Tucker."

Francesca released the seal of Audrey's hood piece and pulled it back, exposing her neck. Audrey took a deep breath, tipped her head, and offered her jugular to the small syringe Francesca held in her hand.

The syringe slipped through her skin and straight into her bloodstream. In and out, like a wasp's venomous stinger.

Francesca helped Audrey secure her hood then donned her own. A perfect rendition of Francesca's face reflected back on her hood's face covering.

That was another cool feature to come out of Francesca's lab. The hood, which was made of a mesh-like material that allowed the wearer to easily breathe even when gasping for breath, could reflect outer surroundings in camouflage mode or paint an exact image of the wearer's face on the hood's outer surface. Once that feature was engaged, if Audrey smirked or stuck out her tongue or if she had a zit, you would see it clear as day.

"Give it a few minutes." Francesca fixed Tucker with a look that could wither the ocean. "Until then, may I remind you to edit your thoughts before sharing with the rest of us."

"Good advice." Audrey said, adjusting her hood.

3

Incompatible

AUDREY WAS BEGINNING TO wonder if testing the nLink with Tucker was a good idea. The guy's mind was going non-stop, bouncing around between mathematical calculations, basic physics, and solving unsolvable technical problems, like how to make the suit work while deep diving. Then he switched to other unrelated and personal topics, like the fact he was buck-naked under the suit and how exhilarating it felt against his bare man bits and the fact he was easily excitable. Inappropriate, non-stop, and distracting.

"I'm wearing the under-layers Francesca suggested and am in total control of my bodily sensations," she pushed to his mind, interrupting his diatribe.

"What? You heard that?"

"All of it, I'm afraid."

"Huh."

Audrey was surprised at how well the nLink worked. Score one for Wantemo! She found herself slipping into the mode of communicating with Francesca and Tucker via thought just as easily has she had with Sinto. Though Tucker obviously hadn't mastered the subtleties of it. She reached for patience, knowing this was an all-new experience for him.

"I got a tip you may find helpful. Start by clearing your mind." If that's even possible, she thought to herself. *"Form what you want to say, as you intend for me to hear it. Push that, and only that, toward me."*

Francesca chuckled, being plugged in as a silent witness to their nLink conversation.

"I want my hat back," he pushed.

"It's my hat, won fair and square."

"Maybe..." What followed his pushed response was a stream of consciousness replaying their challenge on the ship, flowing like a fire hose through the connection: every move she had made, the way she messed with his head doing the unexpected, him falling into her traps, how frustrated he had become, and all the late-night research afterward, obsessing. Him watching YouTube videos of UFC girls fighting, chick flicks, and soap-opera-like shows where women manipulated the men in their lives, and each other, and how he vowed to never find himself under the spell of that manipulation again. His utter frustration at being owned "by a Sheila" for three rounds on the mat in front of the entire *Requiem Sea II* crew, of the crew voting her the winner, of him questioning his masculinity, of how badly he wanted to punch something...

"Stop!" Audrey said out loud. "At least you got one response right, clean and unbridled from your imagination, but that last one... Maybe you should try a Xanax or something before you get plugged in again. Your mind is frantic and exhausting. How do you sleep?"

"Uh." He shrugged. "I don't, I mean, sometimes."

Francesca nodded. "I think we've tested the communications part enough for now. Let's move on to manipulating the suit."

Feeling confident, Audrey imagined herself mimicking her surroundings and quietly slipped behind Tucker, crouched, and wound an arm around his ankles, binding them. She felt a rise of Tucker's heart beat through the team monitoring part of the nLink program; a sudden shift in vitals given as a warning to all connected. Tucker gasped and looked down at her arm, which was mimicking parts of the floor and his uncamouflaged black suit where her arm crossed over.

She stood up. *"Imagine you are one with your surroundings."*

His suit flickered a few times, then he blended into the clean warm light of Francesca's private lab. Shifting from black to white, he became the counter they were standing near, a partially open drawer, and the stainless drawer pull. He placed a hand on the counter and the arm of his suit followed the action, making the movement nearly undetectable.

"Can we try this in the wild?" Audrey asked.

Francesca said, *"Not yet, but I've got a place that might satisfy your request."*

Audrey turned to Tucker, *"You're suddenly quiet, you alright?"*

"Just stayin' out of trouble with you ladies. Best to keep my thoughts to myself and speak only when spoken to."

Francesca chuckled. Audrey whispered a silent thank you to herself.

Francesca opened the lab door. Audrey and Tucker followed her down a stark white corridor, then down a midship circular stairway that deposited them in the bowels of the ship. There was a single airtight oval door with a large wheel.

Francesca spun it open.

Inside was a jungle, bursting with life. It was difficult to determine where it began or ended; the jungle occupied several levels and more than half the length of the ship.

Francesca's hood revealed her smiling face beneath. *"Welcome to my favorite experiment. The beginnings of a self-sustained, fully enclosed natural world."*

A waterfall roared, birds twittered, and bees buzzed—clouds of them bouncing from flower to flower. Clover cushioned the floor beneath her feet. Beetles marched, cutting tracks in fresh dirt. The exotic scent of flowers, damp earth, and tender new foliage permeated the air. There was a pond with lilies, frogs, and fish. A snake slithered between Audrey's feet, flicking its tongue and disappearing into a pile of rock. Light beamed from above and cast shadows beneath trees with moss hanging from their leafy branches, the ground below exploding with fungi. An entire world contained within the bowels of a ship so real Audrey was momentarily pulled back to the time she once spent in the vast jungles on Merluma.

Her adoration of Francesca burst the seams of her conscious mind. "*How can this be?*"

Francesca beamed, clearly proud of her accomplishment. "*I've always been fascinated with nature. We live in a world where the wrong people have the power to destroy it and everything living that depends on it. This has been a pet project of mine for many years. To build a floating island able to sustain an entire ecosystem. I hope we never have need to use it.*"

"*Like the underwater cities the Merahvu created.*"

"*Wantemo was impressed when I showed him what I've been working on. I hope to learn a great many new things from him. I've only had success when working within one climate but hope to evolve into more. At least we can grow fresh fruit and vegetables for the crew since we strive to be independent and always at sea. Animals are a little messier to deal with so we've kept it to flora and limited species of fauna; fish, insect, snake...*"

While Audrey and Francesca were distracted in conversation, Tucker slipped away. Francesca flipped her suit into camouflage mode and the light in the room slowly dimmed until it was lit by a sliver of light like that of a partial moon.

"*Find him,*" Francesca said before slipping away into the darkness.

Audrey found it amazingly natural to invoke the goggle and suit features through the nLink, as if they were true extensions of her body. More kudos to Francesca and her team! The goggles covering her eyes came alive, automatically slipping into night vision, picking up the subtlest of light and rendering everything around her as visible as if in daylight.

Audrey sought for the two others in the nLink network. Francesca was twenty feet away and moving quickly in the opposite direction. Tucker was literally on top her. She switched on infrared tracking and looked up. He was sitting on a tree branch, his feet swinging a foot above her head, clear as day through her goggles' infrared tracking.

"I see you, a blazing heat register."

"As are you, Buttercup."

The red glow of his body faded to nothing. Another defensive feature of the suit: masking heat. Audrey made a note to pin that feature on full-time. Merahvu had evolved naturally to use infrared as part of their sensory sight.

It was her turn to practice hiding and disappearing, and soon she and Tucker made a game of it, wandering through the jungle, tracking each other, and silently conversing through the nLink connection.

After an hour of fully testing the suits' masking capabilities, Francesca gathered them at the door and led them out into the corridor.

"Vitals next." She led them up a level and toward the front of the ship to another lab with medical equipment, including a couple of treadmills.

Audrey and Tucker hopped on and started them up.

After another hour of testing, Francesca announced they were done for the day. But she encouraged them to continue working their suits and refining their communication through the nLink. They had an hour or so left before it would dissolve and cease to work.

Audrey thought it might be a good test to determine how well she could share with Sinto while the nLink was active. Francesca assured Audrey that had been tested between herself and Wantemo with great success. So Audrey tried it herself.

She channeled the Mark buried within her right forearm, the same Mark Sinto carried within his. A unique connection they shared across distance, no matter where they may be. She sensed him across the harbor in the command center, mapping every known portal between Earth and Merluma with Captain Stokes.

The Mark warmed and hummed with life, reaching for its mate buried in Sinto's arm. The connection was made and—

A sudden high-pitched ring filled Audrey's head. She collapsed to the floor. Harmonic vibrations rattled her brain and the tiny bones of her inner ears. Francesca fell to her knees, grasping her head. Tucker grappled with his hood and tore it off, his face frozen in terror as he pawed at his ears and face. Francesca crawled across the lab to a set of drawers and pulled one open.

Francesca tried to stand, failed, tried again, rummaged randomly through contents in the drawer, pulled out a syringe, and jabbed it through her suit and into her neck. After a few seconds she stood gasping, grabbed two more syringes, raced over to Audrey and Tucker, writhing on the floor. She jabbed them in their necks.

The nLink dissolved. The ringing stopped, but echoes and vibrations continued to bounce around inside Audrey's head, as painful as a migraine. The Mark in her arm was on fire, alarm rippling back from Sinto. The last thing shared between them was an unfinished thought—then nothing.

It took several minutes for the three of them to fully recover; to catch their breath, calm their hearts, and overcome a wrenching headache. Francesca took notes on a digital keyboard mapped on the counter with shaky fingers, attempting to record every detail of the experience.

Audrey reached for Sinto. "Are you there?"

Nothing.

"Sinto! Did you feel that?"

A long pause, then "Acutely. Ow."

"Oh shit," Audrey stuck out her arm, "The Mark—I was curious what would happen, so I reached out to Sinto. What does it mean?"

Francesca sighed. "Fatally incompatible, I'm afraid."

4

Sidelined

It took over an hour for Sinto's head to clear. Wantemo had been standing beside him when the mind-numbing sound exploded in his head, liquefying his legs and eating away his consciousness.

One minute they were huddled around a table, discussing the map of portals between Earth and Merluma, and the next he was lying on the floor with a debilitating ring in his head and the Mark in his arm on fire. He had no idea what caused it until Audrey reached out afterwards.

Wantemo whisked Sinto to the *Masquerade Ball* infirmary to join Francesca, Tucker, and Audrey, all of whom were pretty shook up. Dr. Wickman raced over from the *Requiem Sea II* to help and was actively monitoring their vitals. Wantemo scanned their heads with his mind. No permanent damage. During their hour-long recovery Dr. Wickman, Wantemo, and Francesca discussed the possibilities of what happened and why.

If Francesca had not injected the solution that dissolved the nLink instantly, Sinto, Audrey, Francesca, and Tucker may have endured permanent brain damage or possible death.

It was concluded that the Mark and the unique connection between Sinto and Audrey amplified or interfered with the functionality of nLink. As to why remained a mystery. This new discovery about the Mark dumbfounded Wantemo and he suggested Sinto consult with his mother for insight into what it might mean.

"Don't bother," Francesca said, "It means incompatible, thoroughly and completely." She gave Audrey an apologetic look. "I'm sorry, hon, but I'm going to recommend you be banned from participating in any and all nLink operations."

Dr. Wickman gave Audrey a sad smile. "It's most unfortunate, but I stand behind Francesca's assessment."

"I agree," Wantemo said.

And that was it. Audrey was banned from participation in an area she had been trained for most of her life, and that she was most anxious to be a part of. The nLink and the wonder suit Francesca developed was key to Larkian success, and their most promising technology would be employed in every operation moving forward in their battle to neutralize the Orankai.

Sinto struggled to imagine Audrey sidelined to a desk and a headset. That reality cut deep. He felt Audrey's disappointment and distress as acutely as if they were his own.

Sinto reached across the aisle between his gurney and Audrey's where she lay on her back, gaze pinned to the ceiling. He reached for her hand. She took it briefly, squeezing back. Then she gave him a sad smile and rolled to her side, her back facing him.

He closed his eyes. The Mark was always top of mind, especially for Sinto. Why it came to be and where it may take them. Would the Mark draw them closer or rip them apart? The mystery of the Mark thrummed, a growing source of frustration and conflict, mentally and physically. It was an undeniable wedge growing between them.

And now this.

From the day Audrey invoked the Mark and chose him for her lifelong mate, Sinto was both elated and confounded.

The Mark represented a fated and rare connection between two people chosen for a noble and important purpose. By whom or what was a great mystery, as was their intended purpose. The concept of the Mark and the subsequent Joining, in which essences are melded, was a belief passed down through generations of Merahvu. It was a fate so rare that some believed it merely a myth, reserved for propping up the importance of those who led the people, such as a soothsaying queen and her chosen—politically powerful—mate. The fact the Mark chose Sinto and Audrey proved the myth was more than that. It was *real*.

And it had happened once before, long before Sinto and Audrey had been born, between a Merahvu and a Sapien: Sinto's older sister, Leela, and Thomas, an original Larkian, who had since changed his name to Blake—who was currently Audrey's good friend, and as she recently learned, was also her adopted brother. Sinto's mother had discovered the Mark between Leela and Thomas, and in a panic, attempted to sever this mysterious bond. Leela died and Thomas was left in a mental ruin that took decades to overcome. That event reverberated hundreds of years later and was the spark that ignited the rise of the Orankai.

The second part of the myth told of the Joining—which may or may not coincide with the presentation of the Mark—described as an intimate affair where the essences, what Sapiens thought of as "souls," are melded for a common purpose. The ceremony usually ended with the act of celebratory copulation.

The Sapiens might say the mystery of the Mark wasn't a mystery at all, but the luck of two people discovering their soul mate. That it was a concept as old as the universe. Regardless, the Merahvu believed it was something more, much more. Something divine; something that carried great responsibility.

Sinto was beginning to have doubts and wondered if their Mark was a curse. All one had to do was ask Blake if uncertain.

Sinto and Audrey had yet to Join, though Sinto, not fully understanding what it meant and the timing of it, had misread the signs and tried to initiate it early on in their relationship. The timing had been less than ideal, with Audrey having no idea that she had Marked him in the first place. Sinto was thankful for that spectacular failure to this very day.

And Sinto was just as clueless today as he was then as to the when and the how of it.

Joining was an intimate act, both mentally and physically, and one that was causing Sinto and Audrey a great deal of sexual tension. While sex seemed a natural part of it, Audrey argued whether it mattered—that sex was just a joining of bodies that anyone could do, and that what Sinto described was something so much more. Sinto would argue that the *thought* of sex brought on a certain urge for him to initiate that something more. Then she would suggest he lose himself to the physical and keep his head out of it. These arguments and grave questions hung over them every time they touched; would giving in to their sexual desire trigger the Joining? They couldn't agree on that answer no matter how much they tried.

Added on top of that was the rise of the Orankai and the growing presence of Orange in the Pacific that threatened the Sapien world. In sum, it had added up to a certain chilling affect on their budding relationship.

And now this.

Audrey lay with her back to him, hugging a black blanket around her body. Her dark braid hung limply toward the white linoleum floor. He felt that chill growing stronger and wondered if it meant the nLink failure might be the last straw that would eventually tear them apart.

But Sinto refused to accept that possibility. He would do everything in his power to keep that spark alive. The Mark was not the only thing that bound them. *Love* bound them—a seed planted the first time he met Audrey and gazed into her eyes when they were merely ten years old and innocent younglings unaware of the danger and familial conflicts that ensnared them, then and now.

They both acknowledged that spark planted long ago, privately, when seeking out stolen moments of warmth and companionship, regardless of their agreed upon physical boundaries. Chastely sharing the same bed and knowing Audrey was safely cocooned in his arms every night kept him going. He dreamt of the day the Orankai would be defeated and Orange destroyed. A day when they could focus solely on each other, complete the Joining, and live the life they deserved, together.

But dreams didn't always play out the way you expected.

It had been a month since Sinto and Audrey were reunited and the Larkians and Merahvu joined forces. They shared a two-part mutual goal: to defeat the Orankai and to stop the spread of Orange in the Pacific; dual situations in which either—or both—could result in global catastrophe. One where Arkis succeeded in eradicating Sapiens from the face of the Earth, and the other if Orange reached Sapien shores, consuming everything petroleum-based, like plastic.

Both were potentially silent killers that would radically disrupt the Sapien world. No one could be certain of what would happen next, of how the Sapiens would react. But Sapien history tells of the potential for religious upheaval and end-of-the-world lawless panic, of finger-pointing and accusations between Earth's superpowers, and of twitchy fingers hovering over nuclear arsenals. A situation the Larkians and Merahvu wanted to avoid at all costs.

Their mutual goals were clear, but the strategy for achieving those goals was much less so. They were facing a multi-pronged conflict of human against human, and human against nature, with a minuscule number of bodies and minds to throw at it. Even so, both the Larkians and the Merahvu agreed that containing and destroying Orange was the highest priority. Without Orange, Arkis' stores of orange nectar would dry up, greatly hindering his ability to rapidly breed and maintain his slave army, the Orankai, and diminishing his ability to attack and destroy Sapiens.

The Sapien world was oblivious to the existence of the Merahvu and Earth's sister world Merluma. There was a time not long ago when the Merahvu believed this truth should finally be revealed to the Sapiens. Now they believed the opposite—that it would be best for the Sapiens to continue living with their limited world view of Earth and *only* Earth, while the Larkians and Merahvu saved it along with Merluma from the Orankai slipping seamlessly between them. It would all hinge on the unsung heroes who quietly disappear in the aftermath of war, dead or alive.

Heart heavy, Sinto grappled with these realities and what the Mark, the concept of Joining, and his future with the woman lying on the gurney beside him meant, and why they had been chosen for such an important and noble purpose that no one understood, even themselves.

And now this.

After another hour of monitoring their vitals, Wantemo and Dr. Wickman released Sinto and Audrey from the ship's infirmary with a clean bill of health and orders to take it easy for the next twenty-four hours.

They left the ship and headed to the compound's dining hall located on the other side of the harbor, past the village. They ate dinner alone and in silence, surrounded by Larkians and Merahvu socializing and conversing as if another normal day had passed.

When they were done, they slipped away in their electric utility terrain vehicle—UTV, the Larkians called it—back to the house on the south end of the island where Audrey grew up and that she and Sinto now occupied.

They sat on the sofa of the small living area sipping chamomile tea, trying to calm jangled nerves from the day's disheartening event with the nLink. It was hard to ignore Audrey's frustration and guilt. Everyone involved in the design of nLink was rattled by what happened. They learned that after the incident, the Larkian Council called for a quick vote and the project was officially put on hold indefinitely, much to Francesca's dismay. Losing the nLink and its potential as a weapon against the Orankai was a major setback for which Audrey felt personally responsible.

"It's not your fault."

"Not true. Because of our damned Mark the whole project was scrapped!"

She was close to tears and Sinto ached to comfort her, to distract her from this unfair discovery, but she had grown aloof and distant and had wormed herself against the far side of the sofa. The void of space between them was icy and vast.

Night had fallen and the sea had calmed. The lanai doors were wide open and the briny scent of the sea wafted into the room. Stars winked on the horizon. The gentle *shush* of waves and the occasional *slurp* of tea was the only sound filling the small living room.

Normally Sinto would have his fingers twined through Audrey's during these quiet moments before they retreated to the bedroom for more twining of bodies and eventually to sleep. But what had happened disturbed them both and they sat apart, respecting the invisible barrier the day's event erected between them.

"*Should we not be touching either?*" They simultaneously thought.

Audrey and Sinto had not agreed yet whether to seek out his mother's advice as to why the Mark triggered such a devastating effect, and more troubling, if it could happen again without an nLink interfering. Sinto was feeling more strongly that they should.

He said, "We should go see my mother tomorrow. Knowing the truth is better than not."

"So she can tell us what?" She held out her right arm where the prominent outline of a swirl, a circle, and a line connecting them lay just beneath the surface of her skin. "That this Mark is a mistake? That *we* are a mistake? I'm not sure I want to know the truth."

Sinto broke through the invisible barrier between them and slid to her side. He brushed his fingers across the crush of her brow, tracing the worry line etched in between.

"We are not a mistake." He brushed his lips across hers. "If it was, then why do I want to do this." He kissed her gently. "And this." His lips traced the side of her neck. "And so much more." He pulled back, tipped her chin until her eyes found his. "Nothing has changed except maybe the fact you are destined for a different role in this conflict."

She pulled away and crossed her arms. "You mean behind the scenes, watching at a safe distance?" She rolled her eyes. "Like my father made me do growing up?"

"Maybe, maybe not. Where is safe?" He tapped her head. "Wars are often won by what happens behind battle lines. For example, helping find a solution for neutralizing Orange, mapping out strategies, and training those who will fight in battle. Regardless of where we find ourselves in this conflict, we must be realistic. Is anywhere safe? Are we merely delaying the inevitable? That we all might die tomorrow, or next week, or as two old and regretful people who lived in fear of loving each other the way we were intended? I lost you twice already. I want no regrets. Not now, especially after I found you again. And if we die tomorrow, then so be it, but no one can take you away from me, now, in this present moment."

"What are you implying?"

He took a deep breath. "Maybe we question the physical boundaries we've set."

"As in..." Her brow quirked.

He pulled her onto his lap with her legs straddling his legs. "As in... this." He hitched her up against his hips. Her breath quickened and his blood sang when she nestled herself against him.

Their lips hovered, fevering. She softly said, "Do you think that's a good idea after what happened today?" He looked up, capturing her gaze. "I mean, don't get me wrong." Her fingers slipped through his hair. "I'm just as anxious and sexually frustrated as you."

Her words sank in and doubt and uncertainty reared its ugly little head. He released his grip on her buttocks. He was so sure when he suggested it, but now...

She extracted her fingers and gave him a sad look, her disappointment screaming in the silence.

He sighed. "I don't know how to solve this... this thing wedged between us. More so every day."

"Maybe we should see your mother before we cross a line we can't uncross."

"And hope we don't die tomorrow?"

She kissed him tenderly, then slipped off his lap. "Agreed."

She took his hand and led him to the bedroom for another night of warm snuggles, frustration, and nothing else but rest.

5

Things That Are Sacred

THE FOLLOWING MORNING AUDREY and Sinto traveled to the home his mother shared with Audrey's father. Ianthe must have known they were coming and welcomed them at the front door with open arms.

Her recovery from Ramasis' and Arkis' violent attack and abandonment in the Winterlands was progressing. Her color had returned. Audrey heard that Poe had cut her hair shoulder length, adding layers to help cover the spots where it had been yanked out. The fuzz of new growth blended in naturally. Every day she stood a little bit taller, and the physical wounds in her abdomen were healing fast with Wantemo's help.

Psychologically, the wounds inflicted by Ramasis were much deeper and Audrey wondered if they would ever heal, though Dr. Wickman had taken a role in helping her overcome her most recent trauma and the fact her daughter was in the clutches of her once-trusted mate.

Like Audrey's father, Ianthe had begun to noticeably age in a slow determined march toward their inevitable end after hundreds of years of living with the aid of the life-extending elixir, sucuvita.

The reserves of sucuvita the Merahvu once freely consumed were nearly depleted, and deemed only to be used for aid in healing. The rare fungal source of the life-extending elixir had become a victim of recent and unprecedented climate shifts on Earth, especially in the northern climates, with logging and wildfire its greatest threat. It was a rare resource that only grew in a specific ecology within the untouched old-growth forests of North America. It was part of the reason for the migration of Merahvu from Merluma to Earth so long ago. The Merahvu had tried to duplicate the unique Earth environment on Merluma many times over but failed.

Sinto had told her the story on one of the many nights they spent snuggled together. There was a time when living beyond the normal span of a human lifetime was necessary for the Merahvu. Their numbers had stagnated and population diminished because of the Forever War, in which the young and the strong were sacrificed in meaningless and continual conflict. The Merahvu nearly went extinct because of it. Once the Forever War ended roughly three hundred years ago and peace endured, living a long life and producing many offspring had become the custom to increase their meager population to a healthy level.

The Merahvu had recently accepted that extending their lives well beyond what nature intended was a thing of the past. Sucuvita was now employed for its original purpose from when it was first discovered: to strengthen the body with youthful cells necessary to heal the sick and wounded. Its role of increasing one's longevity was an accidental discovery.

Ianthe and Audrey's father had worked to resolve their differences over the past month. It was a tentative thing, their reconnection—they were two broken souls craving connection and belonging with each other, but treading carefully in the wake of what they both had lost. Audrey could sense the subtle tenderness—and caution—they felt toward each other, and though it was difficult to imagine her father with anyone other than her mother, she was happy for them. For him.

Her father had settled with Ianthe in a small house not far from the Larkians' command compound near the mouth of the harbor, where most of the training and preparations for confronting their enemy were taking place. The house was at water's edge with a small beach of lava rock and patches of black sand. The living space was modestly furnished with soft leather easy chairs and a chambray-covered sofa, with a large round table set between them. Bookshelves lined every available wall. It was a mirror image to the small house her father had built for Audrey's mother, which Audrey now shared with Sinto.

Her father had collected his journals, sketchbooks, and log books from his pirating days from the house his original crew had built when they were first stranded on Isla Salvación long ago. They were now stuffed on the bookshelves lining the small living room's walls and gave the room an old library smell. That original house had been built far from the shore, tucked deep into the jungle and nestled at the base of the mountains. Audrey found the old house by chance while exploring the island. It held many secrets and it was there she discovered the truth about her friend Blake Goodfellow, who once was named Thomas Below and was the youngest member of her father's original pirate crew.

Audrey met Blake when she went off to college. At the time she was unaware of her father's true past. Blake had become a close friend and, for a very brief stint, boyfriend. That all changed once she met Sinto and it was soon after that she discovered the old house and her father's journals. They told the story of how Francesca and another woman joined her father's pirate crew in the Caribbean when he stole the ship they were on. They pretended to be men, which was all well and good, until the other woman revealed she was pregnant from a violent rape before they joined the crew. She died giving birth to a son. It was after that they discovered Francesca's true identity, which was another disruptive shock to the crew. But that quickly faded once the crew fell in love with the young tot, especially her father. He claimed him as his adopted son and named him Thomas. Thomas grew up as a pirate on their ship, *Sea Lark*, sailing the high seas. It was decades later that he changed his name to Blake.

That meant Blake had been Audrey's de facto, non-biologically related brother the whole time. Ickiness aside, Audrey and Blake had grown closer as siblings once she learned the truth about his past and his connection to Sinto's deceased sister, Leela.

Blake believed the prematurely severed bond with Leela played a role in the demons that haunted him following her death. It took him decades to overcome the pull of some unfulfilled purpose. Once he found solid mental grounding, thanks to Dr. Wickman, he changed his name from Thomas Below to Blake Goodfellow.

That was the tragedy Audrey and Sinto hoped never to share. And his mother was their best hope for answers.

Audrey wound her fingers through Sinto's, trepidation roiling her belly.

"Please, sit," Ianthe prompted, pointing toward the sofa.

Sinto went to his mother and greeted her with tender kisses to her forehead, nose, each cheek, and then her lips—a traditional way the Merahvu greeted family and dear friends. Her eyes glistened with the depth of love and gratitude she felt for her only son.

Audrey and Sinto sat on the sofa. Ianthe picked up a pillow from a chair across from them and sat, moving slowly and with care. She tucked the long pale-yellow skirt she wore neatly beneath her legs and hugged the pillow to her stomach.

Audrey breathed deep the smell of leather, ink, and musty paper permeating the air. She noted her father had begun sketching again, a pastime that calmed his mind and gave him the space to think. His sketchbook lying on the table between them was opened to his latest drawing. It was of Ianthe caught in a quiet moment of deep thought. It was subtle, but he had captured a deep sense of uncertainty etched across her brow.

Audrey shifted her gaze from the drawing to Ianthe who was gazing intently at Sinto as if there was something important she needed to tell him, and only him. A shift of eye and that gaze fell to her.

"I'm sorry your father is not here. Robert is helping Salvo with the new recruits."

Audrey was so accustomed to hearing her father's crew addressed by their surnames, Culliford and Alvarez, respectively, that it sounded odd to hear the use of their first names as they must have done when they first met Ianthe.

"We actually came to see you," Audrey said.

Sinto sat forward, but before he could open his mouth, Ianthe said, "You have a question about the Mark, perhaps as to its purpose."

He opened his mouth, then paused before saying, "That is one question, but..."

She smiled. "And the other?" Her eyes were alive, crackling with lavender fire.

Sinto shifted, stole a glance back to Audrey.

Audrey cleared her throat. "Ah, we have not—we didn't know if—"

Sinto finished, "—if the Joining must proceed or occur when we..." Sinto's cheeks flushed. "Copulate for the first time."

"That's a perfectly natural question; no need to be embarrassed. You want to know if sex is part of the Joining." Sinto nodded and Ianthe continued, "It can be, and usually is, because of the intimacy of the act of Joining. But it is not required. The same is true with making love; the Joining need not be completed for you to interact in that way. Although the Mark will respond, and it may prove difficult to reject its will. But if you set out with satisfying purely physical desires, then it may abide, understanding the importance of fulfilling your intimate needs.

"Remember that the Mark you share are pieces of each of you, and not some stranger. It knows what you desire and need, and part of that knowing includes when and where the Joining should occur. The Mark will let you know, loud and clear. It is not an act to take lightly, and both of you must be ready and it must take place in the proper environment. One where you are safe and truly alone. The Joining should not be interrupted, and any witnesses may find themselves affected, even harmed."

She paused and shifted her gaze between both of them. "Have either of you felt any urgency from the Mark?"

"To Join?" Sinto asked.

Audrey and Sinto looked at each other. "No," they replied together.

Then Sinto added, "When the Mark first appeared the urge was quite strong, but I may have misinterpreted the sensation, having no knowledge of what to expect at the time. Although the passage of time and the distance we shared recently brought clarity and seems to have calmed that urge."

Audrey added, "Urge to Join, but not the other..."

Ianthe smiled. "Naturally, of course, not the other." Her smiled faded and she drew a deep breath. "The Joining is rare and your Mark is a sacred gift, bestowed to you for a special purpose and not to be rushed."

"How do we know for what purpose?"

She paused a long time before answering, picking at the fringe along the edge of the pillow she was hugging. "I suppose that will be revealed once the Joining is complete, thus the reason for embarking on your journey once the time is right."

Sinto sat back and the room filled with silence. The Mark in Audrey's arm was still and attentive, as was Sinto's, as if listening intently to their conversation and contemplating all that Ianthe had shared. Their hearts beat strongly and in steady rhythm with each other—a level of intimacy that passed between them because of the Mark.

Audrey was burning to learn more. "Can you tell us everything that happened between Blake and Leela?"

A deep sadness filled Ianthe's eyes. "I made a terrible mistake." Her gaze grew distant. "Oh, how I wish I had the wisdom back then that I have now. The truth? They had *never* taken that last step. They were not fully Joined. I discovered this much later during one of my wanderings through the Timeless Dimension. The only reason I could decipher why is that neither of them understood how and of the Mark's importance. They were both so very young, sixteen, maybe seventeen years old…" She sighed. "It is true Leela Marked Thomas, but that was all; they were so very much in love—was that why? Who knows. But I know with certainty they never fulfilled that next step. The bond was incomplete. I was baffled as to why Leela suddenly died. By driving them apart, I believe I broke her heart, literally, and that was what killed her.

"I was distracted by my feelings for Robert and my own desire to pass on my responsibilities to Leela so Robert and I could escape and live the life we dreamed of together."

She tossed the pillow she was holding to the floor and placed her hands across her abdomen. "I have accepted what Ramasis let Arkis do to me. It was unfair of me to disrespect him and violate our vows. I am responsible for the horrible man he has become. I pushed him away and into the arms of another to father your half-brother. That bastard Arkis! Conceived out of rage. Fate has an ugly way of coming back around and snapping you in the ass when you least expect it."

She sat back, picked a piece of lint from her skirt. "I have come to forgive Ramasis, but not myself."

Audrey could sense Sinto's reaction to his mother's words. She knew he wanted to object, to comfort her and reassure her that she wasn't entirely responsible, that fate intervened. But Audrey knew that no matter what they said, she would blame herself till the end of her days. She passed these thoughts to Sinto, and she felt his response die on his lips before it ever left. Instead, he took his mother's hand in his own, sharing a long, sad, and sympathetic look with her.

Audrey stood up and began searching through her father's journals, pulling out the one he had dedicated to Thomas, documenting his struggle and the years that followed. She held it up. "Have you seen this?"

Ianthe shook her head.

Audrey flipped through the passages until she came across the one she found most perplexing. She held it out to Ianthe, pointing at the entry that frequently caused her to wake up in the middle of the night in a cold sweat. "Read that paragraph, out loud so Sinto can hear."

Ianthe looked down, used her finger to mark the words as she read the passage. "It says, 'Thomas had a relapse last night. I found him in the kitchen holding a knife to his chest. It pained me when Marcus chained him to his bed for his own good. I lay unable to sleep as he screamed all night, repeating her name over and over. Claiming something about a wobble, as he does almost nightly.'" She paused, her eyes flickering.

"Keep reading," Audrey said.

Ianthe cleared her throat and continued, "'All Marcus can decipher is that the persistent wobble he speaks of is entirely fabricated in his mind. There is no premise or source of such wobble that we have found, here nor afar. Thomas himself knows not where it comes from. He only insists that it is. With no grounding or proof, we can only believe it the ravings of a madman.'" She stopped, gaze shifting to the window briefly before resuming, "'Marcus and I struggle to placate or calm him, which merely exacerbates his distress. He claims the wobble will end us all, yet claims he does not know what it means, only that we must stop it as it grows more persistent every passing day. A wobble we do not sense nor feel. Please give me the strength to see him through.'"

She pressed the journal closed and handed it back to Audrey, growing strangely quiet.

"I asked Blake about the wobble after I found this and confronted him about his past. He doesn't know what it means now any more than he did then. He thought it was about something unfinished, something about Earth and Merluma being unstable. He believes they are coming apart. What do you believe?"

She didn't answer.

"When I showed him my Mark he was alarmed. Do you know why?"

She didn't answer.

Audrey held out her arm where the Mark was prominent and clear. "His and Leela's was the same symbol as ours: a swirl, a line, and a circle. Sinto's world, my world, Merluma and Earth, connected. Why would they be the same?"

Her eyes fluttered. "I—I have no idea."

Sinto leaned forward, elbows to knee. "Mother, what is the wobble?"

Audrey was struck with a sudden and chilling thought. "Would it have anything to do with the fact they never completed the Joining?"

Ianthe closed her eyes and never answered either of their last two questions.

6

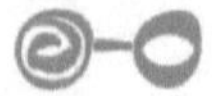

Yin-Yang Frustration

SINTO AND AUDREY LEFT with more questions than answers after visiting his mother. They strolled down to the small black-sand beach below her house. Audrey plopped down, arms cradling her knees, gazing across the open ocean. Sinto sat down beside her, the morning sun warming their backs.

Sinto said, "She's holding something back. Something she's known for a long time. Something tied to Leela's death. Something she disrupted. A big something."

"Why would she not share it with us?"

"It scares her, deeply. Her aura went very dark."

"Peachy," Audrey murmured.

The contrail of a passing jet cut a white line across the pale blue sky. He gazed at the sight, pondering. He guessed the jet to be heading due west toward Japan, roughly thirty-seven-hundred miles away. He guessed it would take the Sapien jet plane roughly seven hours to reach its destination; it would take Sinto less than an hour to tunnel through the sea. The reason for the difference was basic physics. The atmosphere poses resistance, with the engines in a constant fight to push the mass of the jet and its occupants through the air at a speed necessary to give loft to the wings, or else it would stop and fall from the sky.

Sinto could launch a vortex that cuts through the sea; a tunneling void with no water, no air, no living matter, thus no resistance. It takes a burst of electrical energy for Sinto to create that tunnel. Passing through it takes even less. The time it takes for Sinto to travel through water was wrapped up in how long it takes to launch and slow down. Without resistance it takes as much energy to stop as it does to go...

Sinto grabbed his head. Why did he care at this moment? What were these random thoughts? Their world was falling apart and here he was waxing on about distracting rubbish.

Audrey pressed her shoulder to his. He pressed back. Two forces meeting. Resistance. Was that what the wobble was all about? An ever-growing resistance between Earth and Merluma? Two opposing forces pushing or pulling against the another? Energy building until something slips? Like tectonic plates stuck together until neither can hold onto the other, then a shudder and a shake and they slip free, each going their merry way? What could possibly be stuck between Earth and Merluma?

Some Merahvu believed the two earth sisters were never meant to be conjoined as they have been from the initial splintering. An event that should have simply spawned a replicated copy of Earth. But that was not what happened.

The process was interrupted, like the unfinished Joining of Thomas and Leela.

Thomas did not know how so it was left undone.

Was this undone thing his and Audrey's purpose? And if true, what was it? Why did it scare his mother so?

Audrey traced the back of Sinto's hand with her fingers. The look she gave him and the way she was sucking on her lower lip made his heart skip a beat. "What are you thinking?" she asked.

He sighed. "Just random thoughts about resistance and undone things."

"You know she gave us permission."

"Permission for what?"

"Are you kidding?" She smiled. "You know." She slipped her hand to his inner thigh. "For something not done." She wagged her brows. "Yet."

"And here I am thinking about physics."

She walked her fingers higher, making him flinch. "Well, so whatcha think?"

Sinto laid his hand on hers, moved it back to his knee. "We have been *not* thinking about it for so long that I'm not sure what to think."

"Does that scare you?"

"Not sure scared is the right feeling, maybe more of a distraction."

"If we take the plunge or not?"

"Both." He paused to formulate the right way to say what needed to be said without disappointing her. "If we do, we need to consider the consequences."

"Like getting pregnant? Because we have ways of preventing that here in the Sapien world."

"That, certainly, but also... will I have the strength to hold back the Joining?"

"Ah. The consequence of which your mother is so mum about for some reason."

"That, yes." He ran a finger down her chin. "And the fact my thoughts may forever be distracted and focused on that and only that and not the true thing I care about most. You."

"Hmm. For me, I think it may instill a kind of peace in all the chaos. My insides are jangled with anticipation. Just as they have been since I learned you were alive. This anticipation has proved to be very distracting every moment I'm with you. Like you said yesterday, we may be dead tomorrow. I don't want my last thought to be, 'why the fuck didn't we do it!'"

"Nor mine, but the first thing you said is a very real consequence to consider. Not just because of the timing, but..."

"Because I'm a Sapien and you're a Merahvu and we might produce a pretty fucked-up kid."

"Not the words I would use to describe it, but there is a level of uncertainty of what a Sapien-Merahvu child might be like. That and bringing a new life into our lives at this particular moment would be challenging and possibly reckless on our part. Uncertainty atop uncertainty." He blew out an exasperated breath. "Too much distraction."

"I think we can both agree an accidental pregnancy would be bad. So let's say we do what we need to do to avoid that. So once that's done, do we take the plunge?"

He drew figure-eights in the dark sand with his finger, contemplating everything he had been through, the things that had happened to him. From the temptations of Rachel to a near forced sexual engagement with Mianna. The physical part of him he struggled to control when he first met Audrey. Now he had better insight what to expect.

He looked at her.

Could I practice the restraint necessary? Even more terrifying, would I want to?

"This isn't all on you. We're in this together," she said.

Except the Joining. Thomas failed because he didn't know what to do. Sinto had a fairly good idea, but what he didn't know was whether or not he would be strong enough to resist the pull of the Mark. Yesterday he was ready to release the restraints, today he was not. Yesterday Audrey was uncertain, now she seemed raring to go.

Yin-yang frustration.

Is this what all mates go through?

Audrey stood up, held out her hand. "Come on, I think we've talked enough."

"What? That's it?"

"Yeah, now's not the time. I think that's clear. But know this, I plan to talk to Dr. Wickman about contraceptive options, and soon. And once that's resolved, we'll finish this conversation, or whatever may transpire, one way or another."

7

Surprise Guest

Audrey's best friend from the Friday Harbor Labs, Ryan Wood, arrived on Isla Salvación the next day with an unexpected guest. Sinto planned it, apparently, and he was literally tripping over his tongue, excited to introduce this new arrival to Audrey. Audrey had no idea who it was, only that she was a woman and Ryan was pretty enamored with her. So was Sinto.

Audrey hated to admit it but she felt a twinge of jealously toward this unexpected guest Sinto was so excited to greet.

Sinto must have felt her unease and cringed from her red-hot gaze. He finally shared, telepathically, a brief rehash of him meeting this mystery woman he had mentioned to Audrey only once before: Her name was Rachel. She had been an escort he met in Las Vegas, stressing that nothing he would be ashamed of had happened between them. Which, in and of itself, made her a little suspicious. He recounted their journey across America, her cutting his hair to help mask his true identity, then giving him the encouragement he needed to face the unknown and what he might find in the Terrakai's City of Green. He obviously edited his story liberally, except to portray Rachel as offering to help him travel to Lake Superior and then saving his life after he barely escaped from

Arkis and his Orankai and the horrors of the City of Green. It was Rachel who found Ryan on San Juan Island, which led Sinto back to Audrey.

Rachel also taught Sinto to love heavily sugared coffee and cinnamon rolls.

And when he revealed everything to Rachel about the Merahvu, his parents' tumultuous past, and the very real and horrifying reality Sinto discovered in the City of Green, she eagerly offered to join in the fight.

Ryan and Rachel arrived at dinner time when the dining hall was packed with the crews from the ships moored in the harbor and newly recruited Larkians living in houses sprinkled in the hills above the compound. Dyer and Tucker and several others in the crew, who Ryan befriended on their earlier failed mission to find two missing ships in the Pacific, jumped up to greet him and fawn over Rachel.

Once they made the rounds, Ryan and Rachel found their way to Audrey and Sinto's table tucked in the far corner.

Sinto rushed forward and hugged Rachel, a petite little thing he towered over. He lifted her off the floor to kiss her on the cheek, then put her down. They erupted into a running diatribe: What have you been doing? How has Ryan been treating you? How is your wound? Your hair needs a trim! I brought my scissors...

Audrey and Ryan watched as they bantered, ignoring the two of them completely.

Ryan asked, "So how was your birthday?"

The last time she saw Ryan was the day before her birthday, when Audrey and Blake came to Isla Salvación and she knew nothing of Blake's true past. That was over a month ago. And with Ryan busy finishing his fall quarter at the Labs and Audrey busy helping the Larkians grapple with all they had learned, it had been a while since they had a chance to talk, other than sharing brief texts. His were mostly gossip. Hers, well, were much more terse.

Alvarez was quite clear about not sharing Larkian and Merahvu business over the phone or the Internet. She had no intention of breaking confidence after defying his orders the last time. A lesson she would never forget. She had yet to tell Ryan about the deadly attack by Orankai on her much-anticipated twenty-first birthday.

Audrey replied, "Not the birthday I anticipated. I made a few rather big unexpected discoveries. The best of all was that Sinto never died. I can't thank you enough for helping him find me."

"And I can't thank him enough for introducing me to Rachel."

"She's your type."

He smiled. "That's not what I meant. She's one hell of an independent lady. I can't believe how quickly I've come to trust her. She's so easy to talk to. Not judgmental at all and has helped me see the world in a different light. I seem so much happier when she's around."

"Sorry, I assumed."

"Oh, she's the catch of the century, but she's on a relationship sabbatical, says she needs a break from romantic entanglements. She's a great friend and I wouldn't want anything to jeopardize that. So, where's Blake? I was hoping to see him. Is he okay?"

"Blake's good, we're good. It's a long story I'll tell you when there are fewer prying ears and things calm down a bit." She stole a glance at Sinto and Rachel, chattering away. "Blake is on the mainland overseeing some last details on a new fleet of personal submarines. Guess he's been working on this project since last year. Apparently that's what he had been doing when he disappeared for days at a time last fall—that and other things. I learned that he knew my father all along and was instrumental in designing the sailing system on *Requiem Sea II*."

Ryan quirked a brow. "*Seriously?* He knew the other guys too?"

She nodded. "Apparently. Blake has a more colorful past than I could have ever imagined."

"Hmm. He was always a mystery. Must be some story."

She rolled her eyes. "You'd never guess in a million years. He's been through some pretty heavy shit. But he's got a heart of gold and he's like family to me now."

"Family huh?"

She gently punched him in the arm. "Like you. So give me a hug, stranger."

And he did. "Damn it's good to see you, kid."

She pulled back and wagged a finger. "Nah-ah-ah, twenty-one, remember? No more kid stuff."

"You'll always be a kid to me, so get over it."

Sinto and Rachel had been watching them, but for how long, Audrey was uncertain.

Sinto cleared his throat. "Audrey, this is Rachel."

Rachel flashed Audrey a deeply dimpled smile. "How'ya doin'? Sinto has told me so much about you, and what he didn't say I had to wrangle outta him. You know how guys are." She rolled her eyes. "So shy about their feelin's, and his are strong for you!" She stuck out her hand. "Pleased to meet you."

Audrey took her hand, tiny and half the size of hers and very soft and warm. Her dimples accentuated her cheeks when she smiled, lighting up a face framed by short dark hair and eyes that glittered with blue intrigue. Being this close to her Audrey fully understood why she created such a ruckus when they arrived. Rachel was a magnet and even Audrey felt her pull. Disarming and cute and so sweet she oozed sugar. That twinge of jealously she felt earlier evaporated as she understood why Sinto and Ryan had been drawn to her. She felt it too.

Audrey replied, "And I you, what a surprise."

Then she gave Audrey a smile that warmed up the room. "So where's the food? I heard there's a really good chef around here and I'm starving!"

8

Wits And Smarts

Audrey invited Ryan and Rachel to stay with her and Sinto at the beach house. One of them would get the spare bedroom. Ryan said he would be happy to take the sofa.

After dinner they rode together in a four-seater UTV to the south end of the island. They left the bright lights surrounding the compound, the village, and the ships in the harbor, and drove south under the light of a full moon. Twenty minutes later, they were rounding the path lit by downwardly oriented mushroom-shaped light fixtures to the front door of her parent's old house, which her father had gifted to her recently.

Audrey showed Rachel the spare bedroom. It was the room her parents once shared but had been completely scrubbed of the art that once hung on the walls and the colorful quilts that her mother once favored. It saddened Audrey that everything of her mother's had been removed and disposed of after she died. But it was the only way her father could cope—to erase all trace of her. Apparently, he had never set foot inside the house since, and all Audrey had left of her mother were fading memories.

Rachel dropped her bag and walked straight through the living area to the sliding doors leading to the lanai. Outdoor lights highlighted the waves rolling onto the beach from the cove that was part of the property surrounding the house. Moonlight cast an endless highway across the sea.

Rachel nodded in approval. "I hope you like me, cause I'm never leavin'," she announced, firmly.

Ryan shot Audrey an apologetic look. "Maybe I should have taken the bed."

Audrey chuckled. "This house has that effect. Anyone want some tea?"

"Got anything stronger?" Ryan said over his shoulder, stepping out on the lanai to join Rachel.

Audrey rummaged in a cupboard in the attached kitchen and pulled out an old bottle of rum and four shot glasses. She set them on the large table between a pair of reading chairs and the sofa where Sinto was sitting.

He grabbed her by the waist and pulled her onto the sofa beside him and started nuzzling the hollow of her neck with his lips.

"What's up with you?" she giggled.

"Our team is growing."

"Team?"

"Rachel was the one who told me I need a team to help us combat the Orankai."

"What about everyone else who have vowed to join the fight: the Larkians and your people?"

"She meant something more personal, like close friends who watch each other's backs."

Audrey glanced outside where Ryan and Rachel were gazing at the moon-lit sea.

"How exactly did you meet her... and what was it she did in Las Vegas?"

He brushed aside a strand of hair that had escaped from her braid. "I already told you she was an escort, and she showed me a night out on the town."

Audrey leaned back so they were no longer touching. "So enlighten me, with details and *truthfully.*"

"It's not what you think, I mean, well, maybe at first there was some confusion of intent..."

Audrey crossed her arms. "And..."

"We kissed, that's all. It was awkward, we both felt it. Nothing else I regret or should concern you happened. She helped me win money I needed and I agreed to let her come along on my journey. I needed someone to help me travel across America to Lake Superior and she was quick to make that clear. She's merely a friend—actually..." Sinto briefly thought of Naiada. "She's more like a sister the way she gives me advice and calls out my bullshit."

"*Bullshit?* Ha! I think that's the first time I've ever heard you swear."

"Just trying to fit in. I have noticed the use of more colorful words in your language lately."

"It happens when your life gets fucked up and turns to shit."

"Is it still shit?"

She poked him in the belly. "Not right now."

"Then maybe you can stop saying it with crude language."

"Is that what you want?"

Sinto's eyes smoldered. "Actually, I want something else."

The Mark in her arm tingled in a tantalizing way.

"I thought we decided that something you want, we *both* want, was risky."

"It is."

"Why the change of heart?"

"My heart has not changed."

"But earlier you—"

"I have been thinking."

"About what?"

"What you said, and colorfully so, that you did not want your last thought before you die to be, quote, 'why the fuck didn't we do it!', and I agreed, as I still do."

"So…"

He grabbed her hand and began stroking her fingers. "You should see Dr. Wickman first thing tomorrow morning."

Ryan and Rachel burst into the room laughing, then stopped when they saw the stunned look on Audrey's face. "What did we miss?"

Sinto said, "Nothing important." Then he shared an image of that something he wanted to do with Audrey. Her heart pitter-pattered and that place down yonder flared and simmered.

Ryan and Rachel sat across from them. Ryan poured shots. "Tomorrow, what can we expect?"

"Breakfast," Audrey said.

"Seriously? It looks like you guys are settled in as if on vacation, cuddling on the sofa, engaged in pillow talk. I thought the world's about to implode and you called us to help stop it."

"Geez Ry, just taking a break. It's been a little tense around here. We had a serious setback with important technology yesterday and we're outnumbered by a cunning enemy, with more being born every day."

"Huh, so we're the guys carrying a knife to a gun fight?" Rachel said.

"More like a toothpick to a zombie apocalypse," Audrey said.

"Gotcha, so this here is an end-of-the-world scenario."

Audrey looked at Sinto, then said, "To be honest, maybe; at least the world you and I are used too."

"Yes," Sinto said point-of-fact.

"Damn." Rachel gazed around the room and frowned. "Just when things were lookin' up."

Ryan downed his shot and poured another.

Sinto leaned forward, spinning his full shot glass with his fingers. "Orange is our most immediate threat. The Orankai need it to breed their army and control their masses. We must neutralize it, then the Orankai. Keep the Sapien world out of it. That's what's at stake."

Audrey said, "There is one other thing that might just screw us all and there's nothing we can do about it." Sinto grabbed her hand and shot her a withering look to stop, but Audrey ignored it. "The very foundation of everything around us. Earth and Merluma are unstable."

"Like fire-and-brimstone unstable?" Rachel asked.

Sinto sat back and sighed. "Perhaps."

"Wow, and I thought Las Vegas was bad." She elbowed Ryan, who was taking a sip of rum. It sloshed over the rim and dribbled down his fingers. "Whatcha think about all this?"

"I'm going to do what these two tell me to do until we succeed or die."

Rachel sat back. "Well that's depressing. Fightin' with a toothpick's pathetic. Zombies are mean and hungry and never satisfied. There must be some way to punch our way out of this mess with wits and smarts."

"We're open to any and all ideas." Sinto said.

Ryan raised his shot glass. "If it comes to the end of the world, I want to get drunk, find me a woman, and make endless love. If we're going out, that's how I want to go."

And with nervous chuckles and approval from the others, he downed his shot.

9

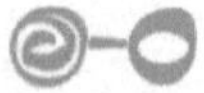

New Perspective

THE NIGHTMARE STARTED THE next morning before first light. The landline from the compound to the house rang loud and insistently, followed by someone pounding on the front door.

Sinto was first to stir from a deep slumber and respond.

The messenger at the front door was a new Larkian recruit Sinto had met only briefly, a young man named Trevor. He was gasping from a surge in adrenaline as he rushed to warn them. His alarm was palpable, his aura radiating bright orange with fear and bewilderment.

He said, "Alvarez intercepted a message from a container ship in the Pacific steaming toward Seattle. Sounds like it's infected with Orange. Everyone is gathering—come quick."

Sinto found Audrey in the kitchen, horror etched on her face, phone pressed to her ear.

A disheveled Ryan sat on the sofa where he had been sleeping and flipped through his cell phone. "Nothing on the news or social media about it."

Rachel, coolly and collectively, began shutting windows and doors, pulling curtains.

Sinto reached a telepathic probe to his mother. "*What is happening?*"

She responded, "*I believe a possible ruse to distract us. Robert doesn't agree.*"

They tore north in UTVs, the sunrise painting the sky red. Audrey drove, riding Trevor's bumper, running the UTV at top speed. No one spoke.

Sinto continued his conversation with his mother. "*Tell me what you know.*"

"*I sense the Orankai may be testing our resolve, Merahvu and Larkian alike, by staging an attack against a Sapien ship with Orange. I believe their true intent is to infiltrate the city of the Arctakai, recruit who they can, and kill the rest—the Keepers of Knowledge, the Healers, innocent families. I fear the Larkians will put all resources toward saving the Sapien ship from Orange and ignore what's happening there. Robert and I could not resolve our differences on this matter. This is exactly the type of divisiveness Arkis would love to create between the Merahvu and Larkians to weaken us. Be aware.*"

"*If Orange proliferates and spreads it will only serve to make the Orankai more powerful.*"

"*That too is true, but not at the cost of our most innocent people. I cannot see a clear path forward. It could be Naiada muddying the Timeless Dimension if she has joined with the Orankai. That or something else, something new.*"

Sinto was conflicted once they arrived at the compound where the Larkian Council of Culliford's original crew, his mother, and Wantemo had gathered.

Audrey noticed Sinto's sudden change in demeanor. "*What is it?*" she pushed into his mind.

"*Troubling news from my mother. How much influence does your father wield over the Larkians?*"

"No more than does the full Council. They all have equal say: Alvarez, Francesca, Dr. Wickman, Leonard. Blake… but he's in Seattle."

"This discussion might get messy."

Audrey never got the chance to ask why. They arrived at the compound and raced inside. The dining hall was dark and empty. Light bled through double doors to an adjoining conference room the Larkians had designated as an impromptu command center. Sinto's mother and Culliford were already there and waved them inside.

Audrey had suggested Ryan and Rachel stay out of the conversation. Ryan readily agreed. Rachel seemed a little put off, but eventually agreed. Audrey suggested they stay within earshot of the meeting. Sinto agreed with the strategy. He might need backup if their discussion came to a deadlock, so told them to stay out of it unless prompted by one of them. One thing he learned from his journey into the Sapien world was to toss previous assumptions aside and switch perspective. Observe, formulate, react. The more varied perspectives the better.

Ryan and Rachel sat at a table just outside the command center. Sinto intentionally left the doors open after slipping inside so they could easily observe the discussion.

Sinto and Audrey sat beside his mother and Culliford at the large oval table that could accommodate more than a dozen people. Wantemo slipped in behind them and quietly took a seat across from Sinto. There was a pile of pastries and coffee available on a side table. The sweet and acrid scents beckoned but he was too anxious to eat or drink anything. The auras swirling throughout the room were heavy and anxious.

All of the Council members had been summoned, except for Blake, who was in Seattle overseeing test trials of a new submarine. Captain Stokes, a fit man of Polynesian descent, was also in attendance. Though not an official member, he frequently participated in Council business. He shot a cocked bright smile towards Audrey, who acknowledged him back. It was Audrey, along with Stokes' verbal assistance, that saved their lives when their submarine was heavily damaged and rendered powerless during the bombing of Sinto's underwater city, Tallamure. It was a time when Culliford and his Council were still sworn enemies of the Merahvu—another fact raising tensions around the table that Sinto's mother alerted him to.

Alvarez called the meeting to order and didn't waste any time getting down to business. "As we expected, the Orankai are meddling in the Sapien world. Francesca's team just intercepted a message from a container ship three hundred nautical miles from the Straits of Juan de Fuca. It sounded desperate. The captain reported that a strange orange substance picked up at sea ate away at their instruments and part of their cargo. No further communications have been sent. Thanks to Francesca's fast work and diligence to scrub the message, neither the authorities nor the shipping company received it."

"I think we would all agree that ship cannot reach port," Culliford said.

No one disagreed.

Stokes said. "We need to quantify how many ships may have been compromised."

"And by who. I suspect the Orankai," Sinto said.

Francesca asked, "If so, why? What's their plan?"

Several eyes shifted to Sinto's mother, who was quietly lost in thought. She gazed back at all the faces looking to her for the answers.

Sinto warned, *"Tread carefully. Speak only with certainty. Do not let them know your ability to see is compromised until we know more as to why."*

She closed her eyes, drew a deep breath. "I believe it is only the one ship. Very likely the Orankai, a distraction to make us look the other way from their true intentions."

Culliford sat forward, "We can't take that chance."

Sinto piped up, "I think we could all agree. But we must think carefully about where to apply our resources. I absolutely agree that we must neutralize Orange. It is the only way to stop the Orankai. So how do we do that before the Orankai overpower us? Both Merahvu and Sapiens."

Alvarez stood and walked over to a large electronic screen mounted on the wall. "What are our vulnerabilities in terms of Orange?" He used his finger to write on the screen. "First, the Pacific is filled with thousands of Sapien ships, each a perfect target for spreading Orange." He turned, "Do we all agree it would be impossible to protect each one?"

No one objected.

He continued his list, "Second, it's a substance capable of attacking essential components of every aspect of modern Sapien life and supporting infrastructure, potentially leading to a complete breakdown of civilized peace between nations, states, cities, and neighbors. Incomprehensible mayhem." He turned for acknowledgment.

Pursed lips and nods all around.

"Third, it's a substance the Orankai are heavily dependent upon for continued success. A key weakness." He turned, prompted for discussion. "Anything else I may have missed?"

Rachel spoke up from the doorway. "Excuse me, I couldn't help overhearing..." She flashed a dimpled smile and turned on her magic charm, capturing the attention of everyone in the room. She waved. "Oh hi, I'm Rachel by the way. Um, am I correct thinkin' that this thing, this *Orange*, is kinda like an out-of-control virus?"

She walked over to Dr. Wickman. "I'm not a doctor or anything so correct me if I'm wrong, but a virus needs hosts and once viable hosts are gone, then, ya know, the virus weakens or dies, right?"

Wickman nodded. "True."

"I read once that plastic literally touches every part of our planet and on any given week us humans ingest up to a credit card's worth of it. That's just outright astonishing and creepy scary! And if we can't keep plastic out of our bodies, then how can we possibly keep it away from something like Orange? Say we call it what it is, a virus, and what do we do with a virus to keep it from spreading?" She paused. "Anyone?"

"Quarantine," Dr. Wickman said.

"Yup." She looked at Alvarez. "There was that other thing you said Mr..." She prompted him with raised brows.

"Alvarez, no Mr."

"Right, Alvarez. Interestin' name by the way." She held his gaze a while longer, then continued. "You said the Orankai need it, and Sinto told me about them caves where they use it to breed their army. That's on Merluma, right?"

Sinto nodded.

"What if we give the Orankai what they want? Save them the work of comin' here and causin' us all trouble. Lure it to Merluma with heaps of plastic and trap it there. Quarantine."

No one said anything.

"Anyway, sorry for interrupting, carry on." She turned to leave.

Rachel elicited a rare smile from Alvarez. "Wait," he said. "Why don't you and your friend join us."

She looked back to the open double doors where Ryan was leaning against the door frame, arms crossed and a smirk forming across his lips.

Rachel grinned. "Us?" Then she looked at the empty seats next to Alvarez. "Sure, uh..." She pointed to the untouched pile of sugary pastries sitting on the hutch. "So long as you don't mind if I snag one of them donuts."

10

Running In Circles

RACHEL BROKE THE ICE in the room. Alvarez had described an impossible situation and Rachel injected a shot of fresh energy and perspective, regardless that what she proposed was an improbable solution to a complicated problem. Their discussion was far from over.

Sinto gave her a wink when she looked in his direction. Rachel's presence chipped away at the hopelessness he sensed earlier. Everyone in the room was suddenly energized.

Alvarez said, "I propose we intercept that ship contaminated with Orange, interview the captain and crew, twist the story in our favor. We must contain any panic from spreading. Secondly, we need to come up with a strategy on how to employ our resources, especially if more ships report similar circumstances."

Everyone agreed.

Stokes said, "Leave the ship issue to me." He pulled out his phone and stepped out of the room.

Sinto looked around the table. "I propose we include the Merahvu, specifically the Circle and other key leaders, in any and all future discussions from this point forward. If we don't, Arkis will take advantage, try to turn them to his side." He glanced at his mother. "If he hasn't already."

Everyone agreed.

Wantemo volunteered to leave immediately for the Arctakai city in the Southern Ocean. Before he left, Sinto pushed to Wantemo, "*Bring the leaders back, and quickly. Before the Larkians make decisions without considering their input.*" Wantemo agreed.

Sinto said, "I suggest we tally up Larkian resources and identify everything we know of Orange and Orankai movements here on Earth before Wantemo returns. We should also list what we don't know but need to know, and soon."

"Good suggestion." Alvarez started summarizing stats on the electronic wall board as he talked. "As far as resources, we have three more ships in the *Requiem Sea* line nearing completion. Coupled with the *Requiem Sea II* here in the harbor, that totals four fast ships for transport and deployment.

"Blake is wrapping up final tests on a single-pilot mini-sub designed specifically for underwater hostile encounters—the Xiphias project. Once they are delivered, training and pilot selection will commence immediately.

"Six mid-sized subs like the one recently damaged beyond repair at Tallamure are on standby and ready for transport wherever we need them.

"Francesca assures me all three research vessels are at the ready for whatever we need to study, research, develop, and deploy. The *Masquerade Ball*, plus one in Seattle, and another en route to here.

"One hundred and fifty recruits just completed their training and are ready to deploy to Seattle to staff the new *Requiem Sea* ships. One hundred more recruits are coming to the island in the next week for training and deployment wherever we deem necessary.

"We have an expansive stockpile of weapons ready to disperse, with plenty of manufacturing resources here, and in Seattle, to replenish and distribute on demand.

"The island has been fully fortified to withstand another attack like the one we had last month. A full detection and defense network encircles the island, assuming any future attacks are from the water. Wantemo is aware to use extreme caution. He knows to identify himself when he returns, along with others that may be accompanying him. The same applies to you, Sinto, should you venture away from the island."

Sinto nodded.

"Anyone coming to the island, whether by air or sea, is detained, vetted, and registered." Alvarez paused. "Beyond that, we have the experience and brainpower in this room, plus whomever Wantemo rounds up. Otherwise, that's it. Not the best odds, but—" He shrugged. "Some of us have been up against tougher odds before, and here we are after all these years." He gave the room a rare smile. "I think that wraps up our current list of assets."

Culliford cleared his throat. "Remember, we have Ianthe and any insights she may provide."

"Yes, of course, sorry for that oversight." Alvarez addressed Ianthe directly. "We value any and all perspectives you may have to provide."

"*Malavee*, my pleasure," Ianthe replied.

Alvarez gazed around the room. "Anything else to add?"

Wickman took the floor. "Wantemo and I discovered Orange accelerates cellular growth in organisms that consume it. That, as Sinto observed on Merluma, coupled with Merluma's accelerated time scale, explains how Arkis is able to breed an army so quickly. As a side effect of consuming a steady diet of this orange nectar, their army should age at an accelerated rate. That's a notable weakness."

Sinto added, "They all consume it, as does Arkis himself. It's like a highly addictive drug. Arkis and my father are drunk on the power of it, and as you noted, I did detect signs of aging. Arkis, who is essentially my age, looked much older than I would have expected."

Leonard raised a hand. "What if we simply let 'em burn out?"

"We did ponder that idea," Wickman said. "But what Sinto reported of the situation on Merluma indicates there could be thousands, maybe many more, and they're continually breeding replacements."

"If Orange is what they want," Francesca said. "Then maybe we give it to them, as Rachel suggested."

Sinto said, "Arkis was clear what he wants. To be king of the Orankai and for the Orankai to take over the world. Both of them, Earth and Merluma. He is obsessed with eradicating Sapiens and mad with greed and power. Beyond that, he seeks revenge for me rejecting his generous offer to rule by his side, which includes hunting down and killing Audrey and probably me as well. He has my sister and the means to produce a queen. That makes him a very dangerous and motivated enemy, regardless of what Orange may be doing to his health."

"Then it is clear we must take him out of the equation," Alvarez said. "Obsession and greed leads to arrogance. Arrogance leads to a heightened sense of infallibility and carelessness. We expose his blind spot. That is how we get Arkis. Cut off the head and maybe the whole thing falls apart."

"What about my father, Ramasis? Maybe he is the one with all the power, propping up Arkis as his puppet. It seemed that way to me reliving my mother's recent experience. Ramasis barked orders, not Arkis. Arkis was the blade that brutally violated her, but it was Ramasis who commanded him to do so."

Alvarez turned to Sinto's mother, who hadn't flinched once when Sinto succinctly described what Arkis had done to her. "What do you think, Ianthe?"

She contemplated before answering. "Ramasis is under the spell of their orange nectar. Take that away and he could prove a powerful ally." She sighed, clearly troubled. "Or not."

Alvarez pressed, "What about Naiada? Is she merely a prisoner? Is there the possibility she'd turn and support the Orankai?"

"Naiada is a hard read. She is like me and very powerful. I have been searching for answers, but am finding a resistance. Is it her? Or is it something else interfering? I don't know with certainty. I cannot untangle the truth from fabrication. I am sorry I cannot be of more help. I will keep trying."

Sinto said, "I don't believe Naiada would join them, willingly. But if Arkis tricks her, if he forces her to consume his orange nectar, then..." He drew a sharp breath. "Arkis will gain the power to persuade her to his side."

Sinto and his mother shared a pained look. She said, "If true, maybe I can confuse the story, paint a false narrative. Tell me what to show her."

Alvarez gazed at the ceiling, tapping his chin with a finger. "Perhaps a red herring..."

"Show her what Arkis might be expecting from us," Francesca suggested.

"Or maybe the opposite." Alvarez stood and hugged his laptop to his chest. "Let's break and resume this discussion at fourteen-hundred hours. Hopefully Wantemo will be back with more representatives by then. We will finish this discussion, as Sinto suggested, once the Merahvu are fully represented."

Audrey and their team of four headed back to the house for breakfast. Ryan whipped up scrambled eggs. Audrey sliced up pineapple and papaya. Rachel laid out a pile of sweet rolls she swiped from the conference room. Sinto brewed the coffee.

Then they filled their plates and mugs and moved outside to the lanai. They sat on the last step leading to the beach, scooping eggs into their mouths from plates they held in their hands, watching birds diving into the surf, their toes buried in sand.

"It feels like we're running in circles," Audrey said between bites.

"We might only get one chance and must weigh all options," Sinto said.

"But at what point do we stop chasing our tail?" Audrey set her empty plate on the sand. "It feels like we're stuck. It's been well over a month, and only now we decide to bring the Circle and other Merahvu leaders into the discussion? The longer we sit around here talking about it, the more the Orankai are multiplying. I understand the need to gather resources and train new recruits and such, but what about the rest of us? I feel like we need to act, to do something, *now*."

"But what?" Ryan asked.

"That's the problem," Audrey said. "What do we do! How many times do we ask that question before we finally figure out we should be focusing on the *do* not the *what*. We need to get moving. I feel rusty lingering around here. Like Ryan said, are we on vacation or what? Am I the only one feeling this way?"

Audrey wished Blake was here for these critical discussions. Toiling away in Seattle on critical technology development, he hadn't confirmed when he might be back. He'd been gone for several weeks.

Sinto took her hand. "I know. I feel the same way too. But I have been there to witness the horror. One false move and you're dead. We need to be patient. What is one of the most important rules Sun Tzu outlines in *The Art of War*? Fight only when you know you can win. I have not heard any winning proposals yet. Have you?"

Audrey released a frustrated breath. "What if there is no way to win?"

Sinto stood and started pacing in the sand. Audrey could sense Sinto's building anxiety through the Mark. "There is always a way. It may not be obvious or elegant or play out the way we plan but as long as we believe in ourselves, cooperate, and remain loyal to what is right for the people we are trying to protect, then the path to victory will continue to show itself. It might be messy, we might hit dead ends, and some of us may die, but as long as we are true to ourselves, we are winning."

"What if they employ the same tactic?" asked Ryan.

"They may at first, but I believe they will fail. Arkis does not care about his people. They're fodder. He only cares about himself. As for my father, he may still be tangled up with emotion centered around my mother, me, Naiada…" He stopped pacing and sighed. "My sister is the one most troubling to me. I find it difficult to believe she would readily flip to Arkis' side unless my father has misled her, and that is quite possible. She is still very young with no life experiences and potentially susceptible, especially if they hook her on their orange nectar. My father and Naiada are very close. Closer than I ever was with him. Plus, she has a power none of us can truly understand except for my mother. That is a wild card we must consider."

"Sounds like a bunch of fights," Rachel said. "You and Arkis, Naiada and Ianthe, Orankai and Merahvu. Don'tcha forget about Orange. That's a fight on a whole nother level, civilization versus nature. Geez, I'm gettin' dizzy just listening to y'all runnin' around in circles."

"A multi-pronged battle," Audrey said. "Where do we start? The top. Lure Arkis with bait, then strike."

"You mean set a trap," Ryan said.

"Exactly," Audrey said.

"Naiada may see that," Sinto said.

"Maybe Ianthe misdirects her, a distraction," Audrey said.

"We're back to red herrings…" Ryan said.

Rachel sighed and threw up her hands. "Here we go again!"

"Let's take a swim and clear our heads." Audrey suggested.

No one objected.

11

New Acquaintances

Wantemo returned as everyone gathered at the compound later that day. Accompanying him were representatives from the Merahvu's governing Circle as well as warrior leaders training the many recruits that had volunteered to join the fight against the Orankai, plus a trio of Scouts Wantemo personally vouched for and trusted as reliable spies.

The command center filled quickly, crowded with Merahvu from all three tribes, Seakai and Arctakai mostly but also a few Terrakai, as well as the Larkians. Regardless of affiliation, everyone was happy to see so many committed to the cause.

Audrey and Sinto's small team stuck together, Audrey and Rachel taking a seat at the table while Sinto and Ryan stood behind. Francesca had invited Tucker. He gave Audrey a smile, twisted by the scar running from his lip to ear. He cocked a finger-gun and pretended to fire from across the room. She returned the gesture, both acknowledging a mutual respect.

Rachel's eyes were wide as saucers as she gazed at the Arctakai in attendance. They were albino in their natural appearance, with extremely long silver hair braided and wound atop heads or wrapped around necks as magnificent necklaces, or a combination of both. Glacial-blue eyes framed by white lashes threatened to freeze you if you stared too long.

The warrior leaders were naked and appeared perfectly comfortable, though their private parts were covered by protective flaps of skin embellished by their unique markings. Others were clothed in traditional skareefs, long pieces of fabric wound around their bodies like a toga or a Hawaiian sarong, according to their tribal custom. The Arctakai always wore white and covered most of their equally pale bodies. The Seakai preferred a flourish of bright color that did little to cover much, using coverings more as an expression of mood or personality. The Terrakai commonly wore animal skins or skareefs in neutral earth tones.

Once everyone found a place to sit, stand, or lean, Alvarez suggested that Wantemo make introductions. He started with the representatives of the Circle standing protectively around Ianthe, who was seated at the far end of the table next to Audrey's father.

Wantemo said, "As you are aware, the Merahvu are governed by a Circle of representatives from each tribe, with assistance from our queen, Ianthe."

He nodded toward a woman with short golden hair and lively ruby-colored eyes. "Surah represents the Seakai."

The woman nodded her head. "*Malavee*—my pleasure."

He gestured to two of the palest bodies in the room. "The representatives of the Arctakai."

The woman of the pair smiled and acknowledged everyone in the room. "I am Lucee and it is an honor to join you in our fight for peace."

The man by her side seemed nervous. He cleared his throat and said, "Sliver. For peace and new acquaintances, uh, thank you very much, uh, mala—my pleasure."

"Three representatives are missing from the Circle," Wantemo said. "No one has seen or heard from Jabal, a Terrakai missing since Tallamure was destroyed. We can only assume he was killed or joined the Orankai. The second missing representative, a Seakai,

Beech, was sacrificed to lamprey as a traitor by Arkis as part of their nightly entertainment." He tipped his head toward Sinto. "We know this because Sinto was witness to this unfortunate tragedy and nearly died in similar circumstances." Audrey felt a sharp jolt through the Mark and a strange tingling sensation on the side of her abdomen—Sinto reliving the moment.

Wantemo concluded, "And I think you are all well aware that Ianthe's mate Ramasis, the last missing representative, has joined the Orankai."

Ianthe gingerly stood up, taking a moment to smooth down the ancient, liquid-gold skareef she wore, the only one she salvaged from the several that were lost in the implosion of Tallamure.

She struck a commanding pose before speaking. "While we are fewer, our purpose and commitment to the Merahvu people remains unwavering. We offer ourselves, and the whole of the Merahvu, to join the fight to defeat the Orankai."

Audrey's father stood and helped her sit, whispering something in her ear that made her smile.

He remained standing, and said, "I never thought I would witness this day again. Larkians and Merahvu gathered in peace, as when we first crossed paths in the Salish Sea. While Larkians and Merahvu have completed a full circle from ally to enemy and back again, I hope we all can bury our past differences." He gazed down at Ianthe. He quieted for a beat as they shared a tender moment. "Just as Ianthe and I have."

The members of the Larkian Council acknowledged with a resounding, "Aye."

"*Sayla!*" shouted the attending Merahvu.

Audrey's father beamed and she felt a jolt of pride she never thought she would feel again for her father. He had truly completed a full circle from her earliest memories of a loving father, to a cold vengeful man, and back again.

He continued, "We have a common enemy, not just the Orankai but the fungus Orange, which their leaders have weaponized as a tool to control their people. The only way to succeed in defeating the Orankai and neutralizing Orange is to fight together."

"Aye!"

"*Sayla!*"

Her father sat. Wantemo gestured to the two Arctakai and one Terrakai proudly baring all, each with different but extraordinarily fit physiques. "Our warrior leaders." They nodded when Wantemo said their names, "Khani, Isden, and Vesna."

Khani, an Arctakai, was a giant of a man who made Captain Stokes and Francesca look like starving adolescents. He had shaved the sides of his head and sported a silver, thick braid that snaked down his spine.

Isden, also Arctakai, was the opposite, tall and lithe and appearing to be unnaturally bendable and a tad underfed. His hair was cut short and lay flat against his skull.

Vesna, a Terrakai, was petite like Rachel and sinewy with taut muscle. Her head and brows were shaved completely.

Each radiated an air of confidence and warrior competence. Audrey would be reluctant to challenge any one of them to three rounds on the mat as she had Tucker.

The trio of Scouts stepped forward. Two females and one male; at least, that was what they appeared to be. If they had been walking through the Larkian village Audrey never would have pegged them as Merahvu. It was unsettling to imagine how the Merahvu were able to wander through the Sapien world, collecting knowledge, secrets, and experiences, without anyone knowing their true origin. Scouts were tasked to integrate into the Sapien world more than their own.

The Larkians had no idea how many Scouts might be living among Sapiens or how deeply they may have integrated into Sapien culture; as teachers, infrastructure management, local police force, or politicians. How many Scouts the Merahvu employed Sinto never elaborated, only saying there were enough to gather the perspective the Merahvu required to fully understand varied

Sapien cultures. They never discussed if that meant wielding influence. She shuddered at the thought of the Orankai deploying such Scouts and the disruption they could easily create if they hadn't already.

One of the Scouts stepped forward. She rocked a high blond ponytail, cut-off denim shorts, and a Blondie T-shirt with the sleeves cut off. It was knotted at her waist, exposing her belly button. She had a hot-pink phone tucked in her back pocket and a pair of purple mirrored aviators propped atop her head. Her skin was cast with the glow of a recent tan as if she came hot off the beach ready to party. She portrayed arrogance and confidence you might expect from sudden fame, akin to the ever-expanding popularity of social media influencers and TikTok stars.

"Hi, I'm Victoria. Howya doin'?" She snapped gum as she swung a bright smile and a crackling blue-eyed gaze around the room. "I live in the Sapien world more than I live as a Merahvu. I've learned to take on many personalities, adapt to different cultures, and am proficient with Sapien technology. I can be whoever I want to be."

She set aside the sunglasses, released her ponytail, and shook out her hair. She easily gathered it into a single braid. The blond faded to black, light skin to a chocolaty tone, eyes to a warm brown. With a trick of shading, her face transitioned from oval to slightly more angular, rounded eye to almond-shaped. Her nose flattened slightly, lips plumped, brows darkened and thickened. It was as if an invisible paintbrush had painted over an existing painting with another image, made possible by her innate ability to camouflage. She fixed Audrey with those warm brown eyes and bunched her brow.

Audrey and her father gasped at the same time.

Victoria rendered a perfect image of Audrey, right down to the worrying scrunch of brow.

Ryan squeezed Audrey's shoulder and whispered, "That's frickin' terrifying."

Victoria's image snapped back to what it was before, instantaneously, then she stepped back in line with the others. She tugged blond strands back into a high ponytail while snapping her gum.

The man beside her stepped forward and spoke with a soft British lilt. "Victoria can be a little dramatic."

Chuckles rippled throughout the room. Victoria popped a loud bubble. Sucked it back into her mouth and grinned.

The man rolled his eyes and gestured with raised hands as if to say, *See, told you.* Then he addressed the room. "I'm Blair, uh, and I too have some tricks of my own. I'm an Arctakai in case you hadn't guessed." His features were anything but, sporting dark slicked-back hair and a dark, neatly trimmed close-cut beard. A popular look of the day. Since Merahvu lack facial hair follicles, the illusion was mind-boggling; a trick of shading and texturing across the surface of his skin. Even up close it looked real.

He closed his eyes and when he opened them, his facial hair faded and disappeared, the skin flattened smooth. His hair faded to the bronze coppery color of a Terrakai, then his skin to a soft bronze. He fiddled with the shape of his eyes, like Victoria had, shaping them with an upward almond-shaped slant, much like Sinto's. He smiled and snapped his fingers, switching his features back to what they were originally.

He wagged a finger, gesturing he was not quite finished. Messed up his neatly slicked-back hair till it hung in loose waves to his shoulders. It faded to a sun-kissed blond, with facial hair to match, but thinner and scruffier. His eyes lightened to a soft green, and his skin was burnished with a deep, golden tan. He shifted his stance, a little slouchy, kicked back and casual.

His lips curved into a skewed grin. "Hear surf's up. Dude, which way to the beach?" he said with the whimsical tone of a quintessential California surfer-dude.

Talk about dramatic! Audrey felt shock and awe swell around the room. So silent you could hear a pin drop.

The last Scout stepped forward reluctantly. Her eyes darted between the floor and the people in front of her, clearly uncomfortable talking in front of a crowd. Her face looked like she could be anyone or no one in particular with no prominent or distinct features. Pale skin that hadn't seen sunlight, ever. Mousy brown hair, parted in the middle, with ragged ends that covered a good portion of her face. One of those invisible people.

"I'm Lizza. I'm best at hiding in plain sight. You can learn anything when no one knows you're watching." Then she stepped back and melted between Khani and Isden, fading to white with silver hair and pale eyes. Was it her natural coloring or another disguise? Audrey was alarmed by the fact she couldn't honestly answer that question.

Wantemo said, "Alvarez?"

Alvarez stopped taking notes on his laptop, set aside his mouse, and went around the room introducing the Larkians, including Audrey and Sinto's tight team.

The entire process of introductions had taken nearly thirty minutes. Thirty minutes too long, as far as Audrey was concerned, and was thankful once the topic turned toward strategy.

"We have a dual-pronged dilemma," Alvarez said. "One which is dependent on the other and one that acts by the whims of nature. Destroy one, weaken the other. We have the unique opportunity to combine Larkian technology with the deep understanding of the natural world. I open the floor to sharing and discussion."

Vesna, the petite Terrakai warrior, stepped forward. "We have learned from our Scout spies planted in the City of Green that the city has become uninhabitable due to their recent population explosion. Arkis has ordered many residents to Merluma to work as slaves in the breeding caves. New recruits and newborns are sent to the city for education and training. Essentially propaganda brainwashing. Where the others from the city went or where he sends those that have been trained, is anyone's guess."

Sinto stood, "Arkis told me he plans to attack the Sapiens. The Eradication, he called it. He may be sending the others to Earth. Have you gathered any information as to where or what he has planned?"

She shook her head. "Arkis has moved his main residence to Merluma. We are guessing it's to be near Naiada. Ramasis is dedicated to her protection and has been by her side ever since they captured her. We have no word as to whether or not she is helping Arkis. Arkis suspects we have spies and is keeping plans to a very tight circle of his most trusted. Nothing has been said of this Eradication among his followers. I can say with confidence Arkis appears to be calling all the shots, and that he moves between his residence and the City of Green via the Deep Lake portal, which is heavily protected."

Khani's voice boomed. "I have a small team restoring the abandoned City of Ice in the Winterlands on Merluma. It is nearly complete. Those in this room and the few working there are the only ones who know. It was one of my warriors who found Ianthe not far from the hidden entry. It is the reason she is alive today."

Ianthe nodded in gratitude.

Khani continued, "A secret network of caves from the city lead to the Terrakai Forestlands and through the Forestlands to the upper region of Inception, near where we believe the breeding caves are located. A portal located not far from here leads to the Sea of Meura, the body of water wedged between our tribal lands. The City of Ice has direct access to the Sea of Meura. If necessary, a quick escape back to Earth would be possible."

Surah from the Circle stood. "A recent survey indicates Orange has yet to spread beyond the original Pacific gyre. Once all the plastic there is fully consumed, we suspect it will migrate. To where is unknown, perhaps to the closest gyre to the north of it. Orankai are actively harvesting Orange and are transporting it to Merluma through the North Pacific portal.

"It is only a matter of time before Orange reaches a coast somewhere in the Pacific Rim or perhaps here. We have encountered some infected sea life migrating through these fields of spread. Dolphin, tuna, and squid to name a few. While we believe these creatures are not spreading Orange, we have observed strange and aggressive behavior after these creatures have accidentally ingested it."

Sinto glanced toward Ianthe before addressing the warrior leaders. "What about Arctakai's southern city? How safe is it?"

Vesna replied, "Not very. We have had breaches. Orankai masquerading as Seakai or as refugees from the City of Green, seeking asylum. Most are detained but we suspect many have slipped through. With all the new arrivals from Tallamure it's been challenging to lock down the city. We fear it is infested with Arkis' spies."

Sinto asked, "What about the Keepers of Knowledge, Healers, and other innocents that fled there from Tallamure?"

"They must be protected," Ianthe said. "Our entire history of knowledge is at stake."

"Agreed," Surah said. "We have not considered where it may be safe to relocate them, yet. We were hoping you may be able to help us with a solution."

"Numbers?" Alvarez asked.

Ianthe and the Circle conferred, then she said. "Fifty, maybe more." Alvarez raised his brows. "As in fifty thousand," she clarified, then glanced at Wantemo. "Understand, we are capable of establishing living accommodations on land as well as in the surrounding waters."

Alvarez tapped away at his keyboard, stopped, pushed his glasses over the beaked curve of his nose, and studied something on his screen. "I think we might be able to come up with a solution, but more on that later. Let's keep this discussion rolling."

Sinto jumped in. "After they leave, the city could be a perfect venue for baiting a trap. See what it attracts."

Alvarez said, "I don't like it. Too great a distance to stage a trap from our base of operations in the northern hemisphere."

"I like the idea of a baited trap, which could be anywhere. What's the bait?" Vesna asked.

Sinto spoke up. "Arkis has a weak spot. He hates me, always has. His resentment runs deep and he is hell-bent on finding Audrey. He would love nothing more than to destroy me by watching her die by his hand." He squeezed Audrey's shoulder as if he never planned to let go. "Vesna, you said it yourself—Arkis is calling all the shots. Cut off the head of the snake. See what shakes out."

Audrey's father glared at Sinto. "No way will I allow my daughter to be bait."

Audrey was ready to object, but Sinto interrupted her.

"I was not thinking of using Audrey."

Sinto gazed across the room to Victoria. "Victoria, do you see a need to involve Audrey?"

Victoria blew a bubble. It snapped. She grinned. "Nope."

12

Laying Plans

SINTO REMAINED STANDING WHILE the top leadership of the Merahvu and the Larkians conferred between themselves. He was pleased to hear the weighing of pros and cons, where best to put their mutual resources, toward which problems, and when. Progress was being made, finally.

While Orange was a priority, Sinto felt stopping Arkis was the one and only way to slow down the Orankai. Create disruption. He was certain his father would find another leader, perhaps even elect himself, but that could take time. Any confusion or conflict within their ranks would be a valuable gain.

And if Arkis committed a fatal error, then maybe his followers would question their leadership, creating fault lines in morale and support. It was Arkis' Scouts who Sinto hoped would be the most susceptible to desertion. Break his spy network.

The wild card in any of their well-laid plans boiled down to Naiada. How much did she know about the topics being discussed at this very moment with the people in this room? How well can she navigate the Timeless Dimension and put together the bits of information she may gain into something real and tangible? Had Naiada been initiated into Arkis' Orankai? If so, what effect would his orange nectar have on her ability to see clearly and without bias? Was it possible Orange could weaken her power, or would it strengthen it?

But most concerning, his stomach lurched because of the horrors his sister might have experienced over the last month—or years, if she is on Merluma at its accelerated time scale. He could only hope his father had enough of his true self left to protect Naiada from Arkis' perversions.

He gazed across the room at his mother who was observing him intently.

"You are thinking of her," she shared privately.

He acted as if he was distracted by others. *"Yes. I fear for her safety and the possibility of corruption. The things I witnessed, how easily Arkis manipulates, how he treats women... It breaks my heart what might become of her, if he is able to convert her. Our most clever plans could be derailed by what she is capable of, what she may see with her visions."*

"We must discuss, but not here. I agree we are terribly vulnerable because of her, not just because of her capabilities, but because of who she is and what she means to us. Arkis could use her as leverage."

Alvarez broke off a private conversation with Francesca and Audrey's father and called the meeting to order. "Sinto has proposed setting a trap for the Orankai leader. Khani has shared a possible secret hideaway on Merluma. I would like to get back to our tabled discussion. How to protect the Merahvu brain trust and innocents currently residing in Antarctica." His glasses had slipped past the peak of his beaked nose. He pushed them up, smudging them with a clammy finger.

"This island is a fortress heavily defended by our most sophisticated technology and the mountain range on the eastern shore. We believe Isla Salvación is the safest haven for your most vulnerable. We would like to offer our island as their refuge. The island is self-sustaining and could easily support an additional fifty thousand residents, maybe more given enough time to prepare. I suggest we set up a process of screening new residents as part of tightened security." He acknowledged the members of the Circle. "Francesca has offered her team to work on this and other security measures."

Ianthe raised a hand. "I offer myself to help you in the screening process."

Sinto felt a jolt of optimism. Having his mother screen the newcomers would most likely be their best bet for ferreting out traitors. No one could hide secrets from her mind probe.

Alvarez continued, "As Khani suggested, we agree the City of Ice could be a launching point for operations on Merluma. With a combination of our technology and your knowledge of the landscape, we could devise an attack on the breeding caves and possibly Arkis' residence once its location is discovered."

Khani said, "I would like to lead that team."

Tucker raised a hand. "Oy, count me in, and I might know a few others."

Khani smiled, "I welcome your assistance."

"As far as setting a trap for Arkis," Alvarez said. "I suggest we put more thought into where and when. Several of us like the idea of using a decoy. I propose Sinto and Victoria formulate a plan and gather a team to implement it as soon as possible."

Dr. Wickman gestured to Alvarez. Alvarez offered him the floor. "Orange keeps spreading. I offer to lead a team in devising solutions."

Wantemo conferred. "I would like to join you."

Ryan tipped his chin. "So would I."

Alvarez smiled. "I believe we have the beginnings of a war plan."

13

Misfit

AUDREY WATCHED TEAMS BEING formed in a quandary. *Where do I fit into all of this?* she wondered.

Sinto was engaged in a conversation with Victoria on how to trap Arkis. Ryan was huddled with Wantemo and Dr. Wickman bantering on about neutralizing Orange. Rachel had wormed her way beside Alvarez, strategizing ideas in her strange and unbelievably practical way. Even Tucker had secured a prime spot on the front lines with Khani and his warrior leaders. Francesca was deep in conversation with the Circle as to what was needed to prepare the island for its new residents. Blake was in Seattle, preparing the Larkian fleet of new mini-submarines for deployment. Stokes had flown to Seattle, and was coptering to join the Larkian ship from Whidbey Island that was en route to intercept the Orange-contaminated ship off the Washington coast.

She felt awkward standing alone, watching the others naturally falling into groups, each with a specific purpose. No one seemed to be seeking her out to join them. None of their chosen purposes sang to her. She felt adrift, invisible, a stranger among friends and new acquaintances.

She flashed back to her first days in college. The awkwardness she felt being on her own in the outside world for the first time. The embarrassing stumbles to engage others in conversation, being snubbed when she said something weird, being ignored when party plans and invites were made. It felt like that all over again. Odd man out. The misfit.

And the misfit had no idea where she fit, if at all.

Something brushed her mind. Ianthe was observing her private struggle. She stood and gestured for Audrey to join her outside.

Audrey followed.

They walked through gardens where a gentle tropical breeze caressed their faces and fluttered the palm fronds soaring above their heads. They strolled along a path to the shore where there was a bench sitting in the shadows of a kukui tree.

A large sea turtle had crawled from the sea and was napping on the warm sand. They sat with the turtle at their feet, gazing back through a slit in its eyes.

"You are frustrated," Ianthe said.

"I don't know what to do."

"I suggest you wait. Soon it will become clear. Meanwhile, offer your ideas and support where you deem best."

"Sinto seems to have it all worked out."

"And that might prove fatal."

"What do you mean?"

"This battle may not be won by the best-laid plans."

"You believe we will fail?"

"I cannot know for certain. Anything is possible. There is a possible role you can play. One strategy is to do what is least expected, maybe what others do not want you to do. Including your father. Be unpredictable. Is that not your specialty?"

Audrey smiled. "You know me well."

"I have heard all the stories and witnessed you in action. Your father shared his memory of you challenging Tucker to three fighting rounds on the ship." She chuckled. "I observed a certain amount of frustration on Tucker's part. When he expected rigid, you went soft; when you started off in a position of submission for no reason, you came back with an attack he was not expecting when he took the bait. You put him off guard and exposed his weakness—arrogance. Flustering your opponent is a good strategy." She swiped aside a loose strand of hair from Audrey's eyes. "Still got that *badass* hat?"

Audrey smiled. "Of course. I intend to keep it forever."

"Badass forever." Ianthe held out her fist. Audrey punched it softly.

"I'm not the only badass. Sinto shared what you endured at the hands of Arkis. After what you've been through, and survived, I'd say you've earned a badass title as well. Look at us, a couple of badass babes! Misfits to the core."

Gratitude shone in Ianthe's lavender eyes. They embraced, laughing, and Audrey felt unexpected tears well. It felt good to release the pressure of uncertainty building inside and to be sitting with Sinto's mother; a woman who had experienced many lifetimes, who had governed and maintained peace among the Merahvu for hundreds of years, and whose mind was as sharp as ever and keen on current Sapien culture; like when to fist bump and the meaning of badass.

Audrey honestly couldn't remember a time since her mother died when she felt like she did in this moment. She missed having a mother during those critical years when she went from childhood, to adolescence, to adulthood, and was surprised at how much she appreciated Ianthe's presence, here and now. She was drawn to this side of Ianthe, as a mother with her comforting nature.

Audrey dug her heels in the sand at their feet. "I remember the first time Sinto brought me to meet you. I was terrified."

"As I intended." Ianthe winkled her nose. "A job requirement, and not necessarily one I enjoyed. But to be a leader, one must portray strength by striking fear; not too much, but enough to maintain respect and power. My role has not been an easy one, and to be honest, not one I would have chosen, knowing everything I know now. I truly wished I could have met your father under different circumstances..." Her gaze grew distant. "But then, we would not have had you or Sinto."

"Put that way, I must thank you. Sinto means everything to me; he is a part of me, and gives meaning to my life." Audrey found herself distracted by a deep ache in her chest, of the reality they faced, of the desire to put it all behind them, of the fear they may fail and having the life she dreamed of living with Sinto crushed before it could begin. Of losing him, again, forever.

Ianthe must have felt Audrey's distress and swept her fingers along the length of her hand and began caressing her palm. Her touch was warm and comforting and Audrey savored the quiet moment and the bond growing between them.

They sat for a moment in silence, watching the surf wash upon the shore, licking at the turtle's tail, slumbering at their feet.

"I'm sorry I rifled your mind the way I did when we first met. I must confess, I was curious about your life, about Robert's part in it... to catch a glimpse of your mother whom he loved so deeply. It was rude and unnecessary of me to violate you that way, without your permission, but as queen one is given certain *exceptions*. One I exploited much to Sinto's objections." She sighed. "Behavior I now find distasteful."

Audrey remembered that rifling all too well. The way Ianthe slipped inside her mind without her being aware, digging out juicy bits, and living a lifetime of memories in a few seconds. It wasn't until Ianthe was finished that Audrey realized what had happened.

It was in that same meeting that Ianthe laid out an ultimatum: get her father to agree to a truce at a time when they were still sworn enemies. It wasn't until after a violent altercation in which Sinto was stabbed and the Merahvu scattered that Ianthe and Audrey's father finally acknowledged their misunderstandings and re-embraced the peaceful and fruitful partnership they had established long ago.

"So how is he?"

"Your father? He is well, finally at peace. Both of us, actually, which I find refreshingly humbling. Though he feels obligated to protect you, as he should."

"Has he accepted my fate with Sinto?"

"He has, but it worries him."

"How so?"

"He remembers what happened to Thomas… I'm sorry, I mean Blake." She shook her head. "I am finally beginning to understand what it means to become old." She smiled. "Beliefs from the past wedge themselves deep in the mind. The longer you live the harder it seems to acknowledge new facts and current realities."

"You're not alone. I'm still trying to accept the fact that Blake was born in the eighteenth century and was once in love with the sister Sinto never had the chance to meet."

Ianthe went strangely quiet at the mention of Sinto's sister, Leela. Audrey noted the short lock of golden hair she twirled between her delicate fingers. "What happened with Thomas and Leela is not all that worries your father. You are a clever girl. Sometimes rash and unpredictable, and that makes you dangerous and potentially vulnerable against the forces we fight. Caring for someone like you care for Sinto, and him you, can lead to irrational action at the most inappropriate time."

"Isn't that true for anyone who loves another? My father of all people should know what it means to be irrational in the name of love."

"And I too." She drew a deep breath, held it, then let it slowly go. "I hope you appreciate what I must say for your sake, for Sinto's." She paused. "You must choose your paths wisely as you have a vital role to play."

"What role? How will we know which path?"

"That will become apparent when the time comes."

"For both of us?"

"Yes."

"And that is what worries my father?"

"Deeply, as for me too. Sinto is my son whom I love with the whole of my heart. It is what we do now, Merahvu and Larkian, that will cast our future fate. Who lives, who dies. What that future may be, if at all."

"Does this have something to do with the wobble Blake told me about?"

She said nothing.

"Are you not concerned?"

"Very."

"Feels like we're running in circles. Everywhere I look, overwhelming problems, a bleak future. What if there is no future? No tomorrow? Do we live now and savor every moment?"

She said nothing, cradling Audrey's hand in both of hers. She splayed Audrey's hand and fingered the lines crisscrossing her palm. Then she rolled Audrey fingers into a fist and kissed her knuckles.

"Listen to your heart. Savor today, but fight for tomorrow. When the time comes, you will know what to do, as will Sinto. I suggest you refrain from discussing this problem of the wobble with others. Including your closest friends. We must sustain hope when the darkness comes, for as long as possible."

And with that, Ianthe gently released Audrey's hands and left her to ponder those parting words.

14

Bitter Farewell

AFTER THE GATHERING DISPERSED, Sinto found Audrey alone, wading in the sea along the beach next to the Larkian compound.

The Mark came alive when she turned to face him, as it always did whenever their eyes met. The jolt of electricity that came not from his merlux but that mysterious connection people in love have universally experienced across the sands of time. Her waist-long braid was wound across her shoulder and tightly clasped in her hands. A worrying sign he knew well. Something was troubling her.

No words were spoken as he came to her and they embraced, Audrey squeezing so hard it made it hard for Sinto to draw a full breath.

"What's wrong?"

She said nothing and pressed her lips to his, her answer ringing loud and clear through their shared Mark. Fear of what was to come, of letting go, of never seeing him again. Her lips quivered when they separated.

"I want you," she said. "Before our world explodes and we're scattered, who knows to where—you and I, Ryan, Rachel... our families, Blake."

"I won't let that happen."

She pulled back. "You can't promise that, Sinto. Time to face reality. We each have a role in this fight and it can't be fighting side by side. Physically, I am vulnerable to what the Orankai are capable of. Francesca and Wantemo tried to give us a technological advantage, but that failed for me. There must be a reason why."

"Perhaps it means you stay here, help settle the refugees from Antarctica."

"Are you kidding? You want me to linger behind while you risk your life with Victoria going after Arkis?"

The venom in her voice made Sinto start. "I, uh, was merely making a suggestion."

Her face wadded up.

"I didn't mean to insult you."

She blinked away tears welling in her troubled gaze. "Why must we face these impossible choices? Why can't we be like normal people who fall in love, put in an honest day's work, pop out a few kids?"

"What's normal? This chaos we find ourselves in is our normal. Time passes, things change, including what you might consider normal. To live is to accept change. Whether for good or bad is a matter of perspective. Nothing is stagnant. Nature is in constant flux, mutating and adapting; Earth and Merluma, the bird, the bee... Orange. It starts with the tiny things, then works its way to the big things. Even in death, what remains breaks down to feed the next cycle in the circle of life."

His gaze dropped to the waves swirling around their ankles. "See how the water flows. The way the sand shifts beneath your feet when a new wave drifts past, how one movement—the lifting of a foot—changes the outcome. Wind creates movement. The ebb or flood of the tide creates movement. The position of the moon in the sky drives the intensity of the tide. Each one of these ever-changing factors affects how the sea moves around your ankles. Never fixed, always adapting."

He pulled her into his arms. "We cannot predict anything with certainty. Not in this fight. There are too many considerations. Remember you and I agreed to ride into the storm, together."

She nodded. "To flow as water, swift as wind."

"Yes."

"But we also agreed to fight fierce as fire—*together*."

"Metaphorically. Maybe that means from different shores."

"And if something happens to one of us? Or both of us?"

He cradled her chin. "We must do everything possible to survive. What else can we do?"

"Must you run off after Arkis? Why not send one of Khani's warriors?"

He gazed into her sad eyes. "It is something I must do."

She said nothing at first, then she looked away. "And there is nothing that will change your mind?"

"No."

Audrey pulled free from his arms and hugged herself. "When do you go?"

He wrestled with telling her the truth, knowing she would object.

"*When?*" she asked more urgently.

"As soon as the others are ready."

"As in right away?"

"Yes."

The full wrath of her despair surged through the Mark and set his heart thundering as surely as her own. How could he convince her that *he* had to face Arkis? That there was nothing she could say that would change his mind. Arkis picked this fight. It was Sinto's responsibility to finish it. He could not rest until Arkis was stardust along with his threat to kill Audrey, and the abduction of his sister was avenged. She was supposed to be the stubborn one; now it was him.

That chill he felt earlier settled between them, like a glacier wedged between two solid and unmovable mountains.

She turned away from him. Her shoulders quivered when she said, "Then go, and be done with it."

15

Timeless Insight

SINTO LEFT AUDREY ALONE on the beach, the Mark in his arm cold and the blood in his veins thick with her bitter, last words. He felt hollow. He wondered if he was making a mistake leaving her, or if he would be making a mistake if he stayed. The weight of this uncertainty weakened his confidence.

He forged on, not looking back for fear he would race back and steal her away, taking them both to the far reaches of Earth and away from the daunting challenges before them. Damned be Arkis and the Orankai! Damned be Orange and the unnatural things on the Earth it sought to swallow!

Rage rumbled deep in his essence. Rage seeded by Arkis and his threats to Audrey, to the Sapien world, and to everything his mother and the Circle had accomplished to ensure peace after thousands of years of the Forever War. That delicate shell of peace, forged over the past three hundred years, had been shattered.

And for what? An insatiable lust for power?

While Sinto was certain of what he must do, he was uncertain of exactly where to begin. Fooling Arkis would not be easy, no matter how well Victoria could reanimate herself to appear as Audrey. He may have spies lurking. Naiada may sense something in the works.

Would Naiada warn Arkis even if it put Sinto in danger?

Sinto missed his sweet little sister. So innocent and mischievous. So full of life and simple reassurances. He hadn't realized until now how much he relied upon her, and how frequently. Would she sacrifice her family for their bastard half-brother? Would their father convince her to join him in destroying everything they had been raised to protect?

Sinto gritted his teeth. Uncertainty, the bane of human existence.

I must rid my mind of its poison!

His last stop before retrieving Victoria for their secret mission was to see his mother.

She was waiting for him on the front lanai of her house. She stood and held out her hand. "Walk with me."

He took her hand and tugged, assuming she meant to stroll along the small beach of black sand.

She held firm. "No, not here. To the Timeless Dimension."

Sinto faced her, toes curling in the smooth hard grain of ironwood at their feet. "Is that possible?"

"Of course." She smiled. "I still hold secrets."

"Have you ever walked with another in that way?"

"Yes. My mother, when she trained me, and again when I trained your sister." She laughed. "Don't be afraid." She brushed her fingers between his eyes. "Keep it up and that worry line will become permanent."

"For good reason. You've nearly killed me several times when you suddenly and unexpectedly journeyed there as I stood by."

"Because you were *outside* the vortex, a very dangerous place to be. I apologize, belatedly, for exposing you to it. I promise you will be perfectly safe by my side."

She led him down the stairs and along a path into a patch of thick jungle growing above the rocky shore. She stopped when they reached a small clearing littered with dead leaves and severed fronds. A circle of trees and vegetation were stripped clean of their greenery; woody skeletons testament that she had been here before to travel into the Timeless Dimension, whose vortex wreaked this devastating damage.

"What do I do?"

She faced him and gathered his hands in hers. "Gaze into my eyes."

Her eyes brightened, pupils swelling until they consumed every part of the iris and whirlpools sucked at wisps of his essence. A wind roared in his ears and sticks and dead leaves whipped in the space around their bodies. The vortex.

She whispered. "Surrender, and don't let go of my hands."

He gripped her hands tighter.

The roar in his ears subsided as did the sting of things whipping past. The expanse of the universe unfolded with a darkness Sinto had never experienced even in the deepest depths of the ocean. A darkness that threatened to fill every cell in his body and still his beating heart. Cold and uncaring, as if death itself had come to take him. Distant galaxies and stars winked back empathetically.

His mother's voice threaded through his mind. *"Beautiful, is it not?"*

Sinto was afraid to reply. Afraid of breaking the tether that held them together, of being lost in this space of nothingness. The Timeless Dimension. This was not a place he belonged and that sentiment reverberated in his bones.

She continued, *"This part might make you dizzy, but that will subside. Best not to focus on the movement but the snippets you may see from the worlds we visit, the timelines we will pass through..."*

His physical body felt no movement. He knew, physically, that he stood in the clearing, holding her hands. It was his mind that was untethered and zipping through a universe of many Earth-like worlds—past, present, and future. Worlds like that of Earth and Merluma and others that felt only vaguely familiar to those he knew. Worlds in various states of growth, change, and near imminent death from an exploding Sun. Their surfaces with continents of different shapes. Some with deep green masses surrounded by blue water, others stripped bare and on fire with muddy seas. Some with gaseous atmospheres so thick he couldn't see what lay beyond.

His mother dove toward an Earth world that looked like a big blue marble surrounded by dark space, like the pictures he had seen in Sapien books and those shared by Scouts of present-day Earth. The same Earth on which his feet were firmly planted, pristine and welcoming in the bitter cold and darkness of space.

They dropped from the sky and tumbled toward the surface.

As they drew near Sinto noticed a slight dimpling in the northern hemisphere centered above the Salish Sea. Ripples radiated across the Pacific Ocean. A subtle movement he wouldn't have noticed if he had blinked or hadn't been looking directly at it. A pulse of energy followed by an irregular wobble.

Before landing on the surface, his mother veered and raced through the sky, counter-clockwise, several times. Then she dove into a vortex burrowing into the ocean and through a portal to Merluma. They burst from the Great Ocean on Merluma and soared like a bird, unseen by man or beast. They swooped and raced over treetops, along the sharp black ridges ringing Inception, to Deep Lake buried deep in the Black Mountains. Up they soared over the top of the highest mountain, then raced down the other side to the fertile plains skirting the Terrakai Woodlands. There was no evidence of disruption or of new settlements.

"*Is this in the past?*" Sinto queried.

"*Yes,*" his mother replied. "A *time before Arkis discovers Orange.*"

They landed in a field of wheat, tender and young; late spring.

At the edge of the field, a blessing of horned horses the Merahvu called *unis* grazed. One moment Sinto was observing from afar, the next they stood beside an old gray alpha mare.

His mother acknowledged the old mare by extending her palm freely for the old mare to take a whiff. The old mare whinnied, pawing the ground. A black stallion approached and stood by her side, guarding and ready to challenge—the proud alpha stallion of the blessing, and the old mare's son, just as Sinto was Ianthe's. He gazed down his whiskered snout at Sinto. The old mare nudged the stallion. He snorted, bowed his head, and dropped to his front knees, offering his horn to Sinto. Sinto ran his fingers along the ridged surface to the end, smooth and shiny like the obsidian from the Black Mountains and honed sharp like the tip of a sword's blade.

"He offers himself to fight alongside us, as will all the other creatures in this world, to protect Merluma. They will not approve of what is soon to happen in the caves near the Black Mountains, nor of the Orankai who will decimate these plains and feast on his flesh."

In the blink of an eye they were airborne and the field and the black alpha and his blessing faded. They screamed along the surface of the Great Ocean at a speed that blurred his vision, moving clockwise. Around and around Merluma they spun, to a time in the more recent past.

They came to a sudden stop above the offshore reefs of Inception Bay, horned in by ancient lava flows from the Black Mountains. The beach where he first brought Audrey to Merluma was nearby. There they hovered. His mother intently stared at the surface of the water, waiting for something.

Arkis and his guards, Taylee and Suevo, emerged with Ianthe bound in their life-sucking bands and bleeding from her belly. Next came Ramasis. They conversed for a moment, then split up. Taylee and Suevo left with Ianthe, cutting through the Great Ocean toward the Winterlands. Arkis and Ramasis swam west, along the shoreline. His mother squeezed his hands until he could no longer feel them as they followed Arkis and Ramasis, past Inception and toward the rocky shores of the deserted Desertlands, once populated by the Seakai during the Forever War.

A steep stairway was carved into the rock where it met the sea. Atop the rocky shore the land plateaued. From there the stairway continued to higher elevations. Orankai guards patrolled, but it was unclear what they were guarding.

Sinto asked, "*Is this where they have taken Naiada?*"

"*I cannot be certain; I do not sense her. But common sense dictates otherwise. They may be using energy sucking devices to block me from seeing her.*"

Arkis and Ramasis scaled the stairway to the plateau and disappeared into the hillside. Sinto was unaware of a cave opening there. The entrance was camouflaged by greenery. Valuable knowledge he tucked away for future reference.

"*What is there?*" Sinto asked.

"*A cave network once used by our ancestors. The Labyrinth. It extends from the sea and up into the Black Mountains. Perhaps into the breeding caves themselves.*"

His mother picked up her sweeping clockwise journey, racing forward to a possible future where the sea boiled over with Orange and Orange smothered the land. Fire ripped through the forests at the base of the Black Mountains where Sinto once saved Audrey from a near-fatal encounter with bluestripe tigers. The sky was tainted with smoke and ash and the shores littered with partially eaten carcasses; fish, turtle, shark, whale. Orange-eyed Orankai fought over what little fruit remained in charred trees.

Busheetails, raptors, and rolly rabbits screamed from cages scattered around the Terrakai Forestlands. Lands that once rippled with golden wheat were barren and turned to dust. Orankai roasted the brothers of the caged creatures over open fires while still alive. Raptors picked the bones clean from the carcasses of the black uni alpha and his mother, who lay where Sinto and his mother encountered them previously in their journey.

Perplexed, Sinto said, "*The Orankai will become like the Sapiens they intend to eradicate!*"

"May *become*," his mother corrected. "*The future is not set. This is but one of several possible outcomes.*"

When Sinto opened his eyes, he was back in the clearing on Isla Salvación. The pleasant scent of plumeria and bird song drifted, and waves crashed on a distant rocky shore. His mother gazed back, eyes pale and lacking their usual spark. The grip around his fingers was weak. Timeless journeys took a great deal of her energy, and with Sinto in tow, he suspected it took more than usual.

He helped her sit against a tree and dropped down beside her. He wrapped his arm around her shoulder. She nestled her head into the crook of his neck. She felt cold and small beside him—a new state of her physical self ever since Arkis had stolen her ovaries.

"I have a spy who can help you set your trap."

"Who?"

"I cannot reveal their identity. There are too many eyes and ears around us; whether the bird in the sky or someone from the Arctakai city in the Southern Ocean, they are anyone and can be everywhere. Ours and theirs. Be discrete with every conversation as I am being with you now."

"I will share this fact with the others."

She nodded. *"Good. Now tell me where you and Victoria plan to set your trap and I will see to it my spy slips the word to Arkis."*

16

Trap Irony

Sinto left Isla Salvación with Victoria soon after his journey across the Timeless Dimension with his mother. As his mother requested, Sinto told her his plan; the where and the when to pass on to her trusted spy. The when being immediately, once they had time to prepare, which didn't feel soon enough. Sinto was losing patience faster than he had admitted to Audrey, both in conversation and through the Mark, which burned with her growing frustration and his festering uncertainty.

Sinto and Victoria raced through the Pacific, heading northeast to the place where all of their troubles began: The Salish Sea. It was there that Audrey's father first met Sinto's mother and began their affair, and where his sister Leela secretly fell in love with Blake and Marked him, triggering a chain of events in which his mother accidentally killed his sister, Leela. A death she blamed on Culliford and his crew. Actions and lies that planted the seed for his father's undoing and the spiteful murder of Audrey's mother hundreds of years later.

Sinto led Victoria to the waters off of Andrews Island, one of many islands in the San Juan archipelago dotting the Salish Sea.

They tumbled to a sudden stop in a fizz of bubbles, once the tunneling vortexes in which they traveled reached their end.

In the cold shallow depths was a lively reef claiming the remains of an old sunken sailing ship from the turn of the twentieth century. Together they swam to the beach that held fond and regrettable memories for Sinto. A place where Audrey once called Sinto from the sea and they had shared a passionate encounter before things unraveled.

The island was owned by the Larkians and was where Culliford's crew settled when they arrived in the Salish Sea in the seventeen-hundreds. The secret cove with its tight and overgrown entrance had been a perfect place to hide their pirate ship from curious eyes.

Sinto often wondered what would have happened if Culliford had never led his crew to these waters and he had never met Sinto's mother. Would Leela be the current queen? Would Tallamure still exist? Would the wobble between Earth and Merluma still threaten the future of both worlds?

Once they reached the beach, Sinto's protective lorica slithered down his body and evaporated into the pebble-strewn sand at his feet. He swung the backpack filled with things they needed to set their trap off his back and dropped it at his feet. He pulled out a stainless-steel bottle of water and offered it to Victoria. She drew deeply then handed it back. Sinto gulped down what remained, recalling his recent conversation with Alvarez and the map he had drawn for Sinto to memorize.

According to Alvarez, there was a bunker carved into a rocky outcropping near the center of the island. The bunker was kept stocked and continually maintained, providing food, water, shelter, and supplies they needed. There was also a large cache of weapons and communication equipment.

The irony of his decision to stage the trap on Andrews Island was not lost on Sinto. It was on this island that Audrey had lured him to her boat for some tea, which she had laced with a drug to put him to sleep so she could kidnap him. A tit-for-tat reprisal for Sinto's role in kidnapping Blake, who at the time she thought of as her boyfriend. Needless to say, it didn't end well except for the fact that they both lived to recall the tale.

That conflict was resolved with much pain and destruction, and here he was, embarking on a new one. The fact Sinto had picked Andrews Island for Arkis' trap was somewhat poetic. Same island, different actors.

At the top of the beach was a path that wound through a meadow sprinkled with old apple trees and filled with tall dead grass from last summer.

Victoria stood at a fork in the path. "Which way?"

The left fork led to the cove. He nodded in the direction of the right fork. "North and up, toward the center of the island."

Since the island was in the Larkians' possession during the discovery and subsequent acquisition of lands from the indigenous peoples, it had never fallen victim to deforestation like so much of the Pacific Northwest.

A forest of centenarian conifers towered. Sinto felt small and insignificant compared to their silent and long-lived history. Peppered in between were birch, evergreen salal, and western fern. Huckleberry bushes took root in rotting stumps. A spongy carpet of coppery needles and cedar flagging cushioned every step and the path was hemmed with moss-covered rocks and fallen branches. Rotting tree trunks nursed the next generation of giants. Strands of silvery moss hung from bigleaf maples whose bare branches were ripe with new buds, readying for spring. Their gnarled trunks spanned the width of Victoria's outstretched arms. A crisp pleasant chill pricked their lungs with each breath.

"Wow," she said. "It feels a lot like the untouched forests on Merluma, except everything's a little bit different."

"Evolutionary paths diverged. Like us, Merahvu verses Sapien."

It was easy to get turned around in this part of the forest in the diffused light, and Sinto was thankful the sun had cut through the canopy to help guide them to the north and the rocky rise of the island. After hiking through the old-growth forest, he spotted remnants of a path used by wildlife and they picked their way around a field of large rocks covered in thick moss. They came across a family of black-tailed deer grazing in a grassy meadow with a pond. Beyond was a dilapidated fenced-off garden bursting with old fruit trees and wild greens that thrived in the cool climes of winter.

Sinto detoured to the garden, passing through an arched trellis missing its gate. The garden had gone wild, self-seeding and spreading as nature intended; wild herbs, winter greens, and root vegetables abounded. He crouched, sampling leaves of chard, arugula, and frilly parsley. Victoria tried a mouthful of arugula, made a face, and spit out a wad of green.

"Ack! That's spicy and weird and just—just *ick!*" She muttered, "What I wouldn't give for a burger and fries about now."

Sinto had to agree and smiled. His thoughts drifted back to the journey he took across the United States with Rachel. It took a couple of days to drive from Lake Mead to Lake Superior, and Sinto had his first experience eating a cheeseburger with fries. Those he could give up, but not the gooey sweet cinnamon rolls and sweet creamy coffee Rachel introduced him to.

Sinto stood. "What is it that makes one crave Sapien food?"

"Everything bad for you." She laughed. "That's why it's so good!" She ticked off on her fingers. "Sugar, fat, salt. The three deadly sins. Bring it and I'll gladly die happy!"

"Alvarez promised there would be plenty of food stores in the bunker. We won't starve."

"Bunker food?" She rolled her eyes. "Yuck."

The entrance to the bunker was just as difficult as Alvarez said it would be to find but true to the description he gave. *Look for the highest rise beyond the garden. Tucked behind a cleft of vertical rock you will find a steel door covered in moss behind a curtain of gray bearded lichen. It has been programmed to open for either of you. Simply gaze into the circular recess along the right side.*

Sinto pushed aside a tangle of silvery lichen that grew from the ledge of rock overhanging a mossy steel door. Beside it was the circular recess Alvarez described, free and clear of vegetation. Sinto bent slightly and gazed inside. A beam of soft light scanned his face. With a click and a whirl the door swung inward. Lights sprang to life, illuminating a short set of steps. Beyond was a short corridor that smelled of dry earth and salty rock.

He turned and smiled at Victoria. "Home for the next few days."

17

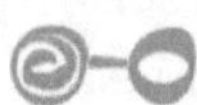

Mystery Of Andrew's Island

Sinto descended the steps carved in rock and into a short corridor of the hidden bunker. Bronze sconces of light came alive and flickered along the walls as they passed by. At the end of the corridor was an elaborately carved wooden door. The intricate carvings on the door depicted a scene of an arched garden trellis twined with wild roses, followed by another trellis, and another, growing smaller and smaller as if leading one on a journey into a garden of infinity cut short only by the limitations of the delicate hand that carved them.

Victoria fingered the masterpiece. "My god, the patience this piece of work must have required..."

Sinto pressed his palm into a hand-shaped recess where a door knob normally would be and pushed. The door swung smoothly and quietly on well-oiled hinges.

More lights came to life inside a low-ceilinged foyer that opened into a living space carved in rock. Defused natural light radiated from several points in the moderately high ceiling. Fresh air burst from hidden vents as if a sleeping giant woken from a deep slumber had sighed heavily.

Dust covers blanketed furniture and muslin curtains covered the walls. They pulled off dust coverings and pushed aside the curtains. The space was livable and accented with art. Books filled shelves. It would take a lifetime to read them all.

A soft deerskin sofa beckoned and Victoria fell onto it, body sprawled with a huge grin on her face. "I hope whatever food they've got is as welcoming as this."

Sinto fingered the various books on the shelves and other fine trinkets collected ages ago. There were feminine flourishes everywhere; antique cut crystal vase, porcelain figurines, a pair of very old dolls. One doll was black skinned with a bald head while the other was pale with frizzy red hair; both had hands and feet carved from wood and bodies of tattered fabric lightly stuffed and holding their wooden extremities together. Thread-thin bodies that threatened to disintegrate if Sinto stared too long.

Paintings of idyllic island scenes covered the spaces not claimed by bookshelves—of a garden in full bloom, of a mist-shrouded old-growth forest, of a rocky shore meeting a lively sea at sunset—places Sinto and Victoria had passed on their way to the bunker and someone had painted long ago.

Tucked into the far side of the small living area was a dining table for two within a small open kitchen lacking any modern amenities. Whoever spent time in this place survived with a potbelly stove and copper sink that required pressing a foot pump to retrieve water. Sinto pressed his foot down several times until finally a trickle of water burst from the bronze spigot. A quick taste confirmed it was sweet and free of sediment and harmful metals. Potable as Alvarez promised.

The cupboards were bare of food but provided an adequate collection of pots and pans, dishes and utensils, knives and cutting boards. Hanging beside the stove were bundled collections of dried herbs and lavender. Based on their muted color and lack of scent it had been a while since they were picked.

An arched doorway opened to a bedroom. The simple double-size bed was covered by another dust cover. Several trunks contained men's clothing from an earlier century, along with sheets, towels, and hand-sewn quilts. An empty chamber pot sat in the corner. A mirror hung on the wall above a table with a wash basin and pitcher. A bare bronze hook embedded into the rock beside it awaited a fresh towel.

Alvarez had given Sinto a brief history of Andrews Island before they had departed. The true name was of possession by someone named Andrew. Andrew's not Andrews. Over time the apostrophe had been lost in the shuffling of official records.

The island was named after Francesca's deceased wife, Andi, who went by Andrew when pretending to be a man, at a time in history when that was necessary. Andi was originally from Scotland and joined Culliford's crew while they were en route around Cape Horn, plucked from a sinking ship that met an unfortunate fate. Francesca had immediately recognized that the new crew "man" named Andrew was indeed a woman. And although the crew had eventually accepted Francesca as a woman after initially thinking her a man, she didn't know if they'd be ready to welcome another woman to the crew. So she and Andi worked hard to keep Andi's secret, even persuading Culliford to marry them. And then one day Andi was caught—literally—with her pants down and the entire crew learned the truth about Andi.

Francesca and Andi found the whole episode amusing. The cunning Captain Culliford had been fooled—twice—into accepting women as part of his crew and then into officiating their marriage. But as unorthodox as their marriage was at that time in history, pirates led unorthodox lives and the crew quickly came to accept their union.

Francesca and Andi were the first to be hunted down by Sinto's father, who wrongly believed Culliford murdered his daughter Leela. It was on the pebbled beach of this very island where Andi died. Francesca barely escaped and managed to swim out to their ship, *Sea Lark*. She was unable to bury Andi and left her corpse on the beach. Having died of sudden heart failure from electrical shock, Andi didn't suffer. Francesca and the rest of the crew fled, believing they had safely escaped.

But that belief was short lived.

After they sailed across the Pacific, Ramasis and a handful of Terrakai attacked them again. Most of the crew was slaughtered. Only six survived and were shipwrecked on Isla Salvación. Decades later, a grief-stricken Francesca built a small sailing ship with Blake's help. She sailed back to the Salish Sea alone to bury what was left of her wife and to live out her remaining days on the island, where she and Andi had planned to settle after retiring from their pirating ways. Francesca had been itching for revenge ever since.

Based on what Audrey told him, he learned that Francesca hired men from the surge of ships sailing into the Salish Sea in the late eighteen-hundreds, paying with her stash of stolen treasure. Hard-working men and the slaves they brought helped her carve out the secret bunker located at the heart of the island. At the time, some of the surrounding islands were named after the men who had discovered them. Francesca dedicated the island to Andi, opting to use her alternate name of Andrew. It was a name she knew would blend in and not stand out from the other islands.

Francesca fiercely guarded her privacy and the shores of the island from intruders, and spent several decades living alone on the island until Culliford recruited her back into the fold. It was then that the remaining six crew members that formed the Larkian Council today formulated a plan to exact revenge against Sinto's mother.

And so began the mystery of Andrew's Island that remained to this day.

And it was here that Sinto, with help from Victoria, planned his own form of revenge against Arkis for destroying so many innocent lives, kidnapping his sister, and threatening his future with Audrey.

Victoria was poking around in the bedroom and came out with the chamber pot in hand. "Are you kidding me?"

Sinto chuckled. "You can always go outside."

She was not amused.

He continued his search for another door Alvarez told him about, cleverly disguised within the shelves. The door to the vault. After scanning several book spines he found the one he was looking for. An old leather-bound book with *Tesoro* stamped on its spine. Tesoro, Alvarez told him with a sly smile, meant *treasure* in Spanish.

Sinto glanced back to Victoria, watching with chamber pot in hand. He wagged his brows and pulled the book out. The entire wall of shelves quivered, then a section slid forward and to the side revealing a solid metal frame and matching six-inch thick sliding door.

Lights clicked on one by one inside a cavernous space filled with storage cabinets and a fully functional modern-day living area with a full kitchen and high-tech communication station. Near the kitchen was a round table with six chairs. An equal number of bunks were secured against one wall with curtains that could be drawn for privacy between each. Victoria squeaked in delight when she peeked inside a bathroom with multiple sinks, a private room with a flushing toilet, and large walk-in shower and a deep soaking tub.

She grinned. "Aye, these pirates are clever and resourceful and appreciate the finer things in Sapien life, like privacy when doing one's business and the simple joy of a hot shower."

"Francesca built the first chamber in the early nineteenth century. This chamber was added ten years ago. Alvarez calls it the vault."

Victoria pulled a bunk down from the wall and claimed it as hers. Sinto opened one of the cabinets and found a cache of various styles of crossbows, spear guns, hunting bows, knives, and collapsible batons. Drawers were filled with barbed spears, arrows, coils of thin rope, darts, and objects that smelled of gun powder. Some fit perfectly into the pockets of a set of sling shots stored beside them. No guns. Audrey told him the Larkians found guns were of no use in water and were much too noisy to be effective against Merahvu. Guns or not, a small and well-calculated war could be fought with the weapons at hand.

A second cabinet was filled with bundles of currency in varying denominations from different countries, as well as sophisticated equipment and specialty paper and stamps for forging passports and other certified documentation.

After claiming her bunk, Victoria buried her head inside a large freezer in the kitchen area. She was digging around checking out individually vacuum-sealed meal packs, an icy mist swirling around her.

"All dated and fresh... Ooh, beef stroganoff, green beans, and—" She rummaged deeper into the mist. "OMG!" she squealed, "Chocolate cake with coconut caramel frosting!" She tossed several packages onto a sterile stainless-steel counter. "I'm starved, you?"

Food was the last thing on Sinto's mind but he was thankful for her enthusiasm and hunger pangs. He hadn't eaten a proper meal for a couple of days, with worry stealing his appetite. He desperately needed refreshment and her choices did sound intriguing. He had never tried beef stroganoff but the sound of her delight made his stomach growl.

Victoria warmed their vacuum-packed meals in a special cooker that used a warm bath of water, what Alvarez described as *sous vide*; a method that worked perfectly for heating up the prepared meals supplied in the freezer.

Sinto sat at the communication station. The computer had automatically switched on when they entered the vault. He found Alvarez on the short list of contacts and hen-pecked a terse message with his index finger. He intentionally kept it brief with few specifics. Alvarez alerted Sinto to the fact that Arkis may have tech-savvy Scouts scanning for their communications. It said: "Successful landing. V overjoyed by meal choices. Two days. We will be ready." He signed with an S then pressed send. He sat back, satisfied. They had two days to prepare before his mother delivered her message to her secret spy.

That night, after gorging themselves with Victoria's picks from the freezer, they reviewed their plan. Ianthe would let slip to her spy that Sinto had taken Audrey to Andrew's Island to hide her away from Arkis and far from the danger of conflict between the Merahvu and the Orankai. Vesna and a team of her warriors would be on standby on one of the Larkian tech ships disguised as a research vessel, anchored in the waters near the reef preserve. An additional team of Larkians was on standby and ready to deploy by air from the Larkians' shipyard on nearby Whidbey Island. Sinto and Victoria would meander the island pretending to be lovers on a long-awaited vacation.

The island was covered with hidden cameras and infrared sensors, and Sinto and Victoria would be notified immediately of any intrusion via ear comms from the network located in the vault. The same network connected directly to the ship. If a rabbit twitched they would all know it.

The next morning Victoria practiced her Audrey disguise. While she gave a compelling demonstration on Isla Salvación, Sinto suggested they perfect it. Victoria's hair was shorter, but Sinto braided it the way Audrey always wore hers. He shared with Victoria nuances in Audrey's various expressions of joy, disappointment, deep concentration, and the way she looked at him, and only him, when no one else was around. Victoria experimented with shading and texturing of nose, cheek, lip and lastly the thickening of her brows.

"Well?" Victoria asked.

Sinto was shocked. She had mastered Audrey's expressions to perfection. He drew a sharp breath. "Close enough." He handed Victoria a pair of jeans, long-sleeved t-shirt, canvas tennis shoes, and Audrey's favorite fleece-lined, hooded sweatshirt; things heavy with her scent. Victoria changed and next she practiced the way she had observed Audrey move.

Sinto gasped from the dip of shoulder and a worried gaze Audrey often made when she thought no one was looking. "That's... perfect." Even the Mark jolted in confusion.

Everything was set.

All they had to do was wait.

18

Cement

Audrey didn't see Sinto after their brief and chilly farewell. Shortly after, he left with Victoria for whatever secret place they had decided was best to lure Arkis into a trap. The last words spoken and feelings shared between them sat heavy on her soul and bitter on her tongue. She struggled with her feelings of regret and frustration, but not as much as her fear for Sinto and what was to come.

And she never felt more alone.

Her house on the south end of the island was quiet. The night was dark and still. And yet she was restless, antsy, and jittery. That feeling of running in circles and getting nowhere. Helpless to stop the inevitable.

Sinto said nothing remained stagnant. Yet here she was, buried in cement while the world revolved around her.

Ryan was whiling away with Dr. Wickman and Wantemo in the lab on the *Requiem Sea II* to dissect and solve the riddle of Orange. Rachel was working crazy hours with Alvarez going over every angle on how to stop Orange from spreading beyond circulating gyres of the Pacific. Blake was still in Seattle, estimated time of return unknown.

She sat on the lanai, gazing up at the first planet sparking into view in the early night sky.

She fingered the Mark buried in her arm. It was cold and quiet like before, when she thought Sinto was dead. Sinto might be a gazillion miles away, possibly in an entirely different world that billions of people on planet Earth had no idea existed.

She wondered if she would be happier to be one of them, blissfully unaware of the trouble brewing in said world and, closer to home, in the Pacific. She wondered what her life would be like if she had been born in another time or place with a different father. Of never meeting Sinto or Ianthe or any of her father's three-hundred-plus years-old pirate crew.

Would she be in college finishing up her master's degree? Would she have met some nice Sapien boy and be bumbling around in a small dorm room discovering each other's bodies with hopes of getting married one day? Living a life many people considered normal?

Sinto said that wasn't normal.

But it was. For lots of people. Why couldn't she be one of them?

The sound of the front door opening and closing startled her from her reverie. The interior of the house was dark, the sun having set long ago. Normally she would have jumped up, found something to use as a weapon, and taken a position of defense until she was certain that who or what opened the door wasn't there to hurt or kidnap her.

Yet here she sat. Stuck in cement. Helpless.

Audrey heard soft footsteps approaching. She whirled around when someone stepped onto the lanai.

Blake startled when he saw her. "There you are! I was hoping to find you—what are you doing, sitting alone in the dark?"

She stood. Her legs tingled and joints had stiffened from sitting for so long. "Yep, here I am, all alone, nothing new."

He gave her a sympathetic look. "I'm sorry. Some people treasure quiet moments alone." Then he gave her a lopsided grin that warmed her soul.

Blake was a welcoming sight; blue eyes alive with vitality and hair swept back from riding in a UTV with the windows down. They hugged. He smelled earthy and freshly showered.

Ever since Audrey learned Blake's true identity, they had grown closer. Siblings raised by the same man in different times. Blake as an orphaned child in an earlier century and raised as a pirate, Audrey as his biological daughter in this present time. Each from one of their father's dual lives. Oddly enough, Blake seemed to be that one part of normalcy that recently entered her life.

"What are you doing here? The compound's abuzz with everyone working late. I thought you'd be there in the middle of it."

She shrugged. "I know, I—I just didn't feel like getting involved."

"Hmm. That's doesn't sound like you." He held up a bottle of wine he had set at his feet. "Would this help?"

She nodded. "Yeah, it's been nuts. Everyone busy or running off to save the world. Everyone, except for me."

He nodded. "I heard about the nLink disaster."

She shrugged. "Guess it wasn't meant to be. So here I am."

They went inside and Audrey switched on lights. She plopped down on a stool at the counter facing the kitchen. Blake dug out a wine opener and a couple of wine glasses.

Seeing him helped clear the fog of depression that blew in earlier in the day.

Blake poured the wine. "I would have returned earlier but Stokes asked for my help with that infected ship. Luckily we were able to intercept without creating a ruckus, and the contamination was minimal. It may have been a sea bird or something else that dropped a chunk of plastic on deck covered in the stuff. We explained to the captain it was an invasive species the government has been quietly tracking and we were a private firm hired to quickly eradicate it, at no cost to him or the company he contracted with. Messed up the ship's electronics, wiring mostly, and gobbled up stuff from a couple of containers. He was ever grateful after we installed new electronics and took the infected containers off his hands. We stressed the importance of not discussing what happened, especially with the company that hired him. He was glad to be rid of it and accepted our generous financial offering to keep mum."

He looked around. "Did Ryan make it to the island okay?"

"Ry is staying on the *Requiem Sea II* and is helping Dr. Wickman and Wantemo on a solution to Orange. Rachel has been hanging out with Alvarez."

"Who's Rachel?"

"Ah, Sinto's friend he met while searching for his father. Met her in Las Vegas."

Blake's brows shot up. "Vegas?"

Audrey rolled her eyes. "Oh yeah. Apparently she was an escort and showed him around town."

Blake laughed. "Escort, huh, I never would have guessed Sinto was the type."

"He claimed it was of pure necessity. She helped him win money he needed to navigate through the Sapien world and offered to drive him across the country to Lake Superior. I get the feeling there was a little more between them, but he claimed not. Strictly friends, he said. Anyway, she's a dynamo and cute as a button with a disarming southern twang. After meeting her, I've come to admire her equally. She came along with Ryan."

"And she's hanging out with Alvarez?"

"She's helping bounce ideas, work through different scenarios."

"Huh, Alvarez usually works alone."

"She has a refreshing perspective of the world, and is surprisingly smart too. Alvarez specifically asked for her help. Not the slippery arrogant fish I once thought he was. Anyway, she's staying at the compound."

"And Sinto?"

Audrey sighed. "Going to trap Arkis with a Scout named Victoria pretending to be me. Don't ask how or where." She made a face, drew air quotes with fingers. "A big *secret*."

"Ouch, sounds like a touchy subject."

She twirled her wine glass. "Don't start."

"So it's just you staying here?"

"Yup."

"Huh, that a good idea? You being all alone?"

She reached across the counter, play-punched his arm. "I can take care of myself."

"Against them—" He shook his head. "Think again."

"Sinto's going to kill Arkis, so I guess I have nothing to worry about." It came out more sarcastic than she intended.

"So, what, you're moping around here waiting for something *not* to happen?"

"Yup."

"I have a better idea." He leaned across the counter. "Stokes and I are fine-tuning some new technology."

"What kind of technology?"

"The mini-subs, single driver. Designed to easily maneuver, fight, and defend against Orankai. Feels like driving a Formula One car but underwater. Flew a dozen of them in on the transport plane that brought me. Crew's unloading them tonight. Training begins first thing in the morning. I think I can convince Stokes to add you to the team."

She grinned at the sound of cracking cement rippling through her mind. "Ah, the Xiphias project. Alvarez mentioned it in one of our strategy meetings." She held up her wine glass. "Count me in."

19

Sibling Secrets

The next morning Audrey rose before sunrise. She had slept soundly for the first time since Sinto left. Blake had stayed with her in the house in the other bedroom. A tiny bit of her was relieved as she realized how utterly alone she felt not knowing where Sinto was, if he was safe or whether or not he would be successful on his mission with Victoria, confronting Arkis.

The new branch in her relationship with Blake was growing stronger. She once felt passionate pangs for him. But that was mostly in name. Circumstances had kept them apart, for which now she was grateful. Blake had offered her support in ways she had never imagined, as a friend and long-lost sibling...

...and that same long-lost sibling was now banging away in the kitchen, retrieving mugs, boiling water, and making fresh dripped coffee. Noises she knew were meant to wake her and she smiled because of it. Acting like she imagined a brother would, using not-so-subtle hints that it was time she got her ass out of bed.

So she did, padding her way to the bathroom and into a hot shower.

"Ready for an adventure?" he asked when she finally wandered into the kitchen in a robe and with hair wrapped up in a towel.

"After coffee."

He handed her a cup, shifted his gaze to the towel on her head. "Want help with that?"

She rolled her eyes. "Please. Been driving me crazy. Braids like before?"

"Mm. I have a different idea. Braids, yes, but maybe we could shorten the length and thin it a little too..."

She rolled her eyes remembering what Sinto told her about change. "Sinto said change is good. Why not?"

Blake slipped into his bedroom and came back with hair clips, a comb, shears, and a shaver. "You sure about this?"

She looked at the shears and shaver, then to his face. "I trust you won't make me look like a freak."

He grinned. "Anything but. I'll make you look like the badass you are."

He led her out to the lanai with a stool in hand and gestured her to sit. She did, facing the cove.

The air was still and water reflective. Rays of sunlight slipped through foliage promising a warmer-than-usual day. He pulled the towel from her head and laid it across her shoulders. She sipped coffee while he combed her hair, swearing several times at the wavy volume and knots that formed just by looking at it. He commented on the fact it had reached the top of her butt cheeks and was ragged with split ends. He didn't bother combing out the last of the tangles along the bottom, opting to cut them off instead.

She tried not to wince at every snip of the shears and the resulting pile of foot-long sections of tangled hair accumulating at her feet. Next he divided her hair into four sections, two on each side, top and bottom. The bottom sections were smaller than the ones on top and extended from her temples across the top of her ears and a couple of inches above the nape of her neck. He secured the larger sections atop her head with the clips.

He snipped off the lower sections on each side to less than an inch. Next came the shears. Her heart pounded, wondering what he had in mind and if she had made a mistake to let him hack off so much hair.

He patted her shoulders. "Relax, you're going to love it." Then he sheared off what remained of the lower sections to a quarter of an inch from her scalp. It felt stiff and scruffy to the touch. The pile of hair at her feet grew to a mountain.

"Want me to cut a design in?"

"Like a UFC fighter?"

He nodded.

She thought of Sinto and their promise, to strike, fierce as fire. "Bolts of lightning. One on each side."

With a few quick strokes with the shaver it was done. She felt it with her fingers, extending from temple to the back of her neck where it kissed the one on the other side. Dual bolts, connected, like her and Sinto.

Strike as lightning and light a fire...

He put the shaver down and released her remaining hair from the clip, then handed her the mirror. "When you let it down, see how it covers the sheared sides, and it's much more manageable." It fell across her shoulders in soft waves, covering the shaved portions altogether and falling to the middle of her back. Her fingers could easily comb through. It felt light and liberating. She handed back the mirror.

He divided the top into three sections and braided each tight to her scalp, then braided the three pieces into one that snaked along her spine.

Her head tingled from the tightly woven braids and she mindlessly reached for a phantom scraggly braid. It felt unnerving now that it was gone, replaced by a much shorter one that barely wound around her shoulder.

Blake handed her the mirror once more.

She barely recognized the woman staring back. A warrior groomed for battle. She was amazed how Blake's creations could make her feel revived, like the time he braided her hair for her challenge with Tucker in which she won his prized badass hat.

Sinto was right. Change was good. It was time to stop sulking and take action.

She beamed at Blake with renewed purpose. "Where did you learn to do this?"

He blushed. "A Hawaiian girl I knew a very long time ago. She had thick wavy hair like yours, drove her crazy too. I braided her hair, and her mine. I shaved the sides of her head the same, and sometimes... other places." His eyes drifted to the tranquil waters licking the pale sand forming the cove. "All I had was a sharp hunting knife, which proved to be quite tricky, and after, we would have the most amazing—" He blinked, gaze swinging back to the present moment and the fact he was sharing something maybe he didn't intend to share with his sister. The red patches that bloomed on his cheeks traveled down his neck.

"You would have what?—*sex*?" She laughed. "And *you* had hair long enough for braids?"

"I had many hair styles in my past; braided, shaggy, buzzed—and yes, that is what would happen, what you said, after we groomed each other."

"Groomed. Each other. As in..."

He nodded sheepishly. "Quite the foreplay. Afterward we would engage in a most vigorous way." He grinned recalling the memory. "And frequently."

Audrey was a bit astonished to be having this frank and honest conversation, but realized that maybe this was what close siblings did in the real world. No secrets or lies or fancy footwork to twist the truth. Especially on the topic of sex, something she knew little about, and which she was embarrassed to admit.

"When was this?"

"Let's just say, long ago."

"Wow. Progressive."

"Not really, you might be surprised what happened back then. Humans haven't changed at all. We merely forget."

Audrey debated not asking her next question for fear of stirring up past emotions, but she was curious. "And this was after your challenging years, after Leela?"

His gaze grew distant and sad. "After I accepted what happened I had to move on. That girl showed me it was possible to love again. She was a well-needed distraction."

"What happened to her?"

He closed his eyes. "She was the daughter of a powerful chief. He gave her away to another. It was the way back then. He didn't know about me. Our affair was a secret, wisely so."

"I'm sorry."

"Don't be. Life is full of twists. Some fair, some not."

"I am beginning to realize that."

"It wouldn't have worked anyway. The Council had made a pact to share neither our secret elixir nor the truth of our past, especially about the Merahvu. Your father never revealed this secret, not even with your mother, though once you were born he suggested we dissolve that pact. Your birth marked a turning point. Watching you grow we all decided it was time to live out the rest of our lives naturally. When you turned eighteen we all stopped imbibing sucuvita."

She gazed at him, recalling the strange and twisted road their relationship had traveled. Once learning of his past, her eyes were opened to a different and more genuine set of feelings. Ever since, her relationship with Blake had grown deeper, not only as a close friend, but as a brother she so desperately wished she would have had growing up. Someone she felt she could share her deepest secrets with and ask the stupidest of questions. Someone she could *trust*. Knowing what she knew now, she realized a romantic relationship never would have worked for either of them. Even if she had never met Sinto.

She zipped her lips with pinched fingers. "Your secrets are safe with me, brother." Then she hugged him. "Thank you for being here, for your tireless support, and for getting my sorry ass in motion." She pressed her hands to her head. "And for this amazing badass creation."

20

Mutual Vows

Sinto and Victoria stayed busy while they waited to spring their trap for Arkis on Andrew's Island. They had two days until word from Ianthe would slip to her spy. One day had passed. Alvarez sent back a reply to Sinto's email that her spy would get the message tomorrow.

Sinto taught Victoria hand-to-hand fighting techniques Audrey had taught him. They practiced firing crossbows, setting up various targets and competing for the most accurate hits. They scouted the entire island, mapping out escape routes should their trap backfire. They were confident and ready.

They read when their bodies felt weary. They scavenged fresh greens from the overgrown garden and mushrooms from the forest. Since it was late winter, there was no fruit to harvest. They ate three full meals a day to fuel their bodies for whatever may come next, Victoria deciding Sinto must try each and every type of Sapien pre-made meal provided in the freezer.

At the end of their sweep on the second afternoon, they climbed to the top of the highest peak of rock on Andrew's Island where Francesca had erected a shrine for Andi. She had artfully stacked large rocks into a cairn and affixed a plaque of bronze cast with

Andi's name and the date of her death. Below she had added a promise:

"Rest in peace knowing,

I dedicate my life to avenging you.

With all the love in the world,

Francesca."

Scattered about were beaded necklaces, silver rings, tattered books, feathers, and shredded wisps of fabric that once must have been colorful scarves or wraps. Trinkets left by Francesca over many decades in memorial.

The memorial peak offered a commanding view to the north across Haro Strait to the Canadian Gulf Islands. Gray clouds blotted out the sun and painted the water a dull gray. Hilly islands were painted a shade darker. Gray upon gray upon gray.

The power of connection in this place was strong between Earth and Merluma, where a portal lay not far below the surface of the Salish Sea. Sinto could feel the thrum of that power within the Mark buried in his arm.

They sat pondering all that gray, whiling away the end of the day. "What made you decide to devote your life to being a Scout?" Sinto asked.

"Maybe the same reason you devour every Sapien book and magazine you can get your hands on. Curiosity, and learning why they do the things they do."

Sinto smiled. "We aren't all that different. Had we not had our physical advantages, we may have done the same." He pointed at a small plane bouncing around just below the cloud layer racing west from the mainland to Vancouver Island before nightfall. "You ever had the chance to catch a ride in a plane?"

She nodded. "A commercial flight, once, from Seattle to Boston. Scared the shit out me being trapped like that for hours in a tin can thousands of feet above the ground. The pressure change is hell on the ears. Took every bit of control not to freak out and toast everyone with my merlux. Ended up hitching a ride back in a car. Don't know what I was thinking. The Sapiens have a saying: curiosity killed the cat. I was almost that cat."

"That happened to me once in an elevator. Nearly lost it in the few seconds it took to go one floor up. Rachel was with me, thankfully."

"That one's a curiosity."

"She sure is." Sinto plucked a blade of grass growing from a crack in the rock where they sat. "Ever wish you could catch a ride to space? To see the entirety of Earth floating in a sea of nothingness?"

"Nope. Some things are best left to the imagination."

"I suppose..." He flashed back to his brief journey to the Timeless Dimension and the multiple Earth worlds he witnessed in various stages of possibility. Parallel versions. Each potentially populated with a different version of himself. He wondered if alternative versions of himself had a tail or came to know the alternative version of Audrey.

"Ever fall in love with anyone?"

She blushed. "Yeah, I had a Sapien boyfriend once. I know we weren't supposed to, ya know, have intimate relations with Sapiens, but I wasn't the only Scout that did it. It got awkward until I finally confessed what I was. I was surprised at how cool he was with it. He was one of those types that gobbled up fantastical fictional stories. But he was good at keeping my secret and quite smug to be dating a *mermaid*." She gazed off and grew quiet.

"And?"

She sighed. "He was in the army and got deployed to Afghanistan. He was on a routine sweep, when uh... a little boy distracted him. It was a trap. Guess it happened all the time over there." Victoria paused, her throat bobbing. "He died." A tear slipped from her eye which she quickly wiped away. "He didn't want to go, but he had to. He took an oath and was bound to fulfill it, just like he vowed to keep my secret. Not all Sapiens I've met are as honorable. Like us, there are good ones and bad ones. Mostly good, like my boyfriend. Never understood why the good ones die and the bad ones live."

"When was this?"

"Five or six years ago."

"Anybody since?"

"Nah. Love bites when you lose someone you can't live without. I learned my lesson. I take care of my own needs and keep to myself."

Victoria's story left a bitter taste in his mouth. Sinto couldn't begin to imagine what it would feel like to lose a partner so senselessly. To lose Audrey.

She must have sensed his despair. She punched him in the arm softly. "But that's not going to happen to you. You got me. We're gonna get that fucker and all the rest." She stood with raised arms, turned in a slow circle, and shouted, "Hear me now—I vow to not rest until every orange-eyed monster turns to ash!"

Sinto smiled at her, feeling the infectiousness of her energy. He called out: "And for Arkis to face the ultimate punishment for his injustice against nature and humanity."

21

Orange Conundrum

AUDREY SWEPT UP THE pile of her cut hair, feeling renewed. Blake did more than style her hair; he snapped her out of a debilitating funk. Gone was her long braid, which she used all too frequently as a crutch to grab onto whenever confronted with fear or uncertainty. Blake reminded her she wasn't alone, that being lost merely meant it was time to seek a new path, one which he offered in the form of Xiphias. And they needed pilots.

Audrey and Blake locked up the house and headed north to the *Requiem Sea* II in their UTV. The morning air was cool. The exposed sides of her head tingled with freedom.

The Xiphias mini-subs had been transported to the ship from the plane Blake flew in on the night before. Audrey was amazed at the dizzying pace in which the Larkians developed, built, and deployed new technology. Though Blake explained Xiphias' development wasn't as last-minute as it seemed. The Larkians had been planning for this day for many years, decades even, by staying on the leading edge of technological breakthroughs, refining and developing new ones strictly for Larkian use, and most importantly, building backup ships to replenish their existing fleet, like the *Requiem Sea* II.

Requiem Sea II's first-generation sister ship was destroyed beyond repair during the attack on the Merahvu's city, Tallamure. The previous ship was scrapped and repurposed for future projects. *Requiem Sea II* was an exact replica with a four-hundred-foot sleek black hull that housed a trio of telescoping "wings" and a drop-down keel. A one-of-a-kind ship that could transition from power to sail with the push of a button. An engineering marvel that Blake helped design. It had been nearing completion when the original ship was destroyed. Apparently, three others were in the works and nearly ready.

The Larkians had accumulated a level of wealth that surpassed many westernized nations, mainly because of advanced knowledge of future events and technology that Ianthe shared with her father. The ratio of wealth to population was obscene. Wealth that size often leads to greed and power struggles. But she hadn't seen signs of this type of corruption among the Larkians or the Council members. Most of their wealth was reinvested for the benefit of all.

As Audrey climbed the gangplank, a flood of emotion came over her. She had experienced firsthand that the Larkians ran their nation like a pirate ship. Every member contributed. Every vote was equal. Why? Because it worked and the original Larkian crew knew of no other way.

Couple that with a stringent recruiting process for new citizens. Alvarez and Dr. Wickman had formulated a screening process that worked with near one-hundred-percent success. Each recruit was chosen based on moral character, adaptability, and commitment. They were respected, regardless of their past mistakes or their shortcomings. Everyone was valued for their strengths and contribution.

To become a Larkian, she had vowed to uphold the Code of Conduct, which she failed to read fully before signing her acceptance. When faced with a hard moral choice, she had blithely defied the orders of a Council member because she didn't agree.

She broke trust, which was a big bad no-no. Only a few ever intentionally met this fate. Audrey had been one of them, but she'd been lucky and got off easy, holding onto her Larkian status. It was a humiliating lesson, especially because she had dragged Ryan into helping her with her offense. It was a hell of a twenty-first birthday wake-up call. Ever since, she vowed never again to act or break trust without fully weighing the consequences, to herself, as well as everyone else.

"Do we have a second for a quick detour? Ryan was hoping to see you. He should be in the lab."

Blake smiled. "And I him."

Once aboard, they passed several crew-assigned cabins then climbed the ship's mid-ship stairway that wound around the drop-down keel housed in a giant cylinder. Inside the ship looked exactly the same; oiled wood, polished bronze and brass, classic nautical light fixtures. The air was perfectly moderated and scented with the brine of the sea that nestled into every nook and cranny.

The laboratory was located on level two, aft, and occupied half of the ship. The door was open. Blake and Audrey stepped inside.

The lab was unrecognizable. Walls had been moved and new spaces added for studying Orange. Additional computers had been added to a wall of electronics that tapped into an all-new data center located in a secret location on the U.S. mainland to support a newly added Artificial Intelligence assistant, Alan, developed solely by the Larkians.

Since Orange would be lethal to pretty much everything on the ship and potentially harmful to anyone who came in contact with it, the working section of the lab had been hermetically sealed off with two staging areas for decontamination. A list of strict rules and procedures for entering and exiting was clearly mounted on the wall, including a short list of who was allowed inside.

Ryan was one of the names on the list. He wore a black, hermetically sealed, rubber-fiber suit with a hood and glass face plate, and was bent over intently studying something under a microscope.

Audrey tapped on the glass viewport to get his attention.

His eyes lit up and he waved back when he saw Blake. A second later his voice crackled from a speaker. "Give me a few minutes."

They watched as he returned the sample he was studying to a sealed glass box. He entered the first of two sealed compartments and stripped off his protective suit, then stepped into another awash with a bright light. He passed through to a third space where he lingered while the system ran a final check for contamination. The door slid open five minutes later once a full scan gave him the all clear.

"Look who I found!" Audrey exclaimed.

Ryan beamed. "Blake! Hey, it's been too long."

They embraced, clapping each other on the back.

Ryan checked out her hair. "Nice!" He regarded Blake. "You do that?"

Blake nodded proudly.

Ryan scrubbed his head. His hair had grown longer, too, popping up in every direction like a porcupine. "Maybe you could do something with this."

Audrey pointed to the inner lab. "Making progress?"

"Not yet. Fungus is highly diverse and can live in the most extreme circumstances. It's everywhere—forests, deserts, our bodies, the ocean... some are harmless, others lethal. Then there's Orange. We haven't pin-pointed where it came from or how it spreads, only that it has a voracious appetite. Between that and what it does to the human brain, it's a nightmare. This is the stuff of sci-fi. Remember that classic horror movie we once watched, *The Blob*?" He shivered. "This stuff reminds me of that, gobbling up everything in its path."

Audrey said, "Didn't they end up using fire extinguishers to freeze it?"

"Yeah, but remember freezing it didn't kill it. The same is true with Orange."

"There must be something that will kill Orange."

"There's the conundrum. We've found nothing that can touch it other than fire, a very hot fire. Even Alan is baffled by the question: How do you burn something at the bottom of the ocean? We found we can control it by offering what it wants, but the more it consumes the faster it grows and mutates. We haven't found a petroleum-based polymer it doesn't like. At this point we hope it mutates itself out of existence." He shrugged. "Hope's all we've got so far. Not so scientific."

"Keep at it. You'll find a way," Blake encouraged.

Ryan laughed. "Thanks for the pep talk."

Audrey said, "Need a break? Blake's been working on a new tech toy. Just delivered to the cargo chamber."

"Sure, a break would be good."

Audrey spun on her heel. "Then what are we waiting for?"

The three of them left the lab with Blake leading the way to the cargo chamber.

22

Lingering Complication

ONE LEVEL DOWN IN the aft cargo chamber, Captain Stokes was directing the final outfitting of the mini-subs Blake helped design. In addition to the one ready to roll off the rails into the sea, there were five more lined up along the side walls. Space was tight. The other six that came with Blake were still in warehouses near the docks.

Stokes was crouched beneath the one on the rails. He looked up, acknowledging them. He winked at Audrey, then addressed Blake. "Final outfitting is nearly complete. Should be ready to commence tests later today." Then he resumed his task.

Blake led Audrey and Ryan around the technological marvel. "Meet Xiphias," he said, beaming. "More are being built to deploy on other ships."

Xiphias looked like a robotic cross between a swordfish and a bluefin tuna. It was eighteen feet in length with a six-foot diameter around the fattest part of the body, which contained an internal sphere made of glass where the pilot sat. Tucked within the tail were dual toroidal-looped propellers for quiet and efficient propulsion. Fore and mid were multiple rotating pod drives for three-hundred-sixty-degree maneuverability. Top speed was sixty knots. Vortex-generating finlets, like those found along the lower-half of a bluefin tuna, and auto-adjusting dorsal-like fins, top and bottom, provided stability and control.

Xiphias was armed to the teeth. The pointed nose housed a retractable sword-like bill, honed to a sharp point and lined with razor sharp teeth for slicing through a net or fending off an attacker. Fore and aft were ports for launching mini-torpedoes. Retractable rotating launchers fired spears and darts in every direction.

Cameras provided the pilot three-hundred-sixty-degree visibility. Sensors captured real-time situational information from every direction, which was mandatory at depths where light didn't penetrate and the pilot was driving blind.

The pilot entered through a transparent hatch directly above the single seat. The rest of the interior was tightly packed with batteries, ammo for weapons, tanks of compressed air, and storage compartments for emergency supplies and additional equipment.

"We added a defense feature specifically for absorbing an electrical shock and funneling that energy back into the batteries. In addition, reverse polarization can suck electrical energy from an electrified organism, like an Orankai. Everything was designed with dual purpose, even the power system, making it a life-sucking weapon."

Ryan asked, "What can't it do?"

"Dive too deep. The weakest point is the hatch for entering and exiting the pilot module. Max depth possible is currently six thousand feet. Sensors restrict the pilot from overriding this failsafe feature, but given more time... we may find a way to overcome this limitation."

"You designed this?" Audrey gasped.

"I was part of the team led by Francesca and suggested we base the design on the most efficient creatures swimming the sea. Tucker programmed the system, and the team in Seattle acquired the necessary materials and fabricated the hull, including the glass sphere. I was there to help put it all together."

Stokes came over and joined them. His short buzz-cut hair was impeccably groomed, as usual. He cocked an equally groomed brow and flashed a brilliant smile. "Want to give it a go?"

"What, me?" asked Audrey, looking around.

"Why not?"

Her heart did a flip. She wanted this, but the memory was as fresh as yesterday. That fateful day she, along with her father and Stokes, dove to Sinto's underwater city in a four-man submarine. Their brief and tense confrontation with Queen Ianthe ended with Sinto nearly dead and the three of them running for their lives. Racing back to the surface, they learned the *Requiem Sea* had been attacked by Orankai rebels. Her father, unaware the Orankai were enemies of the Merahvu, ordered Alvarez to bomb the Merahvu's city with remote submersibles in retaliation.

The subsequent implosion of the city's protective dome reduced the trio of sea mounts surrounding it to rubble, triggered a massive earthquake, and launched a shock wave that nearly destroyed their submarine and generated tsunamis across the Pacific Rim.

Her father endured a head injury. Stokes fractured several ribs, an arm, and his clavicle. Fortunately, Audrey escaped injury and under Stokes' guidance was able to use the last of their air reserves to fill the ballast tanks. It was a risky choice and their chances for surviving were slim. They were sipping their own carbon dioxide by the time they reached the surface and would have died had a Coast Guard rescue ship not been there to cut them out before suffocating.

Stokes must have read her thoughts. There was a rolling stairway with a platform at the top, snugged up to Xiphias' side. He patted a step. "Best to get back on the horse."

Audrey swallowed. "Right."

Stokes climbed up first. Audrey followed. From the platform he pointed out a toehold carved in the hull below the open hatch. "Step there, then swing your other leg up and find the step inside."

Audrey did as he suggested. Once she found her footing inside, she wiggled into the pilot seat.

Stokes leaned in and helped her secure the five-point harness, pulling it snug. "To keep you secure. I think you understand why."

She nodded. "Been there, done that."

Stokes said, "I hope you're not claustrophobic."

"Does feel a little like crawling into a coffin."

"Best not to think about it that way."

"Right." She knew all too well what it felt like to be trapped in a dark coffin deep in the ocean.

Stokes pointed to a pair of goggles hanging beside her. "Put those on and speak to make adjustments to your view. Talk aloud and we'll hear you." Then he closed the hatch. Her ears popped from the change in pressure.

Her attention was quickly diverted from her morbid memory by the smell of leather and new electronics. Blake was right. It felt more like slipping into a race car. A very nice race car with extraordinary capabilities. The soft leather seat hugged her from shoulder to leg.

The glass sphere embedded into the heart of the submarine made for tight quarters. Everything essential was within easy reach. Dual joysticks, one for driving, one for employing weapons. The goggles provided overlaid views from the many cameras. With the shift of an eye she could see every corner of the cargo chamber, Blake and Ryan standing below, the sea beyond the open transom. It was like having the eyes of a fly.

A screen on the dash kept a running tally of the submarine's system status, navigational charts, and a record of what the sensors were picking up, like the heat signature of the bodies milling around the cargo chamber.

"Check?" she said.

Stokes replied, "Hearing you loud and clear."

It didn't take long for the smallness of the space to sink in and she struggled to wipe the image of being entombed at the bottom of the ocean from her thoughts. A flashback she hoped to forget but her mind refused. Her heart raced and hands shook.

She grabbed the wheel to open the hatch. It didn't move. She pounded on it in a panic.

Stokes' voice boomed over the speakers. "Button on the right to unlock the wheel. It's marked."

She found it, pressed it, then the wheel spun free. The hatch popped open. She unfastened the five-point harness and slithered her way out, feeling her way down to the foothold molded into the side. She dropped onto the platform and scurried down the steps in the blink of an eye.

Blake grabbed her arm. "Hey, you okay?"

"Just a little shaky that's all." She forced a smile. "Ry, go on up. Hop in and check it out."

Blake helped Ryan up and inside. He lingered in the hatch, pointing out controls and systems to Ryan.

Audrey paced, trying to calm her heart, swallowing excess saliva filling her mouth. She had no idea how close to the surface her trauma lay and feared she would be stuck here, settling the migrants, instead of participating alongside Blake and the others in the fight.

Stokes noted her distress. "Maybe you should catch some fresh air."

She nodded. "Good idea." She waved to Blake. "I'll catch up with you later."

Blake acknowledged. "Cafeteria in thirty?"

"Hopefully," she said, racing for the inner chamber door.

23

Sage Advice

AUDREY WORKED HER WAY up the mid-ship stairway, one level up to the lab. There she found Dr. Wickman, staring at his computer screen, chin propped in a hand, deep in thought.

"Dr. Wickman? Do you have a minute to spare?"

He spun around in his chair. "Certainly. It's been far too long since we've had a private moment together." He smiled once his gaze made a full sweep of her newly styled hair.

"I just had an episode. Being closed up inside a Xiphias. Rapid heartbeat, sweaty palms, nausea." She held out her hand. It was shaking. "And this."

He closed the outer lab door, pulled over a chair next to his, and gestured for her to sit.

"Sounds like classic onset of a panic attack." He pulled open a drawer, retrieved a pen light, and shined it into her eyes. "Slightly dilated."

He put the pen light down and cradled her hands. "Let's do some calming breaths. In for four, three, two, one. Now hold." He counted to seven. "Now release slowly for eight."

He had her repeat that breathing sequence three more times. Then he asked her to close her eyes and imagine her favorite place.

She thought of the little house she shared with Sinto and the beach where they met long ago.

"Better?"

"A little, I think, um," She looked around the lab. Her vision was much sharper. "Yeah, better."

He looked in her eyes again, felt for her pulse at her wrist, and smiled. "Yes, better." He released her arm. "Maybe we could talk about what triggered the attack."

"I felt that same debilitating fear and helplessness I experienced when I was trapped with Stokes and my father in the submarine. I thought we had worked out those issues, but it was like I was right back in my seat quietly screaming inside my head while my father insisted I was my mother. I really want to participate with the others, but..."

"But what?"

"I can't fail. I must do this, something. Sinto wants me to stay here, help settle the migrants."

"A wise suggestion. It is a very noble contribution."

"But that's not me! I mean, I know it's important but—but that's not what my father trained me for. I'm stuck. I don't know what to do. Staying here is a waste of my skills and driving me crazy. I'm trained to keep moving, not to console newcomers and hold hands."

"And you believe running headlong into the heat of the battle and risking your life is the best solution?"

"You know what I mean."

"I do not. Enlighten me."

She sighed. "I'm afraid something terrible is going to happen to Sinto."

"Do you think you're the only one who can save him from this imagined fate?"

"I don't know, maybe. Yes! I mean, I can't lose him again. I'm not sure I could recover if something happens to him. Ianthe, she said—she told me Sinto and I have an important role to fulfill, together."

"And what if something happens to you?"

It felt as if she'd been poked with a red-hot stick. "Me?"

"Yes, you. Both of you exposed to danger raises the stakes one or both of you may encounter unfortunate circumstances."

"At least we will both die trying."

He raised a brow. "And this helps how?"

She was speechless. What could she say?

Dr. Wickman sat back, patiently waiting for her to figure it out.

She sighed. "It doesn't."

"Correct."

"So you think I should stay here too?"

"Not necessarily. I would suggest you weigh all the considerations before making a final decision. I saw Xiphias. Amazing technology. I would love the chance to whiz around in that thing, being a hero." He smiled. "But for me, my best contribution is to stay here and solve the problem of Orange." He pointed at the bank of blinking and humming electronics lining the walls. "Not a very exciting environment, but required for my critically important task."

"If I decide to join the Xiphias team, can you help me overcome my fear?"

"You are the only one who can do that. I can only provide you advice and maybe something to take the edge off if it becomes a problem."

"I want to do it but I must keep my senses sharp. No drugs."

"Then the best thing you can do is face that fear head on. Exposure is a powerful tool. And remember the calming techniques we practiced before to manage your anxiety. Maybe Blake can help you too."

Blake spent years with Dr. Wickman wrestling his demons after Leela died. Leela was everything to Blake. He literally went insane and Dr. Wickman helped him climb out of that hole and reclaim his sanity. Blake even went one step further. He reinvented himself, changed his name, and buried the damaged man he once was in the past.

"Of course."

"Is there anything else I can help you with?"

Audrey blushed, recalling the delicate conversation about birth control she had with Sinto before he left. Not that she expected needing it now, maybe not for a long while. Maybe never. But still, it was a promise she made. One she intended to keep.

"Actually, there is." She cast her gaze to the ceiling. "Um, Sinto and I, we..."

"You seek a form of birth control?"

She exhaled a loud breath. "Yes, um, not only would an accidental pregnancy be poor timing, but we have other reservations about it happening at all. I think for obvious reasons. So something with high probability of success."

He nodded. "Good considerations to ponder, with the current circumstances and the potential result of cross-breeding between Sapien and Merahvu. I'm pleased to hear the two of you have discussed this topic *before* it was too late."

She rolled her eyes. "It hasn't been easy to... abstain."

He chuckled. "It usually isn't. To be honest, I was expecting you might inquire about this subject and I wholeheartedly recommend you choose a birth control method that works for both of you.

"As for your second concern, if a pregnancy results, planned or accidental, then think of it as nature finding another way to evolve the human species. It is fact that Neanderthals and Homo-Sapiens crossbred. I have a small percentage of Neanderthal embedded within my DNA and you may also, from your father. It's even possible Merahvu-Sapien crossbreeding has already happened. The Merahvu were close allies with the indigenous people when we first arrived in the Pacific Northwest in the seventeen-hundreds. Human nature dictates that somewhere along the line the two species may have integrated already. We just don't have any proof."

Listening to Dr. Wickman, Audrey felt a deep sense of relief and the lifting of uncertainty she had been carrying around for the past several weeks. She was surprised at how much the topic of a possible pregnancy was weighing on her conscience and wondered if it had also weighed heavily on Sinto's too. Every intimate encounter was a struggle of resistance. Guilt and uncertainty wrapped around the what-if.

He stood. "Let's start with your immediate concern. With your active lifestyle, something that you can forget about for several months is best. There are a couple of options."

24

Love Letter

SINTO LAY ON HIS bunk unable to sleep, reading the same paragraph from the classic story of *Moby Dick* for the sixth time. He finally gave up. He was too distracted, the words on the page meaningless and muddled.

Victoria was asleep in a bunk a couple of spots over. He eyed her enviously in the faint light cast from electronics across the room. She was a natural at dealing with high tension situations, something she said she first learned when she became a Scout and set out to live in the Sapien world. She told him if she had lost sleep over worry then she would have never slept at all. She was heavily seasoned to the constant light and noise and uncertainty a new day may bring. Nothing ruffled her. Nothing interrupted her precious sleep.

The vault smelled lightly of roses. Victoria had squealed in delight when she found a very old bottle of rose-scented perfume, buried deep in one of Francesca's old trunks. Sinto had been more delighted by the half bottle of rum Francesca had stashed near the bottom. The rum was long gone. The rose-scented perfume was not and Sinto's head swam with the fragrance.

He got out of bed and quietly padded past Victoria and out the vault door to the original bunker. He lit an old oil lamp and sat at the small table adjacent to the modest kitchen. He had never taken up writing letters before, but something drove him to write one now. Maybe it was from immersing himself in Francesca's old world. The ways of her simple life were taking root—from tending to the garden, to reading classic fiction, to writing letters to those you love.

He had found old parchment among her things as well as a pot of dried ink and a quill. He used a small amount of water to revive the ink and practiced writing the alphabet in a bold script. He perfected his signature, something he had never needed before.

Once he mastered the dip-and-scratch flow of writing with ink pot and quill, he set out putting the words that swirled in his mind since departing Isla Salvación to parchment.

My Dearest Audrey, his letter began. Regrets that had plagued him since their last encounter flowed easily from the pen. He felt that if he could express his true feelings, he might finally be able to get some rest. He took care and gave painstaking thought to each word, for each and every one mattered.

When he was finished, he signed his name.

He blew the ink dry and carefully folded the parchment into thirds. On the outside fold he wrote her name. A tear found the tail of the y, smudging it before it had the chance to dry.

In all his boredom the past few days, Sinto had carved the symbol representing their Mark—a swirl, a dot, and the line connecting their respective worlds—into a small round of wood. He retrieved it along with a stick of black wax he had found with the ink and the quill. He now had a use for it.

He melted a thick puddle of wax with the tip of his finger, crackling with fire drawn from his merlux. He pressed the small round of wood with the Mark's symbol into the puddle of soft hot wax.

He sat heavy hearted until the wax had completely hardened, hoping that Audrey would never read the words he had written and that he would personally recite them from memory once they were reunited and free to love and hold one another.

He quietly returned to the vault and found a safe place to tuck Audrey's letter on a hidden shelf below the counter of the communications center.

He crawled into his bunk. With his mind finally at peace, he slumbered.

25

Fortuitous Accident

Audrey lined up with the other Xiphias test pilots along the aft wall in the cargo chamber on *Requiem Sea II*.

There were a total of six test pilots, including Audrey and Blake. Tucker was one of the six, as was Dyer, whom Ryan had adopted as his new best friend the month prior. Dyer was in charge of maintaining the cargo chamber and offered light-hearted comic relief when Audrey felt insecure or things soured. He was a handsome devil who could hold his own on the silver screen, tall and suave with a smile that made your knees go weak. Sometimes it was unclear which way he swung, partner-wise. He made advances toward both Audrey and Ryan. Whether in jest or for real, both were uncertain. But that didn't matter. He was a good soul and would lay down his life for you.

Each contender was required to run through a preset, realistic, virtual-reality simulation over the past two days. They covered every system and pushed the limits, both of Xiphias as well as themselves. Audrey was grateful that the simulation didn't trigger the same panic response she had felt when she sat in Xiphias the first time. Facing her fear head on, as Dr. Wickman suggested, seemed to be working.

Audrey finished third out of six. Today they would be testing their skills in the open ocean.

Depending on their performance, Stokes would determine if they were ready for the field. Of all of them, Audrey was probably the most disadvantaged. The other test pilots had previous experience operating submersibles, ship tenders, and other deep-sea submarines in the Larkian fleet. But she had scored high in the simulations. It helped to have Blake's advice and support.

Isden, the lithe and sinuous Arctakai warrior leader, offered to help test Xiphias; mainly how well Xiphias could handle an electrical attack and how well reverse polarization worked to neutralize an attacker. The risk factor for possible injury to Isden was high though he didn't appear too worried. This would be the first time Xiphias would be tested with a live subject. Blake reassured Audrey they had run rigorous tests in Seattle and was confident Isden rightly had nothing to fear.

A test grid was mapped out and programmed into the test unit. It included situational circumstances to measure pilot skill in the open sea. Each pilot would be given three chances to complete the test if necessary. It was expected the first couple of runs could be a little sloppy since none of them had ever piloted a single-person submarine like Xiphias before.

"Are you ready?" Stokes yelled.

"Aye!" they all answered.

The Xiphias test unit had been given the short name *Xiph1*. It was queued up on the rails. Dyer engaged the winch that dropped the aft hatch, which was integrated into the transom of the ship. Once opened it served as a platform hanging three feet over the water.

First up was Burns—a nimble, middle-aged man of Indian origin with shots of gray at his temples. He swiftly climbed the ladder and disappeared inside *Xiph1*. The hatch swung down. Dyer and Stokes released the stops and *Xiph1* rolled down the rails, off the end of the platform, and slipped into the water. It floated for a moment, then nosedived beneath the surface.

Screens mounted on the wall above a work bench tracked Burns' progress as he powered *Xiph1* out of the harbor at a depth of sixty feet. On one screen *Xiph1* was depicted as a moving red dot on a topographical map of the surrounding waters. A second screen showed the feed from a camera mounted behind and above the pilot, capturing every movement and a view through the transparent dome. A third displayed *Xiph1*'s instrument panel. A fourth displayed everything Burns saw through his goggles. A fifth showed a list of test maneuvers each contender must adequately perform to become a certified Xiphias pilot.

Burns gave running commentary as he navigated. "*Xiph1* slips through water like hot knife through butter. Seat fits like glove. Stick offers realistic feedback, better than simulation."

After a few minutes of getting a feel for the controls, Burns dove to five hundred feet, where it was dark, and completed the first set of maneuvers. Rolling, spinning in place, then high-speed turns and reversals. Free-form was encouraged to gain a better sense of oneness with the controls.

Burns aced every one.

Next came weapon engagement. One of the ship's tenders was deployed above the testing site outside the harbor. Weighted wet suits were dropped into the water. Once they reached four hundred feet, pressure-activated air canisters exploded and filled the suits. They bobbed, neutrally buoyant. Because of the darkness, they were impossible to see. Burns had to rely strictly on Xiphias' sensors and what was displayed on the navigation screen.

He lined up and commenced firing. Barb-tipped arrows flew at a dizzying speed, essentially shredding the intended target. Then he launched a mini-torpedo from an aft tube at another target bobbing behind, disintegrating it instantly. Audrey and the other pilots whooped and hollered as the targets disappeared. Isden's brow cocked with curiosity and eyes widened with horror.

Burns returned *Xiph1* to the platform. Dyer and Stokes attached a cable and fired up the winch. *Xiph1* slipped effortlessly along the rails into the chamber. Salt water rained from its hull. The ladder was pushed up against its side. Burns popped the hatch, climbed out, and slid down the handrails of the ladder on his hands. He flashed a brilliant smile. High-fives were passed around.

Stokes said, "Audrey, you're next."

Her heart pounded as she ascended the ladder.

Stokes followed. "You got this," he whispered, before she slipped inside and melted into the contours of the pilot seat. She secured the five-point harness and snugged up each strap until she was locked tight against the seat. Stokes nodded his approval. "Good luck."

She closed the hatch, ratcheting the wheeled latch to the stops, engaged the lock. She checked it again as Blake suggested. The wheel was locked and secure. She took a shaky breath. "Good to go," she announced through the comm, linked to the ship.

Xiph1 rolled down the rails and jolted once it hit the water. Her breath caught and she felt the pings of rising panic. She forced it down, pretending it was no different than the simulation. Once she feared being anywhere near or in water. But she overcame that fear with Sinto's help and being forced into situations where she was fully exposed to water. This was no different.

Move in harmony with force of life, flow as water, like stream around rock.

She navigated out of the harbor. The sea darkened as she descended. She rigged for red to preserve her night vision. The cabin filled with an eerie red light. The cameras were no use in the dark. She had no choice but to trust the navigational map and sensor feedback that were projected through her goggles.

She pressed forward, eyes locked on the topographical map. It felt unnatural to rely solely on technology and not on one's own eyes. She had experienced the sensation before when navigating a boat in the dark and through thick fog, of which she was now grateful.

She followed a different tactic from Burns. While he performed his maneuvers in the open water at a mere five hundred feet, Audrey wanted to test at a deeper depth.

Isla Salvación was formed from a dormant volcano that rose from the bottom of the Pacific Ocean roughly twenty-thousand feet below. The further she ventured from the shore, the deeper the bottom fell away.

Stokes had the test Xiphias programmed to halt descent at three thousand feet. Anything down to that depth was game for the test. She wanted to test close to that limit. Blake assured her Xiphias was capable of what she planned to do when she reviewed it with him.

She had studied the topographical map of the ocean floor and discovered an elevated shelf with a series of sea mounts at two thousand feet, well above the three-thousand-foot depth limit. That was where she ran her simulations and where she planned to execute the test—with real obstacles where utmost trust was put into *Xiph1*'s sensors and her own gut instinct.

Because this was her first open-water test, she opted to flip on the external lights. The bottom came into view. She leveled off and guided the sub along the bottom at a safe distance. The small range of sea mounts emerged, varying in height by a few hundred feet as experienced in the simulation. She surveyed the entire area first to ensure the simulation map she trained with was true to reality. It was. With renewed confidence, she flipped off the external lights to get ready for the test.

Rolling, spinning, and turning wildly was easy in open water as Burns demonstrated, but Audrey knew from past experience that didn't equate to reality. She wanted to demonstrate a more realistic scenario.

She began ticking down the list of test maneuvers.

She rapidly ascended the tallest sea mount, flipped over the top, and dove down, racing for the bottom. She navigated by sensors, barely skimming the side of the sea mount. Once she reached the sea bed, she pulled up, then surged forward toward more obstacles. She rolled Xiphias sideways and slipped between two other rising sea mounts—a maneuver she had perfected in simulation.

Her breath fell into a calm and consistent rhythm as she channeled the flow state-of-mind meditation she practiced while training in the forest or the gym. A mindful presence ever aware of potential danger while moving autonomously, ready to react to whatever may present itself. Flowing, like water or the wind, around whatever obstacle presented itself.

The joystick felt smooth in her hands with just the right feedback. It sent a slight vibration as warning when she ventured too close to a solid mass, and stilled when no danger was present.

She rolled Xiphias to the side, then spun nose over ass three times, coming to a sudden halt upside down. She hung there for several seconds before rolling over slowly with control, then back again.

She flashed back to the time Sinto took her for a wild ride through the Great Ocean on Merluma and how the laws of gravity meant nothing; how fish swam in whatever direction they wanted. There was no reason other than habit for keeping your head pointed toward the surface while underwater. And that is what she did, maneuvering through the obstacles presented in this part of the ocean, rolling upside down, with the dome grazing a few feet along the shelf where the occasional sea creature scuttled out of her way.

After performing all the expected maneuvers, she demonstrated her ability to flow freely through her environment. She swooped around sea mounts, through an arched cave, and avoided colliding with innocent sea life. All in total darkness depending solely on Xiphias' technology to guide her.

Weapons deployment was next. At her present depth, the targets dropped from the ship were no good. So she zeroed in on the sea mounts void of sea life and let it rip. She maneuvered up and over, firing spears from the front at one spot of rock, flipping up and over and repeating her attack from the rear.

As if in real battle, she made a run for it to the surface.

Her depth ticked off, fifteen-hundred feet, one-thousand feet...

"Drop targets," she said.

"Targets released," a voice replied.

Multiple targets registered on the sensor screen and began rapidly descending to four hundred feet. She engaged torpedoes to stand-by and circled at distance. The first target bobbled at the intended depth. She lined up the shot and stealthily released a torpedo from the darkness. Before the target was struck she flipped and released her aft torpedo. Both shots hit their intended targets at the same time.

Muffled booms and shock waves rocked the submarine seconds later.

Stokes' voice broke the silence. "Well done, your test is complete." Pause. "Uh, Isden suggested we test with a live subject. You up for that?"

"Absolutely!" she exclaimed.

"Remember, rules of engagement apply. I shouldn't have to remind you of consequences."

She nodded to herself.

Been there, done that, no thanks.

The next thing she saw was Isden's slender white body slither across the dome above her head and around the rear end of the submarine. She picked up his movements seamlessly through the cameras and sensors. He came back around and mounted the dome, gazing down, waiting for her command.

The first test was for electrical defense. She pinched her thumb and index finger close together, then flashed her fingers.

Small shock.

Isden held up a thumb, acknowledging. His eyes brightened. She felt a small shudder. The battery charge notched up a tick.

She gave him a thumbs up, then signaled for more voltage.

A second jolt hit the sub, this time with a gentle nudge. Another couple of ticks on the battery charge. The system was absorbing the shock as designed and utilizing it to boost the batteries.

She spread her thumb and index finger wide, then flashed her fingers.

Max voltage.

Isden paused to fully charge his merlux. His eyes glowed white hot. Her heart raced in anticipation.

She heard a loud crack and *Xiph1* jolted. Threads of white light crawled across the dome, blinding her. The electronics went black for a second before powering back on, absorbing the power surge. The batteries were pegged at max charge.

She gave Isden a double thumbs up.

"Shock test successful!" She shared over the comm link with the ship. "Batteries at full charge. That last one knocked out the electronics momentarily but all systems fired back up and are fully functional."

Isden pushed off and started swimming in figure eights. Their prearranged signal for the dog-fight chase to begin. For Isden's safety it was agreed no weapons would be deployed. Audrey double checked all weapons were locked down with safeties firmly in place.

She flashed Isden a zero with her fingers followed by a thumbs up.

Weapons disengaged.

Then she waved the bladed edge of her hand forward.

Go!

She gripped the joystick ready to chase.

Isden took off, diving to the depths. The external lights would be useless so she tracked Isden solely by sensors and soon caught up, racing straight down just shy of Xiphias' max speed of sixty knots.

Isden descended, ascended, and looped in figure-eights. Xiphias was delightfully nimble, sticking to Isden's tail as if attached by an invisible cable. She marveled at how the rotating pod drives and toroidal propellers worked seamlessly with the joystick she held in her hands. She switched on the autopilot and locked onto Isden's heat signature. Xiphias took over, spinning tight loops, accelerating and decelerating while sticking perfectly on his tail.

After ten minutes, Isden slowed to a stop and hovered, the glow of his eyes piercing the darkness. The autopilot matched his movement. Xiphias hovered fifty feet from its target. The gentle whir and bob of the pod drives held Xiphias static.

Then he did something none of them had planned for. He flicked a wrist, cut a hole in the sea, and dove inside. *Xiph1*'s autopilot was still on and responded. Every prop bit water. *Xiph1* was snagged by the tail end of Isden's tunnel vortex and was sucked inside.

The sudden g-force stuck Audrey to the seat. Props whined with no resistance. She shut off the autopilot and pulled back on the throttle. No response. *Xiph1* flew by the residual force of being sucked into the tunnel and the lack of resistance once inside, like an asteroid, flying through space.

Isden seemed to be oblivious to Audrey bearing down. Since *Xiph1* was heavier than Isden, she soon caught up. *Xiph1*'s nose nudged his feet. He startled and looked back. His mouth gaped in surprise and he momentarily lost his concentration. The tunnel veered wildly, whipping *Xiph1* side to side. Isden slithered atop with his pale belly pressed to the transparent dome. He gazed down at her once he regained control of the tunnel's trajectory.

Grinning, he gave a thumbs up. Audrey raised a pointed finger and circled. Then waved the raised blade of her hand backward repeatedly.

Turn around, go back.

Isden nodded. Belly to the dome, he shifted his gaze forward, eyes aglow and in deep concentration. The tunnel curved, a little at first then more sharply. Audrey was pressed hard against the harness as they completed a high-speed U-turn.

She double checked that all the sensors were working. The topographical map indicated they had looped far to the southeast around Johnston Island, a little-known island used for chemical weapon disposal and other secret government tests, roughly sixty-eight-hundred miles from Isla Salvación. The system recorded every detail of their journey.

The Larkians had yet to solve the mystery of how the Merahvu were able to travel the ocean at unfathomable speed. Audrey experienced the logic-defying phenomena several times with Sinto. He compared it to the concept of a wormhole in space he once read about in the Sapien books he had collected. By cutting a vortex in the sea, it opened a void of nothingness with no resistance. Acceleration was the result of the vortex's spin and the speed in which one dove inside. The trajectory of the tunnel was guided by the mind with the use of echolocation, Earth's geomagnetic field, and memory.

No one had thought to test a human-made object hurtling through one of the Merahvu's underwater tunnels. If Audrey had switched off the autopilot before Isden made his unexpected escape, they may have never discovered this new and game-changing possibility.

Her heart pounded with renewed hope.

26

Speechless

AUDREY AND ISDEN WERE spit out into the bright blue sea surrounding Isla Salvación. Audrey slammed forward against the harness straps that held her fast to the seat. Isden tumbled from his perch atop *Xiph1*.

The radio came alive with Stokes' frantic voice. "RS2 calling *Xiph1*, repeat, RS2 calling *Xiph1*!"

Audrey was breathless from the sudden impact. "This is *Xiph1*!" she replied, gasping. "Holy shit! You won't believe where we've just been!"

She quickly checked the systems. Nothing was amiss from what she could tell. The data from their adventure was seared into *Xiph1*'s memory. It was a miracle. A frickin', fortuitous miracle. She could barely sit still as she guided *Xiph1* to the surface, Isden swimming alongside, appearing as ecstatic as her.

"Tell Blake I didn't hurt his baby!"

Stokes' voice boomed through the speaker. "Where the hell were you?"

"Took a loop through the neighborhood. Ever hear of a place called Johnston Island?"

A pause, then. "Did you say *Johnston* Island?" She could hear commotion in the background.

"Yes... Johnston Island, it's about sixty-eight-hundred miles southeast from here."

"I'm fully aware of where Johnston Island is. RS2 requests you return. *Now.*"

Peachy. She winched. "On my way."

She piloted Xiphias to the cargo platform with the rails awaiting her arrival. She spun the tail end around and gently guided *Xiph1* back until it kissed the rails. Her crewmates were quick to hook *Xiph1* with cables to rings molded into its tail end and engage the winch that pulled it out of the water. She ticked through all the possible violations to the stated rules as the whine of the winch reverberated through the hull. She couldn't identify a single one.

She wondered what kind of reception she would receive. It wasn't the first time she bent Larkian rules. She was certain there wasn't a rule that stated travel via a Merahvu's tunnel was forbidden. A quick glance back over her recorded depth showed her bouncing just above the three-thousand-foot limit.

Thank you, Isden!

Xiph1 recorded everything. If Stokes tried to reprimand her, she had evidence that no agreed-upon rules were broken. And Isden was not harmed in the process. Rules of engagement were properly met.

Xiph1 came to a full stop inside the cargo chamber. She released the five-point harness, took a deep breath, then opened the hatch. Stokes gazed down from above. He held out his hand. She took it and he yanked her up and out with such force her feet were airborne for a few seconds before landing on the stairway platform beside him.

His dark eyes bored into hers. No smile, but no furrowing of brow either. A face transfixed by shock. Stokes, speechless. She had rendered him *speechless.*

"Um, something wrong?" she asked.

Ah, that got a reaction. His brow dipped lower than she had ever seen it dip before. If the depth was any measure of his fury, then damn, it was maxed.

"Did I break a rule?" She tried her best to look confounded. "I didn't go below the depth limit, and um, you didn't say anything about speed."

You could hear a pin drop. His mouth opened to say something but nothing came out. She raised a brow. His eyes closed for several seconds, gears churning, and everyone in the chamber waited for his response.

His eyes cracked to slits and a noisy breath exploded from his nostrils like a pissed-off bull. But he said nothing.

Audrey patted Stokes on the back. "Appreciate your confidence, Captain. Mind if I slip past, I've really got to pee."

Stokes nodded numbly and stepped out of her way.

Audrey climbed down to the deck where Isden was waiting. He gave her a quick smile and a wink. When she passed by he leaned close and whispered, "You took the bait. Ballsy."

And that was it. Audrey gracefully slipped away. No unproductive yelling or threats of punishment. Just a sudden outburst of multiple conversations; of what-ifs and hadn't-thought-of-that types of debate. Blake was in the middle of it, animatedly engaging in each and every discussion. Whenever anyone tried to complain or refute the fact that no rules were broken they were shot down, mostly by Blake. And Blake being a member of the Larkian Council gave his support credence.

By the end of the day, Audrey graduated top of class out of all the contenders and was fully certified to operate Xiphias in upcoming missions.

Blake was ecstatic by the fact high-speed travel as a companion with the Merahvu was possible, calling it a "fortuitous accident," to use Audrey's words. It opened up a new set of possibilities for the Larkians to join the Merahvu in the fight against the Orankai. The last and final question was if Xiphias could survive the delicate passage through a portal between Earth and Merluma. Bringing Larkian technology into the fight on Merluma could prove to be a major advantage over the Orankai.

The Merahvu were capable of passing through a portal via traveling tunnel. *Xiph1* proved it was capable of passing one aspect of that test.

Passing through a portal was something else entirely. There was the element of acute stress; heat, a significant change in pressure, and the sensation of being ripped apart limb from limb. How those things would affect an inanimate object like Xiphias was an unknown. Though the passage was brief, it may or may not rip Xiphias apart with potentially catastrophic consequence to the pilot.

Stokes called an emergency meeting to announce the breakthrough and determine next steps. Audrey as well as the other pilots marched up to the ship's library shortly after the remaining pilots completed their tests. Isden and the entire Larkian Council were in attendance. Since Tucker was one of their top techs, Stokes asked him to attend. Even Ianthe tailed along with her father.

Once her father found his seat he turned and locked eyes with her. When he heard what she had done, he fumed. He had called the ship upon hearing the news, scolded her, and questioned why she felt compelled to join the fleet of Xiphias pilots in the first place. She calmly reminded him that he was the one who trained her and raised her to be a warrior. She also reminded him she was an adult. It was her life and her choice, not his.

She heard later that Dr. Wickman backed her up. So did Ianthe. Blake confirmed it could have happened to any one of the pilots, including him. It wasn't a reckless act. It happened and they gained valuable insight. A new door of possibility had been opened.

Once everyone had settled, Stokes stood and quickly reviewed what happened while Audrey was testing the autopilot system in a cat-and-mouse chase with Isden, including video of Xiphias disappearing and a screen of data captured during Audrey's wild ride. He concluded, "The question on the table is whether or not Xiphias can endure the passage to Merluma."

"Our best option is to test it," Blake said. "A quick survey indicates *Xiph1* incurred no damage during Audrey's recent excursion with Isden."

Tucker shrugged. "Easy enough to program one of 'em to do what Audrey did. Target the autopilot to lock on one of 'em and let 'er rip."

Isden raised his hand. "I volunteer to be the bait."

Stokes turned to the members of the Council. "Thoughts?"

Francesca spoke up. "I would like to say one thing before rendering my opinion." She nodded toward Audrey and smiled. "That was one hell of a discovery, and I want to commend Audrey for keeping a cool head under the circumstances." She spread her hands wide. "There's no question in my mind that we test it, unmanned of course."

Her father pinned Audrey with a glacial stare. "I suggest we use more caution in the future. While the situation didn't result in injury or death to either Audrey or Isden, a fatal accident could have resulted."

Audrey felt mixed emotions. While Francesca commended her for her cool head, her father couldn't quite cross that bridge. It was as if she would never be good enough, no matter what she did. *Damn him.* She nibbled her lip. Someone had to say it. They were at war with dual, formidable enemies.

She rose from her seat. "Based on my observation, we would be mulling over this possible idea, *ad nauseam*, while Arkis breeds monsters and Orange spreads, if we had not made this accidental discovery." She turned to address her father directly. "Someone once told me a warrior must be spontaneous, focus on every opportunity, and take calculated risks. My discovery has given us a huge potential advantage. Was it risky? Sure, but it happened and

I'm here as witness. Why stop now? As a Culliford, I vote we run the test as soon as possible. Enough talk; it's time to act."

The room fell silent for a beat. Audrey noted many quick smiles and tipping of chins.

Alvarez had been strangely quiet until that moment. He said, "I put Audrey's suggestion to test Xiphias, as soon as feasible, on the table for a vote. Those in favor?"

The room resounded with a chorus of "aye's" coming from all present except one. Her father.

He glared at Audrey. He knew she was right; she even tossed his words back at him. Audrey could see the budding realization in her father's eyes: He wasn't the hardened cutthroat in charge like he once was. She was the rising star; in respect, rapport, and achievement within the Larkians' ranks. The dynamic was shifting, and Audrey could see that her father struggled to accept that fact.

She knew he wouldn't hear it, but she pushed the thought anyway as if sharing it with Sinto.

Time to let me fly, Daddy. Be proud of what you've taught me, of what I discovered. Of what I am capable of accomplishing.

Ianthe smiled and nudged her father, having heard her message loud and clear.

Her father looked up, exhaled loudly, and said, "Aye."

Blake and Tucker hopped from their seats and disappeared out the door, Isden hot on their heels.

27

Xiphias Go-Go

THE TEST TO SEND Xiphias through a portal to Merluma was scheduled for the following morning. That night Audrey slept restlessly and woke before dawn, nerves jangled with trepidation and eagerness. She felt a deep and indescribable feeling that her fate was tangled up in the results.

She quietly slipped out onto the lanai to catch the reflection of the nearly full moon cutting a swath of light across the water as it prepared to set.

She walked the beach to calm her nerves, the sand cool and silky at her feet. The sea was still and reflective and surprisingly warm against the cool air. Before she knew it she had shed her pajamas and was in neck deep, floating on the surface.

She gazed up at the sky. Indigo fading to pink. She thought of Sinto, wondering where he was, if he was happy or sad, if he missed her as much as she missed him. She was thankful to be consumed by the Xiphias project as it kept her mind from wandering and worrying about where he was, whether Arkis had fallen for their trap, whether something had gone horribly wrong. The Mark warmed as if answering her plea; Sinto was safe and as lonely as her.

"I love you, Sinto," she whispered to the sky. "Come home soon. I'm uncertain how much longer I'll be here." She yearned to gaze into his eyes, to hold him in her arms, and to feel his heart beating, sure and true, against her own.

The sun cracked the horizon. Her fingers were pruned. She rushed from the water naked, stopping only to gather her pajamas, then slipped around her side of the house and into the outdoor shower outside her bathroom.

Fifteen minutes later she emerged from her room, dressed and ready to go. Blake was in his boxers sipping a cup of coffee. She dropped her packed duffle by her bedroom door.

"I'm reclaiming my bunk on *Requiem Sea* II. The vibe is more stimulating there and I expect we'll be busy with all the tests and planning and, hopefully soon, some real action."

Blake leaned back. "What's wrong with the vibe here?"

"Nothing. It's just not conducive to planning for war. Way too laid back." She pinched the tip of his nose. "I took a dip. You should too. Help you wake up."

He rubbed his eyes and gulped down the rest of his coffee. "No need. I'm ready."

She laughed. "You're going in your underwear?"

"I just might, or maybe nothing. Pants are overrated. The Merahvu do it, why not me?" He laughed and scurried to his bedroom, leaving Audrey smiling to herself in the kitchen.

Twenty minutes later they locked up the house and hopped in the UTV with Audrey driving. Blake liked Audrey's idea and decided to relocate to the ship as well. Their bags jostled in the open trunk as they bumped along the well-worn road past the wetlands. Once they hit the smoother sand-colored pavement near the airport, Audrey picked up speed. The cool morning air flowed through open windows, buffeting their faces.

Twenty-five minutes later they dumped their bags in their adjoining cabins.

Five minutes after that they were in the cargo chamber, performing a routine survey of *Xiph1*'s underside. They started with the exterior, checking cameras and sensors, spinning propellers, and looking for any stress cracks in the outer structure. They found none.

They scaled the rolling stairway. Blake crawled inside with Audrey on the stairway platform, leaning in through the hatch. They scanned every square inch of the inner orb where the pilot sat. They found no cracks or evidence of stress. Next to test were the electronics. Audrey grabbed the systems checklist from a clipboard that she could reach. She read off the list while Blake checked the equipment. The entire process took less than ten minutes, which included Blake describing the design of each feature and the hard trade-offs that had to be made to make them work in such a tight space and under moist conditions. Then Blake climbed out and locked down the hatch.

"Did you check the hatch seal?" Blake asked.

"You just closed it," Audrey replied.

"Check it again, if it fails… sayonara. I always check it twice."

So she did.

She and Blake hopped down. Tucker was at the work bench, installing a final fix to the software he wrote to operate *Xiph1* remotely. Dyer stood by ready to assist.

"Gooood Moooorninnnggg, Sunshine!" Dyer's greeting reverberated through the chamber. He hugged her.

Audrey grinned. "And to you." She ribbed Tucker. "And you too."

"Oy," was all he said. His eyes were bloodshot but perky.

"Pulled an all-nighter?"

"Yup. Been at it with Isden all night." His fingers were a blur on the keyboard. Tucker was like a machine. Once on a project it didn't matter to him whether it was day or night; when he was ready, he pounced on it. Sleep be damned.

"Speaking of which, where is Isden?"

Dyer flicked his thumb toward the open platform. Isden was fast asleep, curled up in a beam of sunshine like a cat. "Guy's been well trained. Sleeps on demand. Ten minutes here, twenty there..." Dyer yawned. "Me, I endure."

"Sounds like Isden's the smart one."

No one knew what they potentially faced if they reached Merluma, or once they implemented their attack on the Orankai, or where they might find shelter, or find time to rest. A true warrior stole sleep whenever or wherever, even on the battlefield.

Others on the Xiphias team slowly filled the chamber, including Stokes and Francesca.

Tucker gazed up at the screen, noting that his latest software update was complete. He turned and punched the air. "She be ready. Someone wake up Isden."

Isden woke at the mention of his name. He stretched and rose to his feet. He smiled when he saw Audrey.

Blake and Dyer rolled the stairway back from *Xiph1*. Dyer flipped a switch. *Xiph1* slid down the rails and into the sea. Isden dove in after.

The entire Xiphias team and Francesca watched *Xiph1*'s progress on the main screen, displaying images from the cameras and sensors, mirroring *Xiph1*'s progress and location.

Once *Xiph1* reached the open waters beyond the harbor, Isden began his game of cat and mouse. *Xiph1* tracked every movement perfectly, then disappeared. The screens went black and a loud alarm sounded. *Xiph1* was off-line, either out of communication range or obliterated.

Audrey could imagine the distress that must have filled the chamber when she disappeared for ten long minutes the day before. The alarm felt by her father and the other pilots. That sickening fear and shock that rendered Stokes speechless upon her return.

Tucker and Isden estimated the test would take fifteen, maybe twenty minutes. Everyone tried to find tasks to pass the time.

Blake paced. Tucker ripped off rounds of push-ups, planks, and standing kicks. Audrey wondered if maybe he really was some sort of machine, always pumped full of energy and never needing to sleep.

Francesca used the free moment to pull Audrey aside.

"I have some good and some bad news. First the good. We ran exhaustive tests and found no flaws with nLink. It will be deployed with the team going to Merluma provided the Xiphias test succeeds."

"And the bad news?"

Francesca sighed. "We have concluded there is an incompatibility. Wantemo and Ianthe agree with near one-hundred percent certainty. The unique connection you share with Sinto through the Mark is the primary cause."

"So what does that mean?"

"Well, it means you will not be able to participate in the nLink network."

Her heart pounded. "Are you saying I can't join the team?"

"Not necessarily. It means you can't participate in the nLink network."

"But—"

She held up her hand. "Yes, *but*." She smiled. "I tweaked the suits. I added an input device so you can manually control its full capability—defenses, ability to camouflage, etc.—but what you will lack is the ability to communicate with other team members, telepathically. You will essentially be deaf and mute in situations where silence will be the matter between life and death when encountering the enemy."

She watched Audrey closely as she absorbed these new facts.

"Mute and deaf people adapt. I'll find a way to make it work. Hand signals maybe?"

"In battle, while camouflaged? I think not. Look, I'm not going to tell you what to do but I want you to know the risks, and they are high. Losing communication with your team can be catastrophic in dynamic situations. A failed warning, friendly fire, you name it, it happens and can be deadly."

Audrey mulled over what Francesca told her. With the ability to control all aspects of the suit, Audrey still had key advantages against the Orankai.

She could hide.

She could fend off an electrical shock.

She could wield a deadly weapon.

A lone wolf.

And lone wolves don't normally work or communicate with anyone.

"Will I still be able to identify other team members and them, in turn, me?"

"Anyone wearing a suit will show up on the suit's monitoring system."

"I'll make it work."

Francesca smiled. "I hoped you would say that."

There was a sudden eruption of static followed by a very loud and enthusiastic holler from Tucker. "She's back!"

As Tucker had programed, *Xiph1* returned to the stern of the ship and circled once before settling to a stop. Blake hooked the cable to *Xiph1*'s stern. The winch squealed as *Xiph1* slid up the rails and into the center of the chamber.

Isden burst from the water and landed gracefully on the platform. Glistening lorica slithered down his skin and from his short flat hair like water rolling off the oiled feathers of a duck. Bone dry, he joined Tucker and Blake, scanning every square inch of *Xiph1*'s hull.

"No stress cracks, not even a scratch!" Blake hopped down from the stairway after rummaging around inside.

Stokes said, "Looks like Xiphias deployment is a go-go."

After *Xiph1*'s successful test, the plan was to launch the next day, once supplies were loaded and the modifications to Francesca's suits were complete.

The chamber filled with a flurry of activity. Dyer helped Blake organize teams. Anyone not assigned a task was asked to clear the space. Each pilot ran system checks on their assigned Xiphias. Then they loaded vacuum-sealed boxes with weapons, ammo, emergency supplies, food stores, a medical kit, and extra clothing. No one knew how long the mission would take or the conditions in which they may find themselves. The Winterlands temps could drop well below freezing.

Audrey ticked through Sinto's war plan in her mind:

Neutralize Arkis. Destroy the breeding caves. Round up the Orankai.

She took a deep breath. It sounded simple. But anything could go wrong. Audrey sauntered out of the chamber with a confusing blend of hope and anxiety roiling in her stomach. But she embraced it.

Better than feeling stuck or running in circles.

28

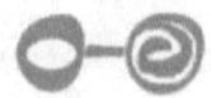

Dark Warning

THE NIGHT BEFORE AUDREY and Blake's scheduled departure for Merluma, they stopped by their father's house. Since they would be gone for an unknown period of time, and most likely encounter many dangers, they both felt compelled to formally say goodbye.

Her father was especially quiet. Ianthe sat bright-eyed by his side, in the same chair she occupied when Audrey and Sinto last visited, which felt like a lifetime ago. This time it was with her brother Blake, sitting where Sinto had sat on the sofa before.

Audrey asked Ianthe, "Any insight regarding Sinto?"

"No, nor do I dare inquire. It is best not to risk alerting Naiada what I seek. We can only trust he will use wise judgment and return once it is done."

"I've tried to reach out, through the Mark..." Audrey shook her head.

Ianthe smiled reassuringly. "I'm sure it's nothing to fear."

"Do you know what he has planned? He wouldn't tell me anything before he left."

"We are all in the dark as to what he has planned and where." Ianthe's smile faded. "We run the risk of a spy slipping through our defenses no matter how hard we try. Sinto was fully aware of that possibility."

"How about *our* spies? Any word from them?" Blake asked.

"Only that the Terrakai settlement in the Forestlands of Merluma is growing," Ianthe said.

Her father finally spoke up. "Alvarez has been in contact with the Scout Lizza, who reported a rash of deaths occurring in a small community around Lake Superior; substance abuse perhaps. The locals fear it may be due to a new drug crossing the Canadian border. As a consequence, there have been a rash of suicides and higher than normal occurrences of violent outbursts by normally rational people; random shootings, hit and runs, intentional poisonings. He's monitoring the situation closely."

"How does that have anything to do with us?" Audrey asked.

"Alvarez suggested it might not be an accident. This fear of a new drug is a very real possibility. Perhaps it's Arkis' nectar."

"A leak from the City of Green?"

Her father sat forward. "He thinks it might be intentional. Imagine if Arkis could infect Sapiens through their water source and order them to do whatever he wants."

A cold shiver slid down Audrey's spine. "Is that possible? We know Orange can cause Sapiens to behave aggressively, but could he actually control them?"

"These events might be a test of just that. Especially considering Sinto's brief exposure and what he described of a hive-mind connection, which he believes is how Arkis controls the Orankai."

Ianthe added, "There is nothing I am aware of that would hinder Sapiens' ability to learn and adopt this hive-mind form of communication once under his nectar's spell."

Audrey recalled a recent conversation, one where Sinto revealed what happened to him in Lake Superior. "Sinto told me he saw Orankai scouts all over the city of Duluth as he and Rachel were racing to escape. Maybe Arkis has been testing its effects on Sapiens for some time and these events prove he's found a way…"

Her father reached for Ianthe's hand. "Wickman and Wantemo both believe it is possible based on their observations of its effects. Imagine Arkis infecting innocents on Earth; send his minions, seed exposure, enlist Sapiens to help encourage their self-destruction. Arkis' dirty work of his planned *eradication* could be accomplished by Orange with no way to trace its source, neither to Merluma nor to his city at the bottom of Lake Superior. Very clever, and an absolute nightmare."

"Arkis is not a stupid man," Ianthe said. "An outright attack would provoke the Sapiens. Done quietly and randomly through smaller communities would not invoke federal government action."

Blake added, "Not a reach to imagine them targeting local police and first responders. After that, he could begin targeting more populated areas. His method of eradication would spread like a silent virus."

Audrey's heart pounded. "If Arkis is that smart, how can we believe he'll fall for Sinto's ruse? What if Naiada senses what Sinto has planned? He could be walking into a trap!"

"Sinto is aware of the risk," Ianthe said. "We must trust he has taken this possibility into consideration. We must also remember we don't know which side Naiada has chosen, willingly or otherwise. She may be in their possession but that is no guarantee they fully control her. They may fear that subjecting her to Orange could greatly diminish her power."

"Or enhance it," Audrey suggested.

"Mm. I believe the opposite but I have been wrong before..." Ianthe's gaze grew distant. Her voice a pitch lower. "There is also Ramasis to consider. He may hate me, but he cares for Naiada, deeply. I am certain he made clear to Arkis no one is to harm her."

Audrey certainly hoped she was right, but that didn't make the burn in her stomach subside. If anything, it only exacerbated the fiery pit in her gut. "What happens if we fail on Merluma?"

"That is a topic keeping Alvarez awake at night," her father said.

"Has he considered alerting the United States government?" Audrey asked.

Blake intervened. "If we revealed the existence of Merluma and an out-of-control substance threatening national security, the word is bound to go public. Then we would certainly have an apocalyptic-scale panic on our hands. So no, Alvarez has not even considered that an option."

Audrey drew an exasperated breath. "So we hole up here and wait for the end of the world?"

"That may be exactly what needs to happen." The tone of Ianthe's voice made her blood run cold.

Their eyes connected. Ianthe was dead serious. Not a passing thought. A command. Audrey wondered if what she suggested had anything to do with what she told her and Sinto. That once the darkness descends they would both know what to do. As to what that meant, she didn't have a clue.

Audrey stood. "Let's hope Sinto is successful. We have to stop that monster."

Everyone concurred.

Ianthe and her father stood and walked them to the door.

"Tomorrow we head to Merluma. Any parting advice?"

Ianthe said, "Stay alive. Come home."

"I doubt either of you will consider not going, so..." Her father squeezed both of their shoulders. "I believe in you both. Take care of each other."

And with that, Audrey and Blake bid Ianthe and their father farewell, knowing it may be forever.

Stay alive and come home.

Take care of each other.

Simple advice easily stated, difficult to promise.

29

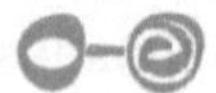

Odd One

GAME DAY. THE CARGO chamber on *Requiem Sea II* was bustling with nervous energy. Everyone was ready to go and suited up. Team Xiphias was clad in Francesca's high-tech suits, newly updated with manual controls. Dyer, Stokes, Tucker, and Burns nervously milled about. Audrey hung back with Blake, who was cool as a cucumber.

Stokes insisted he go first. Backup team member, Tobe—a tall red-headed, bushy-bearded Scotsman—was on standby should any of the other pilots decide to back out at the last minute.

No one had heard from Sinto, and Audrey was anxious about not having the chance to see him before she left. Audrey believed they were cursed, briefly crossing paths before embarking on different, distant and dangerous journeys. She tried not to focus on that unfortunate truth and turned her sights back to the mission at hand: her return to Merluma and their mission to find and destroy the breeding caves.

Stokes was in charge of managing and dispensing the nLink injections when the time arose once they were on Merluma. Audrey would be at a disadvantage but was satisfied with the adjustments Francesca made to her suit, finding it easy to shift into camouflage mode and manage the electrical defense system using the manual controls.

Francesca confessed that the incident with the nLink malfunction forced her team to rethink the suit's operation. The same manual modifications were incorporated into all suits as backup should the nLink fail or simply disintegrate at an inopportune time. Francesca had used the unforeseen flaw in their technology as an opportunity to trouble-shoot; a bright spot in the darkness of failure.

Isden arrived with four handpicked warriors recently trained specifically for the mission. Two from the City of Ice and two from the Arctakai's southern city. Each was assigned to a Xiphias pilot as their guide. Since Stokes was going first, Isden was paired up with him. They would be first to pass through the portal. The plan was for Isden to return, providing all went as planned, then take Tucker next. The remaining pilots would be assigned one of the other four guides for the passage through the portal. Blake would take the third run, followed by Audrey, then Dyer and Burns.

Isden worked with Tucker to draw up maps of Merluma's single land mass and the Great Ocean. Ianthe added details she had accumulated over her lifetime. These maps were downloaded into each Xiphias and the internal processor of each pilot's suit. Once on Merluma, they would navigate to an underwater cave system that linked the City of Ice in the Winterlands to the Great Ocean.

Each pilot was assigned a Xiphias numbered one through six. Blake was assigned *Xiph1*, Audrey *Xiph2*.

Stokes climbed up and disappeared inside *Xiph3*. The stairs were wheeled back. *Xiph3* raced down the rails and splashed into the harbor. Isden dove in after.

Tension was high as the team waited for Isden's return. The monitors didn't record much, other than the fact that one second Stokes and Isden were there, and then they weren't, as they slipped from this world to another.

Isden returned fifteen minutes later. He didn't bother leaping from the water, confirming Stokes' successful passage with a thumbs-up gesture. Tucker slipped into *Xiph4* and he was off. The monitoring system showed Tucker there, then not.

Blake and Audrey were up next.

To ease the tension, Blake struck up a conversation with his assigned partner, a Terrakai who had escaped from the City of Green before Arkis fully took over. He had no problem engaging his Merahvu teammate.

Audrey was assigned a quiet Seakai named Odwon. She'd been told that he had fought to stop the collapse of Tallamure's dome before barely escaping. She felt awkward having been on the enemy side of that conflict. Though there was no outward animosity from Odwon, she did sense something odd about his demeanor. She couldn't put her finger on it, but she felt a tingling unease. Whether it was her, or coming from him, she wasn't quite sure. She finally concluded it was him because of the partner he had been given: the daughter of their long-time nemesis, Robert Culliford. Had their roles been reversed, she most certainly would have felt the same way. Despite her attempts at conversation, he wasn't particularly talkative and made a point of avoiding eye contact. She brushed it off, assuming he was shy or merely overwhelmed by the deadly technological wonder Blake helped design.

She gave Blake a hug before he climbed inside *Xiph1*. "Thirty seconds behind you. See you on the other side."

"Count on it," he beamed. Blake had told her he had waited a lifetime to experience what Leela had described to him so long ago. Passage through a portal and seeing Merluma for himself.

Audrey turned to Odwon. "Ready?"

He met her gaze. "Never more."

Audrey climbed aboard *Xiph2* resting on a second set of rails beside *Xiph1*. She gave Blake a two-fingered salute, then he was launched down the rails. She allowed one last look at Odwon, who was waiting patiently on the platform to dive into the water. His eyes were on fire, a shifting kaleidoscope of gold and red. She smiled at him. He didn't smile back.

She rushed down the rails, past Odwon, and splashed into the water with a familiar jolt. She engaged the props and dove into the clear blue sea. Odwon swam by, taking the lead, fully enclosed in his gelatinous lorica.

Once they reached the open water they lined up behind Blake and his Terrakai guide. It was sudden and alarming when they literally disappeared in a blinding flash of light and burst of fizzy bubbles.

Odwon was at the ready. She set *Xiph2* to target his body and flipped on the autopilot. Audrey counted down the seconds, bracing for a sudden acceleration and the g-force that came with it.

Thirty seconds passed, then a minute. She wondered if Odwon was aware of the plan. He was supposed to launch his tunnel thirty seconds after Blake and his partner departed.

Another minute passed. Audrey grew impatient and frustrated. If they waited too long they may end up far from where Blake made entry. She wondered if Odwon had chickened out. She had no way of communicating to find out for sure.

She called the ship, "RS2, *Xiph2*. Not sure what's up, Odwon is lingering for some reason. Wasn't he briefed on the thirty-second intervals?"

Tobe came back, "He should have been."

"Any ideas on how to communicate?"

"Try flashing the exterior lights."

She did. Odwon turned to face her, gave her a wave and an apologetic shrug, then cut a swirling hole in the sea. She blamed it on nervousness. Her own insides were certainly roiling.

She braced for what was to come next. Seconds later she was sucked inside the vortex and at the mercy of her guide, Odwon.

30

Duped

Audrey flew like a bat out of hell through the ocean in a high-tech mini-submarine that looked like the cross between a swordfish and a bluefin tuna. If one was to describe a badass, she would certainly like it to be her, here and now.

Once Odwon leveled out the tunnel he had cut through the sea, he straddled *Xiph2*, gripping the toe holds molded into the sides of *Xiph2*'s body. Audrey looked up at him through the transparent dome. His intense gaze bored into her as he gave a thumbs-up before returning his focus forward. Audrey's stomach lurched as she noticed a flicker in his eyes; she could have sworn the color darkened from gold to a simmering sienna, but he had looked away before she could be sure.

She tried to ignore the unease rising in her chest, from Odwon's delay in launching his tunnel, the sudden change in his eye color, and the fact she was about to pass from one world to another.

A sliver of light emerged in the vast darkness of the deep sea. Odwon's tunnel was aimed directly toward it. A blinding crack of white light: the portal to Merluma.

She had passed through a portal several times with Sinto. Each time Sinto had rendered her unconscious to lessen the full impact of the experience. Shortly after, she gained consciousness and felt dizzy, achy, and like her head was going to explode. This time she would be fully aware during the entire passage. She tried to relax but found her fingers gripping the arm rests.

Xiph2 shuddered when they burst through a gelatinous-like membrane filling a crack of light. The sudden transition set off a high-pitched hum and a violent vibration that rattled the tiny bones within her inner ears. Pain shot through her head. She gaped her mouth but it didn't help ease the building pressure against her eardrums. She flinched against the five-point harness pinning her to the seat.

Xiph2 remained steady, although the systems registered a rapid increase in temperature, but otherwise everything was working as expected with the exception of the mapping system. It was blank. The transition appeared to only affect the human body.

Odwon's tunnel bowed around dual orbs of fire that circled one another. One was larger, the other a third smaller. The larger one pulsed to a slow and determined beat. The other pulsed fast and sporadically.

Intense heat filled the circle of glass in which she sat. Sweat streamed from her temples. It was a struggle to breath normally.

Yet still, *Xiph2* remained steady, the ride smooth.

The harmonic hum building in Audrey's ears became unbearable. It spread to every joint of her body. It felt like red-hot needles stuck into every joint all at once. After the fire came the pull, as if she was being torn apart, limb from limb.

Then it was over. They were spit through a second gelatinous barrier to the other side.

Audrey sucked air and patted her chest where her heart thrummed. She had survived and *Xiph2* held together. She questioned why she may have had any doubt.

The heat subsided and cool air filled the cabin. The darkness of the deep engulfed her and Odwon, who clung to the dome above her. His gaze was locked forward as his tunnel cut through Merluma's Great Ocean.

The electronics came to life. The map on her screen switched automatically to reveal Merluma, the Great Ocean, and the single island of land. Other than these rudimentary features, detailed topographic data for this part of the Great Ocean was sparse or missing altogether.

Audrey was jolted back in her seat when Odwon's tunnel took a sharp upward turn toward the surface. She breathed a sigh of relief when *Xiph2*'s sensors picked up Blake in *Xiph1* several hundred feet above. Odwon was heading straight for him.

Xiph1 was in motion with all weapons deployed and firing. Multiple pings of life forms surrounded it.

Odwon looked down, eyes burning bright orange. He grinned, vile and deceitful.

"Got you! Arkis will be so pleased."

Audrey gasped from his words threading through her mind. She had foolishly ignored the signs: his aloof and nervous manner, the delay in following Blake, the changing color of his eyes...

A trap!

Fury fueled her, and not just for her own sake. Blake was in serious trouble.

She pushed back to Odwon, *"How about you and me tangle for a bit?"*

Then she engaged the electrical system and gave Odwon a high-voltage shock. His traveling tunnel disintegrated and *Xiph2* came to a sudden and violent stop from the density of the sea. She slammed against the harness then back in the seat.

Odwon slithered off.

The sensors detected a heartbeat. He was stunned, but alive. She was surprised by how quickly he recovered. He swam toward her. She prepared for reversed polarity, opposite of a shock. She flipped off the safety, finger hovering over the button.

Come on you son-of-a-bitch, come get me...

Odwon stopped before making contact. Wising up to Xiphias' tricks.

She lined up for a shot and let a volley of spears rip. Odwon was fast to react, zipping up and over the top of *Xiph1*. She fired a torpedo from the rear. He dodged. It missed. Odwon landed atop the dome above her head, face twisted by rage. He ran electrified fingers around the hatch's seal, attempting to pop it open.

She blew him a kiss. *"Give Arkis my best."*

She pressed and held the button that engaged reverse polarity. Odwon's eyes widened and mouth gaped. *Xiph2* sucked the energy from his merlux, from what remained in his bloodstream. The batteries ticked up significantly. Odwon twitched, stilled, and burst into ash. The shocked look on his face was forever burned into her memory.

Thanks for the charge, asshole.

She grabbed the joystick and aimed for Blake. *Xiph2* jolted as props bit water.

"Hang on Blake, coming to you!"

"Audrey, it's a trap," he replied. "I'm surrounded, stay back!"

"How many?"

"Too many to count. They're all over me!"

"Reverse polarity."

"I've tried that! The batteries are about to blow—too much charge. Can't outrun them."

"Shock them!"

"Tried, not working—they're tearing *Xiph1* apart!"

She raced for the surface. The ocean brightened and *Xiph1* came into view. A swarm of Orankai crawled across its surface, ripping apart the pod drives, breaking off fins, pounding on the transparent dome. A pair were straining to rip off the rear toroidal propellers.

"Got you in view—oh god... Spin your toroidal propellers!"

Blake began to sink nose down. "Trying—stuck."

"Full speed, reverse!"

Xiph1 shuddered and the toroidal propellers flew away from the main body and began sinking.

"I'm dead in the water!"

Audrey was momentarily frozen with fear and confusion from the sudden transition following the portal passage, killing Odwon, and seeing Blake rendered helpless. Her hands wavered over the weapon controls. Which to use? Which one would be safe to shoot directly at *Xiph1*?

Darts! She zeroed in on the switch and flipped off the safety. The element of surprise was on her side but not for long. She wasted no time and fired a round of poisoned darts, sweeping across the field of bodies covering *Xiph1*, once, twice.

That got their attention. Several came after her, the poison not yet coursing through their bodies. She slammed into reverse and once she was clear of *Xiph1*, fired a sweeping round of spears. The Orankai reacted swiftly, darting to and fro. Many of the spears whizzed past; a few hit their mark. The unlucky ones experienced a one-second delay before the spears' tips exploded into a star of flesh-shredding barbs. Blood stained the water. The injured twitched before stilling and disintegrating. Clouds of ash and blood bloomed.

Orankai kept coming.

She released the razor-edged bill from *Xiph2*'s nose. It snapped into place, sending a slight shudder through the hull. Audrey released a war cry as she sashayed wildly, pod drives and toroidal propellers whining. The razor-edged bill slashed flesh, ripping limb from body, spilling guts from torsos. Blood and ash clouded the water until she could no longer see *Xiph1* or the bodies she was beheading and dismembering.

From the depths came the balancers of the sea—a shiver of sharks driven into a frenzy by frantic action and blood. Slowly she backed away from the massacre until *Xiph1* was visible below her, slowly sinking.

She could hear Blake screaming through the comms. Her initial fear that he was injured faded as she realized he was screaming with elation.

"Woohoo! You got 'em!"

Audrey didn't share his enthusiasm as she watched the tail end of *Xiph1* slowly fade into the dark depths, Orankai attached to its surface like malignant tumors.

31

Dead In The Water

Xiph1 was sinking with Blake trapped inside. Orankai yanked relentlessly at whatever parts they could get their hands on. Audrey and Blake's early enthusiasm dimmed as the reality of his situation sunk in.

Audrey dove, firing a second round of poisoned darts, fearing anything of more substance might puncture the damaged outer skin and accelerate Xiph1's descent.

The poisoned darts started to do their magic. Orankai slipped from Xiph1's surface and disintegrated. Audrey fired until her stores were depleted and the last Orankai was dead and the sea was dirtied with ash.

Audrey pulled alongside Xiph1. Blake was pale and shaky but alive and grateful to see her.

"Can you drive at all?"

He tried again. Nothing but a shudder. He shook his head.

"It's only a matter of time until she drops like a rock." His voice sounded exasperated.

"Tell me what to do."

"Get beneath me. Push me to the surface where she'll bob like a cork."

Audrey dove and maneuvered around until she was below *Xiph1*'s underbelly.

"Retract your fins and the bill."

She did. They retracted with a quiet whir and a satisfying *thunk*, signaling that all the pieces were fully intact.

"Angle your nose up and gently push me up, very slowly. Avoid pushing with the hatch at the top of the dome. I think you know why."

"Affirmative."

She rotated the pod drives until *Xiph2*'s nose made contact where *Xiph1*'s bottom fin dangled by wires. She tapped the pods. Slowly they rose past the frenzied sharks finishing off headless attackers and dismembered appendages.

"Where are we?" Audrey asked.

"No idea. My map doesn't cover any detail in this part of the Great Ocean."

"Neither does mine."

She huffed. *Peachy.*

They broke the surface. The ocean extended as far as she could see. Thankfully, it was calm at the moment.

Audrey came alongside *Xiph1* so they could see each other through their glass domes. "Are you taking on water?" she asked.

"Not that I can tell."

"Now what?"

"Tow to the nearest shore or—"

"You hop into mine, right?"

He paused before answering. "Didn't think to test that scenario."

Audrey squirmed in the seat and tried to image the two of them sitting side by side. Impossible in the form-fitting seat. One would have to sit atop the other. Luckily, they were both lean. It would be possible but more uncomfortable than cozy.

"Is there a pilot weight limit?"

"Three hundred pounds when Xiphias is fully loaded with supplies."

"Hmm. I'm one-thirtyish... when dehydrated."

"That's cutting it close."

Audrey didn't like the direction this conversation was going. "What about oxygen?"

"How much do you have left?"

"Seventy percent."

"For two, pushing it. Unlikely we could travel below the surface for long."

Audrey tapped the screen. "Looks like land is a hundred miles to the north. At a tow speed of eight knots it will be dark before we make it. If it's just us stuck here with no backup, we're gonna need the supplies on *Xiph1*."

"Agreed."

"I say we tow and if things go wrong we switch to plan B and things get cozy."

He smiled and tipped his head. "Sounds like we've got our new team leader."

She laughed. "Me? I'm the outsider here, limping along with manual controls and no way to communicate. Like a lone wolf. Watch your backside, I might just bite if things go sideways."

"I'll take my chances. Besides, Stokes has my nLink, so I guess we're equal in that respect." He circled a finger. "Bring your rear end around so I can snag the cable."

Blake wasted no time, popping open his hatch and hopping onto *Xiph1*'s deck as Audrey did as he asked. She glanced at the screen, recording the shiver of feasting sharks below.

She muttered, "Please don't fall in and become dessert."

Her wish was granted. Blake successfully connected the recessed cable from *Xiph1* to the rear end of *Xiph2*. Then he hopped back inside and closed the hatch.

He gave her a hopeful smile. "Move forward, super slow."

Blake waved as he was pulled away from her side and fell in line behind her, stern to stern. *Xiph2* jolted once she picked up the slack.

Towing him this way meant they were facing opposite directions. Seeing nothing but open ocean potentially filled with Orankai monsters triggered that deep-seated fear even Dr. Wickman couldn't help her ferret out.

She shivered, recalling the look on Odwon's face when he gazed down on her with his fiery-orange eyes. A mole who somehow slipped through the Larkians' defenses. If one was able, there could be more. She tried not to think about it and focused on her and Blake's current predicament, which was looking more and more dire.

The tight confines of the cabin closed in. She started to hyperventilate. "Um, Blake, I'm feeling—feeling—a little distressed..." Her vision danced with fragmented images of reality, unable to focus on anything solid, an ocular migraine setting in. Her breathing was reaching a crescendo. The harder she sucked air the less it fed her need for oxygen. The taste of warm electronics and her own fear-tinged sweat lingered on her tongue.

Blake sensed what was happening. "Whoa. Calm down. I'm here, right behind you. I want you to do me a favor. Can you do that? I need you to switch to outside air. We need to conserve what you have for diving. Do you know where the switch is? It should be just above your right knee."

She fumbled with the panel. The fragmented images from the ocular migraine made it impossible to read anything. She used her peripheral vision to scan the control panel, caught part of the label, OUT, then AIR. She flipped the switch. The cabin filled with the cool briny scent of the sea.

Blake asked, "Got it?" She nodded in response even though he couldn't see her. "Okay, remember you're not alone, I'm right here behind you. Breathe with me..."

Blake talked to her the entire time, counting a calming breath sequence and marveling at how they were alive and the warriors who deceived them were not; at how proud he felt watching the way she wielded *Xiph2* like a sword in battle, not once flinching from danger; and at how she was the reason he was behind her and not entombed at the bottom of the Great Ocean, counting down his air supply, or worse, crushed to a billion bits.

Slowly she calmed and her vision cleared with the sad and angering thought that the others on the Xiphias team may have faced the same fate. Her heart lay heavy as they slowly steamed toward the unknown.

32

Double Cross

FIVE AGONIZINGLY LONG DAYS had passed since Sinto and Victoria arrived on Andrew's Island: two days waiting for his mother's message to be passed to her secret spy, three waiting for something to happen. No Arkis. No curious Scouts sniffing around. Nothing out of the ordinary had been detected. Sinto contacted Alvarez, wondering if the message got lost. Alvarez confirmed it had been delivered as directed, three days prior.

Victoria was getting antsy too. Both of them were equally frustrated. Even the meals she prepared from the freezer tasted redundant and of the plastic they were stored and warmed in.

Like today and the day before and those before that. Sinto began to understand the frustration and impatience Audrey had felt before he left. Running in circles. Only he wasn't running. He mindlessly paced, polishing an oval path on the stone floor in the outer chamber. Precious time wasted while Arkis' tribe grew larger with each passing day.

He missed Audrey terribly. Victoria's jokes grew old. The books lining the bookshelves no longer interested him.

They dared not spend too much time wandering around outside in the off chance Arkis would show up, catching them off guard.

They were growing stir crazy in the bunker's tight windowless confines.

Another restless night.

On the morning of day seven the entire team, including those from the disguised research vessel, gathered on the beach. Vesna was the first to admit failure. "I say we abort and regroup with the others. Ianthe's spy may have been compromised. We need a new plan."

"Let's wait one more day," Sinto suggested.

They did. Nothing happened. Almost a week had passed since his mother sent her message.

The research vessel pulled up anchor and steamed back to port on the south end of Whidbey Island, north of Seattle, where the Larkians manufactured their ships and other sea-going vessels. Vesna's team tunneled back to Isla Salvación. Sinto and Victoria were the last to leave, tidying up after themselves, packing up their things and locking down the vault and bunker.

They took no chances and kept up the facade for the trek back to the beach. Victoria wore the clothing Sinto had borrowed from Audrey, her disguise firmly in place. Sinto was fully camouflaged. Other than the back pack he carried, he was invisible.

As they hiked through the old-growth forest toward the beach a large black bird swooped overhead. Sinto thought of Moonstone, and how eerily similar in character and size the bird was to his trusty bird Scout. He had seen many large eagles and ravens frequenting the forest in their first days here, which was expected. The islands were thick with them.

He decided the bird was just an eagle, nothing else. A trick to a tired eye. He had been unable to sleep due to the stress from waiting and the disappointment of failure.

A barred owl swooped low and directly overhead and landed in a tree above. It hooted. A series of high-pitched chitters answered. Not from another owl, but from another species of bird, and not from one but many.

Owls talking to eagles?

Or were they something else?

Sinto and Victoria froze and gazed up; her Audrey-face exposed to the birds' sharp gaze, Sinto's invisible behind his camouflage.

Sinto slipped the pack from his shoulder. It fell to his feet and he quietly stepped away, pressing his body against a massive fir's trunk, camouflage locked in place.

The sky beyond the forest canopy was dark with clouds. Sporadic drops of rain slipped through, peppering the ground at his feet. The only other sound was Sinto's thundering heart. What they sensed could be something or nothing of consequence.

Victoria stood firm, a mirror reflection of the one he loved. The same stubbornness he had grown to expect from Audrey was etched clearly on Victoria's face.

"*What are you doing?*" he pushed in mind-speak.

She looked to the sky. "*Scouts. Isn't this what we were waiting for?*"

"*We have no backup! Too risky!*"

"*Stick to the plan.*"

"*They know I'm here.*"

"*But not that there aren't others.*"

Sinto's gut burned with warning. Were these the same birds he had seen over the past several days? Bird spies that had been observing their every move, including the departure of the Larkian ship and Vesna's team? If so, the two of them were in great danger.

He mindlessly reached for his ear. The high-tech ear buds they had come to rely on to monitor every inch of the island had been safely returned to their charging stations moments before they locked up the vault. They were cut off from the team and the feed from cameras and sensors installed around the island, eliminating their key advantage.

He searched the treetops for the birds, looking for the leader, and locked his gaze on the owl intently watching Victoria's every move.

"Now love, stop playing games and let me have you! I know you are there! Come out, come out, wherever you are..." The way Victoria said it out loud was meant to be seductive, as if they were lovers, playing a game of hide and seek. A trick to lure whoever may be watching to make the first move.

She meandered around, poking at bushes and peeking around tree trunks. She huffed and sat down. "I give up. You're much better at this game than I am. Not fair!"

The owl spun its head and hooted.

Deeper in the forest another responded. Different, not echoed. The returning hoot was stiff and unnatural as if dictating a predetermined code. Then another in the distance answered the same way.

"You hear that?" she whispered in his mind.

"Yes. Bird Scouts."

Victoria swung her gaze to the owl and a flash of fear rippled across her Audrey features. She stood and made her way to the pack. She had asked Sinto to pack a knife she had taken from the vault. She retrieved it, unsnapped the sheath opening so the blade could easily be removed, and slipped the sheathed knife into the back of her jeans, her fingers resting on her hip not far from its hilt.

"Ah Sinto, come on. Stop being a tease!" She circled as she spoke, scanning every movement, keen to the possibility they were surrounded. He heard her merlux fire and emit a soft buzz like a disturbed bee's hive. Sinto's was already buzzing madly in his chest, charged and ready to go.

"You think you're gonna get some of this?" She slapped her butt. "Think again!" Then she turned and stomped her way along the path that led back to the bunker. It was a gamble. Bunker or beach, they were halfway in between. Escape in the Salish Sea or hunker down in the bunker till help could arrive.

The bunker was programmed to open for Victoria as it was for him, once she dropped her disguise. Either could run for it and open the door.

"Good call. Right behind you. Get as close to the bunker as possible," he told her.

Sinto followed discretely, lingering behind to avoid drawing the Scouts' attention. The birds took the bait and pursued Victoria.

She continued her diatribe, pretending to be upset. Her pace quickened as she neared the dilapidated garden and the crack in rock masking the bunker door.

Sinto broke into a jog, sweeping wide through the open forest of grand old trees, grateful for the soft bed of coppery needles masking his footfalls. As they drew closer to the heart of the island, Sinto joined the path and closed the distance between him and Victoria. She stopped halfway through the garden to remove a tangle of vines from around her feet.

Birds gathered in the trees that circled the old garden where Victoria stood. A lone owl hooted, a different pattern than last time. There was no response.

The foliage surrounding Victoria shifted. She sensed it. Her hand reached for the knife at her back.

Sinto edged his way closer, closing the gap between him and Victoria, with access to the bunker door a short sprint away.

Arkis emerged from the foliage. He appeared more fit, which seemed odd considering his lifestyle that Sinto witnessed. Perhaps he had wised up and realized leading a rebellion required hard work. His face was the same, but more lined with age. His black hair was wild as ever and his fiery orange eyes were ringed with kohl. He wore the same red silk shirt and black leather wrap he wore in the City of Green.

Seeing Arkis ignited deep rage, primal and untethered as if that small amount of Orange he was forced to consume during his brief imprisonment had lingered in his bloodstream. A memory so real it threatened to take control against his better sense. He tamped down the urge to explode from hiding and rip Arkis apart limb by limb. That mistake would risk Sinto's life as well as Victoria's. He sensed others hiding nearby. Arkis wasn't alone.

The two of them were in grave danger.

Arkis meandered casually around the garden, picking a leaf here and there as if on a simple stroll.

"So you are the one Sinto made such a fuss about," he said to Victoria.

She stood with her back toward Sinto still as a statue, fingers curled around the hilt of the knife.

Arkis stopped several feet back and scanned her head to toe. "I must say you are rather attractive, for a *Sapien*." He sniffed deeply. "Though I find it hard to get over the stink of your kind. Like, hm," He cast his eyes to the sky and snapped his fingers. "Oh yes, like burnt rubber! And in your case a little rose water sprinkled on top to mask the putrid smell."

He paced before Victoria, back from easy reach, his finger tapping his front teeth.

"You know, I could make an exception with you. Yes, oh yes, I can see the allure. And what better gift then to return to my half-witted and naive brother a *violated* mate."

He howled in laughter and grabbed his genital sack. "Maybe even plant a little Arkis seed inside! I bet your daddy would love that too!" He looked around. "Speaking of whom, where is the mighty Culliford? Is this not one of his properties?" He took a step closer to Victoria. "No daddy here to protect you? And Sinto—" His eyes rolled and lips fluttered. "What a dullard! Maybe it's time you stepped up, dump the loser, and take a tumble with me. I think you might find the experience *sat-is-fy-ing*."

Victoria was breathing hard. The dark skin tone of her disguise had slipped from the hand gripping the knife and was working its way up her wrist.

"*Don't,*" Sinto pushed. "*There may be others. Play along. Move for the bunker.*" As an afterthought he added, "*There is something odd about his mannerisms. Overly dramatic, even for him.*"

Victoria eased her grip on the knife and the skin of her hand flushed brown. She laughed. "Sinto can be a bit dull now and again. Shall I find him for you?"

Arkis grinned. "I don't think that's necessary," He dropped the grin and pinned her with his fiery gaze. "I actually came here for you."

Victoria whipped the knife forward, burying the blade in Arkis' chest. Shock froze on his face and he dropped to his knees, flueox and blood puddling at Victoria's feet. The features of his face shifted into a strange puzzle of Arkis' face superimposed with someone else's.

A body double.

Whoever it was crumpled to the ground and imploded. Ash rained across the overgrown garden.

Victoria froze, bloodied knife in hand, poised for another attack. Sinto scanned the sky, the foliage of the garden. Silence. Stillness. Nothing.

Victoria turned toward where Sinto crouched not far from the bunker door. A second Arkis emerged from behind her. "Shall we try that again?"

She whipped around, knife at the ready.

A third stepped forward. "Yes, I say we should."

A fourth. "Definitely."

A fifth. "This could prove quite interesting."

They surrounded her. Four against one. The second Arkis lunged and slipped a parasitic band around her torso, pinning her arms to her sides. The knife fell to her feet. The third Arkis picked it up. A second band was slipped around her chest. Her knees wavered and she gasped from the sudden draw, sucking life from her merlux.

A sixth Arkis emerged. "And quite fun." This one was exactly as Sinto had remembered. Soft paunch and arrogant swagger. He threw back his head and burst into howling laughter.

Ice coiled in Sinto's stomach. His movements, the tone of his howling laughter—Sinto had no doubt this one was the real Arkis.

"We know you're there Sinto, come out and play! Join us in the fun!" real-Arkis said.

The fake Arkises pulled Victoria to the ground. She thrashed against their hands pinning her down. The one with the knife slashed her cheek; blood rose and trickled past her ear. "Oh boy, that's sharp!"

Another Arkis unzipped her jeans and tugged them off.

Sinto's gut lurched. He felt powerless. He was outnumbered. Revealing himself now would be suicide.

I need a weapon!

"What do we have here?" One of the others waved at real-Arkis. "Come look! She's not a Sapien!"

Real-Arkis tsked. "A trick? My, Sinto, maybe you aren't as asinine as I thought, but then again..." He grinned. "Maybe I knew what you had planned all along. Spies! You can't always trust them."

He grabbed Victoria's braid and the knife-wielding Arkis lopped it off at the base of her neck. The six-inch rope of braided hair instantly turned gold, Victoria's natural Seakai coloring. The real Arkis held it up. "Isn't that right, *Victoria*?"

He tossed the braid of hair aside and began a slow sweep of the garden. "Poor Sinto! I can hear your heart beating like a scared little bunny." He snickered. "Here bunny, bunny. I promise I won't harm you, you silly little wabbit."

There were too many of them. Victoria banded and weakening by the second meant impossible odds without the advantage of a weapon. Sinto took a few more steps toward the crack in rock shielding the bunker door.

Sinto tried to calm her. "*Distract them—talk, fight, plead... just stay alive! I'm heading to the bunker for a weapon.*"

Victoria was surrounded by a circle of crouching Arkis'. She squirmed in the crushed greenery beneath her as he slipped through the crack masking the bunker door. He pulled aside the mossy curtain and pressed his face toward the concaved scanner. He held his breath. He feared they would hear the click of the lock release.

"Here bunny—What was that?" real-Arkis said.

"That was me, you asshole," Victoria said, clicking her tongue. "You think you're such a big man, hiding behind your impostors. You're a fucking loser."

Sinto heard her hawk and spit, followed by a satisfying splat as it made contact with what Sinto hoped was Arkis' face.

She kept talking. "I look forward to the day you die, you worm."

Sinto could tell that she had successfully captured their attention. But what followed made Sinto's blood run cold. Though he couldn't hear anything audible coming from her, he was chilled by the repressed cries that leaked through her thoughts. They were hurting her, badly. And yet, she refused to give them the satisfaction of hearing her suffer.

Sinto bolted into the bunker chamber and yanked the leather spine of the book that opened the vault door. The vault door slid open.

He ran inside. He grabbed an ear bud, charged and ready to go, and a crossbow, preloaded with a semi-auto firing barrel from the weapons cabinet.

He slipped the ear bud into his ear, calling for help as he sprinted from the vault, stopping only to tip the book back to seal it. "S here, we're under attack, five enemy. They have V. In garden near bunker entrance."

He slipped from the outer chamber and stopped inside the bunker door long enough to gulp down several breaths and lock on his camouflage.

"*Hang on Victoria!*" he pushed to her mind.

"*Save yourself... they're draining me... sucking me dry. Blood and electricity.*" Her response was weak and desperate.

Sinto held the crossbow behind his back, blocking it behind his camouflaged body. He slipped around the rock and stifled a gasp when he saw what they had done to Victoria.

Stripped of her clothing, her bound body was awash with blood. Hundreds of cuts crisscrossed her body. Across thigh, breast, face, genitals. She was missing some fingers and they had hacked off the ends of her fluked tail. Intestines snaked from her abdomen. Tears streamed from her eyes. She ground her teeth to keep from screaming, fighting that urge to give them what they wanted. The sound of her suffering.

"*Give it to me! Give me reason to kill them!*"

Her screams exploded in his mind, reverberated through his skull, rattled his bones.

He swung the crossbow into position, sighted, and shot, unleashing a volley of barbed steel. Steel cut through flesh and barbed tips shredded. Four bodies crumpled. Four explosions of ash. The four fakes, he was certain. He swung the crossbow, searching for the real Arkis.

"Scan!" Sinto barked, the command to engage the network of sensors.

"No other life forms near you," came a computerized female response.

To be certain, Sinto quickly double-scanned for the real Arkis and his bird Scouts—listening for the sound of a heartbeat, the glow of an aura. Nothing. The treetops were quiet and bare. Arkis, gone. His feathered Scouts, gone.

He heard the pound of a helicopter approaching.

Sinto ran to Victoria and dropped to his knees. Her face and coloring had returned to her own. He grabbed the knife slick with her blood. The parasitic bands crackled with the life force they had stolen from her when he cut them away. He ignored the electrical burns the bands left on his hands and cradled her in his arms. He pinched shut the slit in her stomach with his fingers. He bent with his face beside hers. "Hold on Victoria, hold on."

He yelled to the sky, hoping Alvarez, or whoever was listening to the tiny electronic bud stuck in his ear would hear. "Hurry, she's dying!"

Victoria gasped, "Did you get him?" She sucked for air. Bloody bubbles gurgled from several holes in her chest. "Please—tell me—you got him." Her eyes were dull yet sought an answer.

The whip of a helicopter's rotors grew louder.

Her aura dimmed. More blood than he had ever seen soaked the ground beneath her. She had seconds before she would begin her final trek to the stars in an exploding ball of ash.

He lied. "I got him. You were brave, Victoria. Hold on. They're coming."

She cracked a bloody-toothed smile and wheezed. "Save his ash—" *wheeze*, "I'm gonna piss on—"

She wheezed one last time. Her lips stilled and the light in her pale eyes vanished. The tightness in her face relaxed and Sinto saw her true face for the first time; the steely strength and quick wit that defined her. The satisfaction reflected in her features, believing the lie he told her.

A black helicopter with the Larkian symbol grazed the treetops. A pair of darkly clad men slid down ropes snaking from the mechanical bird's belly.

Sinto burned Victoria's face forever in his memory, vowing Arkis and his minions would pay for this and all the other atrocities they had inflicted. He choked. "You will be honored and remembered." Then Victoria's body crumpled in his arms until all he held was ash.

PART TWO

33

Sneaky Gamble

"AUDREY? YOU THERE?"

Audrey startled at the sound of Blake's voice. The cockpit was bathed in a soft, red light. Cool briny air flowed and a sliver of moonlight cut through the transparent dome above her head. She sat up, yawning, shaking cobwebs from her mind.

Sitting in the glow of red light in a tight and confined space briefly felt like those tense moments on *Discovery* as she ticked down the last of their remaining air. But, here and now, the air was fresh and she was bobbing on the surface of the Great Ocean after tackling an all new set of problems.

Setup by Orankai spies. Blake sinking. Dismembered bodies and feasting sharks.

She shivered from the memory. "I think I fell asleep. What time is it?"

"Middle of the night. Sun won't be rising for several more hours."

She yawned again, drawing a deep lungful of briny air, and visualized Blake sitting in his mangled Xiphias, facing the opposite direction as she towed him under the cloak of night.

He said, "We're a few miles offshore from the Desertlands. Explains why our maps are vague on detail. We're far south of where we should be."

She rubbed the sleep from her eyes and activated the navigation system. The only outside light was from the partial moon peeking around wisps of cloud cover. She winced at the sudden flash of light when the map of Merluma came to life.

"My readings confirm."

"While you were snoozing I was thinking."

"About what?"

"Why they chose this side to attack us. The obvious answer is to place us as far away from the Winterlands as possible. But what if it's for a different reason? You looking at the map?"

She sat up and focused on the screen with the map. "Yeah."

"Zoom in on the southwest coast."

She fiddled with the touch screen, zoomed in tight to the coast. "Got it."

"Zoom in on Inception Bay. Isn't that where Sinto took you after we were attacked by the orcas last fall?"

She sat up, looked closer. She traced the dark ridges that extended from a mountain range. A perfect horse shoe that hemmed in the land with the sea on one side and a formidable mountain range on the other. She traced along the reefs offshore and the crescent-shaped beach that edged the large bay, then the jungle and woodlands reaching up to the Black Mountains. Dual rivers cut across the beach. She'd been landlocked between them and the mountains with no means of escape except to swim in the ocean. Which, at the time, was something she was not capable of because of her past fear of the water.

"That's it. Seeing it from this perspective, it appears that Inception Bay may once have been a massive volcanic cone that collapsed at the edge of the ocean."

"You said it was unpopulated, that you saw no one else, right?"

"Mm-hmm."

"And Sinto told you that the Terrakai had claimed the plains and lands beyond the mountains, inland, right?"

She zoomed out. Studied the dark ridge of the Black Mountains with a large lake nestled between the peaks and the forest lands and great plains that extended to the northeast. Beyond the mountains stretched the Winterlands, covered by a massive glacier and year-round snow pack. "Yes."

"Did he tell you anything about the barren peninsula along the southwest coast?"

"Not that I remember."

"Zoom in along the shore west of Inception Bay. Do you see something odd?"

Audrey fiddled with the zoom and focused in on something human-made along the rocky shore on the west side of the ridge enclosing Inception Bay. "Are those stairs coming out of the ocean?"

"That's what it looks like to me, like stairs intentionally carved into the cliff. Keep scanning up the coast. Not many sandy and easy-to-access beaches, but these stairways appear all along the rocky shoreline."

Audrey pondered. "If the Terrakai tribal lands are beyond the mountains and in the high plains to the northeast, and the Arctakai claimed Winterlands beyond that, then maybe the peninsula forming the Sea of Meura once belonged to the Seakai. The Desertlands, Seakai territory."

"Exactly what I was thinking."

"But it's barren. Where would they live?"

"I suspect there may be caves peppered along the coast. Leela once mentioned she preferred the dry of the desert over the dampness of the Pacific Northwest. It would make sense if this was where the Seakai came from."

She was thinking out loud. "So if your enemy was imprisoning someone important—hide them where no one would expect..."

Blake finished her thought. "And away from the breeding caves or Terrakai tribal lands." He clicked his tongue. "So why would they want to strand us along the shores of Seakai territory?"

"Because Arkis wants to kidnap me to get back at Sinto." She paused, then gasped. "Damn! Seems too coincidental. I bet Naiada's there too." She did a quick calculation. "Just one problem. The Desertlands are vast, and if he's hiding in a hidden cave... It'll be like searching for a needle in the proverbial haystack."

"I would be willing to bet Arkis doesn't want to wander too far from the ocean or the breeding caves and the portal to the City of Green, but far enough to be safe from an attack. If I was to place a bet on where he's hiding I would gamble he's headquartered just north of Inception Bay in Seakai territory, just on the other side of the ridge and near that first stairway with access to the ocean."

"How far is that from where we are now?"

"Couple of miles. If we keep going in this direction we'll run straight into that stairway."

She huffed. "And he'd be thanking us for being so stupid."

"There's a cove about six miles north of it. It's small, well-protected, and it has a beach. That might be our best bet for getting ashore. We need to offload the supplies in *Xiph1* and find somewhere we can hole up for a while and come up with a new plan. Besides, my ass is killing me and I could use a good stretch."

"Sounds risky, you sure?"

"We're stuck here, so we might as well make ourselves useful."

"Good point."

"What's that mantra you learned from your mom?"

"Move in harmony with force of life, flow as water, like stream around rock."

"A big force just drove us to that rock. Let's flow with it."

She smiled to herself. "Flow as water, sneaky as mouse. Setting a new course now." Audrey set the autopilot for the cove Blake pointed out. *Xiph2* responded immediately and began a slow steady turn. "Should be there within an hour and a half at this speed."

She could hear Blake yawn through their radio connection. "Good. Wake me before we reach shore."

34

Harsh Warning

Sinto tunneled his way back to Isla Salvación through the lonely Pacific, heartsick and defeated. He tried not to dwell on what Arkis and his body-doubles had done to Victoria. The atrocities inflicted with Sinto's knife. Victoria's bravery. The lie he told her before she died, that Arkis was dead. How sincerely she believed him.

He tried not to dwell on the fact that he had come up with the plan and recruited Victoria to help. Now she was dead. Guilt overwhelmed him.

His tunnel spit him out just outside the ring of defense buoys surrounding Isla Salvación. The buoys monitored the comings and goings of Merahvu team members and were a key piece of the Larkian defense system against an Orankai attack. It didn't take long for a small submarine to find him; it was armed to the teeth and ready to defend. He showed his face and gave the hand signal they had devised. After a moment, the pilot acknowledged and he was waved on to proceed through the line of defenses with the submarine following closely behind. He entered the harbor and swam to the dock where the *Requiem Sea II* was moored.

Normally he would run up to the surface with several thrusts of his tail, break the surface, then fly through the air and land on the dock triumphantly. Not today. He sucked in his foot fins and climbed up a metal ladder dipping deep into the water. He may as well have tucked his tail between his legs for full effect. Arkis won. Sinto failed. Victoria paid the ultimate price. He tucked his tail against his back with a powerful damning slap.

No one was there to greet him, to offer congratulations or sympathy. He paused, wondering what was left for him to do now, where to go. He felt lost and alone.

He reached out for Audrey, hoping she was near, maybe helping Ryan or Rachel. In his haste to leave on his failed mission he had failed to ask her which project she had chosen to pursue. His inquiry through the Mark as to where she may be yielded nothing in return. Not a spark or joyous welcome. He tried again, but the Mark in his arm lay cold and still.

Why isn't she here? Where could she have gone? Then it struck him. *She joined the team heading to Merluma.*

Please, no.

He knew of only one person who would know for certain: his mother.

Dread motivated him and he dove back into the water and swam with determination to the black-sand beach steps from the house where his mother lived, using care to stay far inside the Larkians' ring of defense encircling the island.

Once he emerged neck deep in the water, he took powerful strides to reach the dark sandy shore. Water streamed down his body as he ran to the stairs leading to the lanai wrapped around the small house.

She greeted him at the back door. When he saw her, dread and guilt consumed him, and he lost it. She pulled him down to a bench built against the side of the house facing the ocean. He buried his face into her embrace and sobbed. He couldn't find the words to describe what he had witnessed, the guilt he felt for Victoria's death, the rage toward his half-brother, and the disappointment in his father who had chosen to join their enemy. He felt like a half-man unable to protect a new friend and companion who had put her trust in him. The fear that Audrey might share Victoria's fate should Arkis find her was overwhelming.

His mother whispered, "Show me what happened."

He did, reliving the nightmare. New details too horrible to imagine emerged the second time around.

"He is a monster," she said. Sinto felt her body tense. "And he has your sister."

That reminder stabbed deep. He was helpless to do anything about it, at least while he was here.

"I must go and get her."

"No."

"We cannot just leave her."

She said nothing.

He gasped. "You have already given up."

"No."

"Then we must get her back."

"No."

"She's not safe!"

"She is with Ramasis."

"Why do you still trust him?"

She said nothing.

"Was he your spy?"

She said nothing. She didn't need to. Sinto's blood boiled, refusing to believe she could trust his father after everything that had happened.

He let out a frustrated breath. "There's something you're hiding. I have felt it from the start. Why?"

She sighed. "Nothing about our future is set. For me, you, Audrey, Naiada, your friends... everyone, Merahvu and Sapien alike. It is what we do now that will dictate the quality of the outcome."

"And you believe Ramasis can be saved? You believe he is worth sacrificing everything we are fighting for?"

"Ramasis is a good man. He deserves a chance to redeem himself."

"He is rotten to the core. You did that to him. He felt no remorse for killing Audrey's mother. An innocent woman. And your short-sightedness killed Victoria."

"Arkis killed Victoria."

"Someone warned him. He knew it was Victoria pretending to be Audrey."

"How do you know for certain it was Ramasis? Arkis has many spies. Those bird Scouts were watching you. He merely waited until you lost your patience. Perhaps you underestimated his cunning."

He jumped to his feet, unable to contain his rage. "So it was *my* fault?"

She held out her hand. "Calm down, sit, there is more to discuss."

He struggled to contain his anger. It took several moments of pacing and gazing at the quiet sea and the lovely flowers growing along the edges of the lanai to calm himself enough to look at her, to continue this conversation. The truths she spoke cut deeply, and he wondered if he had the courage to go on. To fight this fight against the impossible.

His mother rested her hand back in her lap and sat patiently, giving him whatever time he needed to settle. It took a while for his heart to return to a steady beat. Finally, he sat with his hands tucked beneath his thighs, attentive but ready to flee. "Out with it then."

"Who do you think helped you in the City of Green?"

Sinto was taken aback. It felt like ancient history since his visit to the City of Green when he was on a mission to find his father. A mission that led to his near-forced recruitment by Arkis into the Orankai, and when he refused and fought back, to his near assassination. Ramasis was there, standing by Arkis' side as the lampreys feasted on Mianna, an innocent young woman caught up in Arkis' sick game of control. The same lampreys who nearly ended Sinto.

"No one helped me. I escaped, barely."

"With a strength you otherwise would not have had if someone had not disabled the parasitic draw flooding your holding cell."

Sinto had forgotten that fact among the horror. At the time he did note it had stopped but thought no more about it, that maybe it was because of a fault by Arkis' guards.

"Ramasis did that?"

She said nothing.

"You don't know for certain, do you?"

Her lips pressed into a sharp white line. "Who else could it have been?"

"If it had been Ramasis, it was merely a minor assist. Arkis could have successfully recruited me or I could have died fighting it." Sinto pointed to the scarred circle of skin on the side of his torso. "One lamprey got me; if another had, I would have been fish food."

She persisted. "Ramasis is flawed and not a whole man. He could have allowed Arkis to kill me, but he didn't. I am certain Arkis wanted to, in one of his awful ways. Ramasis is all we have on the inside. He will not let anything happen to Naiada. I believe that with all my heart."

"I do not share your confidence. If he is all we have, then we are doomed and Naiada is lost, unless..."

"Do not fantasize about going after her."

"Why not?"

"Arkis is expecting you to do that. Do you want him to make a fool of you again?"

"Then what would you have me do!" he yelled.

"You are needed here."

Frustration and fury stewed. He reflected back to Audrey's sentiment that she felt they were running around in circles, losing ground with each lap. He felt that way now. Chasing his tail. Victoria was dead because of it.

Silence fell between them. The breeze caressed his skin. Birds twittered their merry tunes in bushes and trees. While the natural things surrounding them were pleasant, he had to know. The real reason he came to see his mother.

He sighed. "Do you know where she is?"

"Audrey?"

"Yes."

"Merluma," she confirmed.

The blood in his veins turned to ice. So it was true, his greatest fear. She decided to join the warrior teams in the City of Ice on Merluma. The same team going after the breeding caves and Arkis. He stood. "I must go."

His mother grabbed his hand. "No. If you go now with vengeance coursing through your veins, you will most certainly die, and so will she."

35

Strange Bedfellow

SINTO LEFT HIS MOTHER'S house in a paralyzing quandary. With Audrey on Merluma he was unsure of where to go. The little house on the south end of the island where they had spent weeks together was empty and held no personal attachment. He had no home to call his own. His had been destroyed months ago and Merluma was overrun by Orankai. He had been living day-by-day and week-by-week, going from one crisis to another. It was a nomad's life that he once accepted while traveling the lands of North America. And while it had been exciting and educational, he was growing weary and bitter.

He was unsure what to do. His mother's harsh warning frightened him. The intensity with which she delivered it, the roil of fire in her eyes as the words spilled from her lips. She must have seen something on one of her journeys through the Timeless Dimension. One or more possible outcomes if Sinto chose to ignore her warning.

He sauntered toward the main compound where Rachel had settled and was helping Alvarez strategically plan their next moves. He hoped she was there. He needed a heavy dose of Rachel's practical advice and reassuring dimpled smile.

The dining hall was empty but the kitchen was a hub of activity. The smell of sautéing onions and freshly baked bread awakened his hunger. Leonard and his Larkian kitchen companion, Poe—a woman who helped raise Audrey—were busy preparing the nightly dinner, debating the best way to cook the meal's main meaty course, whether to braise or roast.

Sinto wandered over to a set of double doors, partially open, where a different type of frenzied activity was unfolding. He peeked inside.

The conference room had been converted into a full-fledged command center, abuzz with purpose. The room was filled with a dozen Larkians making plans and carrying on multiple conversations. Several electronic screens were mounted to the main wall, displaying charts listing changing numbers, maps of ships sprinkled across the Pacific Ocean, a map of the Great Lakes region spanning the United States and Canada, and another of the west coast of North America. Each had a combination of solid orange or blinking red dots. Clusters of orange dots surrounded Lake Superior and around ships passing through the North Pacific Gyre where Orange was first discovered.

The table was covered with piles of paper, open laptops, and buzzing cell phones. Wires snaked and fed power to several towers of electricity-sucking computers. The air was still and hot and filled with the scent of burnt coffee and bodies in desperate need of a fresh water dip.

Rachel was in the thick of it working alongside Alvarez, both bent over his laptop; her mouth twisted in concentration, his brow crushed into a knot.

Sinto suddenly felt self-conscious. He was the only Merahvu that he could see in the room filled with Sapiens. One lacking any form of clothing. Before joining the Larkians in their fight and venturing into the Sapien world where he met Rachel, he felt perfectly at ease intermingling with the fully clothed while in his natural state. The scene unfolding inside was in a semi-state of controlled chaos. Entering naked might tip their progress over the edge and cause an unexpected disruption.

He stepped back from the doorway. Regardless of his state of undress he wondered if he should disturb Rachel at all after seeing the intensity of her involvement. He didn't share the same level of knowledge of Sapien technology. He felt uncomfortable and out of place.

He turned to leave and smacked directly into Audrey's father.

Culliford regarded him with a steely gaze, the same steely gaze he gave Sinto right before he shoved a knife into Sinto's chest and nearly killed him. Though Sinto resolved his ill feelings for Culliford and both had come to terms with what happened, that place where the knife entered tingled every time he gazed into those steely blue eyes.

"Sinto," Culliford's gazed softened. "Welcome back."

"Culliford—I—"

He smiled. "Please, call me Robert. Ianthe's use of it lately has grown on me. Seeing that she is your mother and you have captured my daughter's heart I believe it to be better suited for you to call me by my first name."

"Robert, then."

"So, what are you doing here?"

Sinto blew out an exasperated breath. "I was asking myself the same question. I'm not quite sure. Everyone seems to be scattered and focused on critical tasks. I honestly don't know where I belong."

He gave Sinto a sympathetic frown. "I am sorry about what happened on Andrew's Island."

Sinto stared at his feet. "I was so certain we would get Arkis. I never considered that we might fail. Victoria, she..." Sinto drew a sharp breath. He could not say it or think it. He pinched off the raw memory, vanishing the bloody images that came to mind.

Culliford looked around the dining room at the empty tables and chairs. "You hungry? Care to join me for a quick bite?"

Sinto's throat was a knot. All he could do was nod. The last meal he ate was with Victoria, her last, and from sealed plastic bags. The irony was not lost on him.

Culliford was keen to Sinto's distress and led him through a set of open sliding glass doors to a table on the lanai set next to a small waterfall and pond with koi fish, lazily swimming among water lilies. The sound of trickling water soothed.

Sinto sat.

Culliford stood over him, hesitated for a moment, then gave Sinto's shoulder a gentle squeeze before leaving for the kitchen. A kind and comforting gesture, one that felt odd considering their history.

A koi burst from the surface of the pond to snatch a flying insect. Ripples radiated across the mirrored surface. Ripples that touched everything in their path. The single action disrupted a small frog innocently slumbering atop a lily pad.

Sinto contemplated how ripples from the actions of others had turned everything in his life upside down. A single point of disruption that started it all. Culliford and his mother's affair. How twisted it all became. The man who hunted them and destroyed their city was now an ally and close companion of his mother's and the father of the woman he was meant to be with for the rest of his life. That man was now accepting that fact with a kind and comforting gesture.

Culliford returned with a large sandwich stuffed with roasted chicken, cut in half and shared between two plates. Sinto's plate had a generous slice of avocado, tomato, and a shell-shaped hunk of crisp lettuce added on the side.

"Not sure if you wanted a sandwich with bread. Your mother prefers to wrap it all up in rabbit food."

Another thoughtful gesture. Culliford had become a new man since his accident. Maybe someone should whack Sinto on the head and set his life straight. How convenient it would be to have all the bad things you have ever done erased from your conscience in an instant and everyone forgiving every mistake you ever made.

Sinto was starving and wolfed down the sandwich, bread and all, then rolled up the avocado and tomato in the lettuce and ate it too, just like a ravenous rabbit.

Culliford watched in amusement as he finished his own. Leonard wandered over from the kitchen with a couple cups of coffee and cream and sugar on a tray balanced on the palm of his hand. He picked up their empty plates and gave them a white, toothy smile. He winked at Sinto. "Aye, here's a little somethin' to light a spark in yer eye." Then he left.

Culliford drank his coffee black. Sinto loaded his up with cream and sugar.

"Ianthe told me Audrey's on Merluma, nothing more." He looked up, hoping Culliford would offer more detail.

Culliford sat back, worry etched on his face. He nodded, acknowledging Sinto's question.

"Do you know where she is, what she's doing there?"

"Fighting the fight I suppose."

"That's all? You know nothing else?"

"I know that she is fiercely independent and neither of us can change that."

That truth was what terrified Sinto and made him love her all the more.

"She joined the Xiphias team."

"What is *Xiphias*?"

"Mini-sub, one pilot, super maneuverable and capable of defending itself from your kind. Blake was instrumental in the design. They went together."

"To Merluma? How? When?"

Culliford closed his eyes and drew a deep breath. "They teamed up with Khani's warriors to pass through the portal. That was three days ago."

"If I hadn't wasted those extra days on Andrew's Island, I wouldn't have missed her."

Culliford looked away. "There's more you need to know." He drew a deep breath, then fixed Sinto with his gaze. "Stokes reported Audrey and Blake were the only two who failed to reach the agreed-upon destination. They have not heard from either of them, nor the warriors they were with. He suspects foul play, that it was Arkis' spies who slipped through Khani's screening and led them through the portal to Merluma. God only knows where they ended up."

Sinto's heart raced. He could hear the howling laughter as if Arkis was sitting by his side. Arkis was toying with them. It didn't matter how many people were employed in the Larkians' command center or how many warriors were deployed to the City of Ice. He was outmaneuvering them with a handful of spies strategically placed while his Orankai masses covertly attacked the Sapien world.

"How is he able to cut through our screening and defenses?"

"Ianthe and I have had long discussions about this topic. You are not the only one distressed about the situation. But Ianthe believes Audrey and Blake are safe, for the moment. As for how Arkis is able to stay out of our reach, well, Ianthe has a theory."

"What theory? She hasn't shared anything with me. Only to warn me not to go after Audrey on Merluma."

"Wise advice."

"And?"

"She suspects Arkis may have successfully used her eggs."

"What proof does she have?"

"None. She can only sense at the truth. One truth, anyway. The last time she entered the Timeless Dimension she felt she was not alone."

"It could have been Naiada."

"No. She is most certain it was not."

"But how can that be? She was attacked, what, three or more months ago?"

"You should talk to Wickman and Wantemo. They are learning some disturbing things about Orange."

"Like what?"

"Mutations. Its life cycle is accelerating. The good news is it may mutate itself out of existence. The bad news is that Arkis can breed faster. Did you notice those maps in the command center?"

"The Great Lakes, ships in the Pacific Ocean, west coast of North America..."

"Each orange dot on those maps represents some form of confirmed contact with Orange. Blinking red represents what is thought to be an active attack. It's happening, whatever Arkis has planned. He is cunning, that one, and he has one hell of a weapon in his hands. Spreading out and randomizing his attacks. How well do you know him?"

"More than I care to but I am surprised by his sudden rise in popularity. When we were younglings others liked him until they got to know him. He pulled mean tricks. I was the one to clean up his messes afterwards, if I was around. I believe the only reason he is successful today is because of the power of Orange."

"Leave Arkis to the others. Perhaps you should put your energies into solving the Orange problem."

"You mean leave Arkis to Audrey."

"I am just as unhappy about her choice as you are, but..." He shook his head. "I encouraged her, so here we are. *Both* of my children are taking risks. Though it gives me some solace knowing that they are fighting together. Blake is just as capable of taking care of himself as Audrey is. He won't let anything happen to her."

"I hope you're right."

Sinto downed the last of his coffee. It was time to stop moping and do something.

He gazed down at his naked body. "Um, this may be a strange request, but do you have some clothes I could borrow?"

36

Hideaway

AFTER ANOTHER HOUR AND towing Blake in *Xiph1*, Audrey guided *Xiph2* through a narrow channel with Blake tethered to her tail. The small cove on the south-western shore of Merluma they had discovered was just that, small but well protected from ocean swells.

Before arriving ashore, she came to believe that Blake's theory was dead on. These arid lands where the Seakai once lived and abandoned long ago would be an excellent location for Arkis to hide Naiada and run his campaign of terror. It was a gamble, but one that made a great deal of sense. It placed Arkis away from the breeding caves and Orankai encampments where the teams in the Winterlands were staging an attack.

As she drew closer to the shore, the glow of a pale sandy beach came into view, set alight by the partial moon. The depth sounder showed the bottom slowly rising beneath them.

She heard Blake stir. His voice crackled across the comm. "Retract your fins and park the pods. You should be able to come up sideways to the beach without damaging anything."

Audrey did as Blake suggested then heard Blake scramble atop her sub. He knocked on the hatch. Audrey opened it. "Take it in slow. I'll guide *Xiph1* onto the beach from the water. When you hear me whistle swing your nose out." Then she heard a splash.

Audrey took a quick thermal scan of the beach and waters in the cove looking for warm bodies. She only found Blake's.

She heard a clank, then Blake whistled. She glued her eyes to the navigation screen and tapped the toroidal propellers in opposite directions until her nose was pointed away from the beach. She waited for Blake to come back.

It took a few minutes for him to return. He climbed up the footholds and leaned inside the hatch opening. His hair was wet and slicked back.

"Unless you want to stay there all night, you're gonna have to swim."

Audrey feared the water ever since her mother drowned on her tenth birthday. It was a mantra that her mother taught her that helped her to overcome her fear anytime she went out on a boat or was forced to swim. Sinto changed all of that by helping her face that fear. While she still felt a niggling tremor at the thought of swimming, she no longer felt the need to repeat the mantra, or freeze with panic.

She popped up through the open hatch, and said with confidence, "I can swim."

He pointed to a large remote controller with a small screen and what appeared to be a waterproof silicone sleeve completely encasing the device. It was tucked in a pocket on the dash. "Grab that and hand it to me please."

She did.

"Pocket your goggles."

She zipped them up in a slot designated for them in the folds of her hood.

"Take a swim."

She swung her legs out of the hatch and slid down the side of the sub feet first and landed in the water. Too deep to touch the bottom. Her head dunked under. She treaded water after popping up. The suit kept water from leaking inside through the snug seal around her neck, like a scuba dry suit. Her head was another matter. Her eyes burned from salt water.

Blake reached in and switched off the electronics. Then he pressed a button on the remote. The hatch slid shut and he slipped into the water beside her. It was dark, and without her goggles, she easily lost direction.

Blake grabbed her hand. "This way." He pulled her into the shallows and the soft sand where his disabled sub lay on its side. They crawled ashore and plopped down on the sand.

"Goggles will help your night vision."

They removed their goggles from the watertight seal built into their hoods and put them on. Everything was cast in a soft green.

Blake pressed a button on the waterproof remote and the screen came to life. So did *Xiph2*. He guided the submarine away from the beach and toward the center of the cove by manipulating the remote and following its path on the small navigation screen. Then he guided it to descend and bob weightlessly just below the surface. He fiddled with a couple more buttons, engaging the sub's camouflage mode.

"That should keep her safe for a while."

"What now?"

"Set up camp and offload supplies from *Xiph1*."

They were surrounded by sand and stone. The beach was a mere sliver along the shore. Rising up behind them were fifty foot cliffs of sandstone whose faces were pocked with erosion. Where the cliffs met the shore, they were carved by time and rough seas and offered little protection from the elements.

Blake was determined to find a place where they could hide supplies and rest. He ventured off, poking around at each possible opening along the shore. Audrey went the other way, finding nothing other than shallow caves with an ocean view. When she looked back, Blake was gone.

He emerged from an opening. "I found something," he said excitedly.

He had found a hidden cave. She had to duck down to enter the opening, but once inside the ceiling soared.

Faint beams of moonlight cut through openings in the cave's ceiling, illuminating the space. A fire pit ringed by rocks was filled with ash. A well-worn log for sitting was laid beside it along with a pile of old fish bones. Deeper inside the cave was a bed of furs lying inside a carved-out section of sandstone. The furs were covered by a thick layer of dust and sand. At least that was all Audrey hoped it was, imagining the cave's last occupant dying in their sleep and disintegrating into ash as Merahvu are programmed to do.

"This should work splendidly," Blake said. "Let's get to work."

They labored. Blake handed out boxes stored in the tail end of *Xiph1*. Audrey stacked them on the beach.

The last thing Blake grabbed was a shovel, small and half the length of a typical one, and tossed it beside the stack of boxes.

"What's that for?"

He grinned. "You'll see. Glad I thought to grab it at the last minute."

They stood, arms crossed, studying *Xiph1*, bobbing gently in the shallows.

"What if someone sees it?"

"That is a problem. For now I'll anchor it out and sink it below the surface."

Blake rummaged around inside and pulled out a small folding anchor with about fifty feet of line. He fetched *Xiph1*'s remote, passed it to Audrey, and sealed the hatch. Though *Xiph1* was inoperable at sea, it could still camouflage.

Blake waded out into the darkness and tied the line to the ring on *Xiph1*'s tail end. Audrey pushed and Blake pulled and eventually *Xiph1* broke free from the sandy bottom.

Audrey waited while Blake dove under and set the anchor in deeper water. He swam back and used the remote to sink *Xiph1* beneath the surface.

They labored more, carrying boxes from the beach to the cave. Some of them were heavy and by the time they finished both of them were gasping and sweating. Afterward, Audrey was ready to settle and rest.

"Not yet," Blake said.

Blake pulled aside a box labeled "Emergency Essentials," and set it by the log next to the firepit. Audrey opened it up. Inside was an odd assortment of things: nutrition sticks, first aid kit, hunting knife, set of throwing knives, bar of soap, pair of tiny toothbrushes, iodine tablets, solar blankets, a funny looking contraption with solar cells, a UV light and rubber tubes, plus a couple of boxes of water. She pulled one out, drank half of it, and handed it to Blake, who finished it off.

"Now we dig."

"For what?" Audrey asked.

"Not for what. To bury."

"Geez, was that for real, pirates burying treasure?"

"Yep," he said. "Pirate's law: Never leave valuables lying around." He found a spot along a wall and attacked the sand with the shovel. After several minutes he was standing in a knee-deep hole. He tossed the shovel to Audrey. "Your turn." He bent at the waist, catching his breath.

"Ever forget where you buried stuff?"

"We did once. Rum stash, drank it while we hid it." He rolled his eyes. "Never happened again."

She tried to dig with the same rigor as Blake but found she was panting after digging a few inches deeper. "Damn, this is hard work."

"But worth it. Don't want the weapons getting into the wrong hands."

Once the hole was four feet deep and four feet square, they lined it with one of the solar blankets from the emergency essentials box. They stacked the boxes neatly inside the hole using care to keep an inventory of what was stacked where. They placed a box of weapons on top for quick access.

Blake tucked a second solar blanket across the top and along the sides of the neat stack. "We used to use old sails to keep the sand out."

They took turns filling in the rest of the hole and spreading the extra sand around the cave floor. Blake dug a smaller hole off to the side for the essentials box they planned to bury later, then he buried the shovel in a shallow grave a few feet away. They used their hands and feet to smooth the entire area. No one but them would know an arsenal of weapons and survival gear was buried there.

Audrey sat on the log and dug out a couple of nutrition sticks from the essentials box they had set aside. She took a bite. It was packed with a highly condensed mix of nuts, dried fruit, flax seed, whey powder, and ground-up greens. It tasted just like you would expect, healthy and weird. It left her teeth feeling fuzzy, like after eating spinach.

She said, "It's not a Leonard meal but better than starving."

"Agreed."

After they ate, Blake stood and patted her shoulder. "We rest till dawn. You get the bunk."

37

Undocumented

Sinto ran his fingers across the small white logo embroidered on the chest of the black T-shirt Culliford gave him. An oval imposed atop a flattened X, the same Larkian symbol printed on their national flag and painted on their ships. Audrey said it represented a modern-day Jolly Roger; a human skull atop a set of crossbones, made to be less morbid.

Sinto never imagined wearing the uniform of his once sworn enemy. Now he wore it with pride after successfully accomplishing a secret mission assigned by his mother several months prior: to turn their arch enemy into an ally. Since then they'd managed to recruit Culliford and his Larkians to join their fight against Orange and the Orankai. A success far beyond what Sinto had initially imagined. He suspected the same sense of success was true for his mother.

The black shorts he wore were made of some wonder material that whisked with each step he took. Like the shirt, they were designed to let the skin breath and wick away sweat, something that was meaningless to Sinto with his Merahvu anatomy. The Merahvu cooled down by releasing a layer of lorica and they usually stripped off all coverings before doing so. Culliford had offered

Sinto a pair of shoes but he preferred to leave his extra-large feet bare. The gritty feel of sand and dirt between his toes reminded him of Merluma.

As soon as Sinto left the compound he noticed a loud buzz that reminded him of an obnoxious bee. He looked up. A mini-drone, mirroring his movement.

The *Requiem Sea II* and *Masquerade Ball* were moored together in the harbor on the other side of the compound. Sinto rounded the shore at the innermost part of the harbor where a wood-planked boardwalk extended over crystal clear water where schools of fish circled in the shadows.

Across the street, markets were filled with villagers, both Larkian and newly settled Merahvu gathered from the Arctakai city in the Southern Ocean. They shopped for fresh produce and Sapien-made clothing and toys for their children. Larkians and Merahvu whizzed by on electric bicycles and in UTVs. It was a miraculous sight—Merahvu and Sapiens respectfully living in harmony. Something he never would have imagined a few short months ago.

A large, wide-bellied plane circled low and slow just over the ocean. The way it moved seemed to defy gravity itself. He stopped to watch it line up to the airport's landing strip parallel to the harbor, then touch down. With a squeal of rubber and the roar of massive engines, it drew to a shuddering halt. Beeping front loaders and large trucks rushed in to offload whatever the Larkians were transporting from the mainland.

The drone hovered. He peeked up. A single red eye glared back.

Sinto kept walking—swerving around bustling people on foot, skateboards, electric scooters—with the drone determinedly trailing behind.

The dock was alive with activity, with a pair of Larkians clearing everyone and everything aside to make way for the new shipments to be loaded on the ships. Sinto continued his trek along the edge of the dock until he reached the gangplank leading into the belly of the *Requiem Sea II*.

It was guarded by a friendly Larkian of Polynesian descent and a young Merahvu of Seakai tribe like Sinto, neither of whom Sinto had met before. The Larkian wore the same uniform Culliford had given to Sinto, slick black T-shirt and shorts. The Seakai wore a colorful skareef with smiling sharks printed on it, like those sold in the village markets, and which the local Larkians called sarongs.

The Larkian said, "Hi, I'm Kekoa and this is Junon." Junon nodded in acknowledgment. Sinto sensed Junon's merlux fire, readying to attack if necessary.

"Sinto."

Kekoa raised a small electronic device and swiped it along Sinto's arms. It emitted a harsh sound. "Have you been documented?"

"What do you mean by documented?"

"Did you receive an ID implant, a dChip?"

"No."

Kekoa touched a button on the high-tech communicator hooked around his ear. "Call off the drone. The undocumented guy we're looking for is here. He says his name is Sinto and is requesting to board. Has no dChip." His eyes gazed at nothing in particular, then locked on Sinto's face. "Got it." He addressed Sinto. "What traditional gift did you make especially for Queen Ianthe?"

Sinto was initially confused by the question, then it dawned on him. A test to prove his true identity. Simple and smart and one not requiring technology. "I adapted a special strain of strawberry to prosper in the simulated environment of our underwater city Tallamure. She loves strawberries."

"How old were you and why did you give it to her?"

"My thirteenth birthday. It was my appreciation gift for the life she gave me. A Seakai tradition once a youngling enters puberty."

Junon's merlux calmed. "I remember those. Delicious!"

Kekoa broke the connection to whomever he was speaking to. "Welcome, Sinto." He gestured for Sinto to proceed up the gangplank. "Someone will meet you at the top of the gangplank. You've been ordered to get a dChip, and right away."

Sinto climbed the gangplank stairs. As Kekoa promised, someone was there to meet him, someone he hadn't seen in too long a time.

"Wantemo!" Sinto said.

Like the others Sinto had seen in the command center, Wantemo looked like he was in need of a long rest. Sinto wondered if he looked the same. The past several months had taken a toll on all of them and the battle had only just begun.

Wantemo grabbed Sinto by the shoulder and smiled. "Good to see you alive, *mentee*. Follow me." He led Sinto a short distance through a wood-walled hallway to a circular stairway that wound around a giant metal cylinder. Sinto lagged behind to gaze inside a round window cut into its side. An oval-shaped metal object was contained inside and dotted with crusted salt from the sea.

Wantemo stopped. "This ship is a technological wonder. That which you see is the ship's keel." He placed his palms together. "It can run on fossil-fuel power or by the wind. When they raise the ship's carbon fiber sails—*wings* they call them—the ship tips over, then—" He tipped his pressed palms to a forty-five-degree angle, then slid his palms apart, one stacked upon the other. "The weighted keel drops to counterbalance the pressure of wind against the wings. It's what keeps the ship from falling over. The sleek design of the hull helps it slip efficiently through water. Very fast for a Sapien sailing ship."

Sinto was impressed. He had read up on sailing ships in the Sapien books he collected, including the fast ones pirates preferred for a quick escape after pillaging the slow stubby things many traders in the seventeenth and eighteenth centuries used to travel the seas. Pirates from those days may have been feared but they were cunning and resourceful. True survivors. The Larkians were proof of it and he could understand why his mother had been intrigued by Culliford so long ago.

They exited the stairway and entered another wood-walled hallway running the full length of the ship. A sign announced it was "Level 2". Multiple doors lined the sea-facing side. Names stamped on brass plates were mounted beside each cabin door. One of them was for Ryan, another for Wantemo.

Wantemo stopped suddenly, turned and asked, "Where are you staying?"

"Before I left I was staying with Audrey, but she is..." Sinto shrugged. "I have nowhere at the moment."

"Ah. Then stay on the ship with me." He stopped before one of the doors with a blank brass plate. "We shall put you here." The door was built of solid wood and took effort to open. Wantemo stepped inside. Sinto followed. "Your new home."

It was a modest-sized cabin with a single bunk against the hull below an oval porthole, looking out to the airfield. Sunlight streamed inside, lighting a set of folded bed coverings and a pillow. Everything Sinto needed for a night's rest.

Wantemo pointed to a stack of drawers. "You can secure your things there."

Sinto thought it funny. He had no things to secure except the clothes he wore.

Wantemo placed his hand on the knob of a closed door. A small green light was above the knob.

"Green means vacant, red that someone else is inside, automatically detected." Wantemo opened the door. "On a ship, the Larkians call this the 'head'. I'm not quite sure why. You share it with the occupant in the adjoining cabin, which currently is vacant."

Sinto peeked inside.

The head consisted of a Sapien toilet and a sink. Above the sink was a mirror. A set of drawers were below, one on each side. Wantemo opened a drawer closest to Sinto's cabin. An assortment of personal hygiene products were inside.

"These are yours." Wantemo pulled out a toothbrush and a tube of toothpaste. "I find these much easier to use than a furry stick, and I like the minty taste."

He held up a stick of deodorant. "Not so much need for this." It was true. Merahvu didn't sweat like Sapiens and shunned the use of anything that would interfere with the natural flow of lorica from their pores.

Sinto had learned of these hygiene products from Rachel, and Wantemo was right about the toothbrush and toothpaste. He ran his tongue across his front teeth. He was long overdue for a good brush with minty paste.

But Wantemo had something else in mind.

"We must get you an ID implant. No wandering around without it. Plus, it helps us keep track of everyone. The Larkians designed it not to short out when you fire your merlux or if one of them accidentally gets shocked." His brow furrowed. "The Larkians vehemently dislike accidental shocks, so be careful."

"I'll try to remember that."

"Yes, do. They have technological ways to shock back or suck your merlux dry. The Larkians believe in giving harsh lessons, lest we forget."

They left Sinto's cabin and continued down the hall. Wantemo stopped at the only door on the other side of the long hallway. "This is the lab where we study Orange. Be forewarned, strict rules apply."

He opened the door and they stepped inside. The air was cool and the lighting soft. The space was large and the walls were covered with electronics, quietly humming. Ryan sat with his back to them, silhouetted by a large screen mounted to the wall. He turned when he heard them enter and cracked a smile. His gaze swept across the shirt and shorts Sinto wore. "I see you're one of us now." He stood and gave Sinto a one-armed hug and gentle squeeze to the shoulder. "Good to have you back in one piece."

"He got away," Sinto said bitterly.

"Sorry to hear what happened."

Sinto nodded. "Let's hope Blake and Audrey have better luck."

Ryan puffed out his cheeks, exhaled. "I'm trying not to think about it. See Rachel yet?"

"Saw, only. She looked busy."

Ryan scrubbed his head with his hands. His coarse hair stuck up, pointing in many directions, and stayed that way. "Like us all. Sleep is a rarity."

"What can I do to help?"

Ryan stole a peek at his watch. "We report our findings to Rachel and Alvarez in a half hour. You should join us. Good way to get up to speed on where we stand, which isn't encouraging. We need all the brainpower we can get."

Wantemo spoke up. "Perfect. Should give us enough time for you to get your dChip. Come, this way."

38

Documented

Wantemo led Sinto deeper inside the lab, past the wall of blinking electronics where Ryan had returned to his work. A door was open to a small room tucked on the far side.

Dr. Wickman stood when they entered. The room was not much bigger than a walk-in closet. He smiled and offered Sinto a seat on a round padded stool he rolled from the corner. Wantemo took guard by Sinto's side.

Dr. Wickman smiled. "Welcome to my humble office."

The space was brightly lit and tidy, and one of several closet-sized spaces in that part of the lab. Upper cabinets and modest surfaces wrapped around two of the four walls. A desk was shoved against a third where Dr. Wickman's laptop was open. A fourth was covered with drawings of Sapien anatomy. Various medical equipment and supplies were neatly organized on the countertops, in racks, and in well-labeled drawers. There was a sink with a mirror and a roll of paper towels at the ready.

"Normally I do this in the infirmary on level zero, or the medical center at the compound, but I like to keep my office well-stocked for medical emergencies." Dr. Wickman washed his hands, then pulled a stainless-steel tray with a scalpel and surgical tweezers from an ultraviolet sterilizing unit on the counter. Then he pulled a small metal object sealed in plastic from a drawer near his computer and a syringe filled with a small amount of clear liquid from another. He rummaged for a pair of surgical gloves, cotton pads, and a package of bandages. He set them on the tray.

Dr. Wickman scanned something imprinted on the side of the small metal object with a device connected to his laptop. It beeped, then he opened a file with a long list of names, found Sinto's, and selected it. Sinto had previously provided skin and hair samples for DNA testing along with blood and flueox types as part of the medical records kept for every resident on the island, Sapien and Merahvu. A project in which Wantemo assisted. The code for the dChip he was about to receive was added as part of his record.

Dr. Wickman pulled on the surgical gloves, squeezed alcohol onto the cotton pad, and wiped it along the inside of Sinto's upper arm. It felt cold and the sharp smell made his nose hairs stand on end.

"First, we numb the insertion site." He gently stuck the syringe in Sinto's arm where it was still damp from alcohol. It took less than a minute for the surrounding flesh to go numb. Then Dr. Wickman made a small incision with the sharp scalpel. Clear lorica oozed from disrupted pores in the densely packed layer of Sinto's fatty skin.

Dr. Wickman pressed a sterilized pad against the incision. "Press this down for me. One finger will do, careful not to touch your skin."

Sinto did as instructed.

Dr. Wickman removed the metal object from the plastic wrapper. It was an inch long and about a quarter-inch thick, like a sleek bullet. He held it up between his gloved fingers. "Sealed inside is a specialized chip and a battery that should last about twelve weeks. Since we insert it just beneath the skin we can easily extract it when the time comes to replace it. We'll know who and where you are at all times as long as you are on land or break the surface of the water or are near one of our submerged buoys in the security network surrounding the island."

"Does it work on Merluma?"

"Ah, not so well. The tracking system requires one of our satellites. The team has erected several receiving dishes in the Winterlands but unfortunately they are limited to line-of-sight reach. It is of some use there, but mostly we use them for security purposes here and on and around our ships."

"Did Audrey receive one?"

A pained look flashed in Dr. Wickman's eyes. "Unfortunately, no. We started implanting dChips after they left. It was because of the security failure the Xiphias team encountered that led to its mandatory deployment. That and a much tighter screening process."

They basked in a moment of silence, then he pulled the sterile pad Sinto was holding away from his arm and inserted the dChip implant between the muscle and the thick layer of Sinto's skin with surgical tweezers.

Wantemo knitted the dermis together with an electrified finger. Then Dr. Wickman added what he called "butterfly bandages" on top to make sure the top layer of skin wouldn't split open before the underlying tissue had fully healed.

"These should peel off naturally in a few days."

Sinto could feel the implant beneath the skin with his finger. He winced. The insertion point was tender.

"The tenderness will fade in a few days. Then we'll do it all over again in twelve weeks," Dr. Wickman said.

Sinto wondered if replacing his implant would be relevant at all. Twelve weeks from now they may be dead or trying to outrun the Orankai and the spread of Orange.

Ryan stuck his head in the door. "Time to go. Meeting starts in two minutes and you know Alvarez frowns on those who are late."

Sinto stood, documented and ready to get to work.

Ryan gave a running update as they rushed from the lab and off the ship. Sinto learned that each day had brought distressing news from the Sapien world, of random and violent acts popping up in the least-expected places, like a grocery store or a doctor's office. The number of suicides, sudden heart attacks, or random shootings by normally peaceful people had increased in rural communities. Events the Larkians were certain Arkis was responsible for, possibly by introducing his mind-controlling, drug-like nectar to the Sapien population.

Sinto knew firsthand that Arkis' orange nectar made its users feel infallible and superior to those deemed the enemy. Join his Orankai tribe—Sapien or Merahvu, it didn't matter—or die by mysterious or violent means.

Wantemo added to the story. "Our spies confirmed the breeding caves continue to produce more Orankai. We believe they are funneled directly to Earth once full grown. Possibly to harvest Orange or to seed trouble among the Sapiens."

They jumped into a waiting UTV at the bottom of the ship's gangplank. Dr. Wickman drove, Ryan by his side. Wantemo sat in back next to Sinto.

Ryan spun around sideways in his seat. "No one has heard anything from Audrey or Blake. Not even a blip from their suits or radio response when called. Though Alvarez said that doesn't mean much on Merluma. The dish works in the Winterlands but a lot of interference is emitted from the Black Mountains. Not only are they mostly glass but there's a hell of a lot of magnetic metal buried there."

Sinto nodded. That was true about the mountains, a source of peculiar metals known to disrupt the geomagnetic field in that part of Merluma. In fact, Merluma only had one true pole. Only one point guided every creature on Merluma in their migrations. No north or south, only Inception, located at the heart of Inception Bay. It was there a great mountain of many such metals collapsed into itself during the Great Upheaval and burrowed deep into

Merluma's core. Over hundreds of thousands of Merluma years it filled with sand and rock and water. Its outer lip formed the ocean reefs protecting the present-day bay.

If Audrey and/or Blake were anywhere near the Black Mountains or Inception Bay they wouldn't be able to contact or detect them. It was possible Audrey and Blake were alive, perhaps near the Labyrinth where Arkis and his father retreated after kidnapping his sister, as he observed while traveling the Timeless Dimension with his mother.

Or else the Orankai succeeded and they met their doom in the Great Ocean shortly after passing through.

Or else Arkis found them and was holding them for some other reason.

These were things Sinto couldn't dwell on at the moment. The Larkians were behind in the fight. Too many lives were at stake and Sinto was needed to help save them.

He watched the Larkian world slide by with trepidation as they raced toward the command center.

39

Nutshell Idea

RACHEL GREETED THEM IN the compound breezeway. Dr. Wickman parked at the curb and they climbed out of the UTV.

When Rachel saw Sinto she smiled that dimpled smile he sorely missed and threw her arms around his torso, her head barely reaching his chest. He leaned over and wrapped his arms around her tiny shoulders and buried his nose in her hair, drawing deep her scent and bright aura. Sweet, funny, smart, intuitive Rachel. She tipped her head back and gazed into his eyes, her own eyes watering. It felt good to know she was safe. She deserved the best.

Her brow furrowed as her eyes searched his. "Ah, honey, I'm so sorry about what happened to Victoria. I know there's probably nothin' anyone can say that will make you feel better. But I'm truly sorry, nonetheless, and I'm glad you're safe now."

Rachel kept her arm around Sinto as they followed Ryan, Dr. Wickman, and Wantemo inside. The kitchen crew was setting up the dining hall although dinner wouldn't be served for a couple of hours.

They passed through, trying to stay out of the way, and slipped through the double doors to the conference room turned command center.

Sinto felt a wave of guilt and loss. The last time he stepped through those doors was with Victoria in preparation for their mission to trap Arkis. Rachel must have noticed the tension crippling his forward movement. She slipped her hand into his and tugged him along.

Alvarez was the only one seated at the table typing on his laptop. Rachel dragged Sinto to the far side of the table where Alvarez sat. She gestured for Sinto to sit one seat away from Alvarez, then she sat between them. Alvarez gave her a sideways glance and quick smile before flipping the lid of his laptop closed.

Alvarez cleared his throat. "Please, everyone have a seat."

Dr. Wickman, Wantemo, and Ryan sat across from them. No one else joined.

The screens on the main wall were black. A fresh breeze flowed through the room's open windows and sliding glass doors. The air was tinged with the sweet scent of succulent flowers and sea spray. The mess of papers and electronics and wiring that had littered the large table had been tidied since Sinto had peeked in on the activity an hour earlier. A pitcher of water and glasses sat in the center of the table. He suspected the tidying and addition of water was Rachel's doing.

Rachel poured a tall glass of water for Sinto and looked to Alvarez. He shook his head. She prompted the others, then poured one for Ryan, Dr. Wickman, Wantemo, and finally for herself. She sat. Her aura glowed bright.

Alvarez sat forward. "We need to be honest about where we stand with Orange."

Wantemo tipped his head at Dr. Wickman. Dr. Wickman took the lead. "Our options are few. We've found nothing to neutralize Orange other than to starve it or burn it. It needs petroleum-based compounds, which are found everywhere here on Earth. We tried drying it, freezing it, and suffocating it. It regenerates once exposed to water and air and above-freezing temperatures.

"Once ingested, it passes through the blood-brain barrier and infects the frontal lobe, effectively hijacking its host's higher cognitive functions. We're talking emotion regulation, impulse control, social interaction, motor function… just to name a few. In addition to this, it disrupts cellular division through the rest of the body, accelerating it and causing malignant neoplasm. Cancer. Where these malignant tumors manifest depends on the unique makeup of the individual and the amount and frequency ingested. Could take a few months or several years before the full effects become fatal, we just don't know at this time."

Ryan piped up next. "It's highly addictive and basically turns whoever consumes the stuff into an obedient belligerent beholden to the one who provides their next fix."

"I concur with the violent and addictive aspects." Sinto said, "I only had a small amount in my stomach for a short period before I expelled most of it. I felt a depth of rage I never felt before. Feelings that lingered long after, along with the desire for more Orange. Now that you mention it, and I am disgusted to admit, I did find myself questioning why I had not simply succumbed to Arkis' will."

Wantemo looked at Sinto. "It is highly probable that we may not be able to save anyone who has fallen under its influence for an extended period of time. If at all."

Sinto knew exactly what Wantemo intended him to hear. It may be too late to save Naiada. Certainty, his father was too far gone.

He closed his eyes, angered by his mother's choice of ally and how it may have led to Victoria's tragic death. And the thought of losing Naiada was too much for him to bear. "So what are you suggesting? We burn it all down along with my sister and my father?"

Rachel grabbed his hand. "That's not what they're saying, Sinto."

He stood and paced impatiently, trying to quell his frustration.

Alvarez clicked his tongue. "Rachel had an idea." They looked at each other. Alvarez raised a brow and gave her an encouraging smile to continue.

Rachel said, "Instead of fighting Orange, we give it what it needs. We manipulate *it*."

"With what?" Sinto asked.

"Plastic. Every country's overflowin' with it with no easy way to get rid of it, other than clog up landfills or ignore the problem and let it find its way to the ocean. I'm sure they would be more than willin' to give it to us. All of it."

"Help Orange *proliferate*?" Sinto was feeling exasperated. "Great idea, Rachel."

Alvarez raised a hand and his voice. "Hear her out."

Sinto sat and took a deep drink of water. Rachel waited until he had calmed a little. She held his hand. It felt warm and motherly and it was in that moment he realized how utterly isolated and helpless he had felt since the incident with Victoria, and the very real possibility that he may never see Audrey again, or his sister. He had nowhere to call home. He felt untethered and uncertain of his future. That state of being affected his ability to keep his emotions in check and to think clearly.

He drank more water, drew a deep breath, let it go, and gave Rachel a sad smile. "Sorry. I—"

She patted his hand. "I know," she said softly.

The room fell quiet except for the clanking of dishes coming from the dining room and bird song drifting through open windows. Sinto shut out the unnatural noises and focused on the innocent feathered creatures carrying on their simple lives, unaware of impending doom.

"Where was I?" Rachel asked Alvarez. He leaned over and whispered in her ear. "Oh, right, we manipulate it." She sat forward. "Lure it, trap it, then cut it off from what it seeks. Essentially, starve it out of existence."

"Therein lies the conundrum," Alvarez said. "How, and more importantly, where."

Sinto understood what Alvarez was asking. He could think of only one place that would work. The one and only place where what Orange needs did not exist. "You mean on Merluma."

"One possibility." Alvarez countered. "But it doesn't solve the problem of containment. Portals. There are too many of them. It would be impossible to seal them all. I suggest we scratch Merluma."

"What is it them climate scientists are always suggestin' about reducing carbon dioxide in the atmosphere?" Rachel asked.

"You mean the theory of carbon capture?" Ryan asked.

"Yeah. Suck it out of the air and pump it right back into the ground where it came from."

"Bury it," Sinto said.

Rachel grinned. "That's my idea in a nutshell. Lure it where we want it and bury it."

Ryan's eyes bugged. "Whoa, bury it where? Don't you think that's dangerous? We have no idea of the long-term impact." He ran his fingers through his hair. "We could potentially create an all-new problem."

Rachel kept pushing. "In your tests how long did it take to starve?"

Ryan stammered. "I—I'm saying we need to consider all options and the consequences of each…"

"To answer your question, Rachel; we don't know." Dr. Wickman said.

Rachel said, "Well, maybe we should find out, and soon. Knowing that might help us devise a probable solution."

Alvarez smiled. "Do we agree Rachel has a suggestion worth investigating?"

Everyone nodded, even Ryan.

Alvarez said, "Good, let's get to work."

40

Sinto Gets A Clue

RACHEL ELBOWED SINTO IN the ribs. "I sure could use a dip before dinner." She raised a brow when he didn't answer. "Well?"

Sinto had been deep in thought pondering what they just discussed about Orange. Starvation was the simple solution. It was the how and where that poised the greatest challenge.

Rachel persisted. "Know what I think? You need a dip too. You're grouchy and look wrinkly."

"That obvious?"

"Duh! You know what else? You made me a promise once."

"What promise?"

"You would take me on an underwater adventure and show me things that would blow my mind."

"Now? That would be risky and reckless, considering."

"Maybe we could call it a routine check of the defense systems. Ya know, a little trip around the island, close to shore. Give me little teaser, for later."

Ryan, Wickman, and Wantemo had returned to the *Requiem Sea II* to run a new round of tests with Orange to determine exactly how long it would take to starve it. Alvarez was typing on his laptop beside Rachel. Sinto wasn't sure what to do next other than wait or go exploring for a place to contain Orange which, without an idea of where to start, seemed like a waste of time. Rachel was right. He needed a break, and this might be his only chance to give her a quick tour of the underwater world. Who knows when they may have the chance again, if ever.

And the idea of diving into the ocean was enticing.

"You should take her," Alvarez said, without skipping a keystroke. "I'll let the techs know. Circumnavigate the island. Perfect opportunity to test your dChips and run a routine check of the underwater defense network."

"See, even Salvo thinks it's a good idea." She gave Sinto a giant grin, dimples boring deep into rosy cheeks.

Sinto thought he detected a slight flush of Alvarez's cheeks at Rachel's mention of his first name. No one called him Salvo except Rachel.

Rachel stood up.

"Stay inside the buoy network." He stopped typing and cut a sideways glance to Sinto. "Please." Then he shifted his gaze to Rachel, his dark eyes softening. "And take good care of her."

It was as if time stopped. A shared gaze lingering longer than usual. Sinto was intrigued by the way their auras suddenly flared; a swirl of yellow and pink enveloped them both. Sapiens were blind to this venting of self. A reveal so subtle that even Alvarez and Rachel may not know what was happening. A perfect chemistry match and deep growing affection, akin to falling in love, passed between them. The gaze itself revealed the same truth. Whether Sapien or Merahvu it was easy to see that shared spark. He had seen it before with practically everyone Rachel interacted with, but with others it was one-sided—Rachel being the one receiving not giving. This was different. It was mutual. Dual auras twined. She gazed at him with a keen level of interest he had not seen her display with anyone else.

Sinto smiled to himself.

Interesting development.

He turned to Alvarez. "A short excursion, perfectly safe, and I will take excellent care not to harm her."

Sinto followed Rachel out the back door. He noted what she wore. A pair of cutoff denim shorts and a white T-shirt, not the usual Larkian coverings. "You might get wet."

She whipped off her shirt and dropped her shorts. She stood before him in tiny scraps of fabric that barely covered her breasts—which were notably smaller than before—and private parts below. She spun around proudly displaying her bare buttocks. A tiny strip of fabric flossed her butt cheeks and wound around her hips to the tiny triangle in front. "No worries! Like my new bikini? Never know when the opportunity will strike! I'm never going back to the desert. I love it here and take a dip as often as possible."

He fought the urge not to stare. Apparently, he wasn't the only one. He could see Alvarez through one of the conference room windows, eyes bugged, craning his neck like a giraffe to steal a good look.

"Hmm," Sinto said, "And I thought Sapiens were the modest ones."

She laughed, whisking him along the path that led to the sandy shore. "I don't know what's got your britches in a bunch. Covers all the same parts as them extra flaps of skin and exotic markings y'all got. Doesn't seem to bother y'all to run around naked."

They navigated around black lava rock poking out of the cream-colored sand. Sinto stripped off his shirt and shorts. They left their clothes on top of one of the rocks.

"My heart's a pitter-patterin'. What do I?"

"Stay close, no panicking." He spun her around so she was facing away from him and pulled her back against his chest. "Help if I ask."

"Okey dokey."

A thick layer of lorica seeped from his pores as they stepped into the shallow water. It rolled up their bodies and over their heads, sealing them inside its gelatinous cover once they were head-deep in the water.

"Uh," she gasped. "Oh my, what's this stuff?"

"A protective cocoon."

"It tickles my lips and tastes funny when I breath."

"That's the taste of the sea."

"I'm breathin' water?"

"Oxygen extracted from the water, whipped up to be breathable by the lorica surrounding us. We call it oxywater."

She giggled. "Anybody ever tell you you're the most awesome friend ever?"

"No."

"Well ya are," she said, looking up. Then she kissed him on the underside of his chin. "Now what?"

"Observe and follow my lead." He pinned her legs between his and his tail. Then he took off, his tail and their legs, moving in a rhythmic motion, propelling them through a crystalline sea. They circled the offshore reefs bursting with life and color sixty feet below the surface. The snap and pop of activity assaulted their ears. The savory and the sweet and the not-so-pleasant scents of the sea slipped through his lorica like a heady perfume.

Sinto delighted in pointing out the various corals and colorful fish and creatures tucked inside dark little caves, their eyes aglow. Turtles nibbled on green algae covering lava rock and turned their heads when they swam by. These were things Sapiens could easily see when swimming on the surface and diving down a few feet. What Sinto really wanted to show Rachel dwelled on the far side of the island where the mountains plunged deeply into the sea with a sheer wall that bored straight down thousands of feet to the darkest depths, teaming with sea life. Life Sapiens rarely witnessed, because their only means of doing so was through clumsy mechanical intrusion into this dark and quiet world.

The sun would be setting soon so he decided to speed things up. He extended his hand and flicked his wrist. A spinning thread of electrical fire burst from his fingertips and cut a hole in the water. Its mouth yawned open and sucked them inside.

Rachel gasped and gripped his arms wrapped around her torso with such strength his hands went numb. Wide-eyed she sucked it all in. It was the second time Sinto recalled rendering her speechless. The first time was when he told her who he was and where he came from.

He whipped a hard right around the north end of the island using care to stay within the bounds of the buoy network the Larkians had deployed for detecting movement within the waters surrounding the island. Sinto imagined the techs, monitoring their progress, recording their speed and depth, even listening to their conversation through their underwater sonobuoy network.

He circumnavigated the island several times, though the journey lasted only a few minutes. He whipped his tail to ease the impact of being spit out of the tunnel on the mountain side. Going from zero to water-dense resistance can be shocking the first time one experiences it.

"Holy shitake!" Rachel exclaimed when they jerked to a stop.

"Ready to do it again?"

She nodded and wrapped both hands around his arm.

"This time we go down." He launched a new tunnel directly below their feet and suddenly they were free-falling. Rachel drifted upward until her head was even with his. They descended cheek to cheek as rays of sunlight piercing the surface slipped away and their world turned black.

Rachel whispered. "I can't see anything."

"You will, just wait."

"How deep is it?"

"Very."

"I'm scared."

Sinto squeezed her to his chest a little tighter. "Don't be."

He sensed the bottom thousands of feet below rising up. The vertical tunnel disintegrated and he began pumping his tail and working his legs in tandem. His feet landed gently on the soft bottom. Rachel slid down his chest until her feet hit the seabed.

"Oh!" she said, "It's squishy."

"Shh," he said. "If we're real quiet they will reveal themselves."

"Who—oh," she squeaked when a softly glowing squid swam into view. It tracked along the bottom then swiveled, swimming vertically up a wall of rock smothered with many life forms. Slowly the wall of rock came to life with bioluminescent color. A living, breathing painting of alien life.

Rachel's eyes were wide as saucers. She whispered, "I had no idea—it's so beautiful, so different."

"They only light up in total darkness. It's what makes them elusive and undiscovered by Sapiens diving with lights; even the most dim light imaginable makes them skitter away."

They watched in silence, Rachel pointing out her favorites and Sinto giving her a rundown of what they were and how long they could live.

After answering all of Rachel's questions, Sinto launched a tunnel and they zipped upward and to the south, rounding the tail of the seahorse-shaped island where the house he shared with Audrey skirted the ocean. Once they passed the harbor, they emerged in the shallows from where they started, awash with a setting sun. His lorica dissolved when their heads popped above the surface. The refreshing slip of water across his skin felt like coming home.

Rachel was ecstatic. "Oh my God, that was *amazing*. Consider my mind officially blown!" She rolled to her back and floated on the surface. Sinto did the same. They watched wisps of clouds catch fire from the last embers of the day, bobbing in gentle waves kicked up by a gentle breeze rolling in from the open ocean.

Rachel sighed a calming breath. "Never imagined I would be here workin' with the Larkians to *literally* save the world. My life in Vegas... what a tragedy it was, what a gift you are. I was dyin'."

She stood up in the waist-deep water, waves lapping against her flat stomach. "Ya saved me, Sinto. You saved my *life*." He rolled from his back and kept low in the water, knees buried in the silky sand looking up at her. Rachel was right. He needed this, a recharge from the sea and the company of a good friend. The world would literally need to be burning to draw him away.

Rachel reached out and brushed her fingers through his hair. It had grown several inches since she had cut it in Duluth. "We're gonna win, we have to. And Audrey... honey, she's one tough, determined, and independent lady. Y'all must trust that she'll be okay."

Then her lips bunched up in a stern way he had not seen before, like his mother's did whenever she was telling him something important.

"Now I'm gonna be frank." She gazed deeply into his eyes. Gone were the pearly whites and the dimples. "Get your shit together, Sinto. Get your head straight, and *focus*. Forget about goin' after Arkis to avenge Victoria. Nothin' good will come from it. You'll just be diggin' a hole, a deep one, with no other purpose but to bury both you and Arkis, together. It'll kill what good you got inside, forever. There'll be no goin' back." She paused. "Ya hearin' me?"

His throat felt thick. He nodded.

"The others are searchin' for your sister. Audrey can take care of herself. Blake too. Right now I need you to help us deal with Orange. We all need you. Real bad." Then she kissed him on the forehead and cradled his chin in her tiny hands. " Can ya do that for me? Will you promise to try?"

He drew a shaky breath. "Yes." Tears pricked his eyes. "I promise. I'll try, Rachel."

She pulled him into an embrace and held him like a child being a consoled by a mother. His vision blurred and tears rained. It felt like coming home. And that was when he realized home was not a fixed place to store things. It was where one felt safe, surrounded by friends and family who supported and loved him, and he reciprocated. An endless circle made stronger by establishing trust and commitment. Home was in Rachel's arms or a small cabin on the ship with his name stamped on a brass plaque, down the hall from Ryan and Dr. Wickman and Wantemo. Home was wherever the next phase of his life took him, which, at the moment, was with Rachel and the others to solve a mutual problem that would benefit all. And soon, from the depths of his heart, he hoped for a future home to be shared with Audrey.

Rachel released him. "Good, I'm starving. Hate to miss dinner. How 'bout you?"

It took a moment for him to find his voice. "Go along without me. I need to stay here for a while."

She turned to leave.

He snagged her hand. "And Rachel…"

She turned to face him. "Yeah?"

"Thank you."

He was rewarded with pearly whites and dimples.

41

Plan B

Daylight came a few hours too soon but Audrey welcomed any reason to get up. Sleeping on sandstone was hell for a side-sleeper even atop a couple of layers of thick fur. Her hips and shoulders ached. Hauling heavy supply boxes and burying them four feet in the sand had been harder work than she realized, and her muscles were tender from the effort. In sum, she felt like shit. And there wasn't anything for general pain relief accept morphine in the essential supplies box.

Early morning light bled from various openings in the cave's low ceiling. In the light of day, she could see thick tubes were drilled in the sandstone and plugged with quartz-like stones, pale and milky. Plugs that kept rain, debris, and pesky creatures out, but let natural light in.

She worked out the kinks in her body by stretching and moving her joints. By the time Blake stirred she had worked out most of the creakiness and was ready for whatever the day may bring.

She dug around in the emergency essentials box. They were running low on water, something Blake told her not to worry too much about. She wondered what he meant but trusted his lead. He knew more about what was contained in the boxes they had buried.

She passed on drinking the last box of water and choose a box containing a coffee substitute instead. It was too sweet and creamy for her taste but was packed with caffeine that she desperately needed to clear the grogginess in her head.

She tossed one to Blake. He caught it and grunted when he saw what it was but chugged it down anyway. She gobbled down a nutrition stick. It contained fruit and nuts with a hint of bacon. Blake made a face after taking a bite of his. They both ate with little enthusiasm. Bacon never tasted so wrong.

"We're stuck here, aren't we?" Audrey asked, using a fingernail to pick a sticky piece of fruit from one of her molars.

"Pretty much, unless we can get to the Winterlands and find the others."

"There's no way the two of us can squeeze into *Xiph2*. Towing *Xiph1* would take forever to get to the other side of the continent."

"Unless... one goes, one stays."

"I'm not sure separating would be a good idea."

Blake nodded. "True, but it's an option."

"What if the other team members met our same fate and the City of Ice is overrun with Orankai?"

"We know Stokes and Tucker made it, that is if we fully trust Isden."

Audrey considered his suggestion. "Hmm. I believe Isden is sincere. He seemed fully committed to our cause, unless he's one hell of an actor. Odwon gave me the creeps from the start. I should have trusted my instincts. I should have said something."

"If Isden had been a Scout he could fool us every which way and sideways. Pretend is their specialty."

"Well, someone did. Someone who knew of the Xiphias project. That same someone who set me up with Odwon and you with your Terrakai partner."

"Odwon could have been a lone wolf, a mole that slipped through our defenses, recently or before. Maybe when they attacked the island, or shortly after, before our defenses were fully employed. And *if* Isden was involved, then the others…" He winced.

"Either way, we're stuck. We need to make our *own* plan. Plan B."

Blake stared back, then sighed. "You're right."

"So maybe we go after Arkis ourselves. Find his lair, find Naiada. We've got our suits and lots of weapons."

"Maybe Sinto has already defeated Arkis."

Audrey closed her eyes and focused on the Mark and the connection she had with Sinto. It felt neutral. Neither distressed or joyful. No clues as to what may have happened. She could only take comfort in knowing the Mark remained fully formed. It gave her hope Sinto was alive.

She said, "I think we should assume he did not. Expect the worse possible scenario."

"I agree."

"What do we do about *Xiph1*?"

He rubbed his eyes. "Caffeine hasn't kicked in yet. Got any ideas?"

"Before you woke up, I was thinking…"

He quirked a brow. "Let me guess, you already have a Plan B."

She smiled. "Maybe. What if we set *Xiph1* up to crash on the rocks near that stairway where we believe Arkis is staying? Let him think his team was successful in their attack and we're dead. Leave on the cameras and sensors, maybe gather some valuable intel."

Blake's eyes brightened. "After setting it up, we start walking in that direction. See where it takes us."

Audrey stood and brushed grit from her butt. "Beats living here for the rest of our lives."

They collected their garbage and stuck it back in the box. Blake stashed the Xiphias remotes in hidden pockets of his suit.

She said, "Should we toss a coin for who goes?"

"Don't have one. Besides, I'm best qualified."

She opened her mouth to object.

He said, "No arguments."

They put on their goggles and pulled up their hoods. They switched their suits to camouflage mode as they exited the cave. The sky was brightening. It felt weird to be hiding in plain sight.

Blake retrieved *Xiph2* with the remote. Audrey watched his progress from shore by tracking the disruption of water as he waded in to retrieve *Xiph1*. After wrestling the anchor from the sand, he stowed it. He attached *Xiph1* to *Xiph2* with a cable, popped the hatch, and climbed in. It was weird watching inanimate objects seemingly move on their own.

"Give me a couple hours before panicking."

Peachy. "What do I do beside panic?"

"Desalinate water. The kit's in the emergency box. Follow the instructions. Fill the bladders plus spares. We're going to need it in this dry climate."

"Sounds fun," she said, jokingly serious.

"Stay camouflaged and keep your eyes peeled for baddies."

"Aye, aye captain." She saluted even though he couldn't see it.

He pushed off, flipping *Xiph1* and *Xiph2* into camouflage mode where the outer skin reflected the modulating color of the water as closely as possible. Once he hit the open sea it was nearly impossible to see them.

They were able to chat over the comm for a time, but eventually Blake's voice crackled and faded as he rounded the rocky point that enclosed the cove, leaving Audrey in silence.

She was alone with nothing but her thoughts and the task of making drinkable water from the sea.

42

Walkabout

Blake returned one hour and fifty-one minutes later, much to Audrey's relief. She had felt vulnerable, stuck on a barren beach sandwiched between the ocean and a sandstone cliff, regardless of her camouflaged suit.

He stashed *Xiph2* in the depths of the cove, same as before.

The wind had kicked up. Feathery clouds streaked across a brilliant blue sky. White caps peppered the ocean beyond the protected cove. The sun rapidly warmed the crisp morning air. The temperature was a pleasant sixty degrees Fahrenheit. It might not be so pleasantly cool once the sun rose higher.

Audrey had filled four bladders with fresh water while Blake was gone. As he instructed, she had found a desalination kit in the emergency supplies box. It was a high-tech contraption that ran on solar energy. A foot-high cone covered by solar cells, like those embedded in their suits, spun on a single ball bearing, capturing maximum sunlight. A pump sucked water through a super-fine filter. After spitting out the briny waste, fresh water passed through a glass tube of UV light to kill live bacteria.

They drank their fill of the sweet and refreshing result before flushing the filter and dismantling it.

Afterward, they surveyed the ridge to the south and saw no easy way up. Blake had confirmed that fact by scanning the ridge while he was towing *Xiph1* along the surface.

"There must be a way up from inside the cave. Whoever occupied it must have needed fresh water and a source of food."

Audrey recalled the pile of mummified bones by the fire pit. "Unless all they ate were fish from the sea."

"Let's hope they craved for something else."

"Won't know if we don't try."

They tucked the bladders in their attached backpacks and trudged back inside the cool darkness of the cave.

They collected their garbage and stuffed what remained in the emergency essentials box into their attached packs. They left the desalination kit, which would be too cumbersome to carry. They had their bladders and iodine tablets, and were confident they would find a freshwater source. Audrey handed Blake a knife and slipped one for herself into her thigh pocket for easy access.

Blake buried the box in the hole he dug previously. Audrey swept the cave clean of their tracks and tossed sand and dirt on the furs and log where they sat. The cave looked exactly as they found it.

They slipped on their goggles but left their hoods down. Blake handed Audrey a small LED flashlight which she tucked inside a pocket. He clicked his on the lowest light setting so they could see more broadly with the night vision built into their goggles. He took the lead and ventured deeper into the cave.

The cave shrank to a narrow tunnel, boring deeper into sandstone. They hunched to avoid bumping their heads. Fifty yards in it became pitch black. Audrey was thankful for Blake's weak light and the technology embedded within their goggles. But still—

The walls pressed in. Cold sweat broke from her temples and she suddenly felt sick to her stomach.

Panting, she asked, "It's getting a little too cozy in here. Are you sure there's a way out?"

Blake took her hand. "I feel air movement. Don't think about where you are, focus on holding my hand."

She squeezed his hand so hard she felt the bones grind, backing off when she heard him stifle a grunt.

It helped, but only a little. She was on the precipice of a full-blown panic attack. She felt any progress she had made rapidly backsliding. She silently cursed the Merahvu and their obsession with tunnels. She hoped this would be the only one they encountered.

She focused on the cool fresh air flowing from the direction they were heading and on Blake's hand that she held in an iron grip.

After what felt like forever, a distant glow emerged in the darkness. Blake clicked off his light and looked up.

The tunnel abruptly ended at a set of circular stairs carved in the sandstone. Light streamed down from above. Thankfully, the treads were wide to accommodate the extra-large footprint of a Merahvu, which made the climb easier.

And they climbed, and climbed, ten, twenty... fifty feet or more before emerging from a hole in the ground marked by a circle of large boulders.

The boulders were out of place in the barren landscape. Someone must have intentionally set them to mark the stairway opening, to keep unsuspecting animals or humans from accidentally falling down the hole, or both. She imagined it would have taken great effort to move them there.

The landscape was stripped of vegetation, a peninsula of nothing but sandstone that stretched from the Great Ocean to the Sea of Meura. If this wasteland had indeed been claimed by the Seakai then they certainly got the short end of the stick. No means to farm or grasses for animals to graze or melted snow pack to drink. Only rock, sand, and salt water.

Blake pulled out the *Xiph1* remote and connected it via a signal to their goggles. A blinking red dot indicated *Xiph1*'s location where he crashed it atop a rocky shelf not far from the stairway leading into the ocean. It was roughly six miles toward the dark ridge and a line of green in the distance.

"As Tucker would say," Blake said. "Primed for a walk'bout?"

She laughed at his impersonation of Tucker's thick Australian accent. "Do we have a choice? No way am I going back down that hole."

They pulled their hoods over their heads, flipped on their camouflage, and started their walkabout to the east.

The solar receptors intermixed with the LED modules in the skin of their suits reflected their pale bland environment and kept the batteries charged.

The sun was much higher in the sky and bore down, hot and relentless. Audrey was grateful for her suit's ability to regulate her body heat. Coolness pressed down through the thermal layer she wore underneath, tempering the temperature of her skin.

"If we happen upon Orankai, then communicating is going to be a problem," Audrey said.

"I know."

"Maybe it doesn't have to be."

"What do you mean?"

"Did you ever communicate with Leela, telepathically?"

He didn't answer right away, and when he did his voice was tight. "All the time, mind-speak."

"Me and Sinto too."

He stopped walking and faced her. It was strange looking at someone without actually seeing them but knowing they were there gazing into your equally hidden eyes.

He said, "You think you and I could master mind-speak?"

"Why not? I mean, it did take some practice but was easy once I figured out how to form the message. A thought wrapped with words and delivered with intent and purpose. How about you?"

"It's been a very long time. I'm not sure I remember what it felt like, how I was able..."

Audrey smiled optimistically. "Well, we've got six miles of walking to try."

43

Harbored Loss

THE SUN BORE DOWN. Heat waves rippled across sandstone. Audrey and Blake had covered three miles across the Desertlands on Merluma with three more to go before they reached the jungle growing along the distant ridge. Her throat was parched and she found it hard to imagine a water-loving Merahvu making this same trek.

When Audrey and Blake began their journey, the terrain was flat and barren with random outcroppings. As they drew closer to the obsidian ridge that hemmed in Inception Bay the landscape quickly evolved. They wound around randomly strewn rocks, scraggly bushes, and tufts of grass claiming each and every crack in the sandstone. A stream trickled from the direction of the mountains. Green shoots traced its edges.

"Let's try that again," Audrey said.

She opened her mind. Bits and pieces of concepts popped up and she knew it was Blake attempting to communicate telepathically. They had been working on it for the past forty minutes and making little progress, mostly passing gobbledygook between them.

Blake sighed. "I just can't remember how. It seemed so easy before."

"The first time I tried with Sinto he said I was trying too hard. I remember now, he told me to look into his eyes until I figured it out. Maybe we should take a break and try that."

They found a large bush and sat on the shady side of it, facing each other. They pushed back their hoods and removed their goggles. With the suits set in camouflage mode, their faces floated above the landscape. The sight was so bizarre it made Audrey laugh.

"This is weird," she said, grinning.

"Ha! My whole life has been weird."

"Maybe this is normal and everything else is weird."

"What is normal? Ours or a bird's? Who is to say?"

"Exactly. I read a book on the topic once." Audrey said. "Our sense of normal is perceived, what we gain through our sensory bubble. Every living organism has a unique view of the world, so to claim that ours is the one and only truth demonstrates our ignorance. The fact the Merahvu can sense things we cannot and can communicate telepathically sets our sense of normal apart from theirs. German scientists call this concept 'umwelt.'"

Blake gave her a lopsided smile. "Cool! Let's expand our *um-welt*."

"Okay, um, maybe we should hold hands too." A new round of laughter lightened the mood as they bumbled around for each other's camouflaged hands. Once their hands were firmly clasped Audrey said, "I'll go first. Look deeply into my eyes."

Audrey had forgotten how truly mesmerizing Blake's eyes were, like a tropical sea whipped up by a fierce wind. Ever changing shades of blue alive with vitality, much like her father's. She locked onto the dark of his pupils and imagined diving inside and exploring a whole new world that was his mind.

She concentrated on a simple topic, one that made her feel safe and whole and loved. She formed the words, keeping them simple and true, and wrapped them with feeling, forming a memory she never wanted to forget. Then she pushed her message through the gaze they shared.

"I am grateful you are my brother."

Blake drew a sharp breath and he blinked, tears suddenly welling in his eyes. Not from the shock of receiving her message but because of his reaction to it.

She kept going. *"I am not afraid, because of you. I would be lost without you here."*

Blake gave her a gentle squeeze acknowledging he received her message loud and clear. He blinked a couple of times and his brow furrowed from concentration. A minute passed as they gazed into each other's eyes.

It was a soft brush like a distant thought, but it broke through clear and bursting with feeling.

"Love sister."

It was her turn to gasp. "I love you too, brother," she said out loud. Then they rose to their knees and hugged. "We're going to get through this."

They stood, donned their goggles, and pulled their hoods over their heads. They resumed walking toward the ridge.

Audrey pushed, *"Let's practice by telling stories from our pasts."*

It took a while before Blake's voice threaded through her mind. *"How Sinto met?"* The words were rough but decipherable.

"The month before my tenth birthday he approached me on the beach. The cove where my mom and I went every morning so she could hunt for fish. I was forming sea creatures from the sand. He frightened me. I didn't know where he came from. I had never seen him at the village school. I grabbed his hand and demanded to know who he was and what he was doing on our private beach. I didn't know what was happening at the time, but he nearly shocked me..."

"Nearly?"

"I think it scared him too. He tried to pull his hand away but I held firm. I can clearly remember the loud buzzing coming from his chest.

Then his eyes flashed, blinding me. You know me, I was intrigued and asked him how he did it. He told me it was a secret."

"Leela secrets too."

"Did you know she was different?"

"Not first—soon—impossible to hide."

"Were you scared?"

He paused. Trying to form the right response. He was getting better the more they shared.

"I thought cool! Especially after swim through Salish Sea. I was afraid of what lay below. She lost my fear. We slip into the water and—we would—"

Audrey's body tingled and she gasped from the sudden surge of dopamine passed along through their connection.

"Would what?" she pushed.

Blake chuckled softly out loud, then pushed. *"We hid our affection from others. Beneath ship, many months. Not from Francesca and Andi. Figured it out right away. By looking at me."*

"How old were you?"

"Sixteen."

"So young! I guess that was common back then."

"Relevant for that time. Life expectancy was half as today."

"Hey, you're getting better?"

"What do you mean?"

"Sharing, your words are forming more naturally."

"You sound just like you talk."

She chuckled. "You too, mostly."

They walked in silence for a beat.

"Did our father know she was Ianthe's daughter?"

"No. Was a secret till Ianthe caught us. Leela mostly came alone. We pretended she was a local native."

"Is that the only secret you kept?"

There was a long silence and Audrey thought maybe that last question got garbled. But then she felt it, a surge of emotion crossing the telepathic wire. Panic and elation and a profound sense of despair that made her heart clench and knees buckle. She stumbled. Blake sensed her duress, found her arm, and caught her before she fell.

They stopped walking. Their little game of telling stories was suddenly taking a dark and emotional turn. They faced each other but there was nothing to see except the landscape painted across their bodies. The air rippled slightly as Blake fumbled with something on his arm. A perfectly rendered picture of his face played across the front of his hood. Audrey pressed the button on her suit's control panel to do the same. They gazed into each other's eyes.

Blake's voice shook with emotion. "I never told anyone this secret. As far as I know, Ianthe never discovered it either. Leela never told me, but I knew. I sensed it through our sharing, through the Mark." He drew a deep breath. "Leela was with child when she died. She died with that secret. I—I eventually came to terms with her death, but not of our child's."

It was Audrey's turn to go silent, recalling her father's journal chronicling Blake's struggle after Leela's death. A tormented phase of Blake's life that lasted more than a decade and at times required Blake be chained to a bed to keep him from killing himself. Brutal tactics that would be shunned today, but in the eighteenth century it was all they knew. Blake was tortured by not only the loss of his chosen mate for life, but by the loss of their unborn child. A secret he harbored all that time, until now.

"I'm so sorry. And I'm sorry for prying," she finally said.

"You've nothing to be sorry for." Blake let go of her hand. "But I think we've shared enough, for now."

Ahead, the ridge loomed and the previous line of simple green became detailed with varying textures of foliage.

"We need to focus on finding Arkis," he said.

They clicked off the reflection of their faces and forged on in silence, swimming in a sea of private thought.

44

Leonard's Secret

SINTO SPENT THE NIGHT curled up beneath a reef in the soft sand without his lorica, with revitalizing sea water flowing freely through his gills and energizing his body. He woke before dawn and emerged from the sea feeling rejuvenated. Water slithered across his skin and once he was dry he slipped on the shirt and shorts he had left on the rock the day before.

He made his way along the path to the command center, hoping to find someone there. He had a few questions about Earth's geography. Nothing important except a need to expand his knowledge and become an active participant in discussions regarding solutions on where to possibly bury Orange.

The command center was dark, as was the dining room. The only sign of life came from Leonard, who was whistling away and punching down floured dough in the kitchen. Sinto watched from the doorway, intrigued by the way the large man lovingly rolled the soft dough into skinny long loaves, tender as a lover's caress with his remaining eight fingers.

"Ah, come on in young Sinto. What brings ya out so early?" Leonard asked. "We missed ya for dinner. You must be hungry."

"I am, but no need to fuss."

"Pfff. Fuss ya say? It's what I do, fuss. I fuss fer all of ya's." He grinned. "Me, I like to fuss."

He set aside the dough he was manipulating, walked over to a large sink, and washed his hands, drying them on his red apron. He leaned against the spotless counter. "Eggs, bacon, that healthy Swiss stuff they call muselix, whatever ya want, we got it."

"Muselix?"

"Crushed up grains I soak with coconut milk and honey till it's good and soft. Add seeds, nuts, and dried fruit. Keeps the ol' bowels regular."

Sinto shrugged. "Sounds good."

"Have yerself a seat, could use the company." He kicked a stool out from under the counter with his foot. "Yer looking particularly perky this mornin'. What's yer secret?"

"A long soak in the sea."

"I 'ear that about yer type. Me? A tall shot of rum and a fluffy pillow. Though a well-endowed lady to snuggle up with don't hurt none either." He added with a chuckle.

He pulled a large jar half-filled with something lumpy and colorless from the refrigerator. He scooped a large serving into a bowl. He put the jar back and pulled out a pitcher of cream. Then he waddled across the kitchen with the bowl and the cream to another set of cupboards, where he pulled out jars filled with seeds, nuts, and dried cranberries and apricots. He sprinkled a generous helping of each into the bowl.

Leonard dug a spoon from a drawer and slid it, the bowl, and the cream in front of Sinto. "That'll stick to yer ribs. Coffee comin' right up."

Sinto took a bite. Leonard was right. The texture was a little different but it was good. Sinto wolfed it down before Leonard started the coffee to brew.

Leonard returned with a couple of cups of steaming fresh-brewed coffee and sugar to go with the cream. He sat on the stool next to Sinto.

"Like mornin', nobody's up to tell me what to do." He gave Sinto a toothy smile, rosy cheeks beaming. "How 'bout you, ya one of them mornin' types?"

"I wake when I feel like it. Usually early."

"Spoken like a free man."

"I suppose."

"Speakin' of free speakin', I been meanin' to ask yer..." Leonard looked around, then leaned in close and said in a very low voice only Sinto could hear, "Did yer mum ever tell ya 'bout the Salish Stone?"

Sinto had never heard of such a stone. He shook his head.

Leonard continued in a quiet voice. "Ah, right, cause it's a secret." He rolled his eyes. "I aren't one for keepin' 'em, most pirates aren't. Anyways, the captain hasn't seen it since the old days, back before, when the captain and yer mum were, shall I say, *close*. The first time. Close like now."

"I have no idea what you're talking about, this Salish Stone."

"Ah, just curious, shame to have lost such a thing." He sat up and fingered his wiry white beard. "Rumor among us crew was it was some kind of magical thing. Size of a cantaloupe and like a diamond with an amber fire glowing inside. Blindin' if ya stared at it too long."

Sinto shook his head. "Huh. I haven't seen or heard anything about this stone."

A furrow of brow. "Hmm, I'm surprised. Supposedly the stone helped her enter that place where she saw the future and such, which she shared with the captain."

"You mean the Timeless Dimension?"

He snapped his fingers. "Ya, that was it." He tapped his head with a gnarled finger. "Years catchin' up. Not as sharp as I used to be." He stood and collected their empty coffee cups. "Got bread to bake and eggs to scramble. Ya take care of yerself, young Sinto."

Sinto stood and watched him shuffle across the kitchen, whistling the same tune he was whistling before.

Sinto left and headed straight to his mother's house, determined to learn about this fabled stone and if Leonard's musings had any weight to them. Sinto shook his head, slightly annoyed. He wouldn't be the least bit surprised to find the Salish Stone was yet another secret his mother had kept from him.

45

Key To The Timeless Dimension

SINTO'S MOTHER WASN'T IN her house or on the black-sand beach steps from the lanai. He traced the path he had previously taken with her to the clearing in the thick foliage of the jungle, northeast of the house and far from the shore. Sinto approached the clearing slowly so as not to disturb her if she was venturing into the Timeless Dimension.

She was not.

She sat cross-legged in the dirt at the center of destruction from all of her previous journeys, meditating. Her eyes were closed and strange words flowed from her mouth soft as a whisper. He lingered on the edge of the circle where the greenery had been spared from the vortex that shredded everything else that had the misfortune of growing within its swirling path.

While he waited for her to finish, his mind raced with what this rumored stone may mean, and if the rumor was true, why his mother had never revealed its existence. She had always been secretive, which frustrated him greatly. He never understood why she believed it best to withhold critical information from those most affected. He did understand the importance of holding it back from a wider audience, for obvious reasons. But why withhold it from those whom she trusts?

Whatever it was, it felt like a game, one that may have worked during her reign as queen and while governing with the Circle. But the situation had changed, and playing political games hindered their ability to solve the ever-growing and insurmountable problems facing them.

Since the destruction of Tallamure and Arkis' attack, she had been rendered weak and powerless. The reins had been ripped from her hands, and the Circle trivialized, by new and young leaders, Merahvu and Sapien alike, who stood up to take action. It was time for her to let go, like Culliford seemed to have done, difficult as that may be.

She had enjoyed her power for hundreds of years. If he was in her situation, what would he do? He knew what *not* to do. He wouldn't sit on vital secrets, especially now.

But then again, he was twenty-something in years. Never having the power she once had, he couldn't imagine the struggle she must face to let go under difficult and humiliating circumstances.

He looked up. She had left her meditative trance and was staring at him, the emotions on her face unreadable. It was a well-practiced game face she had perfected over the years, always in self-control no matter what she might be feeling. It was a tool she employed to navigate sticky situations and sway negotiations to her favor.

A practiced game face he tried to replicate, but at this moment he found fleeting. His curiosity had morphed into something more acute.

"Tell me about the Salish Stone." It came out as a demand, more so than he intended.

She put her finger to her lips. Her voice threaded through his mind. *"Sit, and I will tell you."*

He stood his ground. *"So it's true? The stone exists?"*

She nodded.

He was quick to anger, something that had come over him recently following the attack on Andrew's Island. Victoria's death hung heavily on his heart.

He snapped back, "*Something as important as the key to unlocking the Timeless Dimension and you failed to tell me about it? What if it is the key to solving our problems? What if this stone fell into the wrong hands? Does Naiada know of the existence of this stone?*"

His breath was shallow and useless for calming his frustration. Catecholamines flooded his system and his merlux sparked to life. He was losing it. Again. He once cherished his ability to remain calm. Lately he found himself more exasperated and tense and apt to lose control of his emotions.

He had snapped at Rachel the day before, and now, at his mother. He recalled what Rachel suggested in her form of nutshell logic, succinct and expressed quite sharply:

Get your shit together.

He repeated it to himself three more times like a mantra, breathing deeply and purposefully. Surprisingly, repeating the words helped as did the fresh oxygen filling his lungs.

His mother said nothing in reply, a sly smile curling the corners of her lips. He knew she sensed his struggle and was waiting patiently for him to become calm.

They gazed at each other as he continued to breathe fresh oxygen to the depths of his lungs. Big breath in, soft release, until his heart settled and merlux silenced. Sucking the magic of oxygen to restore himself.

She patted the ground. Sinto sat across from her, cross-legged, feeling calmer but mildly agitated.

"*You are upset about Victoria's death. I am truly sorry it happened. She was of good heart and did not deserve to die by that monster's hand.*"

She reached out and cupped his cheek. "*It is true, I have withheld many secrets. All for good reason. I would never withhold information that would jeopardize our fight to defeat what threatens us. I will answer your questions and tell you everything about the stone, but first, I must know, who told you about it?"*

Sinto paused unsure if she would be upset if he told her, after gaining Leonard's confidence. "Leonard, but—"

She rolled her eyes. *"Pirates. Minds leaky as a sieve. Once they obtain a nugget of valuable information they cannot seem to keep quiet about it. I am fond of Leonard and harbor no ill will against the man. I suspected Robert told his merry band of pirates about it long ago. If anything, he is at fault of breaking my trust. Certainly would not be the first time..."*

"So not such a secret?"

"Oh, it is a secret, a very important one. I have known all along they knew about it. Rest assured, they are a tight group and as much as they feel the need to share valuable information, they tend not to let those secrets circulate beyond their tight circle. I believe to the depths of my essence that Robert's original crew can be trusted."

She paused and took a deep breath.

"The Salish Stone was discovered long ago when Robert was my ally. It was before Leela's death and Ramasis' vengeful attack. I had wrongly believed they had forgotten about it. Alas, I am thrilled Leonard remembered, for good reason."

"What good reason?"

She smiled. *"To tell you, of course. You learned of the stone through casual conversation as I had foreseen. I also anticipated your vitriolic reaction, especially towards me. And now you are here confronting me about it. That too I foresaw. The timing could not have been more perfect. I accurately predicted you coming to me at this exact moment in time. Perhaps I'm not as weak as some believe."*

Sinto was stunned. Though the more he thought about the words she shared the more he understood. He had learned that his mother rarely presented information until it was necessary. She had a peculiar knack of waiting until the last most possible moment to reveal what must be revealed. And she relished his reaction as a confirmation she still had the power to divine what others cannot see or have yet to discover.

Sinto took a moment to relinquish his annoyance and frustration. He'd had a lifetime of mind-dizzying interactions like this with his mother. Only this time he sensed she wouldn't hold back the next part.

"Tell me more."

"I bent the truth regarding my power of foresight. While it is true that my ability to sense things—be it from studying the aura of the natural world and the many creatures and humans occupying it, or by accessing the accumulated knowledge passed down from my ancestors—my true power of foresight was gained only once I broke into the Timeless Dimension. The Salish Stone was the key that unlocked it and offered me guidance to target that which I sought from the past, present, or future. With the stone I was able to predict with clarity a future nearly aligned with the one we now occupy. The details differ but the essence is the same—a new conflict with the Terrakai. Though the introduction of Orange was not foreseen.

"Without the stone, I can see possibilities, but an alarming clutter of them, and with much less certainty. Once the stone unlocked the Timeless Dimension, I have been able to enter without it, akin to one learning a pathway on which to travel. One I was able to show Naiada. But as I demonstrated to you without the stone, a certain level of refinement is lost. I can only capture pieces of what may or may not be vital."

"So you no longer possess it."

"Correct."

"What happened to it?"

"It was lost when Robert destroyed Tallamure."

"Did Father know of the stone?"

She didn't answer.

"Did he?" He pressed more firmly.

A worrying line cut between her eyes. *"I am not certain, but it is entirely possible Ramasis may have found it among my things. Or—"*

Her gaze grew distant. Sinto watched as a multitude of past memories played across her face.

"*I possessed the stone for a very long time and holding that secret dear from your father took great restraint—it is entirely possible the existence of it may have slipped through my thoughts by accident in one of our many private conversations or more intimate interactions.*"

"*Did you tell Naiada about the stone?*"

"*No, she was not ready, and it would have been meaningless to share that knowledge since I no longer possess it.*"

A much more concerning emotion rippled across her face. Fear bordering on pure terror.

Her eyes cut to his. "*Which means...*"

"*If Father knew about it and believed it lost at Tallamure, he could have found it.*"

She drew a sharp breath. "*And Arkis could use it to great advantage.*"

46

Franzaboana Bevor Slumpjam Gemtaker Buttmist

THE DESERT SCRUFF SOON intersected with a thriving jungle. Blake took the lead, darting between leafy bushes and squatty palms. They passed through a grove of banyon-like pillar-rooted trees, whose roots dropped from branches to the ground. Mango-like trees with smooth white trunks exploded with young fruits too green to consume. Monkeys with bushy white tails swung between the higher branches, oblivious to their presence. Evergreens similar to the ironwoods on Isla Salvación towered in between. Shrubs with fragrant flowers brushed their knees. Birdsong filled the air and small unseen creatures scurried among the leafy ground covers.

This was the wild of Merluma Audrey remembered, and she breathed deeply its vitality.

Now that they were in the jungle with many textures and shades, the surface of their camouflaged suits were a flurry of movement. Sunlight was intermittent through the thick canopy, adding dancing shadows to the mix. Under these conditions the charge on their batteries drew dangerously low.

Blake must have been thinking the same thing. *"We should set the camo mode to still, save our batteries,"* he said through mind-speak.

"Double tap the control button to set it to still, single tap turns active camo back on, tap again to turn it off."

He fiddled with his wrist controller. His suit froze with a random pattern of like colors and shapes, like military battledress designed for this particular jungle. Audrey tapped her camo button twice. Now they were a matched pair.

Blake stopped to look and listen. He tried to connect to *Xiph1* with no success. What they were looking for, they were not entirely sure. A trail, footprints, an entrance to a cave or other protective shelter. Arkis' lair. At least that is what they hoped if Blake's hunch was right. Audrey would be ecstatic if they could at least find a trail. Whacking through the jungle was a lot of work. The suits were working hard to keep them cool.

They forged on through the brambles and bushes. Audrey searched the ground for footprints or other disturbances that would indicate recent passage by one of many creatures on Merluma, or by Orankai.

They finally stumbled on a narrow trail, too small to be made by humans. Blake knelt. Audrey knelt beside him, looking for telltale prints. The soil was too dry for detailed impressions, just random disruptions in the dirt from something passing through, recently or long ago.

They stilled and listened. Beyond the cacophony of birdsong she thought she heard the rustling of leaves, something coming towards them.

She grabbed Blake's hand, pointed down the trail, then to her ears. He nodded. They flipped on their active camo.

They crouched lower. Whatever it was was definitely drawing closer.

Audrey's heart pounded.

Blake pushed, *"Prepare to defend, follow my lead."*

"Affirmative," she pushed back.

The sound of rustling leaves seemed nearly on top of them but yet they saw nothing.

"Orankai camouflaged?"

"Possible."

"Can they see our thermal signature?"

"No, the suit neutralizes your body's heat, matches its surrounding environment. We're invisible."

Now it sounded as if whatever was making the rustling sound was right on top of them. They dropped low to the ground, looking up. Still Audrey saw nothing.

"What is it?" Audrey asked.

"I don't know!"

When the thing rustling the bushes emerged, she gasped.

The creature froze and eyes darted, wide-eyed and fearful, its body quivering. It stood no more than a foot and half tall, appeared to be male and was featured like a mini-human. Two arms, two legs, and standing upright on two feet. His arms were a little long for his height but he had gnarled hands with four fingers and an opposable thumb. He was clothed, if that's what one would call it, with a strip of brown fabric wound around his hips and between his legs and tied at his hip. His chest was hairy and bare, nipples pert with fear.

Slung across his shoulder was a string of fish and a short wooden pole strung with a shiny barbed hook. Sporadic strands of wiry gray hair sprang up from his bald head. A scraggly white beard hung limply to his belly and a mustache jutted outward beyond his equally hairy ears. The soft brown eyes were extraordinarily large for his weathered face, and his brows were dueling nests of wiry gray hair. His nose was bulbous and shiny with sweat. Sticking out from all the hair were plump rosy lips in the shape of an O and was the source of his panting breath.

The poor thing was utterly terrified.

"What do we do?" Audrey asked.

Blake didn't reply. He simply switched off his camo and slipped the hood from his face at the same time. He held up his hands, in a gesture of peace and surrender, and gave the small terrified thing a friendly smile.

The creature leaped back, dropping its fishing pole and freshly caught fish. He clasped his beard with his dirty gnarled fingers. His brow furrowed as his dark curious eyes swept across Blake's exposed face.

Blake dug out a nutrition stick from a pocket in his suit. He unwrapped it. Took a bite. Rolled his eyes and made moaning sounds of utter pleasure.

Then he offered the rest to the small human-like creature.

The creature stepped forward cautiously.

"What should I do?" Audrey asked.

"Stay hidden, let me gain its trust first and try to communicate."

The creature snatched the partially eaten stick from Blake's fingers and jumped back. He sniffed then licked it. His brows quirked. He took a bite. Then he sat down next to his catch and pole and gobbled the rest down in a few quick bites.

Blake pointed to himself and said, "Blake."

The creature pointed to his chest and said, "Franzaboana Bevor Slumpjam Gemtaker Buttmist."

Blake faltered and stumbled through repeating it.

The creature pointed to his chest and repeated it very slowly. *"Franz-a-bo-ana Bev-or Slump-jam Gem-ta-ker Butt-mist."*

Blake looked flabbergasted.

The creature waved a hand. "A mouthful, I know, just call me Franz. Everyone else does. Besides, it makes me feel old, hearing my full name. The older I get, the more names that get tacked on."

The look on Blake's face was priceless. The words and the manner in which they were spoken by this strange and human-like creature was entirely out of context of what he was expecting.

Blake held out his hand. "Pleased to meet you. I mean no harm."

The little creature ignored his hand. Rolled his eyes and said, "That's what they all say."

"You mean the Orankai?"

The little creature sat back. "Is that what they're calling themselves now? Hard to keep track."

"I'm not alone. I brought my sister with me." He brushed his hand across Audrey's shoulder. "You can come out now," he said to her.

Audrey turned off her camo and pulled the hood off her head. "Hello, I'm Audrey."

Franz's eyes widened. "Wow, that's some trick. Just like those other guys." He crawled forward and stood, scrutinized her face, sat back down. "Pfff. She doesn't look like your sister."

"We're not blood related. Do you know what that means?"

"Sure, you both got different mommies or daddies or whatever. So she's your sister, I can accept that."

He pointed to the lightning bolt cut into the shaved part of her hair above her ears. "Those some kind of tribal markings?"

Audrey laughed. "No, just something I like."

"So, Blake and Audrey, easy enough to remember." He sniffed the air. "You don't smell like you're from here."

"We came from the other place, Earth. Do you know about Earth?"

Franz burst into laughter. "That place where your peoples put ceramic sculptures of us in their gardens? Of course! Ha, they believe we're gods that'll bring good fortune." He fluttered his lips and patted his small rounded belly. "If only they knew."

"What do you call yourself, I mean, not by name but what you are," Audrey asked.

"Oh please, don't get started with Snow White and the dwarf thing. We're small but not *them* and certainly not a *gnome*. Who came up with that one? It's so negative—*gnoooome*. Why not *Yessirea*? Or something important and powerful like 'Masters of the Universe'?" He rubbed his bald head as if shining up a precious jewel. "And what's with the pointy hats! Sheesh! Never owned one."

He shrugged. "Anyways, we call ourselves Wekeep. Rolls smoothly off the tongue, don'tcha think? Besides, it's what we do, lest we forget. We keep stuff, found and liked."

Audrey glanced at Blake, who picked up the conversation. "Are you aware of what's happening here?"

"You mean the strange goings on in the mountains? Sure, we avoid that business. Stay quiet and hide whenever they're around."

"Where do you hide?"

He grinned. His gums were pink and healthy and his teeth were slightly yellow and extraordinarily large for his mouth. As opposed to his dirty fingers, his teeth appeared to be well cared for. "We hide right under their noses."

He stood and whipped off the sash tied around his hips. His tiny man bits flopped about when he dove for the ground and rolled into a tight ball, butt to the sky.

"What do I remind you of?" His voice was muffled.

Blake asked, "Is this a game?"

"No! You asked how I hide so I'm showing you! What do I remind you of?"

Blake and Audrey shared a questioning look. "Uh..." Blake said.

"A rock maybe?" Franz said.

Audrey said, "You do look a little like a rock now that you mention it."

A rock with a hairy ass.

He unrolled and sat back on his hands, knees hitched up and legs spread, apparently quite comfortable with his man bits hanging out, catching some air. "They don't see us, they're dumb as rocks! I keep tellin' me missus, it's the little things that'll get ya, stay sharp and keep your eyes open."

He crawled over to where his grubby brown sash lay on the ground. He stood and wrapped it around his hips and through his legs and tied it in a knot below his belly. The ends hung down to his bony knees. "I know you're not one of them, so what's that contraption you've got for hiding?"

Blake said, "It's a suit that mimics one's surroundings. We Sapiens, we rely on technology for advantage."

"Oh I know about you Sapiens. Cell phones, Internet... and you're hairy in places the Merahvu aren't."

"How do you know so much about us—the way you speak—you sound like you're from Earth," Blake asked.

He chuckled. "You Sapiens can be so arrogant. You think you know everything, same with those other guys. The Merahvu think they're the only ones who know how to pass between here and there." He looked around, then came closer. He wagged a finger. Blake and Audrey leaned in until their faces were level with his. He whispered, "They're wrong. There's one of them portals not far from here, in the woods. Dumps ya out in a place called Canada."

"Is it possible there are other cracks that lead to Earth, here, on land?" Blake asked.

"Not sure, you might have to ask the faeries."

"I think I met some faeries once in a meadow over that ridge." Audrey said. "I couldn't understand a word they said."

"That's 'cause they speak faerision."

Audrey asked, "Do you know faerision?"

Franz bobbed his head. "Yes, yes, yes, I speak all the languages of the Herbys."

"Who are the Herbys?" Blake said.

His head swiveled between them, then he threw his hands up. "Geez! You two are exhausting!" He gestured dramatically with his hands. "The Herbys are the good creatures, the ones that don't try to eat you. The Carnys are bad, very bad, they slip us down their gullets as tasty little snacks. Now, the Omnys, like yourselves, eh, can go either way, good or bad. Depends on your character."

Audrey wondered if Sinto knew of the Wekeep and their ability to speak so many languages with the docile creatures on Merluma. "Do the Merahvu, Omnys as you call them, know about your relationship with the Herbys?"

"Only the ones who ask, *nicely*."

"Would you help us if we asked nicely?"

He pursed his lips and tapped his chin with a dirty finger. "By nicely I mean getting something in return."

Blake smiled and asked, "What is it you seek?"

He looked down at the string of small fish lying in the dirt, then back to Blake. "More of that sweet treat you gave me. One for me and one for me missus."

Blake pulled his last nutrition stick from a hidden pocket and nudged Audrey to give Franz hers. Gaining the help of the Wekeep was worth going hungry.

Franz tucked their offerings into the front flap of the wrap tied around his hips.

Blake said, "We're looking for someone who calls himself Arkis."

"Oh, *that* one. He's very, very bad. Me and me missus stay away from him and anyone who does his dirty work."

"Do you know where he resides, spends most of his time?" Blake asked.

"Certainly. He's hiding out in the Labyrinth."

"Labyrinth?" Audrey repeated. "Where is that?"

Franz hooked a thumb and pointed behind his shoulder. "A short wander that way."

"Can you take us there?" Blake asked.

"Sure, I was going that way anyway. We moved in after the Seakai abandoned it. Had it to ourselves until Arkis moved in with his lot of brainless tough guys and babes." He shrugged. "The Labyrinth's big enough for all of us."

"Tough guys and babes?" Audrey asked.

"Yeah, the brainless brings him newborns from the mountains for his pleasure."

"Newborns from caves where Arkis is rapidly breeding an army?" Audrey asked.

"Ha! Ya got me, wasn't aware of any army. Surprised you know about them caves too." He stuck a finger in his ear, dug around a bit. "I thought you knew nothing."

"We know many things you may not, as we expect you know many things we do not," Audrey said.

"What's with the mumbo jumbo talk? What you're saying is, I know things, you know things, and they aren't the same. Right?"

Audrey smiled to herself. "Right. Would you agree we can both benefit by sharing these things?"

"Now you're talking straight but depends on what *things*."

"Like showing us how to access the Labyrinth?" Blake asked.

"Hmm, I suppose." He grabbed his fishing pole, stood, spun on his feet and started walking. "Come on. Try to keep up."

Audrey noticed Franz had left his catch of small fish on the ground. She picked it up. "Wait, don't you want these?"

"Nah." He turned and patted his groin where he had stashed the nutrition sticks. "Got these, besides those damn things are too bony for my likin' but you're free to keep 'em of you want." He spun on his heel and continued walking.

"We're right behind you, but will be hiding," Blake said.

Franz waved a hand. "No worries, I know where ya are. I can smell ya plain as a flashing billboard. Got a schnoz like a dog."

Audrey and Blake pulled the hoods over their heads and switched their suits to active camouflage mode.

"*He's a strange one,*" Blake pushed to Audrey.

"*Gifts come in funny wee packages,*" she replied.

"*Should...wekeep him?*"

Audrey stifled a snort. "*Very punny.*"

And with that, they followed their strange new friend through the forest.

47

Costly Retrieval

Sinto was spit out of his tunnel into the North Pacific where the underwater city of Tallamure once stood, vital with life and an active community of a hundred-thousand Merahvu. A place that families had called home for hundreds of years. The place he grew up.

The glow from his eyes couldn't cut through the vast darkness of the deep. He engaged a set of sensors he had no need of in the Sapien world and had not used in a long while, a type of sonar. While a bit rusty from lack of use, he was able to map a detailed image of what now lay on the ocean floor.

A storm of emotions swirled. The city was gone. In its place was an uninhabitable wasteland. A reality he still struggled to grasp.

The trio of mountains that once stood as mighty sentinels around the city's dome were nothing but piles of rubble.

The remains of Club Ballo littered the rocky mount where it had proudly risen above all other structures, ten stories high, round and wrinkly as a brain coral with its electrified surface flashing in a rainbow of color once the mock sun had set. It was there Audrey unwittingly Marked him, altering the course of their lives forever.

Sunken tombs were all that remained of the underground caves where Terrakai had carved a vast network of tunnels and homes in the salty sea bed beneath a simulated forest. One of those homes had belonged to Nawtuga, a Terrakai woman who had watched over Sinto and his sister when his parents were away, and who had opened her home to Sinto and Audrey for a Merahvu-inspired dinner. A date. Their first and only, officially. Sinto had been relieved when he learned Nawtuga survived and had been safely settled among the Larkian community on Isla Salvación.

A geothermal fissure rumbled with activity where the Great Tower and surrounding compound once stood, overlooking the city. Heated water vented from Earth's core, souring the scent of the ocean with sulfur. The swirling foul scent penetrated the thick layer of lorica encasing his body and lingered on his tongue with each breath.

The fissure was a new feature and posed a serious problem. The Salish Stone had been hidden in his mother's residence at the foot of the Great Tower.

Before he left, his mother had described where she hid the stone in her private residence. She was confident the stone would have survived, but the carved wooden box she stored it in would have not.

He pushed aside the grief he harbored for his beloved city and dove towards the fissure.

The fissure was about sixty feet long and twenty feet wide, an opening in a narrow crack that extended in both directions as far as he could sense. The geothermal vent had not been there before, opening only as a result of Tallamure's explosive collapse and the shift of tectonic plates it had triggered.

He sifted through silt and rock around the fissure opening, hoping to find the stone among the debris. He tried to use light emitted from his eyes to see more clearly but it was futile. The water grew murky from his sifting. It was depressing and tedious work.

But he forged on.

Hours later he considered his options.

A massive cloud of disturbed silt and marine snow made his task impossible. He tried filtering for a spectrum of light his land eyes could not see. Regardless, the task was impossible. The stone could be five inches from his nose and he would never know it.

He decided to take a break while the murk settled and to prepare his head for what he knew he must do next—dive inside the fissure. A reality that may or may not be possible.

He swam to the highest vantage point and made a full sweep for other life forms. It was possible Ramasis may return to search for the stone if what his mother feared was true. It didn't take a genius to realize Ianthe would have left the stone in her haste to save herself before the city imploded and that it had been buried along with everything else.

Sinto could only assume his father was fully aware of the stone, where his mother had kept it, and the advantage of foresight Arkis would gain by using it, either with help from Naiada, or the other possibility: a new queen bred with the eggs Arkis stole from Sinto's mother. Given access to the Timeless Dimension, Arkis could predict Larkian and Merahvu movements and keep the Sapiens guessing about his silent and effectively targeted genocide of their species. Sinto suspected the reason Arkis may have learned of his trap on Andrew's Island was because Arkis already had the stone.

There was only one way to know for certain.

Keep looking.

The stone may have fallen inside the fissure because of its weight. He accepted the possibility the stone was lost forever to the fissure's endless depth. But forever lost was better than Arkis and the Orankai possessing it. Or it may have landed on one of the many ridges jutting out from the fissure's walls.

Diving too close to geothermal vents could be deadly, but he had to be certain.

A steady stream of boiling seawater rose from the fissure. He sensed an explosion of sea life had already taken root within, nourished by heat and a concentrated mix of minerals released from Earth's core. He launched from his high perch and dove down through the settling murk to the fissure's edge. Bioluminescent creatures skittered and blinkered as he passed by.

He had no need to emit light from his eyes; in fact, it only hindered his sight. The hydrothermal light from several chimney vents flickered in a light spectrum his land vision could not see. He adjusted his underwater vision until he could see only the faint outline of shimmering streams of heated water. Places he did not want to pass through.

His sonar traced the hard surfaces of the fissure opening and what lie within, confirming it was very deep with vertical walls that plunged straight down. Along the walls were small ledges where the stone may have come to rest. Chimneys teaming with shrimp, tube worms, and yeti crabs sprouted outward from one side of the fissure. The other side of the opening was relatively barren.

He ventured inside, head first, hugging the barren wall as a guide to keep his body from flesh-melting water spewed from chimneys on the other side. He stopped at every ledge that seemed safe. He searched each surface, batting away the occasional stray shrimp or crab. All he found was more mountain rubble and shredded remains from the city. He found nothing the size of a cantaloupe.

Hope faded the more he searched.

More vents burst from the fissure walls the deeper he ventured. The water was much warmer, pleasantly so, but he stayed frosty. One lapse in concentration and a vital appendage may cross through boiling water. The walls of the fissure closed in the deeper he dove.

Then he saw it.

Perched on a ledge ten feet below and next to a roiling vent was the stone. It was tantalizingly close, as if someone had set it there as a challenge for him to retrieve. The stone cast a light of its own, a faint glow of amber from within. Surrounding the glowing center was a crystal-clear shell, like a polished flawless diamond.

A harmonic tremor erupted within the Mark buried in his arm. The sudden sensation was a distraction. He brushed it off as emotional interference, elation at finding the stone.

He dove down and across a narrow gap of cool water but was driven back by fiery water. He retreated, clinging to a small ledge on the opposite side.

The stone taunted. So close yet impossible to reach without enduring bodily harm.

Then something happened, suddenly and violently. His heart raced and skin struggled to maintain his protective lorica. He gasped for oxygen but all he sucked was carbon dioxide. He grew confused. Forgot where he was. His vision faltered.

Venting water—Earth's core. He was breathing pure carbon dioxide.

He flipped over and whipped his tail, hugging the fissure's wall, and burst up and out of the fissure where the water was cool and oxygenated.

His blood stream was thick with carbon dioxide and it took a while for him to regain his senses. He berated himself for being so stupid. The chimneys drew water from the Earth's core, rich with carbon dioxide. The fissure was saturated with it. He should have known.

While his heart settled and breath calmed he replayed the situation in his mind. He needed a plan. A quick in and out, or else risk losing his mind from lack of oxygen and dying a horrible death.

The stone was fifty feet down on a ledge less than a foot from the top of a chimney spewing fiery water. He had the advantage of the near-freezing sea water in this part of the ocean to rapidly cool the water around the chimney. The mussels and tube worms attached along the sides of chimneys where swarms of pale shrimp and yeti crabs feasted confirmed that fact. If he stayed where the creatures thrived he would be safe. That meant diving deeper. Hug the chimney and grab the stone from below.

Easy peasy, Audrey would say. He smiled at that sudden thought. Thinking of her gave him encouragement and a fresh wave of determination.

His plan was solid. But planning and doing were completely different things. One slip and—

He didn't want to imagine the result.

He recalled what Wantemo had taught him to harness fear and quell stress reactions: to breathe calmly and ignore the primal urge to flee. Target fixation was another lesson he taught Sinto. The good and bad of it. His simple instruction threaded through his mind:

Focus where it is safe, ignore everywhere else.

The pathway to the stone was tight with many deadly obstacles. Speed was not critical until he slipped deeper and ran out of oxygen. He tucked his tail along his spine to reduce the possibility of his fluke slipping through a roiling stream of flesh-melting water.

He dove head first with micro strokes of his feet. He followed the path he took before, hugging the barren wall opposite from the stone. Forty feet down, he rolled and pointed his toes to Earth's core. He descended by fluttering his arms above his head until his feet settled on a narrow ledge.

Across from him the stone beckoned. His body urged him to flee, screaming for oxygen.

Hydrothermal light crackled and wavered along the chimney's lip. The chimney walls were covered with mussels and tube worms and a mass of feasting yeti crab and shrimp. The sulfur stench was stifling.

He dropped six feet, swam to the chimney, and hugged it. Mussels and hardened tube worms pricked his body. The water was hot. His protective lorica melted. He sucked water through his gills. Oxygen was sparse and carbon dioxide was thick.

He climbed the chimney, inch by inch, squeezing his body into the tight space between it and the fissure wall. Bits of shell crumbled. Yeti crabs crawled across his body. Shrimp battered his face and slithered through his hair.

His heart raced; each draw through his gills was rich with carbon dioxide, straight-lining directly into his bloodstream. His vision faltered. Wedged between the roiling chimney and the hard stone wall, he panicked. He debated, with what little sense he still possessed, whether to continue or back off and try again.

The stone was within reach. So was the flesh-melting vent. He raised his right arm, climbed a few more inches.

Vertigo set in. His head swam with confusion. Up was down. His arm wavered dangerously close to the vent.

Abort!

He slithered down, across to the other side, up, and out.

Free from the fissure, his gills pumped for oxygen. He wondered if he was on a fool's errand. Then he thought of Arkis. The bastard would sacrifice as many Orankai as necessary to get that stone. He channeled that horrid thought and drew strength from his anger.

Try again.

Sinto bled a renewed layer of lorica. Waited until it plumped with fresh oxygen, siphoned from the surrounding water. He descended on the same path, repeated the same movements; head down, rotate, toes down, flutter of arms, until his toes touched down on the shelf across from the chimney.

He sucked a deep breath and held it. Then launched for the other side. He wormed his body between the wall and the chimney, batting away crabs and shrimp, ignoring others crawling down his body. He reached up with his right hand and wriggled higher, face pressed to rock, shoulder scraping along uneven surfaces. Shells cracked and cut into his skin. He ignored the sharp pain and focused his gaze on the stone.

His fingers edged closer, inches from the stone and from the shimmering fire at the lip of the chimney. The heat was unbearable. His lorica disintegrated.

He reached and squirmed until his fingers splayed across the stone's surface. Fiery water scorched. Skin blistered before his eyes. He shut out the pain and the numbness that followed. He withdrew his arm with the stone firmly clasped in his burnt hand. It was hot and heavy and his first reaction was to drop it. Pain rippled up his arm. The Mark reverberated deep inside. He wriggled down from the gap, broken shells and angry crabs plastered to his skin, with the stone hovering dangerously above his head.

He fought the urge to suck carbon dioxide-rich water through his gills. His vision faltered. He gritted his teeth and held fast, with his blurred gaze locked on his prize.

He slithered to the other side of the fissure, hugging the stone to his chest. He retreated, up, and out. Once free of the fissure, he drew a watery breath through his gills. His heart pounded with elation and shock and a heavy dose of carbon dioxide. He gazed in disbelief at the stone cradled in the crook of his left arm.

He was afraid to look at his burnt hand, but did. In the faint light cast from his eyes, it was clearly charred and shriveled. Pain radiated and thrummed from finger to elbow. The skin along his lower arm was grossly discolored and blistered. The Mark visibly writhed.

He tucked his prize in the pit of his injured arm, launched a tunnel with his good hand, and dove inside.

With the Salish Stone hugged to his chest he jetted straight for Isla Salvación.

48

Grow A Tail

Sɪɴᴛᴏ ʟᴀʏ ᴏɴ ʜɪꜱ side on the black-sand beach by his mother's home on Isla Salvación, vomiting. The stone rested next to him. His right arm was on fire and too tender to touch or rest comfortably. He couldn't feel his hand. The flesh was mottled an angry red and sickly white. His wrist and lower arm were less so, but still pink and swollen and quite painful. The sight of it invoked more vomiting.

The Mark had survived the misfortune of being burned, but it was screaming.

Ianthe and Culliford emerged from the house and came running.

Sinto didn't remember anything after that.

He woke in a sparse, sterile room, lying in a bent bed that elevated his head. A bag of clear fluid was connected to a small plastic tube that was plugged directly into a blood vein in his left wrist.

His right arm was resting across his chest, swaddled with white gauze. His mind was fuzzy and body numb. There was intense pain, deep and throbbing, and rippling in waves from wrist to elbow. He still couldn't feel his hand. It was during those intolerable waves of pain that his vision winked to darkness and gravelly moans involuntarily slipped through his lips. In brief and rare moments of consciousness, he feared he no longer possessed a right hand.

He called out. For Audrey, for his mother, for Wantemo, for anyone who could hear.

It was Wantemo who slipped through the door and came to his side.

"I can't feel my hand." His eyelids felt like cement. "Is it gone?"

Wantemo grasped his good one, gave it a squeeze. "Not completely. But I cannot lie, it was severely damaged. Third degree burns—the skin, the insulating fatty layer, the dermis are gone. The muscle and tendon may not be salvageable. The bones still have life but will be irreparably weakened. The Larkians have treated it as best they could. Even with their impressive medicines and medical knowledge..." He shook his head. "There is a high probability you may lose it."

Sinto nodded gravely, his stomach withering at the thought. "And my arm?"

"The arm is less damaged. Second degree burns. It will heal from the wrist up, luckily."

"The Mark—it's gone silent. Before it—it was screaming."

"That I cannot explain. Perhaps it was in response to its mate."

Sinto's heart leapt. "Audrey."

"Most certainly she felt your duress. What you describe may have been her reaction."

Sinto managed a smile. Not from the depressing news Wantemo just shared, but that the Mark reacted. Sinto knew it meant Audrey was alive somewhere on Merluma. He breathed a deep sigh of relief.

Wantemo continued, "I am sorry to be the one to give you that news but if we are to do anything to save that hand, we must act now. It will not be pleasant."

Sinto closed his eyes. Another setback. Three steps forward, another one back...

"And the—the... *object* I brought back with me?"

"I am unaware of what object you speak. But your mother wanted me to tell you thank you and that it is safe."

His gaze slipped down his chest to the bandaged arm that lay across it. His injured hand was hidden within a wad of gauze. Safe but at what cost?

"Is there anything you can do to save it?"

"You know there is one way."

"Regenerate it."

"But there is no guarantee and it will be quite painful."

"Have you no tinctures you can give me to ease that pain?"

"I do. But." He gazed into Sinto's eyes expecting him to explain what came after the but.

"You need me conscious."

"You remember your lessons well, my apprentice. You must participate for us to achieve success."

There was no need to consider. Sinto had made up his mind. "I want to keep my hand."

"Hold close that determination. You will need it."

The reality of what Wantemo was implying sank in. Sinto was about to embark on a journey like no other. He suddenly felt nauseous. "Understood."

"We need to move quickly. Are you ready?"

Sinto nodded.

Wantemo pulled a small translucent bladder of red liquid tied beneath the folds of his skareef. He held it up. "Sucuvita, some of the last from our stores. I need you to drink it. All of it. Now."

He held the bladder to Sinto's lips and he drank. Sucking it down to the last drop.

The effect was immediate. Fire spread through his belly and raced through his bloodstream. His vision sharpened as did the pain. Sucuvita would energize cell reproduction, boast his immunity, and help regenerate damaged tissue.

Wantemo placed a hand on Sinto's shoulder. "Dr. Wickman asked if he could observe. Do you consent? He could prove a helpful assistant." Then he leaned over and whispered, "I highly recommend you agree."

Sinto nodded. "Absolutely."

Wantemo left and returned with Dr. Wickman a few minutes later. Both wore green baggy pants and short-sleeved shirts that tied in the back. Green caps covered their heads and light blue masks covered their noses and mouths.

Dr. Wickman came alongside the bed. His pale eyes were sympathetic and sharp with intelligence. The aura surrounding the doctor was bright and sincere. "We're going to do everything possible to save your hand."

Sinto's head swam from sucuvita, having never ingested that much all at once. "Thank you for..." His voice sounded whispery and distant. "Whatever the outcome."

Wantemo pulled back Sinto's bed coverings and folded them down at his waist. His upper body lay bare on the bed. Both of them washed their hands in a sink across the room and splashed them with a sterilizing solution.

Dr. Wickman approached the bed with raised hands. Wantemo rolled over a tray table from across the room with stainless-steel surgical tools, sterilized and ready to use. They each slipped on a pair of surgical gloves.

Dr. Wickman pored a generous splash of orange liquid onto a ball of gauze. "Where shall we take skin for the graft?" he asked Wantemo.

Wantemo studied Sinto's abdomen, skipping over the place where a lamprey had once taken its own skin graft for a snack. It had grown back but was still slightly concave where the fatty layer had yet to fill in. The top layer of skin had not healed perfectly since Sinto had to heal himself. It made his camouflage a bit irregular in that spot. Wantemo pointed to a place on the other side. "There, to start."

Wantemo turned to Sinto. "Dr. Wickman suggested we aid the rejuvenation process by introducing healthy tissue during the knitting process. What we take from healthy places on your body will heal itself naturally and eventually. We may need to take healthy tendon, vessels, and muscle fiber from other places as well. It will be a setback for you physically for a short while. Do you consent to these suggestions?"

He didn't have much choice. The thought of losing his right hand was unfathomable at the moment. More scars merely added to the storyline of his upended life.

Sinto nodded.

Dr. Wickman began rubbing the orange liquid along the side of his abdomen in large sweeping circles. He did the same to the entirety of his left arm. Those were the places where Wantemo suggested they harvest healthy tissue for the rejuvenation process.

"You will be the second to experience the merging of Sapien and Merahvu medical treatment." Sinto could tell Wantemo was smiling by the crinkles surrounding his eyes, peeking from above his mask.

The room had begun to spin. "Who was first?" It came out slurred.

"Rachel. She asked us to remove her breast implants. A simple procedure. Yours will be much more complicated."

Sinto's mind faltered, then he remembered how she looked when she stripped off her shirt the day before. The tiny triangles of her swimsuit that barely covered her small, perfect breasts. When Sinto met her as an escort in Las Vegas she had extra-large breast implants, hair extensions to extend the length of her hair, and long acrylic nails that clicked whenever she touched anything. On top of that she wore high-heeled shoes and looked like she would topple over at any second and stab herself with her fingers. Her transformation back to her former self began in earnest shortly after they met. *Never going back*, she had claimed. Removing the Sapien-made liquid-filled sacks had been the last step.

Wantemo picked up a pair of scissors and proceeded to cut the gauze from his arm.

He talked as he worked. "Remember to maintain calm. Compartmentalize the pain. Lock it away in your mind as you would a secret you wish to hide from your mother. It will do you no good to dwell on it. The only way to stop the pain will be completing the rejuvenation process. Focusing on the pain will make our work take longer. Focus on a rejuvenated hand. Do you understand?"

Sinto thought back to that night when Audrey was dying of sepsis poisoning on Merluma. He had to do something similar to save her life and the use of her shoulder. He knew it would be a messy procedure. Only then he had no hot water or sterilizing solutions or surgical tools. Audrey had lain on a mat on the sand and Sinto had used a knife he had cleaved from black glass spilled from the Black Mountains. He had no way to ease the pain other than to coax her mind from her body and secret it away in his mind. He remembered using those same words—*do you understand*—after telling her that what she would experience would be unlike anything she had ever endured. It worked until she panicked and her consciousness had returned to her own body. It was a miracle she survived with her wits and shoulder intact.

Now it was him lying helpless at the mercy of fate and the experience and knowledge of the two men who stood over him. Like Audrey once had with him, he must place full trust in their ability to fix him, as well as in himself. But he had no complaint. His life was not at stake, only his hand. The same had not been true of Audrey. She had panicked before he could finish, and when she became fully conscious during the final stages of reanimating her flesh all he had to help her endure the pain was a stick that he pressed between her teeth. She endured, and now, so must he.

"I need something to bite down on."

Dr. Wickman rummaged for something across the room. He came back and pressed a hard leathery object between Sinto's teeth, the taste of the beast it came from mixing with his saliva.

Wantemo said, "Remember we have practiced this many times during your training. Envision you are a lizard simply growing back its missing tail."

And then, the agony began.

49

Labyrinth

AUDREY FALTERED. THE MARK in her forearm came to life and burned as if on fire.

"Stop," she said. She stumbled from unbearable pain then fell to her knees. She hugged her arm to her chest, stifling a scream, sucking air through gritted teeth. She added pressure to the Mark, shook her arm, but nothing she did would stop the fire within.

Franz spun on his heel, hands to hips. "We don't have all—"

Audrey whipped off her hood. "Something's wrong—Sinto—I think something's happened." Her heart raced. She felt sick to her stomach.

Blake knelt beside her, pulled off his hood. Their faces floated mid-air in the midst of a thriving jungle.

"The Mark, it's on fire, and I feel sick."

Blake said to Franz, "She needs a break."

Franz plopped down in the dirt. "Whatever. This gig's on your dime."

Debilitating pain and elation surged through the Mark, sensations that were not her own. "Whatever has happened, it's—it's *confounding*. I feel excruciating pain in my right arm and my—my hand, it's—it's numb. I feel like I'm about to throw up, my heart is pounding from the pain, but also—excitement, something good, as if something hard-fought was won."

She looked up at Blake. "What does it mean?"

"It means he's alive, wounded maybe, but alive and pleased about it. Try not to read too much into what you feel. We don't have the luxury to dwell on distractions. I'm sure Sinto wouldn't want you to take any risks worrying about him. Focus on the positive things you feel, knowing he's alive."

Tears welled and she nodded. "The rest is helping. The pain, it's subsiding—he'll be okay—he'll be okay..." She said it mostly to herself as if saying it would make it true. She struggled to catch her breath, took a sip from the tube connected to her water bladder. It was empty. She grimaced. "I need water, I'm out."

Blake offered his but Audrey could only get a sip. Blake's was out too. So were the extras she had filled, emptied on the long hike across the Desertlands.

Blake turned to Franz, who was picking dirt from under his toenails with a stick. "We need fresh water."

Franz cocked an ear. All Audrey heard was the rush of her breath and pleasant birdsong floating down from the trees above. No wind, no rushing water. Franz swiveled his head as if his ear was a receiving dish for capturing sound. He raised an unruly brow, sniffed a couple of times. He stood, brushed off his bum, picked up his pole.

"Not far, this way."

Blake and Audrey got up, slipped on their hoods, and resumed their stealthy walk. The Mark had switched to a low simmer and her heart began to calm. She hoped Blake was right. She clung to the knowledge Sinto was alive, that wounds heal, but death—no one comes back from that.

Franz headed south toward the ocean. They walked in silence. Blake bumbled around for her camouflaged hand, gave it a squeeze.

Audrey tried to let go of the fact that Sinto was in pain. As Blake suggested, she focused on the fact he was excited about some sort of victory. She pushed support and sympathy through the Mark, unsure if Sinto could feel it or not. She got no response.

Ten minutes later they came across a fast-running stream following the curves of the ridge.

Franz waded up to his knobby knees, bent over, and took a sniff. Then he took a sip, flushed it around in his mouth, swallowed it down. "Mmm, tasty, and safe enough." He drank greedily, wiped his mouth with the back of his hand. "Ah, good call, me missus is always pestering me to drink more water."

Blake and Audrey helped each other remove the bladders from their packs and refill them. Before sealing them up, Blake dropped an iodine tablet in each, shook them up. Told Audrey, "Give it thirty minutes to be sure."

"I told you it's safe." Franz rolled his eyes. "Whatever." He waited with his arms crossed and gnarled fingers drumming his well-muscled forearms while they stashed the full bladders in their packs.

"All good?" Blake asked Audrey.

"Considering..." She gave Blake a reassuring smile.

"Time to roll, but first, I gots something to show ya," Franz said.

Franz continued toward the ocean which their internal maps indicated was nearby. He picked up a heavily-used trail with many animal tracks and a few extra-large human ones. Her heart skipped a beat. *Orankai.*

The trail skirted the stream that followed the curves of the soaring ridge. Sunlight cut through the thick canopy. The obsidian ridge sparkled like black diamonds where the sun struck it.

Franz picked up the pace, fishing pole slung across his shoulder, the shiny barbed hook dancing. For a little guy he moved swiftly. They had to jog to keep up.

She was sorry they were in enemy territory in the middle of a war. It saddened her. She would have preferred to savor the beauty surrounding her; the ridge, the various plants growing in the jungle, the array of birds populating the trees. Taking a dip in the river... Would she ever have the chance?

She scoffed.

Maybe in an alternate life.

The stream cut a sharp turn and disappeared into an crack at the base of the black ridge. Franz pointed. "Feeds several chambers including the ones Arkis took over. If others didn't rely on it, I would've suggested we shit in it."

Fifteen minutes later they stood at the edge of a fifty-foot cliff overlooking a patch of rocky land above the ocean. It was there the stairway came up from the sea and Blake had left the damaged *Xiph1* on the rocks. They could hear ocean swells slowly grinding it to pieces.

They squatted. Franz pointed to a cave opening cut into the ridge near the top of the stairway, and whispered, "Arkis uses the ocean entrance exclusively." He pointed back to the trail where they came from. "We Wekeeps use a different entrance. They call us a nuisance but leave us be. We don't wanna get caught pokin' around, specially not you two. Best we move on. Stick close and try to be quiet."

Franz's legs were a blur as they retraced the way they came from. They passed the spot they stopped for water, and kept running.

Franz stopped at a fallen tree, straddling the stream with access to the ridge on the other side. Once they caught up, he zipped across before they could stop and catch their breath. He passed over easily because of his size. It was a precarious passage for Audrey and Blake, for the tree was narrow and flexed under their combined weight.

Franz disappeared like a fleeing mouse into the vine-tangled hillside nestled against the ridge. He stuck his head out from the greenery and waved a hand. "Through here!"

Blake took the lead, ripping a larger path through the tangled vines that tugged at their packs as they wormed their way through.

Carved in the rock face of the ridge was a human-sized opening: a cave, tunneling deep. Franz zipped inside. They followed his tiny silhouette, running toward an arched doorway filled with light.

They burst into a chamber three stories high and a hundred feet across. A waterfall cascaded down the far wall and fed a large pool that filled half of the chamber; the rush of water reverberated. Light bled from openings plugged with opaque rock like the cave where they slept and stashed their supplies and weapons. The ceiling was cleaved obsidian. Some places were honed to sharp points, like the rows of a great white's teeth. The floor was gray and polished smooth from thousands of years of passing feet.

There were pockets of rock and wooden stools scattered throughout, and carved-out spaces along the walls that Audrey imagined were for hawking wares, or serving food and beverages. It must have taken an army of Merahvu to carve out these spaces and the dark tunnels spawned from the chamber.

As Franz had said, it appeared abandoned and neglected. Rodent droppings were everywhere, and a thick layer of dust coated every flat surface. A gossamer of spider webbing shimmered along the walls, in every corner, and dripped from the rough-cut ceiling. The water filling the pool was inviting and crystal clear. Fresh air swirled from the tunnels cut deeper within the ridge. With a little elbow grease, Audrey imagined the chamber would be a well-protected place to live or gather.

Franz waved for them to quietly follow him deeper into the Labyrinth. He would tip-toe up a stairway carved in rock, then down another faintly lit tunnel, stopping periodically to sniff. Then he would wave for them to follow and he would race down another tunnel, traveling in a different direction. And on it went.

The light varied, never growing fully dark, but some places were better lit than others by plugged openings in the ceiling. In some places were reflective surfaces, like mirrors, that captured and reflected the light to others strategically placed.

Doorways opened to other chambers—private living spaces from what she could tell—with dilapidated furnishings carved from wood. All were vacant.

Franz continued in a frenzy of twists and turns, and Audrey lost all sense of direction. At first they were heading inland toward the mountains, then they were backtracking toward the ocean. Thankfully her suit recorded each twist and turn.

Franz stopped suddenly with a finger to his lips and waved them inside one of the dark chambers. They pinned their bodies against the wall. Audrey and Blake donned their hoods and switched their suits to camo mode. Franz's eyes were wide with fear and he signaled for utter silence. Audrey shoved him behind her legs, hiding him behind her camouflage.

Voices, footsteps, grew louder.

A procession of Orankai passed by. A pair of guards dressed in black leather skirts and snug vests decorated with shiny silver buttons towed a group of six young women linked together by rope tied around their waists. Their arms were bound by a thick band wound around their torsos. Each of the young women were of Terrakai origin and uniquely exquisite, their lithe bodies barely covered by silky, peach-colored skareefs.

Franz slipped out from behind Audrey's legs, transfixed by the shiny silver buttons glinting from the guard's chests. She grabbed him by the shoulders and yanked him back, holding him fast with her legs.

"Arkis is going to love this batch of beauties," said the taller guard.

"Think he'll share this time?" said the shorter one.

Audrey's face fevered. *Sex slaves.* The young and innocent bred for Arkis' pleasure. She reached for her knife tucked in a hidden pocket at her thigh. This time it was Blake pulling her back, stopping her from jumping out and inflicting swift justice.

He pressed his arm across her chest. *"Later."*

She sensed his frustration and anger as acutely as her own. *"Later, bet on it,"* she replied.

"Guess that confirms my theory."

"Sure does. Those young women were fresh from the breeding caves. He's here and probably Naiada. Time to formulate Plan C."

"Let's see where Franz takes us first. The Wekeep may be a factor."

"Agreed."

"Flow as water..."

"And drown that fucking rock named Arkis."

They waited before moving along in case there were others migrating from the breeding caves to Arkis' lair by the sea. Then Franz launched into his rapid little trot, drawing them deeper into the Labyrinth. Audrey and Blake jogged behind, quietly landing on the pads of their feet.

Up they rose in elevation, along meandering paths to a second open chamber, dusty and neglected as the one before, then through an arched tunnel that spawned others that split in many directions. Light bounced from reflective surfaces mounted along the upper walls and by their feet. Obsidian teeth bore down from the arched ceiling above. The light never ceased, providing enough to easily see their way. Audrey tried to imagine a bustling community of peaceful people that once occupied these spaces, filled with the scent of humanity.

Franz moved like a man with a purpose, turning left, right, stopping to smell and listen, then racing on again. Audrey was again hopelessly lost, thankful her suit tracked their movement. They passed many doorways and meandering tunnels. A Labyrinth indeed.

Franz slowed. The sound of many voices and busy hands swelled, growing louder as they approached an arched doorway to another chamber. Franz stopped them before entering. "This is it, where Wekeep gather. You can stop hiding now."

Audrey and Blake switched off their camouflage, removed their hoods, and tucked their goggles around their necks. Audrey imagined they looked like black giants with lumpy hunch backs next to Franz.

They followed him around the corner and into a large chamber.

50

Wekeep Hospitality

A BUSTLING OF SMALL bodies. Faces swept in their direction. Eyes widened with fear followed by a flurry of movement. Things clanked, bodies swooshed, water splashed, voices cut off, and screams were muffed.

Then—

Stillness. Silence. The bustling chamber was suddenly vacant.

Audrey scanned around, wondering where all the Wekeep had gone. At first she saw nothing, but then she looked closer. Dozens of tiny bodies were thrust into contorted positions. Balled up like yarn, twisted around table legs, flattened to the floor like a rug. Bodies made to mimic everyday things including a few hairy-assed "rocks" like Franz had demonstrated.

The tiny occupants of the gathering chamber were cleverly hidden and if many had not been trembling so badly she may not have noticed their presence at all. Large shiny eyes winked, shifting from one another and back, assessing the black giants who had invaded their space.

Whispery voices carried in the frozen silence.

"What are they?"

"Is that Franz?"

"Sapiens!"

"What are Sapiens doing here?"

"I peed myself."

"I shit myself."

"Ew! Get away from me!"

Franz raised his hands. "You can come out! These are my friends."

Slowly they unrolled, untwisted, and plumped back to their normal forms. A couple of Wekeeps crawled out of a pool of water, soaked and gasping for air. One by one they revealed themselves and gazed back with curiosity. The brave came forward and surrounded them, some poking them in the legs, others sniffing as if what they observed with their noses would answer all of their concerns and questions about these strange beings.

A particularly brave group climbed atop each other's shoulders, stacking up, two, three, then four bodies high, standing atop shoulders. The one carrying the load teetered forward to get a better look.

The group advanced toward Audrey. "Oh!" she exclaimed.

The one carrying the others tripped and the stack of bodies fell against her shoulder and tumbled to the ground. One clung to her braid.

"Ow," she said, reaching for the little Wekeep. The hanger-oner let go and ran away, trembling.

A gaggle of little ones climbed Blake's legs and swung from his arms, their tiny eyes locked on the shiny goggles hanging around his neck. He did a little dance to shake them free. "Stop! Shoo! Help!" he said.

Audrey laughed and came to the rescue, picking up a little girl barely six inches tall who had perched atop his shoulder. She wore a cloth sack with head and arm holes cut out. She fit perfectly into the palm of Audrey's hand. The girl's blinking bright-green eyes were wide as saucers.

Audrey cooed and said, "Hello." The tiny girl squirmed as if trying to get away.

"Oops!" she said in a high-pitched voice. She looked down and began giggling.

A sharp-smelling wetness dripped through Audrey's fingers.

A haggard middle-aged-looking woman came forward to retrieve her, her head barely reaching Audrey's knees. She reached up with a smile and plump rosy cheeks. Audrey set the little girl into the woman's arms.

"A leaker this one, sorry 'bout that." The woman slung the little girl onto her hip and cooed, "Ah, Wendi, it's alright." Then she pulled a scrap of fabric from the pocket of her skirt and handed it to Audrey. It was no bigger than a square of toilet paper. "Not much for wipin' up the mess, but it's all I've got."

Franz was working the room, recounting his story to the other adults about how he met these lost Sapiens. He waved for Blake and Audrey to join him. He wound his arm around the waist of a shy woman with a shock of white hair and a lifetime of wrinkles etched across her face. She wore a faded flowered dress cinched around her rotund waist by a wisp of fabric like the one Franz wore around his hips. "Want you to meet me missus, Snookibottom Sweetfeet Pudfall Slimbabe Gnatswater." He glared at Blake. "But seeing hows that might be too much of a mouthful for ya, just call her Snooki."

Audrey knelt and held out a finger. "I'm Audrey Culliford, but just call me Audrey."

The woman gripped the tip of Audrey's finger between her palms. She smiled and said, "Audrey." She tipped her head toward Blake. "And who is this handsome fella?"

Blake knelt beside Audrey. "Blake Goodfellow."

Snooki blinked. "Goodfellow? Like that mischievous Puck fella from the forest of mystery and darkness?"

Franz jumped in. "Nah, not that *Goodfellow*." His eyes narrowed. "No relation either, I hope."

Blake laughed. "No, it's just a name I chose a long time ago." He gave Snooki a lopsided grin that made her cheeks blush. "Call me Blake."

"You two, er, intended?" she asked.

"Brother and sister," Blake replied.

Her gaze shifted between the two of them. A brief wave of confusion rippled across her wrinkled face.

"Blake's my step-brother," Audrey added.

Her brow crunched into a mountain range of folded skin.

Blake explained, "We have different biological mothers and fathers but we were both raised by Audrey's father." He hooked Audrey's neck with the crook of his arm. She playfully slapped him away. "We only recently learned we're siblings."

Snookie smiled, though she still looked a little confused. "Oh, I see. That's nice."

Franz quipped. "We're hungry and need to rest. Our guests came from one of the abandoned caves in the Desertlands."

Snooki said, "Naturally, you must stay, it'll be dark soon." She clapped her hands and the others stopped whatever it was they were doing and gave her their full attention.

"Assemble a feast for our guests!"

A ruckus of activity exploded.

"Come, this way," Franz said. He spun on his heel and led them down another tunnel, then another, and slipped into one of the many chambers cut into the walls. It had a sofa and a couple of chairs with a table between them. A thick layer of dust covered everything. Off from the living area was a bedroom.

They followed Franz through a twisty hallway to a shower, the switchback entrance offering complete privacy. A generous rush of water poured from a spigot protruding high up on the stone wall and snaked down to a drain in a concave basin carved below. "You clean up here." Franz flashed a toothy smile. "Good thing we didn't shit in the stream."

They backed out of the small space and Franz continued his tour, out of the chamber and into the main tunnel. He pointed to another twisty entrance across the way. "Ya take care of that other business in there, take careful aim, down the chute it goes. Got a nice system for washin' yer bum after."

He bid them farewell. "I'll send the misses back with soap and beddin' and such. Come when you hear the feast horn blow."

Back in their chamber, Audrey stripped off her suit and padded across the hallway in her under-layers to take care of that other business. It was basically a hole in the floor you squatted over. As Franz mentioned, clean up was hands free with no requirement for toilet paper. There was a well-placed spray of water for washing "yer bum" and a blasting breeze flowed through a small hole for drying off and moderating unpleasant smells. An ancient bidet system. She washed her hands in a trickle of water above a wash basin that drained into a hole in the floor.

Shortly after Franz left, Snooki arrived, leading a parade of Wekeep carrying stacks of thick furs, down-filled pads and pillows, bouquets of flowers, baskets of pleasant-smelling soaps and lotions, and a stack of woven fabrics.

Audrey and Blake watched as they dusted shelves, swept floors, and polished the reflective surfaces, catching light projected from a hole in the ceiling. They cushioned chairs and beds with down-filled pads and furs. They made up beds with soft fabrics and wool blankets. Down-filled pillows were tossed about. Towels were hung on wooden hooks in the shower room. Soaps and lotions were neatly arranged on shelves. A stack of skareefs was left on the spotlessly clean table. Flowers were distributed throughout, emitting pleasant scents.

Snooki beamed at the result. "We've had these items for many years collected from your Seakai friends."

"It's lovely, thank you!" Audrey said.

Audrey and Blake played a quick round of rock, paper, scissors to see who got to shower first. Blake won. He stripped off his suit and padded through the left-right jog into the shower room, wearing only his boxers.

Audrey picked through the skareefs on the table. They were worn and faded but would suit them just fine. The Wekeep must have scavenged what was left after the Seakai vacated the Labyrinth. Worn skareefs, old furs, and chipped vases were given a second life.

She chose a skareef in a faded green. The color reminded her of the natural world, of vitality, of the color of Sinto's eyes. Thinking of him warmed her heart and the Mark buried in her arm and she suddenly felt compelled to send him a message. Not just any message, but the message of *salamora*—one of love and a promise upon parting to meet again. She regretted their last parting. It was anything but a love-filled promise, with bitter words of disagreement. She had no idea if it would work but felt compelled to try.

Salamora was expressed in more than simple words. It was a sharing drawn from the depths of the heart and soul—what the Merahvu call *essence*. It was her essence—the whole of her—which she committed to Sinto the day she Marked him, and him to her by accepting it.

She closed her eyes and forged a connection through the Mark. One that knew no bounds, regardless of which world they currently inhabited. She shared that she was safe. Told of how she and Blake had mastered mind-speak and with their suits could move stealthily in his ancestral world. That their current mission was to find his sister. She shared the story of meeting Franz, of the Wekeeps and their generous hospitality. She told him she missed him terribly.

And after passing her message through the Mark, she clasped her hands at her heart and said the words she needed to say. A prayer, if only for her own benefit. "Dearest Sinto, I promise to return to you and when I do, we will embark on our intended journey and embrace our mutual purpose. I am yours, the all of me, the whole of my essence. *Salamora*, my love."

There was slight tremor in her arm where the Mark lay. She opened her eyes surprised. Saying the words filled a void that had left her cold and empty. She felt whole for the first time since she and Sinto parted. She imagined that those who frequently prayed to a God they believed in must feel the same way afterward. Filled with hope, knowing you were not alone. She hoped the tremor in her arm meant Sinto felt the same.

She felt compelled to send him another message. One much more intimate that made her blush. Strange how one can think of such intimate things or the mere sensation of holding tight to the one you love when the world is falling apart. Thoughts that gave incentive to soldier on.

Blake broke her deep thoughts when he emerged with damp hair and a towel wrapped around his waist.

"Ahh, a little piece of heaven," he said. "Sorry, I left a ring of grime." He dropped his boxers atop his discarded under-layers. "No way I'm putting those back on."

Audrey wiped a tear from her cheek. She patted the stack of skareefs on the table. "Know how to tie these?"

He grinned. "Leela showed me. Been awhile, but I'll manage."

She tossed him a blue one, then twisted her way left and right into the shower.

The water was lukewarm and refreshing and the soap an exquisite blend of every delicious flower that must grow on Merluma. She scrubbed every inch of her body and worked the suds along her scalp between the trio of braids woven tightly against her head, then into the braids themselves, and finally the prickly shaved part at the base of her skull. The grime in the drain bowl at her feet was twice as thick.

She patted herself dry and wound the green skareef around her waist, between her legs and across her chest with a double criss-cross. She secured it around her waist with a double-knot.

She grabbed her pungent under-layers and went back out to the main living area where a couple of women were waiting to take her dirty clothes.

Audrey wasn't sure if it was good idea to give them up. Dirty was better than none. She looked to Blake for advice. He shrugged. "I gave them mine."

Audrey knelt to meet their faces. "Very important that these are returned," she said to the two younger looking women.

"Yes, yes," they exclaimed. "Soon and smelling sweet as a moondew flower!" They turned and scurried out the door with their smelly loads.

Audrey glanced at their suits lying across the chairs, in particular the attached goggles, shiny and very tempting. "What about these? Did you see the way they went for your goggles?"

"And Franz for the guard's silver buttons. They have a thing for shiny objects."

"Should we hide them?"

"I don't think it will make any difference with their sniffers."

"Best to leave them out and make certain Franz understands they're off limits."

"Any way to electrify our suits? Not much, but a jolt that would make them think twice."

He nodded. "Good idea. Hand yours over."

She did. He fiddled with the buttons on her suit until she heard a slight crackle. "Ow!" he flung it across one of the chairs. "That'll teach anyone who touches them!" He did the same electrifying trick to his suit.

The sound of a low rumbling horn resonated through the tunnels followed by the padding of many tiny feet. The call to the feast Franz told them to listen for. They stepped out of their private chamber and joined the steady stream of knee-high Wekeeps meandering their way to the gathering chamber.

51

Franz's Code

The gathering chamber was filled with mouth-watering smells of roasted meat with savory herbs, poached fish, baked bread, and freshly cut fruits. An odd assortment of platters and bowls and utensils were stacked at the end of a long table piled high with a buffet of delectable eats. More things left behind by the Seakai and put to practical use by the Wekeep.

A long line of tiny bodies had formed. Lips smacked and sniffers sniffed. Pleasant murmurs of anticipation swirled with mouthwatering scents.

Franz waved Blake and Audrey to the front of the buffet line. They tried to refuse, feeling uncomfortable cutting ahead of the others. Based on the grunts from some Wekeeps, they agreed. Though most insisted their guests should go first, so reluctantly they did. Franz handed them the largest of the plates from a haphazardly stacked pile of dishes and encouraged them to take as much as they wanted.

Audrey was starved for real food. While the nutrition sticks were highly concentrated and nutritious, they never quite satisfied her hunger. It took great restraint not to over-heap her plate, considering the many mouths to feed.

They sat with Franz and Snooki on woven mats, which were laid in a large circle on the floor. This was not normal, Franz informed them. Usually they ate in smaller groups. But tonight was special, a gathering where stories would be shared once bellies were filled.

A trio of older-looking men came over with two mugs and a pitcher of honey mead. They handed full mugs to Audrey and Blake. The men lingered while they took their first sip. The mead was sweet and delicious and quite potent. Then they gestured for Audrey and Blake to gulp it down, which they did. Their mugs were quickly refilled as was customary with the Wekeep. Others beside them gulped theirs down, then held their mugs up for more.

Audrey set down her second mug full of mead without drinking it, feeling a little light-headed from the first. She decided it best to keep her wits sharp, knowing Arkis and his guards were nearby within the Labyrinth with nothing but meandering tunnels in between.

After they ate their fill, the young ones gathered the mugs and dishes. Wendi, the little girl who had peed on Audrey when they first arrived, waddled up to her and held out her arms. The dress had been replaced by a thick diaper covering her tiny bottom. Soft downy hair covered her body and the top of her head. Audrey picked her up and laid her in the crook of her arm like a kitten. She felt warm and soft and smelled of sugar and spice and everything pleasant about babies. Audrey smiled down at her, fingering her soft belly. The little girl giggled in delight. Sharing a quiet moment with one so young and innocent was a much-needed reprieve from the reason they were here.

Franz said, "This is the part where you tell us a story."

"Us?" Audrey asked, looking up from her new friend.

"Yeah, like why yer here and why it matters."

"Oh." Audrey said, swinging her gaze to Blake.

Blake pushed, *"They need to know the truth. Arkis' campaign affects them as much as us. It's only a matter of time before he stops thinking them a mere nuisance and takes action to recruit or destroy them."*

Audrey set the little girl in her lap. "Our story is a long one, and begins with conflict. A conflict that bloomed into outright war that has united Sapiens and Merahvu against a great and threatening tribe, the Orankai. The same Orankai who lurk just outside these tunnels." Audrey paused as anxious whispers echoed throughout the chamber. "We're here to stop them and eliminate their leader, Arkis.

There was an eruption of undecipherable whispers and hisses.

One voice rang out, "Arkis bad."

Audrey continued once they settled. "Yes, Arkis is very bad, and he resides not far from here, and has kidnapped someone very important. Naiada, the daughter of Queen Ianthe."

The chamber filled with a collective, "Ohh, no!"

Audrey continued once it quieted. "Naiada's father, Ramasis, is helping Arkis, but we're not sure of his intentions, whether he's protecting her or allowing Arkis to use her as a weapon of war. We believe she's being held captive here in the Labyrinth against her will, or worse, she may be helping Arkis."

There were more whispered conversations and Audrey got the sense that the Wekeep were more aware of the situation than Franz may have led them to believe. The Wekeep, while helpful, were very secretive. More reason to win their trust and, more importantly, gain their help.

Blake picked up the story. "Arkis controls the Orankai by forcing them to drink an orange nectar. We believe its source comes from Earth, created from a fungus that is wreaking havoc in Earth's oceans. This nectar is addictive and makes anyone who consumes it susceptible to manipulation. Arkis rules by fear and intimidation, and places no value on the natural world or the creatures that live in it. He is also using this orange nectar to breed an army somewhere in the mountains."

A young male with hair cut in a mohawk raised his hand. Blake gestured for him to say something. "I've smelled it, them caves. They stink of agony and death. He breeds pure evil."

Others nodded and whispered the same sentiments.

Audrey said, "That is just one challenge we face." She told them more about Orange and its destructive spread across Earth's oceans and of the Larkians' fight to contain it. "If we destroy the source of his orange nectar we strike at the heart of his advantage."

"But that is not his only advantage," Blake added. "Arkis also has a secret weapon we are unsure of. He has foreseen every one of our attempts to stop him. It is why Audrey and I are trapped here. Arkis knew of our plans and sent spies to mislead us. We were attacked but managed to defeat them. We know we can win if only we can learn how he is able to predict our every move."

"Witches," someone muttered.

"What was that?" Audrey asked.

"E's got witches," an older woman said in a raspy voice. "Three of 'em."

"Grotesque things, they are," another added.

"And a magic crystal ball," the mutterer muttered.

The room burst with the sound of *oohs* and *ahhs*.

"What kind of *crystal ball*?" Audrey asked.

"A shiny one with a green center that glows," Franz piped up.

Blake turned to Franz. "Where did it come from?"

Franz shrugged. "Nobody knows. One day it showed up, then the witches, then bad things started happening. Little stuff at first."

"When did this start?"

His face twisted in thought. "Many full moons ago, so many, lost count."

Blake said, "That doesn't make sense. It was, what, three months ago that Ianthe was attacked and Naiada kidnapped."

"Yes it does," Audrey said. "You're thinking in *Earth* time. On Merluma time spins much faster; one hour on Earth being one day on Merluma." She ticked off the numbers in her head. "Three months since she was taken, one month training before that... so roughly four months have passed on Earth. Which means—" She blew out an exasperated breath. "Nearly *eight* years have passed on Merluma since Naiada was abducted. It means Naiada is no longer a child but a full-grown adult."

"That's another advantage Arkis has. Time, and lots of it. To convert Naiada, to plan, react, to breed." Blake's face fell as he considered the impossible situation.

"Not if we strike down his primary advantages. What if we—" Audrey stopped abruptly, realizing their mistake; Wekeeps hung on every word passing between them.

Her mind swirled. If Arkis had these so-called "witches" and some sort of crystal ball that allowed him to foresee or observe everything, then he could potentially foresee Audrey and Blake's presence among the Wekeep and the details of their very public conversation, here and now.

She grasped Blake's hand. "We need to change the subject. *Now.*"

Blake's brow furrowed, then shot up as he realized the same thing. "I agree."

Franz sharply picked up the vibe passing between Audrey and Blake. He stood and clapped his hands three times, very loudly. "To bed, wee ones!"

Audrey pushed to Blake, "*How can these witches know everything? I don't believe in magic, but what if there is something special about this so-called crystal ball?*"

"*Remember what Arkis stole from Ianthe.*"

Audrey gasped. "*Her ovaries.*"

"*What if he bred those witches with her eggs.*"

"*Oh shit. Multiply Ianthe's power of foresight by three.*"

Audrey and Blake retired to their chamber, surprising a pair of adolescent Wekeep boys who had sneaked inside. One was hopping around with his hand pinched between his thighs and emitting a high-pitched yowl. They bolted when Audrey and Blake entered.

"Looks like your trick worked," Audrey said.

Shortly after, Franz came knocking. "What's up with them boys? Screaming like a couple of banshees who dipped their fingers in the wrong cookie jar."

Blake gave him a look that said it all.

"Uh, right, sorry 'bout that. We see, we like, we take, we keep."

Blake said, "Well, we *protect*, and there are consequences. That one's thieving hand will smart for a while but he'll live."

Franz sighed. "Gotta do what ya gotta do... anyway, I was thinking, um, um..." His bushy brows wadded in deep thought. "Not sure how to say this thing I must say without really saying it. Ya get what I mean?" His gaze was wandering around the room as if searching for some unseen presence.

Audrey smiled. "Loud and clear."

"Like a code," Blake added.

"Uh huh," Franz said. "I scratched out some ideas." He held out an old chalk board the size of a sheet of paper. The surface was scratched and pale from years of repeated use. The wooden frame wrapped around it was cracked and dented from being dropped several times. It was an object Audrey would expect to find in her world, not Franz's, but then she remembered him telling them he frequented Earth through a land-accessible portal. Probably lifted during one of his many journeys along with who knew what else.

We see, we like, we take, we keep.

Was it possible the theory of gremlins was real? *Not gremlins, but Wekeeps.* She chuckled at the very real possibility. She was staring at it and his name was Franz.

Audrey looked past the object to what Franz had scratched out on the surface with the nub of chalk pinched between his gnarled fingers. Franz presented a simple list of the relevant things they had discussed with an equal sign followed with another word that meant something creatively different but easily remembered. It went like this:

Arkis = cad

Ramasis = nutjob

Naiada = dove
Witches = bats
Guards = birdbrains
Orankai = trolls
Crystal Ball = puzzle
Audrey = butterfly
Blake = lion
Wekeep = bear
Larkian = lizard
Merahvu = fish
Earth = desert
Merluma = ocean
Labyrinth = knot
Breeding Caves = hotbox
Winterland = icebox
Everybody else = fawn

Franz said, "Memorize it. Say the code word instead of the real word when we talk about important stuff. Works with the wee ones when us old ones want a private conversation. We'll make up more as we go along."

Audrey and Blake studied the list and nodded in agreement.

"Oh, one more thing. Bears like the butterfly and the lion and offer to help eradicate the bats and the trolls from the knot."

"And what about cad and the puzzle?"

He grinned. "The bears love puzzles, especially ones with shiny surfaces. Hate to see the wrong party possess 'em. We'll leave cad to the butterfly and the lion to do with as they please."

52

Pure Luck

FIRE. PAIN. AGONY, PURE *and fierce. The creak of leather between his clenched jaws, skull screaming in protest at the compounding pressure between his teeth. The blaze of sucuvita in his system, roaring through his veins and feeding new life into his injuries. Pain unlike anything he'd ever felt. Feeling that if he endured a moment longer of that pain, he would snap. But then, at his breaking point, a mercifully deep and quiet darkness.*

Sinto woke with a jolt, startled by a soft caress across his brow. His mother stood over him; she smiled when he found her gaze.

"My son, how are you feeling?"

It took a few moments to shake off the vivid memory. He lay in the same bed, the room smelling strongly of antiseptic. He tried to smile back but his jaw and cheeks ached from clenching the leather strap Dr. Wickman had placed in his teeth.

But it was worth the pain to smile. He breathed deeply, relieved by the lingering ache deep in his mended bones and the intense prickle of the new skin he felt on his right hand. It meant he still had one. His mother leaned back and gestured to his arm lying across his stomach. He raised his head to look.

His arm was cocooned in a clear plastic bubble from his elbow down, warm air circulating around it. From what he could see he had all five fingers, albeit a bit bonier than before, with a full layer of pink skin. The skin along his forearm looked equally healthy, like that of a newborn.

His pinkie twitched, bringing a fresh round of joy.

The side of his abdomen itched; that place Wantemo suggested they cut away a layer of skin to help accelerate the healing process. Similar patches of tingling and itching erupted beneath bandages on his left arm. The source of tendon, vessel, fibrous tissue, and muscle Wantemo and Dr. Wickman used to seed the rejuvenation process. He embraced the strange and nagging sensations. It meant his body was healing. The combined efforts by Sinto, Wantemo, and Dr. Wickman were a success.

His head dropped back to the soft pillow. "I feel thankful and relieved."

"Wantemo said you were very brave."

"I—I cannot remember much." He worked his jaw. "Except biting down on that strap and focusing on not breaking my teeth while imagining building my hand to be as it was, from the bones up." He pulled his lips back into a grimace.

She smiled. "Well, your teeth appear to be in perfect shape."

He tried to move his right index finger. It was stiff but functional. He moved the others one at a time. All stiff and achy but each joint bent as he hoped. The thumb was the weakest as well as his ability to grip. Sinto wondered if he would ever again be able to hold something as heavy as the stone he had retrieved.

His mother must have been peeking into his thoughts. She said, "In due time. You will gain strength with proper exercises and rest. Wantemo and Dr. Wickman are optimistic you will fully recover the use of your hand."

"How long till then?"

"That will depend on you. Push yourself too soon and too hard..." She shrugged. "And it will take forever."

He scoffed. "Great, sidelined in the middle of a war."

Her brow furrowed. "You are forgetting one important thing."

"What?"

"Wars are not won purely by brawn. They are won by patience, resources, strategy and timing." She tapped him between the eyes. "Use your *brain*."

"You forgot one other important thing. Luck."

With that she smiled and nodded. "Yes, indeed, and luck you found aplenty."

"You mean my finding the stone?"

"Yes."

"Have you used it to find Audrey?"

"No. Using the stone may prove to be a mistake. Arkis is very clever. He has found a way to access the Timeless Dimension."

"Naiada?"

She pondered before answering. "Not sure, but I am certain someone has passed through, besides myself."

"What should we do with the stone?"

"That is a question I've yet to answer. Now rest."

Rest he did. The next time he woke Wantemo was at his side.

"Greetings, young Sinto! Or shall I call you Rip Van Winkle, the one who sleeps through a great revolution!"

"What day is it?"

"Does it matter?"

He tried to sit up but it was cumbersome with the large bubble enclosing his arm.

"Let me help you." Wantemo pressed a button and the top half of the bed began to rise to a sitting position. "Adjustable beds, what a wonderful Sapien invention!"

Sinto's legs were restless and his butt numb. "I feel like I've slept for a lifetime."

"Only two days, but rest well-needed. Your essentials were in need of replenishment."

He squirmed around. "When can I get out of this prison of a bed?"

"Now if you would like."

Wantemo helped him swing his legs off the side of the bed. The rubber flooring felt solid and cool to his bare feet. "Take it slow, you've been immobile for a while. Give your legs a chance to wake up."

Sinto stood. His legs felt shaky, foreign for someone as active as he was, but not for the first time. He felt the same way after Wantemo saved him from his near-fatal knife wound.

Sinto held up his right arm. "And this, how long must I wear this ridiculous bubble?"

"No longer. Dr. Wickman insisted just as a precaution against infection. We kept it pumped with pure oxygen to help the healing process. We both learned a great many new things from each other at your expense."

"No expense, I still have my hand."

"We will see if you have that same enthusiasm once we run a few strength tests."

Wantemo released a plastic tube from the bubble with a loud hiss. The transparent plastic retracted around Sinto's arm. Wantemo slowly rolled it back from the tender skin starting with the end next to Sinto's elbow. Once his hand was free, he tried to make a fist.

"That's a good sign. How does it feel?"

"Like I slept a lifetime and woke up old like you."

Wantemo tsked. "Watch it, Sinto, I can hold my own against cocky young bucks such as yourself."

They shared a chuckle and a hug. "It feels weak but functional."

"The bones were compromised. I suggest you refrain from punching things with your right hand, and I mean *ever*."

Sinto felt a sudden wave of relief and tears welled in his eyes. "That I can do, otherwise, I couldn't imagine my life without such an important appendage as a hand."

"Appendages are important but they do not dictate what one is capable of. It is what you do that determines who you are, hand or no hand. But truthfully, I would agree, life can certainly be made easier when you keep most of the parts you were born with." He reached for his other arm. "Let us get you ready to roar, shall we?"

He removed the bandages from Sinto's stomach and other arm and inspected each of the various places they had taken healthy pieces of tissue. The incisions had healed completely and barely left a scar, including the place on his abdomen. Wantemo must have stitched him up and smoothed the surface, a signature of his fine work.

Wantemo said, "At this rate you will have a full map of life misadventures covering your entire body before you reach your thirtieth birthday."

"Let us hope this war ends soon."

"Then go and make it so. Rachel is waiting for you with the others in the command room. She wanted me to tell you she is pleased you have recovered, but it is time to get to work. They desperately need help."

53

Double Conundrum

SINTO ENTERED THE COMMAND center at a tense time. The room was packed. Most of the Larkian council members were there: Alvarez, Francesca, Dr. Wickman, Leonard, Culliford. Blake was still missing along with Audrey. Sinto could only believe them to be safe, or else he'd go mad with worry and render himself useless. He trusted the Mark and the warm vibrations he frequently felt, which he believed to be messages sent from Audrey. At the moment it was at peace.

Also in attendance were the remaining members of the Circle, plus Wantemo and Ianthe. Ryan, Rachel, and Alvarez lined one end of the table, each of them with dark circles under their eyes. There was a small team of men and women surrounding Francesca that Sinto had yet to meet.

Sinto slipped into an open seat beside his mother. She reached for his good hand and gave him a reassuring squeeze. *"Good to have you among us,"* she shared.

Rachel acknowledged him from across the room with a faint smile, no dimples, aura dim.

Alvarez took the floor. "First order of business this morning." He cleared his throat. "A planned attack against Arkis is under way on Merluma. Communication between the command center and the teams in the Winterlands has been challenging. We're relying on our Scouts passing between the earth worlds for updates. The last message described their current campaign. We won't know the result until it is complete."

He looked down at his laptop. "I received a message from Stokes this morning. It says, 'Arkis is hiding in a cave network deep in Terrakai territory, west of the Black Mountains. He has Naiada and is keeping her close, along with Ramasis. Khani believes the fortifications surrounding the caves are still intact, but we are taking utmost caution knowing of Arkis' reputation of setting traps. Naiada's safety is top priority. A tactical team is tasked to find and free her. Team Xiphias will be deployed offshore. Khani's warriors will approach from land. Then we'll tighten the noose and drive them out.'"

Alvarez looked up and captured Sinto's gaze. "Apparently a fleet of Scout raptors infiltrated the nearby Orankai camps to gain information about Arkis' whereabouts, a fleet led by a raptor named Moonstone."

Sinto's heart leaped with pride hearing of Moonstone's contribution.

Beat swift and cautiously my friend.

"May we wish the team success." Alvarez concluded. "Now we wait."

The auras swirling in the command center were restless and anxious. His mother's simmered hot at the mention of Naiada's predicament.

Sinto's gaze cut to his mother. *"Ramasis is responsible for putting her in the middle of this."*

She closed her eyes, her aura shifting from orange to red.

Alvarez continued, "I'd like to add another troubling development that impacts the mission. Khani's team still hasn't heard from Blake and Audrey, which is distressing, but not surprising with their limited ability to communicate. Without any new information, there isn't much we can speculate regarding their whereabouts or current status. Sinto, is there anything you'd like to add?"

Sinto sat forward. "We must remain optimistic. While I feel uneasy with the situation, I believe Audrey and Blake are capable of taking care of themselves." He looked to Culliford who nodded his affirmation.

"Thank you, Sinto, for your honest words." Alvarez tipped his chin toward Francesca. "We have more business to cover while we wait for news. Francesca?"

Francesca stood and used a remote to switch on one of the TV screens mounted to the conference room wall. On the screen was a map of the United States.

"There are two urgent situations we're tracking." She picked up a pen-like object that shot a bright red laser across the room. She used it to circle clusters of orange dots around the Great Lakes and the entire West Coast. "The first regards an increase of mysterious deaths we believe are caused by a step-up of Orankai activity in these areas, mainly around the Great Lakes and along the West Coast.

"Each orange dot represents a community we suspect they have infiltrated. Note how they are avoiding the larger cities." She zoomed into an area around Lake Superior, where some dots were larger than others. "Some instances occurred on the outskirts of Duluth, but look at what is happening in the more rural communities. The larger the dot the more recorded deaths per capita." She zoomed in tighter, to a small town along the lake's shore with one of the largest dots. "Death happens, but not normally at this rate. Most puzzling is how they die." She pulled up a chart titled, "Top Leading Causes of Death by Age Group."

She shook her head. "This next part defies logic, but the types of these excessive deaths map closely to this chart, with the exception of cancer, which takes time. It's as if Arkis studied this chart and decided to use it as a guideline—accidental injury, suicide, homicide, and heart disease, which we track as fatal heart attacks—down to the most frequent cause by age group. The only reason I can imagine why he's doing this is to confuse the authorities, which is exactly what is happening. It's not random but well-thought out. Except for one method puzzling the medical community: heart attacks. Seemingly healthy people are dropping dead. Their hearts literally stop beating."

"That's not surprising," Sinto said. Every eye swung in his direction. "It takes very little for us to target the heart with our merlux. A jolt precisely aimed at the heart would easily stop it from beating, with no obvious side effects. As far as the other types of death, I could imagine Orange playing a role. Slip it into someone's drink or water source and they become part of the Orankai hive. Once that happens, they can be manipulated to do anything; murder your neighbor, kill yourself, stage any type of accident."

Francesca sighed. "Meanwhile, morgues are filling up. Eventually officials may get involved in a big way. But before then, the Orankai continue to infiltrate the everyday life of innocent people. And we're seeing glimpses of this occurring globally. So we must ask: How do you stop thousands of psycho-serial killers who can shift their appearance in the blink of an eye? Even if they get caught on camera or leave evidence—such as DNA—it would be impossible to identify or track them down, since they're not from Earth."

Surah from the Circle said, "Our only option is to root out Arkis and defeat the Orankai."

"Correct." Francesca switched screens. An entire map of the Pacific Ocean and surrounding shorelines popped up. "Which leads us to the second situation we face; the proliferation of Orange. I don't think I need to remind you of the potential implications. But once Orange reaches any shore, there will be nothing we can do to stop the intervention of local governments, the United States as well as others. How they react may prove catastrophic."

"Bet he's already thought of that." said Leonard. "Probably planned fer it."

"Very possible," Alvarez said. "But let's not get ahead of ourselves, just yet." He gestured to Francesca. "Proceed."

She circled the large orange blob that sat stubbornly between California and the Hawaiian archipelago: the location of the Great Pacific garbage patch with the largest accumulation of plastic garbage.

"Several ships passing through the area have been infected. We've employed every ship in our fleet plus several we've commissioned to intercept each one. So far we've been able to keep up, but it's possible we're unaware of all of them."

She smiled at Rachel. "Our goal is to contain Orange in a singular location until we determine the best way to contain or destroy it permanently, and we believe the best way to do that is to give it what it wants. More plastic."

She clicked a button on the remote. Green dots began populating the map from all over the Pacific Rim and several more, forming a circled pattern around the core location of Orange.

"Six weeks ago we formed a company—Global Coalition, or GC—to collect plastic that has been piling up for years at recycling and garbage collection sites from several Pacific nations. Plastic that would have ended up in their landfills or flushed out to sea. So far we have not made a big stir with our action and have obscured any connection to the Larkian nation. We are quietly relieving participating countries of their plastic refuse. Unsurprisingly, they have been more than willing to give it to us for free. GC has hired every possible ship, barge, and contractor service to aid us in this endeavor. What is collected is heated and compacted into tight bundles. We call these 'breadcrumbs.' These plastic breadcrumbs have been strategically dumped around the gyre to keep Orange from migrating."

She circled the green dots around the gyre with the red laser.

"For obvious reasons we're acutely aware of the need of stealth to avoid catching the attention of environmentalists. We've cloaked our activities under the guise of ocean cleanup efforts, which is not entirely untrue. Orange pretty much sucks up every breadcrumb we dump. Details of which we would rather not explain publicly."

She flicked on a third screen, mapping the various swirls of currents where plastic had accumulated across the Northern Pacific. "There are actually multiple gyres where plastic gets caught. Orange originated here, in the eastern section between California and Hawaii with the largest concentration. We recently witnessed a small finger stretching northward toward a swirl north of the origin."

She pointed to the top swirl and a finger of orange dots leading to it. "We successfully redirected this migration back to the origin."

She refreshed the screen. The finger of Orange that had escaped was gone. "Our goal is to continue our efforts to keep it contained. It's not perfect, nor is it a long-term solution, but one that may buy us valuable time to come up with a permanent solution. Meanwhile, we continue to observe biologic activity around the site. We believe it to be Orankai harvesting Orange and transporting what they collect to Merluma through a portal in the North Pacific."

She prompted for questions. No one had any.

She gestured to a bespectacled young man of Asian descent among her Larkian team. "Hiro is a geologist who has been researching possible sites for containing Orange."

Hiro stood. "Hello," he said, nervously. "Uh." He looked at Francesca, who nodded encouragement. "Our findings are disappointing. We have not yet found a suitable location to contain Orange. Most challenging is the volume to be considered and potential environmental impact."

Culliford raised his hand. "What about depleted oil or natural gas drilling sites?"

Hiro smiled, his confidence visibly building. "Good question. Voids created in earth's mantle from pumping oil and gas were our first targets for investigation and we found many possibilities. Unfortunately, Orange is not an inanimate substance that can be manipulated like water or gas. It is a live organism and with that comes characteristics that must be considered. Like its potential to increase in mass when consuming whatever oil or gas remain in those spaces, which could catastrophically stress the geology around any void we might choose. But the most prominent is its will to survive. It becomes defensive whenever we attempt to manipulate it. Which, of course, would be necessary to pump it into any of the sites we have identified."

Sinto raised his hand. "So even if we could find the ideal location, Orange may reject any of our efforts to contain it."

"While your question is outside of my expertise, it is my opinion that what you say is most likely true." He gestured toward Ryan. "The team studying Orange should be able to elaborate more on this topic."

Francesca said, "Thank you, Hiro, for your assessment and to your team for all your hard work."

Hiro nodded and returned to his seat amongst the others.

Francesca switched off the screens. "We have played through every possible scenario: luring it into large tanks, onto barges, into naturally carved-out spaces in the ground... all with the same conclusion; it won't work. Bottom line, we need to come up with a different solution, and soon."

Across the table from Sinto, Rachel slumped chin to chest. Her tiny body melted into the chair, her perpetual enthusiasm deflated. It was a good idea she had proposed and at least part of it had been the right solution—how to keep Orange where they wanted it—but the core problem remained unsolved: how to contain and neutralize it.

The room stewed in silence, digesting this latest news.

In that moment of silence, thick enough to feel, Isden burst through an open sliding door, blood streaming from his nose.

54

Power Of Connection

SINTO JUMPED TO HIS feet and bolted to Isden's side. Francesca's team backed away as Sinto helped him settle in a chair at the conference table. Wantemo and Dr. Wickman began surveying him for injuries. Others stood back in shock not quite sure what to do.

Isden gasped. "Arkis knew we were coming. It was a trap! He knew about our raptor Scouts long before they were deployed. He tricked them, fed them lies! He knew of our teams hunkered in the City of Ice. He knew about our Xiphias fleet in the Great Ocean. He—he ferreted out every part of our plan!"

Isden was visibly shaken. Wantemo patted his shoulder. "Settle now, catch your breath." Sinto offered him water. Once he caught his breath, he continued, "Khani has ordered a retreat. Those who are able are returning here."

Sinto asked, "Did you see Audrey or Blake?"

Isden looked at him as if he was crazy. "I thought you knew, they're gone." Tears burst from his eyes. "Arkis slipped two of his Scouts onto my team that lead them through the portal, with the order to take them out. We learned Audrey and Blake were specifically targeted. I had no idea. I am so sorry."

Sinto squeezed his shoulder reassuringly. "We believe they survived. How, or where they may be, we don't know." Sinto drew confidence from the Mark, vibrating with vitality. "But trust me, Audrey, at least, is still alive." He glanced at his mother. "And we have good reason to believe Blake is too."

Isden's face rippled as he absorbed Sinto's message, relief tangled up with guilt and angst, a full spectrum of emotion flaring through his aura. The room was awash with it.

Isden said, "I wish that were true of others."

The meeting turned to chaos, some realizing it was time to leave, while others were stunned and stuck to their seats. Alvarez knelt beside Isden, gathering as much information as possible while fresh in his mind.

Sinto sought out his mother's mind among the chaos. "*How can Arkis know these things? We have the stone!*"

"*I do not know.*" Then she slipped out the back door.

Sinto turned to Wantemo. No words were necessary; he waved for Sinto to follow Ianthe.

He bolted after her. "*Where are you going?*"

"*I must learn his secret!*"

His mother rounded the far end of the compound and sprinted down the path that led to her home. Sinto quickly caught up. She stopped and turned to face him. Both of them were gasping from exertion.

He said, "How do you plan to do that?"

She said nothing.

She didn't have to; he knew before he asked. "With the stone."

"Yes."

"But at what risk?"

"Everything we do is a risk. Doing nothing could be the greatest risk of all!"

"Then we take this journey together."

Once they reached her house Sinto waited outside while she retrieved the Salish Stone from its hiding place. She came to the door with the stone wrapped in a forest-green blanket hugged to her chest.

"Wait." Sinto knew they could no longer take any chances and surveyed the sky for spies. The Larkian defense system had not considered the likelihood of spies penetrating their defenses by sky. Raptors, like Moonstone and those he encountered on Andrew's Island, could easily be released by Orankai outside their defense system. The trees were silent. He scanned deeper, relying on senses beyond his vision, such as the flicker of a warm-blooded body or that of an aura venting. He saw none.

"Let's go, quickly," he said reaching for her. They traversed the soft path to the clearing deep in the jungle, Sinto diligently scanning the skies.

Once there, his mother laid the bundle she held to her chest in the center of the clearing and pulled back the corners of the blanket until it was laid smooth with the stone lying in the center. She dropped to her knees and directed Sinto to do the same across from her.

She placed her hand on the stone and gently placed Sinto's weakened hand beside hers. Then they repeated the same with their other hands until the surface of the stone was fully connected to the palms of their hands, with their smallest fingers overlapping.

"Surrender yourself to the stone. Hold nothing back, expose every secret, every painful memory you may have locked away, every want you desire, every fear you hold. The stone only guides those with purity of mind and essence."

What she asked from him went against everything he had fought to conceal from prying minds—inner-most thoughts, weaknesses, and fears. Offensive actions and feelings that ate one's moral conscience. Others that he cherished and deeply wished for. Things he was ashamed of, things he desired, things he was proud of—the totality of the essence of who he was, including his vulnerabilities. What she asked of him was terrifying. An inner stranger revealed. A sacrifice of self, laid bare. There would be no going back.

Her eyes were on fire. *"Do not be frightened. Know I must do the same."*

"How does one let go of those things they have held dear, as secrets from themself?"

"Just do it! Gaze into my eyes, open your mind, and think of nothing but your desire to learn and discover, to understand and feel: What is the universal truth?"

Sinto did as she asked, laid his essence bare and surrendered to the stone.

The stone fevered and quivered beneath their palms. A wash of amber light encircled them, an impermeable bubble of a mysterious force. A force beyond anything Sinto had experienced in the natural world, a force entwined within the essence of the universe into which he was born, of which he was a tiny but significant part.

The stone seized Sinto's essence, laid bare as it was, and ripped it from his physical body.

The jungle faded.

Sinto hovered as an ethereal body within a sea of darkness surrounded by glittering stars.

Those things he cherished and feared seemed intangible and meaningless in the realm in which he found himself, a speck of stardust caught in a gossamer webbing that connected one to a universal place, one entity to another, on and on to infinity. A minute yet critically significant thing intertwined and tangled together with the tangible things collected from the essence of self, his as well as his mother's, and of every other living thing, no matter how big or small—the microbe, the fish, the tree... pieces accumulated into a singular, universal truth.

Without universal truth there would be nothing. The living and the inanimate, waiting to be freed like the core of the stone that delivered him to this meditative state, depended upon it. A universal truth that gifted him a living, breathing body filled with vitality and life. A simple construct that filled his consciousness with the understanding that the good and the bad and the messy parts in between were merely ingredients in the recipe of self. Ingredients not to be judged or dismissed or greedily horded, but accepted, for the essential truth of life depended on each and every ingredient presented, no matter how perfect or flawed.

The universal truth was life itself and its infinite number of connections. At the end of one life, another was spawned by repurposing its scattered elements. New connections ready to form. An endless tangle of threads woven throughout the universe, shifting and changing, growing and shrinking, never ceasing but ever-present.

The universal truth could never be refuted because without life and its tangle of connections there would be nothing. *Nothing* cannot have a say in the parsing of the universal truth because *nothing* was void of the essential elements of argument. Nothingness was nothing, nothing was anti-truth.

And once Sinto and his mother fully embraced this universal truth and its endless connections, they were propelled forward.

The stone prompted in only the way an inanimate form of life could: by seeding a thought into the minds of those possessing it; a question linked to the infinite bundle of universal connections, asked in the simplest way possible.

The stone said, "*Which thread shall I follow?*"

Sinto replied back in thought, not in an ordinary way with words, but as an intended journey, on which he and his mother were ready to embark.

He replied, "*The Mark shared between myself and another.*"

The darkness and glittering stars scattered and they found themselves, animated, in a life situation. Running, light-footed, through a musty and dimly lit space, a series of vast tunnels carved in stone beneath the ground with twists and turns and meandering stairways, descending deeper, but where? The sound of rushing water murmured nearby, fading and growing as they beat feet.

An aged, bald Wekeep ran ahead, leading. He came to a sudden stop when the tunnel they were in met another, more brightly lit. A crossroad. He paused, sniffing as Wekeep do to assess their surroundings. His eyes widened and he pressed flat as a pancake against the dusty stone wall just beyond the light, a dirty finger pressed to lips.

Fear filled his eyes as he gazed back, the message clear: *Danger! Quiet!*

Sinto and his mother, as observers, heard the hushed pant of nervous breath and a wildly beating heart. Stress-sweat twined with a spicy body-scent Sinto recognized immediately.

Audrey.

There was a subtle shifting of the stone wall. Two people camouflaged, effective but not perfect, not like the skin of a Merahvu but like the skin of something Sapien-made. Larkian technology. Two people wearing specialized suits.

She took a sweeping gaze back, shared a thought. *"I'm scared."*

Blake answered back in mind-speak, *"Me too."*

Audrey and Blake had mastered the art of sharing. Sinto found that intriguing and hopeful that it was possible to teach sharing and mind-speak between Sapiens. He knew his mother and Culliford frequently spoke privately. He certainly had with Audrey, and most likely Blake had learned how from Leela. A newfound skill essential to their current situation.

A parade of Orankai guards passed by in the brightly lit tunnel intersecting the one where Audrey, Blake, and the Wekeep hid, unaware of their presence. Orankai guards dressed in the same black uniforms Sinto witnessed in the City of Green; knee-length black wraps and matching leather vests with rows of silver buttons, depicting their status in Arkis' new tribal order.

The guards strolled casually. Deactivated parasitic bands swung loosely from their waists, escorting someone within the tight circle of their bodies. Someone too small to see over them, except for a flash of golden hair. This was not a slave. It was someone important, fiercely protected. Trailing behind the procession was his father, Ramasis, his step light and eyes glowing bright orange from a recent hit of nectar.

"*That's Naiada! Where are we?*" Sinto demanded of the stone.

The stone did not answer because the stone guiding them knew not of people and places, only threads and connections.

"*Which thread shall I follow?*" it asked.

Sinto grew frustrated not knowing how to formulate the right question, to speak in the limited language of connections. The connection of the Mark was obvious, but seeking his answer of a place was not.

His mother intervened. "*Flow as the nearby water, downstream.*"

The stone answered. Audrey, Blake, the Wekeep, and the procession of Orankai guards and their prisoner faded.

Suddenly Sinto was falling. They landed in water, bobbing like a nut that had fallen from a tree and rolled into a stream. The stream wound through a network of caves, flowing through large open chambers and narrow flooded tunnels. They raced in darkness until they were spit out into blinding sunshine. They tumbled over a roaring waterfall, spilling into a faster moving stream that rushed with finality into the sea. There they bobbed atop the lively crashing waves before tumbling toward a cliff where an ancient stairway rose from the Great Ocean to a rocky shore littered with the remnants of a Larkian-made Xiphias.

"*The Labyrinth!*"

And with that discovery they were spit from their transfixed state back to the circle and returned to animate their stilled bodies with the stone turning cold beneath their fingers.

Sinto blinked and looked to his mother for explanation.

"The stone has produced the answer to your question," she said.

"But I never asked it a question."

"You did. You sought to learn of Audrey's current location through your connection with the Mark. I merely provided assistance to help the stone fully form the answer. Only one truth can be sought at a time."

He pressed his hands to the stone. "So let's go again. I think I understand now, how to ask what—"

"No." She pulled his hands from its surface. "The stone determines when and how often you may seek the truths you desire. We will try again, tomorrow, if the stone deems it so. Meanwhile, I suggest you think hard about what is the most important answer you seek and its connection to the universal truth of life."

She remained on her knees, gathering the corners of the blanket and wrapping it around the stone. She looked deeply troubled.

Sinto turned to leave. "Are you coming?"

She drew a deep, long breath. "No." She stood and handed Sinto the heavy bundle.

He cradled it with his good arm, laying his weakened hand on top to steady it.

"Return the stone to our chambers. Hide it in the old chest at the foot of the bed among the other linens. I have unfinished questions the Timeless Dimension may answer. Go on, I must do this alone. I promise if I learn anything, *anything*, you will be the first to know."

"You believe the prisoner was Naiada."

"Yes."

"What do you know of the Labyrinth?"

"I know it is vast and one could easily get hopelessly lost. They could be anywhere. Now go."

He left, his mind a jumble of confusing emotions and filled with more questions about threads and connections than he ever thought possible.

55

Earthshake

SINTO'S MIND REELED. LANGUAGE of connection. Universal truth. Threads. Audrey and Blake with a Wekeep in the Labyrinth. The three of them hiding from a procession of Arkis' guards, surrounding Naiada with his father in tow. Audrey and Blake, communing in mind-speak: *I'm scared. Me too...*

Sinto had known of the Labyrinth but had never ventured deeper than a few chambers inside, afraid of getting lost. The Labyrinth extended from the Great Ocean to the Black Mountains.

The Labyrinth was a place the Seakai abandoned hundreds of years ago once the city of Tallamure on Earth was built. Tunnels had been carved into the ridge by their original ancestors, linking a large network of existing caverns together. Dark, musty, and primitive. And vast. His mother confirmed the upper Labyrinth included the breeding caves he recently discovered. No one had been back since the end of the Forever War. A perfect place for Arkis to occupy and hide.

He followed the path from the clearing where he left his mother to the house she shared with Culliford. As she directed, he placed the Salish Stone swaddled in the green blanket in the wooden chest at the foot of the bed in their shared chambers, making sure to hide it near the bottom beneath stacks of folded linens.

He shut the lid and sat, pondering what to do. The scope of challenges facing them were overwhelming. Surely running off on his own to the Labyrinth would be suicide. The incident with Victoria was a raw and painful reminder of Arkis' advantage. His mother's harsh and stern message rang loudly in his conscience.

You go now with vengeance coursing through your veins, you will most certainly die, and so will she.

Sinto was at a loss as to how Arkis had become so powerful so quickly. Until they cracked that nut, it would be a waste of lives and precious time to attack the Labyrinth based on what he and his mother learned from the stone.

The answer to Arkis' power was buried within the stone that stubbornly held onto it, dishing it out on its own secret timeline.

The stone determines when and how often you may seek the truths you desire. We will try again, tomorrow, if the stone deems it so.

He wanted to punch something.

But that would be unwise.

He worked his weakened hand, forming as tight a fist as possible before stretching his fingers wide. The bones throbbed beneath the newly rejuvenated flesh, soft and tender. After working his fingers, he used his other hand to massage the joints of each finger, working his way up the tendons to each knuckle, then to his wrist and along the muscles of his forearm to the coil of the Mark buried below his elbow.

He traced the lines of the circle, then the swirl and the line in between.

Connection.

He closed his eyes and concentrated on that connection he shared with Audrey. "*Are you there?*" He traced the line, to and fro, between the circle and the swirl. "*Please answer.*"

The Mark responded, warming to his touch. He heard nothing in return to his question, but the Mark began to vibrate. He pressed his finger to the circle, then the swirl. Fire erupted, something happening. Then he pressed separate fingers onto each one, simultaneously.

A force that made him gasp grabbed hold, as if the tips of his fingers were metal, stuck to a powerful magnet. No matter how hard he tried, he couldn't break them free.

The house began to shake, slow at first, then in a frenzy.

The fan above the bed swayed. The floor rocked, the roof squeaked. Things on shelves jostled until they reached the edge and fell. Beyond the sliding glass door, confused waves danced on the sea.

Sinto jumped up, stumbled, and grappled his way to the front door with his fingers helplessly stuck to the Mark.

He burst outside.

Alarms blared. Palms whipped. Rock formations cracked and rumbled into the sea. Larkians and Merahvu streamed from buildings throughout the compound, shouting with concern.

Ships moored in the harbor cast their lines—*Requiem Sea II*, *Masquerade Ball*, and several small sailing and diesel-powered vessels—and swiftly departed, battling a surge of wild waves pouring into the mouth of the harbor. The boats that stayed were smashed against docks and pilings.

The sound of destruction came from inside the house. Bookshelves toppling and glass breaking.

As suddenly as it began it stopped. The ground stilled. The sea calmed. Birds returned to displaced nests.

His fingers pulled free from the Mark.

Sinto gazed at the place in his arm where the Mark resided, confused. Had the shaking started while he was fiddling with the Mark, or before? Did his fingers truly get stuck or had he imagined it? It made no sense.

Was that merely a coincidence?

His mother came running down the path from the clearing, Culliford ran from the command center. The three met at a crossroads of diverging paths.

"Everyone all right?" Culliford asked breathlessly.

Ianthe grasped him by the arm, visibly shaken. "I was in the clearing—the next thing I remember I was laid flat on my back. What happened?"

"An earthquake," Culliford said. "Rare for this island, but not an impossibility. Could have been a ripple effect from an earthquake on the island of Hawaii. Alvarez is looking into it."

"That was more than just a ripple," Sinto said.

He ran to the command center where part of the group from their last meeting were milling around outside on the lanai. Ryan was trying to calm Rachel. She looked pretty shook up.

"So that's an earthquake? Remind me not to move to California." Her hands shook and voice quivered.

Alvarez joined them, holding his phone high in the air, squinting to see the tiny screen. "Cell service is down, no Internet." He shoved his phone into his pocket.

Rachel fell into Alvarez's arms, the shock of it rippling his features. In a rare show of affection, he embraced her, burying his face into her hair, whispering reassurances in her ear. Their brief encounter was over in a matter of seconds. She stepped back, hugged herself. "I'm so sorry. I know you don't like to be touched."

He smiled, sincerely. "It's quite okay. First time experiencing an earthquake can be terrifying." He offered her a chair. "Sit."

She wiped tears from her eyes and gazed up to Sinto, then to Ryan. "Guess I'm not so tough after all."

"Rachel, you're tough as nails," Ryan assured her.

"Well, I don't know about y'all but I'm sleeping outside tonight."

"No shame in that," Sinto added. "Perhaps we will join you."

Alvarez's hand-held two-way radio squawked; he pulled it from his pocket, and stepped away to answer it. From the short distance, Sinto observed his reaction to whomever he was talking to. His face reflected a montage of disbelief, from doubt to more shock. He slipped the radio back in his pocket and returned to their circle.

His brow furrowed. "That was Dr. Wickman on *Requiem Sea II*. They were able to link up with the satellite and establish a connection. That earthquake wasn't an isolated incident. It was felt across the entire globe."

56

Mission Interrupted

AUDREY WAS WOKEN, THE morning after the Wekeep feast, by someone sneaking around their chamber in the Labyrinth. Her heart beat a little faster as she slipped from beneath the makeshift covers where she slept on the floor beside the old bed. Her first thought was that a Wekeep had come to steal their goggles, but with Orankai a short jog and many twists and turns away, she took caution.

Their electrified suits lay on the sofa where they left them the night before, both sets of goggles glinting in the dull light of a new morning, untouched.

She crawled, lizard-like, on hands and feet, crouched close to the ground, out of her bedroom door and around the end of the sofa.

A small figure was standing on tippy toes against the curved wall. It was Snooki, busily coiling up dangling cobwebs with a broom. She startled and fell to her bum when Audrey rose to her knees.

"Oh! Ya scared me. Almost wet me britches!" She stood, brushing off her backside.

Audrey held a finger to her lips, pointed in Blake's direction and gestured, palms pressed together to her cheek. Snooki's eyes popped and lips formed a perfectly shaped O, then she nodded in understanding.

Audrey pointed to the door. They slipped out into the tunnel, careful not to wake Blake.

Audrey knelt. Bringing her face level with Snooki's.

"Oh so sorry! I just couldn't sleep. All that talk of tough guys and witches. Franz is so very brave but I worry about his laissez-faire attitude about—"

Audrey pressed her finger to Snooki's mouth. "You mean about birdbrains and bats?" Audrey emphasized the code names with a wink.

"Right." She winked back. "Them and that, er, other one, the really scary one in charge."

"The cad."

"Oooh good name fer that one! Nasty and unworthy of sharing the same air we breathe. Me Franz came up with that?"

Audrey nodded.

"Anyways, dusting and such keeps me mind off that filth living down the way."

Audrey nodded. "I couldn't agree more."

"How do ya do it, sleep I mean..." She lowered her voice and punched her thumb toward the darkness opposite of the Wekeep's gathering chamber. "Knowing thems—whatcha call it?—er, *bats* are just over yonder? I told Franz it be best we move on, but 'e's insistent we've nothin' to worry about. Me Franz was born without one, ya know, that *worry* gene. I've got it in spades!"

Audrey found herself warming up to this small precious woman. She reached out. Snooki lurched into her arms and tears welled in her eyes. She clung to Audrey's neck and cried.

Audrey patted her back, offering soft murmurs of comfort. "I know what it's like to be utterly afraid. Have the Wekeep considered moving on?"

Snooki leaned back and looked up, cheeks rosy and eyes moist. "This is *our* home they 'ave invaded. Wekeep never run from fear. It's what makes us who we be."

Audrey chuckled. "I guess that's how you and I are the same. Once I would have felt otherwise, but no longer."

"So you will help rid our home of that filth?" She glanced to the forgotten broom lying at her feet. "That silly broom can't do it."

"We'll certainly try. Though we need all the help we can get."

She beamed. "And 'ats where Franz can help. He gots friends in far off places, all he's got to do is ask and they'll come by wing, hoof, or paw. He don't ask often enough in my opinion. Like when those Orankai took over the Labyrinth and brought in those nasty *bats*. The elders always did while all those—whatcha call 'em, uh, *Merahvu*—tribes were a warrin', though they didn't call themselves Merahvu back then. Thankfully them agreed to settle peacefully, as one tribe, and changed their name to prove it. Guess things are a changin' and 'ere we go again." She rolled her eyes. "We see, we don't like, we got ways of gettin' back. We keep our honor to Merluma and what that—that cad's doin' isn't honor. Time for Merluma to stand up and fight back!"

Blake interrupted from the doorway with a loud yawn.

"Mornin' sunshine!" Snooki said to Blake, picking up her broom and slinging it across her shoulder. "Come along for eats when yer ready." She winked at Audrey. "And thanks to you fer listenin'."

She spun on her heel and headed towards the gathering chamber, whistling and coiling up cobwebs bowing down from the ceiling as she went.

Audrey and Blake decided to wear their suits to the gathering chamber. They were keen to explore the lower chambers where Arkis had taken residence, to learn more about these witches the Wekeep spoke of, and maybe find Naiada.

Franz agreed to take them as if sneaking around danger was all in a day's work. Snooki didn't look too happy about it and begged Franz to use caution, warning him that he had become complacent to all the evil rumblings coming at them from both ends—Arkis' chambers near the ocean and the far end of the Labyrinth where it ended at the breeding caves.

After a quick bite, they headed out, moving quickly through tunnels alongside the stream that fed fresh water to the lower chambers of the Labyrinth. The sound of rushing water helped to mask their footfalls and panting breath. They stopped once to sip a cool drink and rest. Then they were off again.

Between breaths Blake whispered, "We've covered at least three miles—not including all the twists and backtracking. We would have reached the ocean by now—if we'd been traveling in a straight line."

Audrey whispered back, "Crazy, right? Without my suit's processor I'd be utterly lost. Look on the bright side—we're getting a week's worth of steps by the hour."

"Excellent! After this, I can sit on my ass for the rest of my life."

They were fast approaching a brightly lit intersection of tunnels when Franz skidded to a stop. He pressed his body against the tunnel wall, cast in shadow. Audrey and Blake did the same and flipped on their suits' active camo mode.

Franz sniffed the air, pressed finger to lip, and melted his body flatter into the concaves in the wall.

The sound of approaching footfalls grew louder, twined with male voices, low and rumbling. Orankai boasting about a trap they had set for the Merahvu and their Larkian companions, about severing heads from bodies and leaving the dead in the fields for their raptor spies to devour.

The procession passed the tunnel opening where the three of them hid. The tough guys Franz told them about—Orankai guards. From the display of brawn and arrogance Audrey agreed that their code name of birdbrains described them perfectly. Arkis says, "Do," and they do it, no thought necessary.

Which made them all the more terrifying.

Her heart pounded, fearing that with one look in their direction they'd be discovered. "*I'm scared.*"

Blake pushed back, "*Me too.*"

They were escorting someone very small, not a child but a young woman with pale hair and dark skin, and when they came even with the opening Audrey caught a full glimpse of her face. Her cheeks were pockmarked with round scars. Her lavender-colored eyes slipped sideways and met Audrey's gaze. They sparked in recognition and she flashed a knowing smile. It felt as if Audrey had been shocked. A connection made, despite the powerful technology Audrey hid behind. Naiada saw right through it.

"*Naiada! Full grown as we suspected.*" she pushed to Blake.

She felt Blake's body stiffen beside her once the procession passed with Naiada fully bound within the circle of guards. Trailing behind was a man of tall stature, an orange-eyed Terrakai with a confident swagger. Other than his age, colorings, and disheveled appearance, he carried himself in a way that made her heart skip. Sinto's father. The similarities were striking.

Blake grabbed her hand. "*That's the man who attacked our ship and murdered most of our crew. He's the one who tortured Alvarez. I—I never felt so helpless in my life. I watched as he cast his flame to Alvarez's torso.*"

"*The same man who murdered my mother. Ramasis... Sinto's father.*"

The sound of the guards' voices and footfalls faded. They held their positions until they were long gone and had calmed from seeing the man who made a profound impact on both of their lives.

Franz sniffed the air. He whispered. "They're close, I can smell 'em." He crinkled his nose. "Bats."

The tunnel was brightly lit. While their suits would provide proper cover, Franz was fully exposed. He didn't seem to be too bothered by this fact and Audrey's heart reached out to Snooki, who was no doubt riddled with worry.

They encountered no one else, much to her relief.

Franz turned left then right through more connecting tunnels—a wee man on a mission, knowing exactly where he was going. At the end of the last turn, they were greeted by an open doorway with a soft green glow bleeding from within.

He pointed, stuck his thumbs in his armpits and batted his arms like wings.

They moved tightly beside one another pinned to the wall. Audrey listening, Franz sniffing. He gave them a hearty thumbs up.

Audrey crouched, ready to sneak inside—

The ground beneath her jolted, and mightily knocked her from her feet.

57

Shaky Complication

IT BEGAN SLOW THEN gained intensity. From the depths below Audrey's feet the ground rumbled. She was pitched to the ground by the violence. The meager light in the tunnel faltered as reflective glass casting light from strategic holes in the ceiling shattered.

Audrey's goggles automatically reacted to the sudden darkness, showing a ghostly image of what was happening around them. Rock tumbled and dust filled the tunnel making it difficult to breathe.

Screams erupted from the chamber they were in the process of entering when the earthquake struck. The chamber with Arkis' witches.

Shouts echoed from deeper in the tunnel network behind them. Pounding feet drew closer. Blake grabbed her and yanked her to her feet, slamming her back against the tunnel wall with his arm across her chest. Franz nestled against the wall between them, arms wrapped around her leg in a death grip. She pushed him behind her, pinching her legs together. Franz flattened his body to the wall, hidden behind her camouflaged body.

The shaking continued for a minute, then two. Audrey wanted to scream, fearing being crushed beneath rock. Her heart pounded in warning to flee.

Arkis' guards entered the jolting tunnel, five, then six of them. One carried a ball of firelight in his hand, barking orders. "Gather the queens, hurry!"

The guards passed by and disappeared into the queens' chamber. More screams, the sound of scuffling feet, grunts.

"*Move!*" Blake pushed.

He gathered Franz in his arms and they ran back the way they came, through lurching tunnels, dodging bits of rock dislodged from the ceiling. They retraced their steps using the path logged by their suits' processors and the faint light picked up by their goggles.

They came to a rubble-filled dead end. The tunnel leading back to the Wekeep chambers had collapsed.

"Where to now?" Audrey asked.

"Go back, take a left," Franz shouted over the loud rumble.

They followed Franz's directions, stopping once or twice as he sniffed. In the dark, it was his only source of guidance.

They burst from the Labyrinth into daylight. They had exited the lower entrance above the roiling ocean. Trees whipped and hillsides slid. Others had escaped the Labyrinth. Guards, whose backs were to the three of them, stood over gaunt slaves and young women hugging themselves and sobbing. No Arkis or Ramasis or Naiada.

The ground shuddered to a stop and an eerie silence descended.

Andrey and Blake wedged Franz between them. They backed their way into the jungle without being seen. Franz pointed to a path next to the stream. They sprinted, Blake carrying Franz. The stream ended at a waterfall.

The path continued up the hill beside it with a series of switchbacks. Part of the hillside had collapsed. Fortunately, most of the path was intact. They used care with each step fearing a misstep would set off another landslide.

Up they scrambled.

Once they reached the top, they ran along the stream, past the place where they first met Franz.

Wheezing, Blake stopped and dropped Franz to his feet. Audrey bent, hands to knees, gasping. Blake circled, sucking in air and chugging it out.

Franz sat, found a tiny stick. Picked his teeth with it. He sucked something from a tooth, spat, and said, "That was a helluva of a thing."

"No shit," Audrey said, rolling her eyes. "I think we got lucky."

"I'm sure they didn't see us," Blake said.

"Let's not wait around to find out," Audrey said.

Franz jumped to his feet and took the lead. Shortly after, they reached the Wekeep entrance to the Labyrinth. He pulled back the tangle of vines that hid the entrance.

"Oh boya, we're screwed." The entrance was filled with rubble. "The next way in is waaay up there." He pointed toward the mountains. "Couple day hike and a doozy of a climb up a sheer cliff. Otherwise—" He made a face. "We go back where we came from and pick our way through the Labyrinth. Thousands of possibilities, less now probably... it ain't called the Labyrinth for nothing."

Blake said, "Guys, code!"

"Uh," Audrey said, recalling Franz's code words. "We stick with the plan. Learn what *cad* is up to with those so-called wit—er, *bats*, and disable his advantage. Find the, uh... *dove*, and get back to the, uh, *desert*, through that secret passage you told us about."

"You people ask for the impossible!" He stomped and huffed and stomped some more, then blew out a long dramatic breath. "Ah, what the hell?" He threw up his hands, stuck them to his hips. "I'm game."

"What about your people?" Blake asked.

Franz fell quiet, pondering his question with a little navel gazing. When he looked up his eyes were moist and his face was tight with worry. "I prefer not to think about that right now. I'm with you two kids, we're like a family, we stick together and do this thing you must do. What is, is, no amount of worrying will change that. Us bears are survivors, that's the best I can hope for."

Audrey knelt and patted Franz on the back. "We don't expect you to make sacrifices on our account."

He shook his head. "This isn't only about you. It's about that monster, and if you think I'm giving up, then you don't know Franzaboana Bevor Slumpjam Gemtaker Buttmist!"

He stuck out a fist. Audrey laid a fist atop it, then Blake. Franz topped the stack with his other. "We go, we fight, we wreak havoc the Wekeep way. Somehow, someway, those suckers are ash!"

Blake grinned. "I like that word, *ha-voc*."

"Ha, sounds like a cleaning device we could market." Audrey lowered her voice. "Got ash? No worries, *hav-vac* will change your life! All yours for the guaranteed low-cost of nineteen-ninety-five. Call now, get the second one free!"

"If only we had a telephone..."

"Ah shit, we've got no stinkin' phone. What a pain in the ash!"

Franz waved his hands. "Ha, ha. Playtime is over, kids." He did a little two-step. "Let's get this party started."

Franz led the way, sniffer raised high.

They retraced their steps back to the lower entrance, discussing their plan in low voices using Franz's code. Blake mentioned they had a stash of weapons and ammo back in the cave where they first spent the night, plus one Xiphias which he quickly described to Franz.

Franz screeched to a halt. "Code!" He grabbed a stick, dropped to his knee, scratched his chin, then used the stick to scratch out new code names in the dirt:

Weapons = fishsticks

Ammo = sauce

Xiffy whatever = dohicky

He looked up, brows arched. "Got it?"

Blake gave him a lopsided grin. "Interesting choice of words."

Franz tossed the stick aside and stomped on the words until they were unreadable. "Yeah, whatever, beat feet!" And off he went, Audrey and Blake running behind.

Franz said, gasping, "After we recon, we'll head out for fishsticks and sauce, maybe take a ride in the dohicky, *comprende*?"

Audrey chuckled between gasps for air. "How do you know so much Ear—uh, desert slang?"

"Wasn't born yesterday, I get around, play some vid games, watch some TV—oh god, all those commercials, you people take a lot of pills!—and the news stories! Sheesh! How do you know what's real, some say this, some say that. Head spinning!"

"How much time do you spend, uh, in the desert?" Audrey asked, incredulous.

"More than me missus knows. Ah, but she never complains, my Snooki, and she sure loves the little things I bring back."

"And how far is this secret passage to Earth, oops, sorry, desert?" Blake said.

"Ya mean, Canada."

Blake quirked a brow. "Sure, how far?"

He slowed down a bit. Audrey was thankful to get a break from all the running, though she still had to walk at a fast clip to keep up.

"Er, depends on how much of the knot is still standing. Before, a day passing through the knot, now and out from here, more." He shrugged his shoulders.

Blake continued, "And once you pass through, how far to civilization?"

"Depends on what you call civilization. I usually just hang out in a cabin not far from where I cross over. Gots the vid games and TV and that thing called Internet. Seems civilized to me."

Blake skidded to a stop. "That's kinda important to us."

"Me too, kick the feet up and munch some popcorn. No missus or wee ones under foot. A man could learn to love isolation with them high-tech gadgets to keep 'em company."

"Not for that reason. For the Internet; we can use it to contact our people."

He stopped running and whipped around. "So, what, ya wanna do that now? Cause it's kinda in the other direction."

"Later, let's stick to this plan," Audrey said, "We need to find the dove, and gather more info on those bats."

He rolled his eyes and started running again. "Whatevs," he mumbled.

They decided to wait until dark before entering the Labyrinth. The grounds around the entrance were quiet and they found a circle of trees with thick bushes growing beneath where they could hunker down for a few hours.

They rested free of interruption, except for Franz's occasional piggish snorts and whispered sweet nothings to his beloved Snooki.

58

Blind To The Obvious

EVERYONE WAS UNSETTLED BY the earth-shaking event that happened earlier in the day on Isla Salvación. It was night and Sinto joined Ryan and Rachel on the beach. They had gathered blankets and pillows and Rachel made nice cozy nests for each of them. All were looking forward to a night under the stars. At Rachel's insistence, Alvarez joined them.

It had been a long time since Sinto spent time with others he cared about. He was tired of being alone, especially after the incident with Victoria.

He missed Audrey. So much so that it made his guts ache and heart pound erratically whenever he thought of her stuck on Merluma with Arkis nearby. He itched to go to her, to seek her out, to bring her back to Isla Salvación where she belonged. But he remained grounded by his mother's sage advice.

And thinking of that made him wonder, once again: where did he belong? Where was his home? That place that sings its song every time you return to it. While Isla Salvación was a safe and beautiful place surrounded by the great Pacific Ocean, it lacked that essential kernel of one's self planted by those who came before. What was that essential kernel? Was it the birthplace of his ancestors? Was it where he spent his childhood?

He felt untethered. He yearned for that place that screamed, "Here is where you belong!" Yet he had no idea how to find it.

Ironically, it was Rachel who brought the topic up. She pointed to the planet of Venus, hanging low in the night sky. "Why is it women are from Venus? What if I want to be from Mars, that inhospitable place where no human being belongs. The man planet."

Ryan said, "It's a metaphor to explain psychological and emotional differences between men and women."

"I know it's—it's a—a"

"Metaphor," Ryan repeated.

"Right, I know it's not real—but what if I want to live on Mars, psychologically and emotionally, like a man? Sometimes I wonder what it would be like to be a man, er, not *physically*—don't get me wrong, I really like being a woman—but just once it would be awesome to be the dominant gender callin' most the shots."

Sinto said, "My mother might be able to help you with that."

"Oh to be a queen! I say jump and y'all jump."

"You don't need to be a queen to make me jump," Alvarez said.

Rachel giggled. "Really? Jump Salvo!"

He looked at her. "Maybe later; my physical self has retired for the evening."

Rachel suddenly grew quiet and when Sinto looked over, he noticed that she had rolled to her side and was gazing at Alvarez lying on his back, looking up at the sky. He had taken his glasses off and it was the first time Sinto had seen his eyes without the filter of round spectacles. They were richly brown and alive with vitality.

Rachel traced the rise of his beaked nose with her finger starting at the crown of his forehead and pausing at the crest of his lower lip. The way she was gazing at him confirmed what Sinto suspected the other day; the spark growing between them was getting stronger. In the darkness, their auras twined red and blue, merging into a sultry purple.

Sinto turned to Ryan. "It's still early, feel up for a walk?"

Ryan looked to Sinto questioningly, then he noticed Rachel and Alvarez lying on their sides facing each other engaged in whispered conversation. "Me? Wide awake and still spooked from today. A walk would be good."

They grabbed the blankets they had been lying on, rolled them up, and left Rachel and Alvarez alone on the beach. They strolled along the shore toward the village. Doors were locked up and the sidewalks empty. Across the bay, *Requiem Sea II* was back and peacefully moored to the dock, deck lights aglow.

Ryan stopped and gazed up at the stars. "Is it possible Audrey and Blake can see these same stars?"

"We believe Merluma shares the same universe. In fact, Merluma's singular land mass intersects the same longitude and latitude as the Salish Sea and sees the same stars as in the northern hemisphere." He pointed to the Big Dipper and traced the two points along its lower edge to Polaris, faint but clearly present. "Same Big Dipper, same North Star."

"Strange coincidence."

"Mm-hmm. If it was night and they were gazing up, they would be gazing at the same stars. What is a mystery is why you can't see satellites or contrails from passing jets in Merluma's sky."

"Don't look to me for the answer." Ryan rolled his eyes around their sockets. "That quantum physics stuff makes my head spin. Is the cat dead or alive? Depends on if you see it. Otherwise, it can be both, or neither, geez... poor cat. And now, this concept called entanglement."

Sinto smiled. "It makes my head spin, too." He raised his right arm. "As does the meaning of the Mark Audrey and I share and how she was able to bind our fates together. We're connected no matter where she may be."

Ryan laughed. "I'm sure I'm not alone in saying men have been trying to figure that out since the beginning of humankind. History got it backwards. It wasn't a caveman dragging his chosen by the hair to his cave, it was a woman spinning her invisible web. One look and we were sunk, groveling on hands and knees ready to do their bidding."

They continued walking. The air was warm and still and the moisture infusing it captured Sinto in its warm embrace. He wanted to shed the clothes he had become accustomed to wearing around the Larkians and dive into the water, savor the slip of the sea across his bare skin, and breath deep its salty essence through his gills.

But he cherished this shared moment with Ryan more than his desire to flee into the sea. He missed his childhood friends from Tallamure. He missed his sister. Every one of them were scattered or dead by the hand of his once friend and bastard half-brother, Arkis.

Ryan broke the silence. "Sorry to change the subject, but I have, what might be to you, a stupid question."

"Wantemo once told me, no question is worthless or stupid. Not asking and formulating a made-up answer is a sign of arrogance and weakness. Best to ask, no matter how worthless or stupid."

"Wantemo is a wise man and I've learned a great deal from him. You were lucky to have someone like him to teach you."

"It was not all fun having Wantemo as my mentor. Some of his lessons were quite painful and belittling. Wantemo made me realize how very little I understand of the world." He pondered. "I truly wish I had been taught many of those lessons by my father."

"We have that in common. I never knew my father, at least my biological father. There were many pretend dads in my life but the only thing they taught me was I didn't want to be anything like them, floating through life numbed by drugs and meaningless relationships."

"I am sorry to hear that."

"It's okay, I learned long ago to ask lots of stupid questions."

"Right, so, what is your question?"

"How were you able to contain the city of Tallamure at the bottom of the North Pacific? Audrey spoke of a transparent dome that was super strong and flexible and seemingly had a mind of its own, choosing who could or could not pass through. A biological lock."

Sinto stopped walking and looked at Ryan. "What did you say?"

"I was curious about the dome containing—"

Sinto grabbed Ryan by the shoulders and howled with laughter. "That was a *brilliant* question!"

"What? I don't understand."

"Finish your track of thought—but first, the answer to your question: the city was contained by a biologically modified version of what we produce to enable us to dive to the deep, our lorica."

Ryan smiled. "Uh, I hadn't really thought about anything specific, I was just wondering—uh, actually, that's not true." He made a funny face with his lips peeled back exposing clenched teeth. "I had this random thought that, uh, maybe that could be one way to contain Orange. In some sort of a giant bubble."

Sinto was stunned. Ryan was onto something. Why had Wantemo not thought of that, or, he was embarrassed to admit, why had *he* not thought of it either? The possibility was so glaringly obvious, was it not? A biological prison.

"That is not a random thought!"

Sinto picked up the pace.

"Where are you going?"

"To the ship to wake up Wantemo. You coming?"

Ryan beat feet beside him. "Wouldn't miss it, whatever *it* is."

Sinto wound his arm around Ryan's neck and gave him a one-armed hug. "The *it* is you! You are a genius, Ryan Wood!"

59

Old Man Owned

WANTEMO WAS NOT PLEASED to be roused from his slumber in the middle of the night. One thing Sinto had learned through the years was Wantemo valued his sleep and the only reason one should disturb it was if there was a critically important reason. Life-and-death type of reason. While no one was in imminent danger, Sinto knew they had better be ready to explain why they were there, and quickly.

Sinto and Ryan stood over Wantemo. He was tangled in the sheets of his single bunk in his private cabin on the *Requiem Sea II*, fast asleep. Sinto shook him. Wantemo cracked a bloodshot eye.

"Ryan has an idea, a thought actually, a really good one."

"You disrupted my rest because Ryan chooses to spend his nights *thinking*?" He swung his legs to the floor and sat up, rubbing his eyes. The braids normally wound around his neck were snaked in rows on the bed beside him like the spaghetti noodles Leonard made from scratch. He also had removed his ever-present white skareef. His skin was so pale it glowed in the darkness. His markings wrapping around his hips resembled sticks and snowflakes.

Sinto clicked on the lamp mounted to the wall beside the bunk.

Wantemo shrank from the light as if it were poison. "More insult to the senses!" He squinted up to Ryan. "This better be a good thought."

"It is, get dressed." Sinto tossed him the white skareef that hung on a hook by the cabin door.

"May I remind you, Sinto, which of us is mentor and which is mentee?"

Sinto grinned. "Not today."

He stole a peek out of the darkened porthole. "It is not day."

"I stand myself corrected. We will wait for you in the lab."

"What about Dr. Wickman?"

"He can rest. If what we discover works, you can be the one who wakes him to give him the good news."

Ryan and Sinto switched on lights throughout the lab. They wasted no time and began collecting a sample of Sinto's lorica in a test tube.

Wantemo wandered in shortly after, wrapped in his white skareef and tugging at the braids he had re-wound around his neck.

"What about this idea is so important?"

Sinto piped up, "What was our greatest challenge in building Tallamure at the bottom of the Pacific Ocean?"

"Convincing the people it was a worthy endeavor."

"I mean, challenging to *implement* once it was approved by the Circle."

"There was choosing the site. I remember many heated discussions."

"No! Think *implementation!*"

Wantemo startled. "Settle down young Sinto, I am an old man and I just woke up. Let me discover the answer to your question my way." He crossed his arms. "It took a great deal of preparation of the sea floor once the site was determined."

"And then?"

He tapped his chin with his index finger. "The atmospheric processing plant. Those jellyfish took many iterations to get right. I remember a couple of catastrophic failures..."

Sinto crossed his arms, wondering if Wantemo was intentionally toying with him. Wantemo looked at him for more. Sinto said nothing.

Ryan had added some of Sinto's lorica sample to a petri dish and was studying it under a microscope. "What is this stuff made of?" he asked.

"What are you looking at there?" Wantemo seemed to perk up.

"A sample of Sinto's lorica."

Wantemo looked at Sinto and chuckled. "So this was your idea, lorica?"

Ryan looked up. "No, I had merely asked Sinto how you were able to contain the atmosphere of Tallamure in the depths of the Pacific Ocean."

Wantemo's eyes lit up. "The dome," he whispered. "Of course, of course." The look of utter shock crossed his face. "Why had I not thought of that?"

"Good question," Sinto said with a grin.

"Ahh. Perhaps I have been asleep all along. I think you are onto something, young Ryan."

Wantemo was fully awake now. His pale eyes were wide and aglow with renewed energy. He paced while thinking. "It took a great deal of resources to form the dome. It did indeed start from the same concept as our lorica, but required modifications. For one, how to hold its form consistently, and of course the locking system—how vast of an area are we talking about?"

"The gyre was huge originally," Ryan said. "Roughly the size of the state of Texas, but that has been greatly reduced. We found Orange spreads while seeking its source of nutrition. Francesca is working on an estimate of the actual quantity we're dealing with, volume wise."

"This Texas, how big is it?" Wantemo asked him.

"Big." Ryan turned to a computer and quickly tapped out a search on the Internet. "Over two-hundred-sixty-thousand square miles."

"Hmm, exponentially bigger than Tallamure ever was."

"The question is, how big of an area are we really talking about? What if Orange was compacted into a tight ball?"

Wantemo sat next to Ryan. "Let us find out. That and if a biologic material could contain it."

60

Sleepless Quest

Sinto left Ryan and Wantemo in the lab, feverishly testing Ryan's possible solution for containing Orange. It was still dark outside with several hours left before sunrise. He was too worked up to sleep, with thoughts bouncing between Ryan stating the obvious solution to Orange and then to the open questions regarding the Salish Stone—both its purpose and the vision it shared of Audrey and Blake hiding within the Labyrinth with the assistance of a Wekeep.

He left the ship and wandered the dock and soon found himself standing outside the front door of the house his mother shared with Culliford.

He reached out to her. *"Mother, are you awake?"*

"Ever since your father let Arkis steal my eggs and he cast me into that icy hell-scape. Sleep brings back the nightmare. Why do you ask?"

"We should try again, bring the stone."

He got no reply and interpreted it as agreement. He was certain she was as curious about what they learned of Audrey and Naiada the last time they used it. He patiently waited until she emerged through the door with the stone bundled in the blanket and cradled in her arms.

"Have you considered your next question?" he whispered.

"Yes."

"Naiada?"

"Yes. I attempted to make contact through the Timeless Dimension but was interrupted by the earthshake."

"Do you think she can help us?"

"Possibly. However, it will depend on the stories Ramasis may be spinning about us and his explanation for what is happening with Arkis and the Orankai."

Sinto recalled the last private conversation he had with Naiada when Sinto was naive about the ways of the world and when Culliford and the Larkians were their enemy. It was Naiada who warned him to take the simple action of leaning to the left. When and for what reason she did not say, only that Sinto would know when. Her advice saved his life. The knife Culliford plunged into his chest barely missed his heart. If he had not heeded her advice, he would have died most certainly.

Naiada also revealed in their last conversation that she was having visions, unprompted, and before their mother had trained her how to invoke them or how to enter the Timeless Dimension. She raised concerns about disturbing things on the horizon that she struggled to fully grasp. She spoke of lies they had been told, lies she did not specifically identify.

She also accurately foresaw the rise of Arkis and the Orankai, as well as unsettling things involving their mother. While it could have been anything, perhaps it was a premonition of the attack orchestrated by their father where their mother was carved up for her ovaries and left for dead, and Naiada was captured to serve Arkis.

He wondered what else her visions and thoughts had revealed at that time and if she had been too young and sheltered to understand their dark meaning. Surely, she must know more now, being in the presence of Arkis as witness to his dark obsessions. Did she know her mother had been violated? Did she believe her mother was dead?

"What if she has sided with Arkis? Is it worth the risk to reach out to her?" Sinto asked.

"I am hopeful she has not. As we learned, Ramasis has been protecting her. If I know anything about your father, I know he would never put Naiada in danger nor would he allow Arkis to take advantage of her. She is still so young!" Tears welled in her eyes and she wiped them away. "I have been seeking that answer whenever I enter the Timeless Dimension. I was so very close to reaching her when the earthshake occurred. This time we will use the stone."

"While we must learn of Naiada's fate, there is another important question we must answer, and soon: How is Arkis able to predict our every move? It will be vital to remove that advantage if we are to defeat him."

"I concur wholeheartedly."

Sinto lit the path to the clearing with a soft glow of green light emitted from his eyes. They encountered a recently fallen tree, loosened from its rotting base by the earthshake. It was quite large and riddled with scraggly dead branches that nipped at their clothing and threatened to poke out an eye. He cradled the heavy stone with his good arm and helped his mother navigate her way through the branches and climb over its massive trunk.

Once they reached the clearing, Sinto set the stone in the middle. His mother went through the same ritual as the day before, spreading out the blanket until the stone lay in the center. They knelt with the stone between them.

"Like before?" he asked.

"Let us try something different. The stone offers more than just an answer to a specific question we may have. We shall let it guide us through the Timeless Dimension. Let the stone tell us its story. I have discovered many unusual things tracing the threads that suspend it. Then, when it is time, let me ask the one question it will allow. What that question may be depends on the journey we are about to undertake."

She gazed into his eyes with conviction. "Surrender completely and quell whatever emotional reaction you may feel. Compartmentalize your feelings until it releases us. Can you do that, no matter what we learn?"

"Do I have a choice?"

She smiled. "No."

"Then I shall do as you suggest."

She nodded her approval and placed her hands on the stone. Sinto did the same with their pinkies twined.

61

The Stone's Story

EARTH HUNG ALONE IN vast darkness, bright as a blue marble, circling a fiery sun. It was a wonder that only Sapien astronauts had had the pleasure to see from space; never a Merahvu, except by the chosen few allowed to enter the Timeless Dimension.

But something was amiss with this image of Earth that Sinto was observing. A peculiar sphere was attached in the northern hemisphere directly above the northwestern portion of North America where the Salish Sea lay. A sphere slightly smaller than Earth, barely visible but distinctly present and covered by water and a tiny speck of land. An apparition, ethereal in appearance, and when you blinked it would disappear momentarily before reappearing as a vapored image, like a ghost flickering from another dimension.

And whilst he watched he observed a second anomaly. The conjoined spheres quivered, sending shock waves through the galaxy; an imbalance in the system, threatening to tear the spheres apart and disrupt the established rotation of every planet in Earth's solar system around the life-giving sun they shared.

Ripples, subtle as they seemed, marred Earth's surface as the ghostly sphere struggled to break free. It was with shock and awe that Sinto realized what he was seeing. The ghostly sphere was real, not an illusion—Merluma, stuck to Earth's core. A portion of it buried within Earth's marbled surface.

Was the push and tug between the Earth sisters causing the wobble Blake spoke of?

What would happen if Earth and Merluma separated? Sinto imagined such an event would spell the end of the delicate balance he was observing. Earth cracked open and broken. Certainly an end to Earth's solar system, and maybe the galaxy in which it resides.

Had one of these quivers caused the recent earthshake felt across the globe?

It made sense to him now. Merluma's presence was never seen by the Sapiens on countless space expeditions or by the thousands of satellites that circled Earth. These technological things passed through Earth's ghostly sister, oblivious. It was only by the stone's guidance that Sinto and his mother were able to see the unvarnished truth: where the earth sisters were linked and the vulnerability of their connection.

Without the stone Sinto would have been blind to this reality. A reality billions of Sapiens and millions of Merahvu and countless other creatures and living organisms were unaware of. A fate more life-threatening than a giant asteroid hurtling toward Earth. If Merluma managed to tear free, both earth worlds would become unbalanced. Earth without Merluma and Merluma without Earth could not exist. The unfolding story revealed that their delicate connection was crumbling.

And that was where the stone's story paused. Nothing more was shown as they hovered above the vision. It was a disappointing conclusion, with the receivers of the story left hanging as to why the connection was crumbling.

Sinto wondered, but did not ask, the most obvious of questions: How to stop it? How would one calculate the consequence of something as catastrophic as a decoupling of conjoined worlds? And without that answer how could one possibly devise a solution to stop it? The question boggled the mind and Sinto wondered if the stone knew the answer, and if it did, whether he wanted to hear it.

The stone remained silent as if waiting for a question. But neither Sinto nor his mother responded, as they had agreed before launching their journey. They waited patiently, prompting the stone to continue the story.

They were soon rewarded for their patience.

They fell from the sky, landing on Earth's surface as one among many early microbes seeding a barren land. A time before Sapiens existed and transformed Earth's surface with their hands, tools, and technology. A time before Merluma was born and Earth was wild and unsettled, its fiery core impatient.

Volcanoes erupted, forming new land masses and creating an atmosphere with the essential elements necessary to foster and sustain new life forms. The enormous, single continent of land tore itself apart, its pieces setting sail across vast swaths of ocean, colliding, eating, and riding atop one another. Mountains rose up and pierced the upper atmosphere. The sea bed cracked open in some places and in others was sucked deep beneath Earth's upper mantel, slurping down great gulps from the ocean and taking it with them to hibernate between the layers at Earth's core.

And it was within the spinning core that Earth's heart beat, strong and steady, readying to birth another, patiently awaiting the trigger.

The core stopped spinning. Earth's magnetic field reversed. Its surface quivered and a seed was ejected from the core. A teeny tiny thing, so small it could not be contained by the crush of rock forming the planet. It passed through the layers of molten lava, hibernating water, and rock to the oxygen-rich surface. It kept going, higher than the highest mountain, and burst through Earth's young atmosphere to the vast nothingness of space.

Onward the seed continued, dragging along other seeds simultaneously birthed from the sun, the moon, and all the other planets in the solar system, joining others from the surrounding galaxy, until the migrating seeds found a vacancy in the vast void of the universe. The seeds cracked open and a new galaxy was born exactly like the one that had spawned it, including a duplicate of every living thing captured from their mothers at the moment of conception.

Sinto had barely caught his reeling mind's breath when the stone took them back to the core of the Earth from which they came. His mind swirled with the feeling of déjà vu. Only this version of Earth was more mature and more stable.

The core stopped spinning. Earth's magnetic field reversed. Its surface quivered and a seed was ejected from the core. But this time something different happened. The seed got lost on its way to the surface and got stuck on a sliver of land that was in the process of colliding with another. There it festered until it cracked open, prematurely.

Another Earth was born, stubbornly stuck atop its sister, smaller and deformed. And ghostly, shimmering, barely visible.

Merluma.

Merluma expanded and fought to free itself from its sister. The struggle was fierce, but roots had burrowed deep into Earth's core from the sliver of land where the seed had festered. Roots that refused to let go.

Merluma reached for its intended home across the universe, straddled between womb and an alternate dimension, yearning for independence. But it couldn't break free from its ethereal state: it was a planet both here and there, its skies reflecting that of a different but duplicate universe.

The duplicity of life never fully bloomed on Merluma since Merluma had only partially formed—an essential process interrupted. Merluma began life as a rock covered with water with a single island of land and a meager seeding of life. Bacteria and microbe, nothing more.

There Merluma settled, in its half state of development, partially stuck in an alternate dimension.

Time passed and Earth and Merluma continued to evolve, each feeding off of the other, and over time they developed a tenuous and symbiotic dependency. Earth at the time of Merluma's birth had spawned new life, thousands of species that had evolved over millions of years, and eventually, early Homo-Sapiens.

Then forty-two thousand years ago, the strain of Merluma expanding within her sister formed cracks. Life forms from Earth wormed through, seeding sophisticated life throughout Merluma's oceans and upon its single island of land. As Earth heated and cooled, seas rose and fell. Cracks—portals—connecting them came and went, burying them deep in the ocean or beneath rubble scratched along Earth's surface by glaciers. Because of these shifting connections, some species—including Homo-Sapiens—got stuck on Merluma. Because of this, evolutionary paths diverged. It was from these early Homo-Sapiens that the Merahvu evolved.

This last part of the story the Merahvu were aware of, but only as bits and pieces of lore passed down from their ancestors. They never knew the complete story that the stone now told, especially the truth about Earth and Merluma's tenuous state.

The stone quieted and expelled a great sigh, or at least that was what Sinto interpreted as a sigh, coming from an inanimate stone. What it was exactly didn't matter, because it was clear:

Story time was over.

Sinto and his mother patiently waited for the stone to ask its question.

62

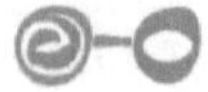

Blood Of My Blood

THE STONE FELL SILENT. Sinto and his mother lingered in their untethered state in the Timeless Dimension, patiently waiting for the stone's question.

Finally, the stone asked, "*Which thread shall I follow?*"

His mother replied, "*Blood of my blood, the most recent.*"

Sinto and his mother were cast to the surface of Merluma to a cliff above the Great Ocean, where an ancient stairway carved in rock dipped into the sea and the remains of a Larkian submarine lay broken. Sinto recognized it immediately, picking up the thread where the stone last left them after answering his mother's question the day before.

Before them was a cave opening. An entrance to the Labyrinth where they believed Naiada to be.

With no prompt from either Sinto or his mother, they zipped inside and through a series of tunnels and into a darkly lit, circular chamber. A circle of light streamed through an opening in the chamber's soaring ceiling, lighting three figures sprawled atop pillows laid out in a circle.

To say the three lounging on the pillows were human stretched the bounds of imagination. It was difficult to determine if they were male or female; perhaps neither. That was irrelevant to the fact of what they were and where they came from.

Abominations from Arkis' breeding caves.

Sinto felt his mother's pinkie fingers twined with his flinch and her grip grow tighter around the stone.

All three of the figures lying before them were horribly deformed, wrapped in silky black skareefs that covered the bulk of their misshapen bodies. But their limbs, if they could be called that, were not covered. One lacked arms or legs but had stubs of fingers and toes sprouting from shoulder and hip. Another had arms that bent backward from the elbow and one severely bowed leg and a blunt stubby tail in place of the other. The third had a huge fluked tail in place of legs and fins instead of arms, appearing more fish-like than human. They each had over-sized bulbous heads covered only by translucent skin, with a tangle of red and blue veins crisscrossing and pulsing visibly beneath.

But that was not what made Sinto's skin crawl. It was their faces. They were perfect—breathtakingly perfect—and an exact mirror of his mother's at the peak of her youthful beauty. His eyes failed to blink, not because his phantom self had no eyelids, but because of shock. His phantom self felt dizzy and nauseated by the horror of what he observed.

He could hear a deep moan rumbling in his mother's throat as they knelt across from one another, pinkies touching. Their physical bodies were stuck in the clearing, but their minds, untethered from body, were bound to the stone and what they were witnessing in the Labyrinth on Merluma.

The trio shuffled, reaching out for one another to form a connected circle as best as they could with the bodies they had been born with. Fluke curled around a backwards hand, hand cupped to fingered shoulder, toed hip nestled to a bowed thigh.

An orb sitting in the center of their circle came to life. Dim at first, then growing brighter. It captured the trio's eyes and they gazed mindlessly at the orb casting a pale green light. Their lips moved in a chant of whispered and undecipherable words that barely stretched beyond their circle.

The air suddenly swirled around them, forming a mighty vortex. A vortex like the one that bound his mother whenever she entered the Timeless Dimension. Their faces looked up, wide-eyed, into the fury swirling around them. The chanting grew louder, a booming sound that bounced around the chamber. Their faces reflected things they must be witnessing—lips twisted, eyes winced, jaws dropped in surprise—followed by wicked smiles.

Their voices stilled abruptly. The vortex dissipated. Grossly bulbous heads hung to chests in exhaustion.

Arkis entered the chamber.

Seeing him filled Sinto with a fury that threatened to unleash him from the stone's tenuous grip on his mind but he held fast to the stone's unfolding story and buried his bitter feelings toward his bastard half-brother.

Arkis had noticeably aged since he last saw him on Andrew's Island. The excessive use of orange nectar was catching up. The soft paunch around his midsection remained and a thick web of wrinkles had formed around his eyes and across his forehead. He wore the same gaudy red silk shirt unbuttoned to his navel and loosely tucked into his black leather wrap. The Orankai leader's uniform.

Arkis' hair was much longer than Sinto remembered, nearly touching his buttocks. It was still painted black and pulled back by a copper chain adorned with precious stones. The chain was like the one Sinto's father gave him when he turned thirteen years of age. Had his father gifted one to his bastard son on his thirteenth birthday as well? That thought made Sinto's stomach roil.

Arkis knelt by the abomination with only a tail and fins. His hand gently stroked her back.

She spoke. "They grow desperate." The voice was deep. She sucked a noisy breath. Every spoken word took great effort.

"Frustrated by your foresight." A deep sucking breath was followed by a chuckle that eerily sounded exactly like his mother's. "Us."

"Yes, my precious queens. What else did you learn?"

"Sinto injured."

Arkis laughed. "Is he in pain?"

"Great pain," the tailed one rasped.

His face was alive with joy upon hearing of Sinto's injury. "Compromised, physically, I hope."

"You mean, can he fight?"

"Yes."

"We were unable to glean extent of his injury. He is alive but weakened."

"I see." Arkis gazed at the ceiling, as if sinister thoughts swirled in his mind about a damaged Sinto. He continued caressing the tailed one's back. She writhed and leaned into his touch, moaning, like a lover seeking a more intimate place to be touched. Arkis' hand slipped beneath its black covering to where the thing might have a breast. "Like that?"

"Yeesss..."

He leaned in and pressed his cheek to hers. The tailed one rolled her eyes and opened her mouth. An extraordinarily long tongue reached out, licked his lips, and probed inside his mouth. He sucked it for a spell.

"Did you plant the information I requested of you?"

The tongue withdrew from his cheek. "Yes, your upcoming visit to the breeding caves, planted for Mother to easily discover. The trap is set." The tailed one's eyes rolled to meet his, her tongue swiping across her lips. "Is there anything else you desire, master?"

"That is all for now. Very well done, my precious queens."

He went around the circle, hands fondling, lips planting kisses, tongues licking. Each of his queens swooning, eyes begging for more.

They spoke as one. "Please, master, stay a little longer. Let us pleasure you."

"Ah, tempting, but I've got a trap to set. Rest. I will return soon and let you have your way with me."

The three things writhed with anticipation.

Arkis stood and bowed to them. It was the only time Sinto could recall Arkis displaying such respect to another. Sinto and his mother now possessed the answer to their burning question: these queens bred from his mother's eggs were Arkis' secret weapon.

Arkis turned to retreat but paused. His body stiffened and he looked around the cave. He walked the outer circle around his queens, breathing deeply through his nose. The queens wriggled from their tight circle, reaching for his feet, begging for him to come back. He shushed them vehemently. They cowered among the pillows, afraid and seemingly ashamed by their need for human connection.

Arkis froze for several beats, teeth clenched and gaze scanning the stone walls with a fiery intensity that could peel back centuries of accumulated grime. It was a tense moment that confounded Sinto, and he too scanned the chamber for whatever had garnered Arkis' undue attention.

He must have found nothing amiss. After several tense moments, Arkis fell back into that arrogant swagger that roiled Sinto's blood. He bent to reassure each of his witches it was nothing, and they've nothing to fear.

At the chamber door, a man observed the entire interaction, hidden in shadow. A large presence with glowing orange eyes and wild unkept hair. The man stepped back and disappeared before Arkis saw him.

Sinto heard his mother gasp.

Their connection to the stone broke.

The answer to her question given.

They were cast back into the darkness of night and the embrace of soft humid air and the sweet scent of night-blooming jasmine swirling in the clearing. A faint glow tinted the sky beyond the thickness of the jungle canopy as the sun prepared to rise in the east.

His mother stood and stumbled backwards, hands clutching her abdomen, horror etched on her face.

She bent and vomited.

63

Batshit Disgusting

GUARDS WERE GATHERED IN a chamber just inside the Labyrinth entry. The slaves and young women they saw shortly after the earthquake were bound by thick bands and were huddled against the far wall. The guards leered at the young women and tossed hunks of bread at the emaciated slaves. When they reached out for the offering, the bands around their torsos would shock them, and they would writhe and cry for mercy before scurrying back to their place on the wall. Scraps of uneaten bread littered the floor.

Audrey seethed at the injustice but Blake pushed her along. The guards and the slaves they tortured for entertainment had to remain a distant thought. Another problem for another day. Franz sniffed in search of the witches, pitching down one tunnel after another.

Arkis and his minions must have been spooked as much as they were in the aftermath of the earthquake. His people filled the chambers closest to the exit.

Wafting smells piqued Franz's curiosity and it didn't take long for him to find Arkis' witches. He made a face and pointed toward a dark doorway.

Franz dropped to his belly and slithered inside like a snake. Audrey and Blake followed, pancaked to the wall with their suits actively camouflaged.

Once inside her goggles adjusted to the darkness, casting everything in the round chamber a faint green. They found a concave section of wall and the three of them melted into it with Franz nestled behind their camouflaged legs.

Pale-skinned figures loosely wrapped in dark skareefs lay atop a mountain of pillows in the center of the chamber. There was something odd about the shape of their bodies and at first she chalked it up to the dim light and the fact they were mixed in with so many misshapen pillows.

Then Audrey looked closer.

She pinched her lips to stifle a gasp once the reality of what she saw became horrifyingly clear. Among the pillows lay three grossly deformed, subhuman beings with over-sized bald heads. Genetic experiments, bred without properly balanced genetics. Arms, fins, legs, and tails—or none at all—sprouted from all the wrong places. Grotesque, except for their faces. Those were perfection, and stunningly exceptional. Bred to be more beautiful than that of their donor mother, who was obviously Ianthe.

Arkis must have picked them specifically for this reason, regardless of their grotesquely developed bodies. The witches weren't witches but queens. Queens he bred from eggs stolen from Ianthe. He had been busy, breeding queens as well as an army. The cruelty was palpable. Bred for one purpose only. She wondered what interventions had been made during the breeding process to improve upon their all-seeing potential, as evidenced by the size and shape of their heads.

She saw no indication of care given to help with their disabilities, no crutches or proper seating apparatus to make them more comfortable. Only a pile of soft pillows that flattened or bulged in all the wrong places. She sensed their discomfort every time they adjusted to a new lying position, faces wincing in pain.

Bed sores festering, no doubt. What she witnessed lacked limb or stamina to stand or move beyond the circle of pillows: His precious queens were left to wallow in their own piss. Audrey seethed, once again, at Arkis' lack of empathy, at the injustice.

"It is time," said one who had no limbs, only a tail and tiny fins wriggling from narrow bony shoulders. The three queens writhed around in a tragic dance to grab onto one another as best as possible with the deformities they had been bred with. Once they had formed a circle of connection they began chanting in a strange language. It was then that Audrey noticed the shiny object set in the center of their circle. The crystal ball Franz had told them of, the *puzzle* per their new language of code.

Franz's face emerged from between her knees, eyes wide and locked on the ball, licking his lips and salivating. She shook him. He looked up and gave her an apologetic shrug before ducking back behind her legs to hide.

The crystal ball began to glow and the chamber was whipped by a frenzied tornado encircling the queens. Audrey felt her body lifting. Blake threw his arm across her chest and they both ground their feet in an attempt to stay planted against the wall. She held fast to Franz whose arms were flailing from between her legs. They were buffeted violently until suddenly it was over. The air stilled. The crystal grew dark and the queens slumped in exhaustion.

The dust settled. Arkis entered.

Audrey had never seen him before. She only had a vague description from Sinto—black shaggy hair, black-lined eyes, the ridiculous clothing he wore, pretending to be a rock star. He had the look of a lead singer from a nineteen-seventies hair band. Sinto had refused to share any memories he had of Arkis, stating "I will not pollute your mind." No amount of convincing had changed Sinto's stubborn stance.

Audrey was taken aback at first. Arkis was attractive physically with a swagger that made you take notice. The energy shifted noticeably when he entered the chamber. A presence wielding great charisma. Someone who set your heart pounding with awe and wonder and the desire to embrace whatever they were pedaling. Potent character qualities Sinto failed to mention, which maybe he was blind to, but Audrey saw it as part of Arkis' magic. It was what made him so powerful and deadly like past tyrants from Earth's long and tumultuous history.

She now understood how Arkis was able to capture the hearts and minds of his people, by turning on the charm, by entertaining them. And once he had captured their attention, he slowly fed them a steady diet of propaganda until they believed with utmost certainty that left was right and the good people were really the bad people who needed to be punished, or worst, unjustly massacred. Add in his special elixir and he had a winning combination. A recycled old recipe for success. Charm then pollute minds, offer grand entertainment and a few niceties, then bind them with a drug capable of numbing minds to the manipulation. Reality and truth be damned. Leave them yearning for more false prophecies. The more outrageous the better.

Beyond the facade of charisma and good looks, Audrey saw the real Arkis. The evil rotting his soul rolled off him in waves and the charming persona wasn't so charming at all. The monster inside made your guts crawl and heart sputter, and as Sinto had warned, "Once you became a target in his sights you might as well be dead."

Seeing how his guards treated their prisoners and the conditions his queens were living in revealed a man who lacked any empathy or remorse. A man who respects only himself and nothing more—human or animal or an entire living system like a planet. A man who would crush and burn, murder and annihilate to get what he wants. Use and use until his disciples were used up. Then breed more. An endless cycle of death and destruction. Utter waste. A man who—

Blake interrupted her thoughts. *"Did you hear that? Arkis is planning another trap at the breeding caves. We must move, now!"*

Audrey startled back to the present. She had been so consumed observing and dissecting the man called Arkis that she had not heard one word the queens may have spoken. Now she watched in utter shock and horror. Arkis was wielding his charm by fondling and kissing the queen with a huge tail in a batshit disgusting way.

"*Did you hear me?*" Blake repeated.

"*Uh, sure. A trap.*"

"*And he's going to be there to watch. We'll discuss later. Right now, we've gotta get out of here.*"

Arkis made the rounds to the two other queens, giving them the same treatment he gave the one with the tail. Hands fondling beneath their skareefs and slurping kisses. Audrey couldn't watch. Their desperation for human touch, for connection, for love, was palpable and heartbreaking.

"*Leave. now?*"

"*At our first chance, follow my lead.*"

Before they could make their move, Arkis suddenly stiffened, like a hunter catching the whiff of potential prey. He circled the room, scanning the walls, the dark recesses of the ceiling. He passed by them, frozen against the wall. He sniffed.

Blood sang in her ears and she held her breath, fearing one move would make the suit react and shift. An inordinate amount of time passed and she was forced to take a sip of air.

Arkis' swung his gaze toward them. His eyes narrowed. She coiled, every muscle braced for an imminent attack. She played out possible scenarios in her mind, cursing the fact that she and Blake had not considered what to do if attacked; her role, his, whether she went high or low...

She felt a tap to her shoulder. Blake's signal to move. Arkis had given up his search and returned to his queens who had been frightened by his sudden and intense loop around their circle. He reassured them that they were safe with more fondling and kisses, and while Arkis was distracted, the three of them moved as one along the wall toward the door.

Peering from the shadows outside the door was Ramasis, silent and observing. He turned and ran away before Arkis saw him.

They too ran away. Out the door and through the tunnel, Franz clinging to her leg.

64

Snake Eats Tail

Ramasis was moving with purpose, winding through the connected tunnels of the Labyrinth unaware of the trio following. Blake went first, then Audrey with Franz hugged to her chest. They encountered no others but could hear plenty of action. Echoes of whispering voices, the tinkle of glass, the occasional scream. Then, something metal striking rock, a fiery explosion, grunts, and rubble crumbling. The clearing of collapsed tunnels.

Ramasis turned down a side tunnel and approached a door at the end, sealed with an opaque gelatinous seal. He pressed his palm to the surface. It evaporated instantly. He slipped inside a well-lit chamber the size of a large bedroom.

Pots of flowers and herbs were sprinkled about. A pile of bedding was tucked beneath a slight overhang against the far wall. The curved interior served as a blank canvas, halfway painted.

Naiada stood on a stool, lost in creative flow, singing a song and painting the finishing touches on a leafy tree laden with ripe fruit. She seemed to not notice Ramasis' presence. He offered no greeting, just crossed his arms and watched.

Audrey felt an instant sense of recognition from Naiada's expressive creation. It was the meadow Audrey discovered the first time Sinto brought her to Merluma. A magnificent waterfall feeding an emerald pond surrounded by wispy willows and rosy iris. A grassy meadow filled with fruit trees with sloth-like creatures draped over their branches, sleeping. A family of furry bunnies, rolled up and bouncing through the bright green grass circling their bases. Faeries hovering over the pond, potent dust falling from wing. The head and neck of a horned horse grazing—and that was where the painting ended.

Audrey imagined Naiada painting what she could not experience locked inside this place. Like the historic rendition of the Salish Sea from hundreds of years ago, a painting she left unfinished in her room in Tallamure after she fell ill and was confined to a bed in the House of Healing.

Naiada dabbed her brush into a jar she held in her hand, raised the brush, and tried to finish a leaf. She brushed several times, failing to fully render the leaf with what little paint remained on her brush. She jabbed the brush into the jar several times, then stomped her foot, clearly agitated. She blew a loose strand of hair away from her eyes, gazed up at the unfinished leaf, and sighed.

She no longer appeared ill; in fact she was aglow with youth and vitality. And she had matured—by eight years, Audrey estimated. She had zipped through puberty—and the awkward transition in between—straight into adulthood in the four Earth months she had been held captive on Merluma. Naiada was twelve when Audrey first met her in Tallamure. That made Naiada nearly the same age now as her older brother Sinto.

Naiada's face had transitioned into a youthful version of her mother's, with high cheekbones, wide-set eyes, pert nose, and softly pointed chin. Her skin was dark like her father's, which stood in high contrast to the shock of golden hair held back by a purple ribbon. Her eyes sparked with life in a soothing shade of lavender, like her mother's when she was happy and calm. Naiada had not grown to the same stature as her mother or her brother; quite the opposite. She was petite and more curvy than lithe.

One thing from her youth remained. Pockmarked scars cut deeply into her cheeks from the toxin that nearly killed her. A toxin released into the waters surrounding a Larkian ship, captained by Audrey's father, when Ianthe had sent Ramasis and Naiada to deliver a message of truce in hopes of ending their grievances. Audrey's father claimed he acted in self-defense when she confronted him after learning of Naiada's illness. If it hadn't been for Sinto sharing his lifeblood, Naiada would have died.

Naiada jumped down from the stool. "Did you get the paint I requested?" She tipped the jar in her hand upside down, shook it. "I'm out."

Ramasis drop to his knee and looked up to her. He gave her a sad smile and shook his head. "Many supplies were destroyed in the earthshake, including your paints."

Naiada looked deeply disappointed. She gazed up at her unfinished creation and pointed to a crack that ran from the ceiling through the painted wall to the floor. "I have no idea how to fix that."

Ramasis slid a finger across her scarred cheek. "Then don't. It is beautiful just as it is, like you."

Naiada pulled her face back. Ramasis was left with his finger hanging. She drilled him with a fiery gaze. "If I can't paint what I crave, then why don't you let me go outside?"

Ramasis stood. "We have been over this, many times. The reason still stands. It is dangerous."

She crossed her arms, brow cocked. "And *why* is it dangerous?"

Ramasis did not answer.

"Perhaps because a certain someone decided to start a revolution."

His hands balled at his sides and body tensed. A bomb about to explode. The transition in demeanor was sudden and explosive. Naiada jumped back, putting a large pot with bright yellow lilies between her and her father. He clenched his teeth, struggling to control his rage.

He lost.

He grabbed the pot Naiada was cowering behind with his great hands, hauled it up above his head and threw it against her painted wall. It shattered, casting pieces of ceramic and torn flowers through the air. Flakes of paint floated down.

Naiada was rattled, knelt, head bowed in submission. "I am sorry. I did not mean to anger you, Father." Audrey had the distinct feeling this had happened before, many times. Her questioning, probing where it stung. Him exploding with violence and rage. Her submitting.

Sucking air, he gazed at his hands, the broken pot, the scattered flowers, the marred painting. He screamed. He scrubbed his fingers through his wild dirty hair. He slapped his face and frantically swiped his arms and his chest, as if suddenly covered in stinging fire ants.

After several tense beats of frantic swiping, he cradled his face in his hands and began sobbing. "I can't help myself—I would never hurt you. You speak of things I cannot accept—Lies. Truths. Who knows what is real, what is not. My mind is failing me. I don't know why." He sat down, pressing his back against a blank part of the wall.

"I speak no lies, Father. It is the nectar Arkis feeds you that is destroying your mind, eating your body like a snake eating its tail. You grow old before my eyes! You must stop. Expel its poisonous toxin from your body!"

He looked up with troubled eyes. "Its grip is firm. I have tried."

"Not hard enough."

"Oh sweet child, you are so innocent. There are things in this world that will break you. That is why I keep you here, under my protection. Arkis may be your half-brother, but you are to stay away from him. He is momentarily distracted by his queens and the young things he insists on breeding to please him. Eventually he will tire of his playthings and his queens' weak visions and he will come for you." He gazed the length of her body, studied her face. "You are no longer a child and there are things men like him do to innocent young women like you. They are not pleasant."

"I was not born yesterday. I am aware of what he is and what he is capable of." Her eyes widened and sparked. "I see more than you imagine. Awful things you never warned me about. I know what is happening, here and on Earth."

His brow furrowed. "You are having visions, now, here?"

She did not answer.

His eyes bulged and face reddened. "Answer me!" he bellowed.

Naiada stood her ground. Said nothing.

He launched to his feet, grabbed her shoulders, and started shaking her. "Do not defy me—answer my question!"

Naiada slowly looked up and met his manic gaze. She smiled and stepped back. Dual bolts of fire burst from her eyes and struck him in the cheeks.

He recoiled, hands to face, and fell to his knees screaming.

It was Naiada's turn to pace. Back and forth, glaring down at her father, babbling and sobbing at her feet. The man was unhinged and possibly a danger to anyone who crossed him, even his sweet young child he was fiercely protecting. Switching between contained calmness and out-of-control fury like Dr. Jekyll and Mr. Hyde. A deeply seated rage invoked by Ianthe's long-ago affair with Audrey's father and aggravated by his addiction to Arkis' orange nectar.

This was the man who had murdered Audrey's mother and who Sinto nearly died trying to protect. Audrey hated him more than she had ever hated anyone or anything before. But she could not deny that other feelings stirred at witnessing the senseless breakdown of another human being. Another casualty in Arkis' senseless war.

"Mother trained me. Obviously, you have forgotten or you choose to ignore that which you fear. That I might learn the truth about you and Arkis. At least Mother came clean, with Sinto, and in time, she will with me, if she ever gets the chance. I am fully able to utilize the Timeless Dimension and have spent countless hours picking around in our family's ugly past, as well as in the present, spying on Arkis and his queens, witnessing all the horrible things he is doing! I've gazed into the future. *All* of them—those Arkis destroys and those without him."

"You can't possibly—"

"Don't interrupt me! I am not finished." Audrey was struck by Naiada's assertiveness and maturity. This was a woman clearly in control, not a bumbling, low-self-esteem, barely-out-of-the-woods teenager. She wielded a confidence and strength Audrey had observed in Ianthe, and a wisdom from all she had seen through her visionary power. Audrey felt proud of how she had matured, and imagined Sinto would be too if he was here to witness this confrontation between his sister and his father.

Naiada knelt and grabbed her father by the hair. Lips peeled back from her teeth as she said, "I dare that vile creature to touch me." She released him and he fell back, stunned by her strength and boldness.

She punched a fist to the sky. A bolt of lightning struck the ceiling. Rock and dust rained.

"I don't need *you* to protect me."

She strolled to the door, where Audrey and Blake were pressed against the wall just outside, camouflaged. Franz was no longer behind Audrey's legs. She hoped he was behind Blake's.

Naiada reached through the doorway, rotating her arm, palm up, then down, before withdrawing. She smiled and teasingly stuck a foot out. She cast her gaze back to her father. "I could leave and there is nothing you can do to stop me." She spun on her heel and set hands to hip. "*Father.*"

He crawled to his feet. "No, no, you must not, Arkis, his guards, must not catch you roaming free. I—I made a deal with him."

Her eyes narrowed. "What kind of deal?"

"Keep you locked up and away from the others, especially Sinto."

"What did you ask for in return?"

He looked away ashamed, mumbled something.

She stepped closer. "What did you say?"

His face wadded. "Nectar."

"I'm stuck in here for your precious *nectar*?"

He winced. Nodded.

"And if he catches me wandering free, what will happen—other than starving your addiction?"

"He didn't say—" He came to her, grabbed her hands and placed them over his heart. "I fear not my death. I fear yours. I would beg you to kill me now, take away this burden, this thing inside me, eating my body and my mind, if I did not believe that he would hunt you down and crush you with a violent, prolonged—and public—death once he had his way with your body and raped your mind of all you know and can see."

She plucked his hands from his chest and held them in hers. "You must stop thinking this way. Accept the burden of what you have created. Locked, for years, in this prison that you claim is for my protection, I have had a great deal of time to ponder. I have seen many *disturbing* things from the past. I watched a beautiful city rot. I watched innocent people enslaved or murdered for refusing to bow to his demands. I watched you encourage Arkis to recruit Sinto, and I watched as you stood by his side while those lampreys nearly killed him. You let Arkis do these terrible things, all of it!"

Ramasis groveled. "No, no, I *helped* Sinto. It was I who disabled the parasitic draw where they held him so he would have the strength to escape!"

"Arkis' nectar has clouded your judgment. What of all the others? Was not Beech your friend? A respected member of the Circle who stood up for what he believed, fed to lampreys for *entertainment*?"

He hung his head for a breath. "You are right to accuse me of encouraging Arkis. He questioned the leadership under your mother and the Circle, as did I."

"So because of you, he became a monster."

"No! It wasn't me!"

"If not you, perhaps you should enlighten me."

"The Terrakai were denied victory at the end of the Forever War. The Seakai offered peace, and the Seakai and Arctakai celebrated. But the Terrakai were deeply displeased, suppressed, forced to retreat from their claim to new lands and to sever our newly formed relationships with our equals on Earth. Those who formed the peace agreement claimed that if Ianthe chose me to be her mate—the son of the Terrakai tribal leader—it would placate our people. It was a joke, a slap in the face."

He scowled. "The bitter taste of that deception has never left our mouths. So it was Arkis who took the initiative. He formed a group of rebels with the goal of gaining greater influence within the Circle. He was going to stop once he got their attention, once they agreed to hear his grievances and his demands that your mother step down and for you to rise up as our new queen. A queen with Terrakai blood pumping through her veins!"

He shook his head. "I never intended for it to go this far. I only wanted to punish your mother for what she did to me. I was never the man I once was after she bedded Culliford. If it weren't for that damn orange fungus Arkis discovered in the Pacific, he never would've accumulated the power he has to manipulate and control."

"Then why don't you stop him?"

Ramasis whimpered. "I told you. He has imprisoned all of us with his damn nectar, including himself. Death is the only escape."

"Then this nectar must be abolished, all of it."

Panic rippled across his face. "Oh no, no, no—that would be cruel."

She grabbed his chin, gazed deeply into his eyes. "Oh yes, it would be. Very cruel, like locking me up here—for *years*."

Naiada glanced toward the doorway. Her gaze shot through Audrey's camouflage and bored straight into her soul. Audrey felt that shocking zing of essences connecting. The same connection Naiada made earlier when she passed by in the tunnel.

She turned back to her father. "And I know someone who would gladly help me." She shoved him and bolted for the door before he could find his footing. She turned to face him from outside the chamber. She waved her hand in the doorway, whispering in a strange language. It filled with an opaque gelatinous seal followed by a pop.

She beamed with defiance. Then turned to Audrey and said, "What took you so long?"

65

Salish Connection

Sinto's mother was inconsolable. Sinto tried to hold her but she shriveled away from his touch and fell to the ground as a quivering heap among leaves and dirt within the jungle clearing.

Culliford must have heard her screams. He came running down the path and gathered her in his arms.

She coiled around him, sobbing into his chest. "They cannot be! Abominations with my blood running through their veins!"

Culliford looked to Sinto, brows arched questioningly.

Sinto said, "Arkis used her eggs to breed a trio of queens. Grotesque mutants. They are his secret weapon."

Gasping, Ianthe declared, "Never—going back—cannot risk—encountering those—those *things*—those monstrosities!"

Sinto quickly wrapped the Salish Stone in the blanket and wrestled it into the crook of his arm with his good hand.

Arkis' queens were right. Sinto was alive but weakened. If Arkis' trio of queens knew of Sinto's injuries then he may learn of how and why he got them. Arkis must not know of the stone. No telling what he could do with it and his trio of queens.

He captured his mother's gaze. "They lack specific details, like how I was injured. Arkis cannot learn of the Salish Stone. We must hide it, far from here and in a secure place. With it, they would grow more powerful."

She nodded. "I agree. Where?"

Sinto nearly let his planned location slip but stopped himself from saying where. Arkis' queens could be anywhere, anytime, watching and spying. "That is only for me to know."

She nodded again, understanding.

Once they reached the house, Sinto had one last burning question for his mother.

Culliford busied himself brewing a round of tea while Sinto and his mother moved to the living area and sat together on the sofa. The stone was on the table at his knees, wrapped in its protective blanket.

"Where did the stone come from and how long have you had it?"

Shivering, she reached for a folded shawl in a basket beside the sofa and wrapped it around her shoulders.

"I found it in the Salish Sea shortly before the incident with Leela, when Robert and I were still lovers. There was a great earthshake, like the one we just experienced here. It was extensive and caused much damage to the shorelines and the indigenous peoples' villages.

"A tsunami rolled through the straits from the Pacific and bounced between the tight land masses. Culliford and his crew were on their ship at the time and wisely sailed from their anchorage to open waters to ride out the disruption it caused.

"I dove to the deep to survey a portal in the Pacific I frequently used. It was gone. Upon my return, I discovered a new one, in the deep waters beside Andrew's Island, linking the Salish Sea to Inception Bay. It was not there before the tremor. On the lip of the portal opening sat the stone, free and clear of sediment as if it had been placed there for someone to find.

"Looking back, I realize that the earthshake must have occurred around the same time Leela cast her Mark upon Thomas, *Blake*. It was right after the earthshake that she started acting differently, giddy and secretive and running off for long periods of time, both of them, together." She gasped as if suddenly realizing something she had not considered before. "Those two events must have coincided."

Sinto sat forward. "You believe the stone was birthed by Earth *because* of their Mark?"

Her eyes danced from the sudden epiphany. "I don't know for certain, but the timing of those events..."

Sinto looked at the stone, then back to her.

"No," she said. "It's too risky to use it again after what we learned. Those monstrosities will be watching for me, and I am not going back, ever again."

Sinto felt anxious, but she was right. They got their answers and more. Pushing too far entailed risk of discovery by Arkis' queens. "The stone has given me much to ponder. We know Arkis' secret. We know what he has planned. We know where he resides." He paused before asking, "Did you see the man in the shadows?"

She looked up, her eyes red and swollen from crying. "Ramasis."

"You're still getting information from him?"

She looked away. Said nothing.

"That's what I thought."

Sinto stood. "Rest, and when you're ready, reach out to him. A test. Ask how Arkis knows so much. Ask him what he has learned recently, what Arkis plans to do next. See if he tells you the same story about the trap he is setting in the breeding caves."

Culliford joined them. Curls of steam rose from piping-hot cups of tea he had in his hands.

Sinto waved it off. "Sorry, but I must go." Culliford set down the cups and gave Sinto a hug. Not the same as if from his blood-related father but damn near close. He reciprocated his new found affection for the man. "Take care of her."

He smiled. "Always."

Sinto bid his mother farewell with a kiss, then lifted the stone with his good arm and left through the sliding door to the lanai fronting the black-sand beach. He dove into the sea with the stone cradled to his chest and cut a tunnel to Andrew's Island.

There Sinto emerged to a cloud-pocked sky tinged pink from the setting sun. He padded through the forest on quick feet to the bunker. He shuddered as he stepped into the small clearing near the bunker's entrance, eyes locked on the patch of ground where Victoria met her wretched fate. Though the more obvious signs of the struggle had softened, Sinto could see hints of dried blood and crushed earth and battered foliage on the ground. Sickness crawled through his stomach at the memory.

Blinking away the prickle of tears welling in his eyes, he went inside and hid the stone within the inner vault, next to the wax-sealed letter he had written to Audrey.

After locking up, he climbed the hill above the bunker, settled on the log next to Andi's memorial, and set his gaze north across the horizon and the stretch of water separating the United States from Canada. Sunlight cut sideways through the clouds. A narrow swath of water danced with sea glitter. He would never tire of this view.

He reflected back to the story the stone told of Merluma's origins. Of the sliver of land where the seed got stuck and festered, firmly setting its roots halfway in this world and to another in a different dimension of the universe where it belonged. The ghost-like sphere sat like a cancerous tumor on Earth's surface. It was not lost on Sinto where this bulge existed. Sitting at the pinnacle of Andrew's Island, he was dead center of it. The Salish portal was the shortest, most direct link between the earth sisters, spilling into Inception Bay not far from the lower entrance to the Labyrinth and the beach where he first introduced Audrey to Merluma.

He pressed the palm of his good hand atop the Mark in his injured arm. It pulsed with energy. He closed his eyes and thought of nothing but Audrey. He channeled the idea of connections, the language of which the stone spoke.

Which thread shall I follow?

He focused on the Mark that connected their souls, their essence. He thought of the scent of her, the sound of her voice, the power of her mind, her stubborn will, the bronze glow of her soft skin, the movement of flesh along her neck when her heart raced, the messy braid lying across her shoulder, the gentle curve of her breasts, nipples pert and wanting. He sang the song of love and longing in his mind, imagining a second voice threading back along the connection in perfect harmony with his.

What he received in return was faint but encouraging. Neither a song nor harmony nor words. Just the tickle of a sense like being wrapped in a blanket made of her. He savored the moment as bursts of joy and sadness, fear and exhaustion, love and a deep languishing yearn passed between them through the Mark. A yearning that made his heart ache and stomach clench at the thought of anything happening to her.

But there was something else he felt. She was not alone; a discovery or someone found. A victory of sorts.

And when it was over he found himself curled up on his side on a bed of moss, cheeks moistened by tears with a heart embattled between hope and the bitter loneliness that engulfed him.

In the west the sun slipped behind mountains forged on Vancouver Island long ago by a colliding sliver of land where an earth seed got stuck and festered.

66

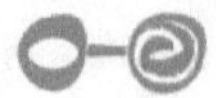

Stolen Treasures

NAIADA SMILED AND GAZED directly into Audrey's eyes through her suit's goggles and camouflage. "What took you so long?"

Audrey and Blake slipped off their hoods and goggles.

"How did you know we were here?" Audrey asked.

Naiada set her fists on her hips. "You are kidding, right?" She laughed. "I've been aware of your skulking around since I first spotted you. Don't you remember? Me surrounded by Arkis' finest?" She made a walkie motion with her fingers. "They treat me like I am his most secretive treasure whenever they move me from one place to the other."

"I do remember."

Audrey stole a glance at the sealed door. Beyond the seal she could hear Ramasis attempting to escape. The crackle of electricity and the yelps that followed. In between attempts, sobbing and apologies.

"That was a very interesting conversation you just had with your father."

She didn't say anything at first. A tear slipped down her cheek and she wiped it away with her palm. Her face denied what she must be feeling inside. Audrey was still trying to accept this new stoic, wise, and mature version of Naiada versus the emaciated young girl she was when they first met.

"My father is broken. I fear beyond repair." Anger flushed Naiada's cheeks. "Arkis," she said with a hiss. "He is truly a bastard."

Blake said, "A fool always finds a greater fool to admire him."

Audrey added, "Arkis is much more than a fool, but I will spare your tender ears from the colorful language that best describes him."

Naiada smirked an Ianthe smirk. "Perhaps later you will enlighten me. I've yet to learn more about this colorful language and how best to use it." She patted Blake on his chest. "Who's this? Have we met?"

Blake gave her that heart-melting, lopsided smile. "I'm Blake. We've not met, but I have a long history with your family."

She searched his features then gasped. "You're *Thomas!*" She grinned. "I can see why Leela was so enamored with you!"

Audrey had never seen Blake's face turn so red.

She bent over to introduce Franz, then stood suddenly, looking around the tunnel. "Where's Franz?"

"Franz?" Naiada asked.

"A Wekeep who's been helping us."

Naiada chuckled. "Wekeep are known to be troublemakers. Perhaps he is off creating havoc. We could use a little distraction to get out of here."

"You saw the way he was salivating over that crystal ball," Blake said.

Audrey gasped. "Oh shit, you don't think he went to steal it, do you?"

"Shall we place bets?"

"He's going to get himself killed! We must find him."

Audrey and Blake slipped on their hoods. Naiada's skareef fell to her feet. She had the same swirl and dotted pattern of markings as her brother. Then she instantly faded into the background.

The three of them raced to the end of the tunnel where it intercepted the main thoroughfare. From the direction of the queens' chamber came Franz, legs a blur, mouth gaped and panting, and rolling the crystal ball ahead of him.

"What are you doing!" Audrey said in an exasperated whisper.

"No time! Go, *go*! Hurry! Follow me!"

He ran by and they followed, sprinting. They used their bodies as best as possible to block their pursuers' view of Franz's small body and the shiny crystal catching light and projecting glittered patterns on the walls and ceiling.

There was a ruckus of heavy feet pounding on stone and deep voices shouting from the tunnels behind them. Arkis' guards in hot pursuit.

"We sure could use some fishsticks about now!" Franz screamed.

Naiada asked, "What fishsticks?"

Blake said between breaths, "Code word, means weapons."

Naiada's voice was calm but firm. "Perhaps I can help." A bolt of lightning burst from thin air, struck the ceiling. It came crumbling down, sealing off the tunnel behind them with a pile of rubble.

"I hope that wasn't the only way out." Blake said.

"It's not," Franz and Naiada said together.

Naiada shed her camouflage and took the lead. Audrey and Blake switched theirs off too. Batteries were hovering at twenty-five percent—dangerously low and working overtime to keep their bodies cool from exertion.

They followed Naiada's lead, running in a full sprint. They passed many other tunnels threading through the Labyrinth, past unoccupied chambers, along a fast-running stream. Their pursuers' voices echoed, distant and close by, distorted by angles in the stone that formed the Labyrinth, threatening to find them, to burst through any one of the multiple tunnels or chambers they were running through. Naiada and Franz ran together, following the same twisted path, taking the same turns. Deeper they ran into the Labyrinth. Audrey and Blake blindly followed, helplessly lost.

Blake asked, "Is there any way out of this maze?"

"Yes, but it's quite a bit farther," Naiada said, "and closer to the base of the mountains. But I know another way. A short cut. Let's hope it was spared in the earthshake."

Franz began to slow down. Panting heavily, body sheened with sweat, still rolling the crystal. "Running on empty. How much farther?"

Naiada smiled. "Not far." She swerved to the right and into a narrow tunnel with a low ceiling. "Watch your heads!"

Blake took the crystal from Franz and hugged it to his chest. "This thing is heavy."

"No shit, Sherlock," Franz mumbled.

Deeper they ventured, steeply angling up, curving left then right then back again, a switchback rising in elevation, until what little light they had faded completely.

Naiada snapped her fingers. A ball of fire bobbed in the palm of her hand, which she used to guide them. The ceiling dropped lower. They were forced to bend over. Their backs scraped the ceiling and they scampered forward with hands pawing along the ground, like their original ancestors.

Audrey felt the walls closing in. She bit down on the fear blooming in her chest. "Guys, I don't do so well in tight dark spaces."

Naiada reached back and grabbed Audrey's hand. "It's an adventure! Be strong!"

"You sound like your brother. Just don't feed me to a megalodon."

She laughed. "He told me about that. You almost peed your pants."

"Is there anything he hasn't told you about me?"

"Not everything. He was fiercely reluctant about sharing more intimate details."

Audrey's cheeks heated, thinking about their passionate encounter the night she Marked him. "Smart man."

Naiada's grip was strong and comforting, as much as could be expected in the current circumstances. Audrey tried not to imagine what would happen if the ground started shaking while trapped in the dark beneath tons of rock. At least she was not alone like Naiada had been all these months. *Years* to her. Stuck in a cave with nothing but her paints and her drug-addicted, manic father.

Audrey swallowed her panic and forged on, crouched low, thighs burning, back aching, and sweat stinging her eyes.

A circle of light bloomed in the distance. The ceiling rose. She straightened, stiff from being bent over for so long. They burst from the dark dusty womb of the Labyrinth into blinding sunlight and a thriving garden. It felt like being born.

Naiada spun with glee. "Just as I imagined!"

A large chamber yawned before them, its ceiling long collapsed. High vertical walls of slick obsidian reached for the opening above. Beams of sunlight streamed down. A waterfall from above cut a stream in the chamber floor, snaking around rock and disappearing down a tunnel like the one from which they just emerged. Thick woody vines hung down from above, tickling the rich soil covering the chamber floor.

Nature had claimed this new fertile space. Berries grew on bushes, a thicket of smooth white-barked trees with peach-colored fruits reached for the light, butterflies fluttered around flowers, bees buzzed and birds twittered.

Audrey and Blake stripped off their suits and underlayers and lay them in the sun to recharge and air out. Audrey's skin tingled from the burst of fresh air and sunlight. She never wanted to put her suit on again.

Naiada stood in a pool of sunlight, arms splayed and face raised to the sky. Tears streamed down her cheeks. "I have not felt sunlight on my face for... *forever*."

"This whole time you've been locked up in the Labyrinth?"

She spun in a circle. "Yes."

Audrey's jaw clenched, a flush of anger creeping over her. "Your father is a sick man, keeping you locked in there for so many years."

"Imagine my relief when I caught a glimpse of you three sneaking around, literally, and in one of my Timeless travels. I witnessed the Orankai attack you both at sea and your humorous encounter with Franz. I would have gone insane if Mother had not trained me how to summon the Timeless Dimension."

They gazed at each other as if meeting for the first time. In reality, they were, as adults with an ocean of misery in between. They fell into an embrace, Naiada's head against Audrey's chest. It felt like coming home. "Sinto's going to be ecstatic when he learns you're alive and free."

Naiada pulled back enough to gaze up into her eyes. "Alive yes. Free, not yet. The road is scattered with many obstacles, for all of us."

As they waited for their suits to recharge and settled into each other's company, the mood lightened. Blake let out a whoop, swinging upside down by a twist of vine wound around his leg, flashing that lopsided grin, flexing his muscles and pounding his chest like monkey. Franz was plucking berries from bushes and stuffing them in his mouth. Purple juice ran down his beard to his belly, a look of pure delight on his face.

Audrey looked at Naiada. They burst out in laughter and joined Franz, munching down berries, tender greens, roots, and mushrooms. Blake had climbed higher on a vine and was swinging toward the upper branches of a white-barked tree bearing ripe fruits. He hammed it up, pretending to slip and making faces, making them laugh harder.

Audrey forgot how good it felt to laugh, to release one's troubles. The joy of companionship and silly antics. Naiada was bringing herself to tears, laughing uncontrollably. Audrey wondered if it was the first time she had laughed, truly laughed, in years.

After several missteps Blake finally snagged a branch. He tossed ripe mango-like fruits to their open hands before sliding down and landing on his feet.

Naiada tore at the fruit's flesh with her teeth. "Mangeleno," she said with reverence, savoring each bite and swallowing it down, skin and all. "Nothing like it on Earth. Merluma perfected it."

Blake slurped one down. "Tastes like mango."

"Better than mango," Audrey added. "And without the stringiness."

After eating their fill, they splashed water on their bodies and slaked their thirst.

Audrey and Blake refilled their water bladders.

Franz quietly snored on a bed of grass, hugging the crystal to his belly.

Naiada pointed. "You know, he won't be able to keep that."

Audrey cocked her head. "Why not?"

"Because of its intended purpose."

"And that would be what, exactly?"

Naiada's eyes glazed over, mulling over the answer. After several moments she said, "That is not entirely clear to me at the moment, only that it has one of great importance." Then she smiled. "One not intended for Arkis, which is why we must keep it safe."

Audrey eyed the strange stone, wondering how an inanimate object could have such important purpose. "Well, I can only sympathize with the one who has to tell Franz he can't keep it."

Blake said, "Don't look at me."

Naiada grew quiet, gaze distant as if seeing something no one else was privy to. She stood, looked up. "We should not linger. We must go."

Blake hopped to his feet, gestured to the sky. "It's a tough climb. I'll go first, help pull you up from above."

"What about the crystal? That thing must weigh thirty pounds," Audrey said.

He looked around, zeroing in on a broad-leafed plant. "We'll wrap it and tie it up with vines, pull it up separately."

"Sure, sounds like a great plan. Have fun extracting it from Franz's grip," Audrey said.

Blake gave her the evil eye. "Not me. I came up with the idea. Someone else can convince him to hand it over."

"I'll do it," Naiada said.

Audrey plucked a giant leaf. Blake yanked down a tangle of vines. Naiada sweet-talked Franz into giving her the crystal.

Audrey stared at the crystal Naiada held in her arms. "I watched him just hand it over with no argument or tears. How did you do that?"

"I threatened to turn him into a toad."

"You can do that?"

She leaned in; so did Audrey. She whispered, "No, but don't tell him that. He thinks I'm a witch."

"He thinks all queens are witches."

"I'm not a queen."

Audrey ribbed her and smiled. "True, not yet."

Once the crystal was tightly wrapped in the leaf and bound by a woven net of vines, Blake tied it to a vine hanging from above. He gave it a good tug. It held firm.

Blake and Audrey slipped on their smelly underlayers, deciding it would be easier to climb without their suits on. Blake tied the suits together with more vines.

Blake went first, easily climbing the seventy-five feet to the top, stopping only once to catch his breath.

Franz went next, ferociously climbing on his own until he reached his limit a quarter of the way up. Blake pulled him up the rest of the way, then dropped the vine back down for Naiada.

Naiada was much stronger than Audrey expected and was able to easily climb all the way to the top without stopping, and with the grace of an acrobat. She suspected the Merahvu were given superpowers somewhere along their evolutionary path. Tackling physical feats seemed to come easily for their kind.

Audrey was last and hefted their bundled suits onto her shoulder. She tied the bundle to one of the vines for Blake to pull up.

Then it was her turn. Determined to climb up on her own, she focused on each hand grab and foot loop around the vine, then on to the next.

Exhaustion crept through Audrey's limbs. The events of the last few days were finally catching up. Her lungs labored. Her muscles trembled as she clawed her way up. She held on by sheer will and was grateful when Blake pulled her the rest of the way up.

She flipped her leg over the lip. She stood up.

The world spun and went dark.

67

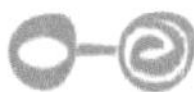

Otherworldly Connection

AUDREY LAY ON A bed of soft moss, sinking, as if lying in a pool of warm honey. Blake, Naiada, Franz, and the woodsy landscape faded.

She was engulfed by Sinto's smell and felt his fingers brush her brow with an emotional intimacy she recognized as coming through the Mark.

His voice threaded through her mind, "*Where are you, are you safe?*"

She answered with glee. "Yes!" Then with less enthusiasm. "*For the moment.*"

She pushed all that had happened since arriving on Merluma through feelings, images, and emotion, since words were easily lost through the Mark. She shared her disbelief and betrayal by Odwon. The elation of saving Blake. The grim realization of their isolation from the others. The deepening of her familial relations with Blake. The surge of hope after meeting Franz and gaining the Wekeep as allies. The utter horror of witnessing Arkis with his queens. Witnessing the demise of his father by Orange's wrath. The elation in finding and freeing Naiada. The terror of being stuck in the dark belly of Merluma. The relief once free of the Labyrinth.

A ghostly image of Sinto emerged. He lay beside her, resting on a similar bed of moss and soft grass, with rays of rosy sunlight caressing his face. His lashes cast shadows along his cheeks and concern was etched deeply in his brow. The expanse of the Salish Sea and pink-tinged snowcapped peaks of the North Cascades and Mt. Baker spread in the distance behind him.

"I see you! Naiada's with us, unharmed and safe, and she's all grown up. She misses you terribly." Audrey extended a hand toward his form, fingertips brushing air. "As *do I.*"

A smile tugged at his lips before he faded. She grappled to hold onto his ethereal image, the feeling of his essence twined with hers. But it slipped through her fingers as suddenly as it had presented itself.

When she opened her eyes, she was lying on her back. Three faces peered back.

Blake waved a hand into front of her eyes. "Hey, you there?"

She blinked. "What happened?"

"You blacked out. Feel okay?"

"I—" She sat up, felt a little dizzy. "I'm okay. Maybe I needed a moment to regroup."

"It was Sinto," Naiada said. Her gaze distant, before looking into her eyes. "Am I right?"

Audrey sob-laughed. "Yes—he—he was lying right next to me, not fully, but in spirit. I saw him as if a ghost."

Naiada pressed her hand to the Mark buried in Audrey's arm. "He reached for you, through the Mark; it's very hot. He's close by, not here, but there, on Earth." She scanned the ground, splayed her fingers in the dirt. "A connection point between the worlds."

Blake pulled Audrey to her feet. She felt shaky but elated. Hopeful and ready to forge on to tackle whatever challenges came their way. Sharing with Sinto what she had survived since coming to Merluma boosted her confidence and spirits. She was alive; Blake and Naiada too. She looked around at their ragtag team, feeling a deep sense of love and connection, of family; something she had craved all her life. She hugged each of them and expressed her gratitude. To Blake for getting her this far, Franz for his bravery and leaving his people to help them, to Naiada for her encouragement.

Franz said, "Let's get this love fest on the road before I start crying."

Blake tossed her her suit. She lifted a foot to slip inside and wobbled. "Whoa, still pretty shaky." She stepped the other foot through, pulled it up to her waist. Standing solidly on both feet, she felt it again.

"It's not you," Blake said, gaze trained on the surrounding trees, gently swaying.

The ground shook once again, starting with a little bump, like a boat meeting a dock, then a slow back-and-forth sway. She stood on bent knees, braced for the movement to grow violent like before. It did not. The ground stilled. It was over in a matter of seconds. If they had been running through the forest they may not have noticed it at all.

Naiada was staring into the pit of the chamber.

"What is it?" Audrey asked.

"The crystal, it rolled and fell." She pointed to the hole where the stream disappeared into the bowels of Merluma. "It's lodged there in the stream, on a concave shelf."

Audrey couldn't see it, wherever it was. Blake knelt on the edge of the pit, ready to grab a vine to go after it.

Naiada pulled him back. "Best to leave it. It is safe there, well hidden, its internal light masked by the leaf. It can be retrieved later. We risk it falling into the wrong hands if we bring it along."

Franz lingered, gazing into the vast hole, his face crumpled in devastation. He caught up to them a moment later, grumbling bitterly to himself, his face slick with tears.

68

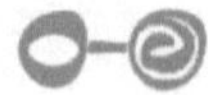

Old Feathered Friend

THE COLLAPSED CHAMBER AUDREY, Blake, Naiada, and Franz climbed out of had been one of many in the upper end of the Labyrinth. They continued their trek north and westward through a dense forest and up several rocky ridges, gaining another thousand feet in elevation, and passed many similarly collapsed chambers.

The air was cool and crisp with the scent of fir and pine. Naiada led, their destination a mystery she kept to herself. The Black Mountains towered beyond the treetops. Audrey suspected the breeding caves were nearby.

It had grown cold, markedly so, in the last mile and with the additional rise in elevation. Naiada was perfectly adapted with the dense layer of body fat incorporated as part of her skin. Blake and Audrey had their suits, moderating their internal temperature. Poor Franz was shivering non-stop in nothing but a wisp of thin fabric wrapped around his hips, goosebumps covering every inch of his body. He tried to put on a brave face but it was clear he was suffering.

Blake stopped, pulled his suit to his waist, and gave Franz his undershirt, long sleeved and thermal and warmed with his body heat. He slipped Franz's arms through the sleeves, which plopped to the ground in tiny piles. Blake used his knife to trim off the excess from the sleeves and along the bottom. He tied a pair of knots on each side to snug it up around his bony knees.

Franz gazed down at the dress-like covering.

"Sorry for the smell, buddy. I could use a shower and a laundromat," Blake said.

Franz took a shivered breath. "I'd rather be warm than smell like a rose."

They continued walking along a narrow game trail at Naiada's insistence. Audrey walked beside Naiada, with Blake and Franz trailing several steps behind.

Audrey said, "Arkis is setting another trap."

Naiada nodded. "I am aware, at the breeding caves."

"Is that where we're heading?"

She didn't answer.

"He had his queens plant a false tip for your mother to discover in the Timeless Dimension."

She smiled. "This is true."

"What about your father? He seemed rather critical of what Arkis is doing. Might he try to warn her?"

"Father won't be going anywhere anytime soon. That lock cannot be broken. It will release him before he starves or dies of dehydration. I'm not heartless. Though he will suffer greatly without his nectar."

"He murdered my mother. I know he is your father, but he deserves to suffer."

She fell silent. "I am sorry about your mother. I love my father but he has done horrible things and I agree he must pay penance. The Merahvu way of justice will not view his acts kindly, I'm afraid."

Naiada stopped and gazed up at the trees. The caw of a raptor captured her attention. Her eyes narrowed. She grew strangely quiet, kept walking.

Audrey felt the brush of something entering her ear, then the prick of a needle slipping past the eardrum, a tentacle sweeping the inside of her skull, soft as a feather.

Naiada, slipped her a message. *"Careful what you say. The raptor in the trees may be Arkis' spy."*

Audrey looked at her, before looking up, and mind-shared her response, *"Then you are in danger."*

"No need to react. Yet. Keep moving and ignore it. Has Blake mastered the way of mind-speak?"

"Leela taught him as Sinto taught me. It took some practice but we mastered it on our way to the Labyrinth."

Naiada turned and smiled back at Blake.

Shortly after, Blake's eyes shot up and he smiled back.

"He is as proficient as are you. Have you tried connecting with other creatures?"

"Sinto never told me that was possible but I would love to learn."

"It is quite different. Creatures don't use words and they sense the world differently. They speak in images, intent, and feelings—very strange ones, I might add."

"Franz says he speaks to the creatures, at the least those that don't want to eat him."

Naiada laughed, lyrical and pleasant. *"Let us hope we don't encounter them."*

"Are you two ladies talking about us guys?" Franz said.

Naiada said, "Absolutely, we're debating the best way to get rid of you; feed you to a Carny or throw you off a cliff."

"Ha Ha. Aren't you cute."

They walked in silence for a long while, Naiada's gaze scanning the trees above where a lone raptor followed, clumsily flying between the trees.

"What else did you learn about the trap Arkis has planned?" Naiada pushed.

"That Arkis will personally be visiting the breeding caves."

"Hmm, I missed that specific detail." She smiled. *"Though my instincts were true and so it must be. We too shall visit the breeding caves."*

"Do you think that is a good idea? Look at us, we have no weapons."

She didn't answer but looked back at Blake and Franz trailing on their heels.

Franz tugged on Naiada's fingers. "Come on! Seriously, my nose is burning. What are you two talking about?" He sounded a bit exasperated.

She stopped walking and knelt beside Franz. She whispered in his ear. His brow furrowed, lips twisted, he hemmed and hawed a couple of times, listened some more. "You want to *what*?" He frowned and looked down at the over-sized shirt wrapped around his body, sniffed, made a face. "Me, fight? All I got is Blake's stink, it's like a force field."

She whispered something else in his ear. His eyes brightened and he burst into a smile. "Brilliant." Then his face sank. "Do we have enough time?"

She stood. "We won't know unless we try."

"Try what?" Blake asked.

She gazed up. "Bring in trustworthy friends. One at a time." A large black bird gazed back, head cocked. Naiada clicked her tongue and the bird responded. She waved her hand, encouraging it to come closer. It dropped down and landed at her feet, battered.

The black raptor bird had been in a fight. Some of its tail feathers were missing and it was covered in dried mud. It looked up. A flash of white-and-blue eyes.

Audrey gasped with recognition and knelt. "Moonstone?"

"Bahak," Moonstone replied feebly. He pressed his head against her knee. A large gash festered on the side of his neck.

"Oh no, he's wounded. What happened?"

Naiada gazed into Moonstone's eyes, then after a beat, she said, "He was attacked by Arkis' raptor spies."

"Is there anywhere Arkis hasn't spread his poison? Moonstone's just an innocent bird!"

"Not just," Naiada said, "He's been helping the warrior teams and your Larkian friends in the Winterlands. He was with others like him but he's the only one that escaped the attack."

Audrey remembered a time when Moonstone had once spied for Sinto. Sinto had sent Moonstone to Earth to spy on her long before she knew of the tangled mess of relations between her father and Sinto's mother.

Audrey gently picked dried mud from Moonstone's head. "Once a spy always a spy, huh?"

"Bahak."

"Maybe he can return to the Winterlands, send a message, let them know we're alive. Stokes must be worried sick about what happened to us."

Naiada laid her forearm on the ground. Moonstone stepped onto it, careful not to puncture her skin with his sharp talons. She stood and hugged him to her chest. "He's exhausted and hungry. I fear he would never make it."

"Ha, join the club!" Franz plopped down in the soft moss at the base of a tree.

"Franz has a point," Blake said.

He threw up his hands. "See, told ya, but nobody listens to me. What, I'm too small to be put in charge? Bah humbug!"

Blake said, "It'll be dark soon, we should find a place to shelter." Blake bent over Franz. "Any ideas?"

Franz looked around like Blake was asking someone else. He rolled his eyes, stood up, brushing his bum. He mumbled, "Careful what ya wish for." He set fist to hips. "First, great idea, the Carnys come out at night and I don't much like sleeping in a tree—wait, some of them are good climbers—scratch that plan. Second, our choices are..." He shrugged. "Um, got none."

"What about that portal you told us about. The one that drops you in Canada by that cabin with popcorn and the Internet."

"Ah, good suggestion." He thrust out a finger, took a deep sniff. "It's…" He spun around, waving his fingers and sniffing. He stopped, pointed a gnarled finger west where the sun was setting. "That way, up and over the ridge. All downhill from there, Canada and popcorn."

"How far to the ridge?"

"That's the thing, it'll be dark before we get there."

"If we run?" Blake asked.

Franz said, "Kidding, right?"

No one answered.

He fluttered his lips. "Maybe. Well more like dusk-ish *if* we run."

Blake turned to Audrey and Naiada. "Still got some juice in you?"

Naiada looked down at Moonstone. He gazed up, dropped his head on her shoulder. "Someone would have to carry Moonstone."

"I can help," said Audrey.

"Me too," said Blake.

Though neither sounded too enthusiastic about the idea.

Naiada, the sensible one, stated the obvious. "We'll never make it before dark." She smiled, looked at Franz. "But I've got an idea."

"What?" Blake asked.

Franz rolled his eyes. "Oh boy, more friends." Franz plopped back down under a tree shivering. "And more mouths to feed."

69

Unis

Naiada found a clearing in the forest and warned their ragtag team to stay back.

Audrey held Moonstone and Blake held Franz. Franz hugged a ball of electrical fire Naiada gave him to keep him warm. They braced themselves against a mother tree among a forest of saplings.

As Audrey, Blake, and Franz witnessed with Arkis' queens, Naiada summoned a vortex that cut a hole between this world and the Timeless Dimension. A circular wall of swirling energy crackled with electricity and a soft lavender glow sprang up around her.

Naiada's ability to command her power with such ease and control was mind-boggling. She needed no crystal to seek answers like Arkis' queens. Hers was a power given naturally, not forced or genetically manipulated by a mad man. Unlike Arkis' queens, Naiada's body wasn't still. She waved her arms and danced on the pads of her feet, as if a weaver spinning a web and gathering up fibers no one could see.

Her body suddenly stilled, intently focused on something found. Her eyes blazed and fingers were a blur stroking the air as if pulling on an invisible thread. She pulled and pulled and pulled until she smiled and snapped her fingers. Then she raised her arms, fingers wrapping around the top of the vortex. She wadded it up and hugged it to her chest as a swirling ball of electrical fire, absorbing it fully and completely.

The three of them watched, awestruck.

The darkness of the forest returned. When Naiada opened her eyes, they were alive with purple fire. She was breathing hard. Her breath fogged the air. She walked to them, a smile spreading across her face.

"We have an hour or so to rest."

The hour slipped by slowly. The rest was restless. The air felt heavy with anticipation, waiting for something, for what Audrey was unsure. More waiting, still nothing.

Naiada sat still as a statue, gazing east.

Franz sniffed the air. "Is your idea what I think your idea is?"

"That would depend on what you are thinking," Naiada said.

"I'm thinking you should tell us."

"That would ruin the surprise!"

"It's not someone's birthday, come on, spill!"

"Patience, wise Wekeep."

The silence of the forest was broken by a distant rumble, growing louder with each passing breath.

Naiada stood, facing east, anticipating. Audrey stood beside her, curious as to who she had summoned.

The answer presented itself on thundering hooves.

"Unis!" Franz screamed.

A blessing of horned horses burst from the dark forest into the clearing—thirty or more of them. They pranced and circled and snorted, tails held high, ears perked. The ground shook with their mighty presence.

Their leader, a mighty black alpha, approached Naiada. He bowed his head in greeting. She scratched his whiskered snout with her fingers. He pawed the ground before lowering himself to his knees. Naiada grabbed a fistful of his mane, kicked a leg over, and settled on his back. Moonstone winged up and snuggled against her belly.

The alpha stood and whinnied to the others.

A mottled gray one with a gleaming black horn pranced up to Blake and circled, measuring him up. A mare with a mischievous twinkle in her eyes. Blake must have met her approval, for she lowered to her knees, inviting him to mount. Blake hopped up and held out his hand for Franz. Franz scurried up with Blake's help and settled in front, the gnarled fingers of one hand wrapped in the uni's dark mane, the other hugging his warming ball of fire.

A caramel-colored mare strolled over to Audrey. She whinnied and shook her head, as if saying hello. Her eyes were soft and warm and wise and her horn gleamed like polished ivory, its tip sharp as a thrusting sword. The mare rolled her head sideways, encouraging Audrey's fingers to find that place around her ears that needed scratching. Audrey obliged. She whinnied merrily in response and dropped to her knees.

Audrey's heart pounded. She had never ridden a horse, only a pony her father had rented for her eleventh birthday. It was a sweet gesture, looking back now, but a prime example of how utterly out of touch he was to what mattered to her. It had been a bit of joke; her legs had grown gangly early on and she rode with knobby knees pressed to her shoulders and bent over the horn of the saddle. It was embarrassing and unnatural and she was thankful once the whole thing was over.

That pony was an ant compared to the mare waiting for her to mount.

Audrey grabbed her uni's mane and slung her leg up and over. The mare's back was slick with a sheen of sweat and Audrey nearly slipped off the other side. Her hands shook, fisted in the mare's mane, unclear what to do next. The mare stood. Audrey hovered five feet off the ground atop a live wire of pure energy, unpredictable and capable of inflicting great harm should Audrey slip and fall and end up beneath her hooves.

"Use your knees to hold on," suggested Blake.

Audrey squeezed and the mare lurched a few paces. She nearly toppled off but held fast with her knees and her grip on the mane. Blake gave her a thumbs up of encouragement. She released an exasperated breath and adjusted her weight, leaning slightly forward. Fingers white and eyes popped with fear.

Blake continued, "Whatever you do, don't let go of her mane. Stay low, follow her lead, like waltzing with a partner."

That was well and good advice but Audrey wasn't exactly experienced in waltzing or dancing of any kind. The last time she was asked to dance was when Sinto took her to Club Ballo for a thing the Merahvu called the *Ballorue*. The Ballorue was nothing like Sapien dancing. It entailed a roller coaster-like ride akin to being a herring swirling around in a ball with dozens of others, mind-linked and avoiding predatory danger. Darting and swerving to avoid crashing into one another. She had clung to Sinto as if her life depended on it.

So she hugged the mare with her knees, melding her body to the curves of the mare's back, just as she had melded against Sinto's body.

"Let's go fast!" Franz exclaimed. "Loves me a wild ride!"

Audrey didn't share Franz's enthusiasm.

Naiada and Moonstone took the lead, heading toward the setting sun beneath a canopy of giant evergreens. The alpha set the pace with a slow grinding gallop through the open forest floor, rounding trees and leaping over fallen trunks or glacier-deposited boulders. Audrey's mare was hot on his tail. She kept her eyes open to anticipate every swerve and launching leap, clinging to the mare's back and mane for dear life.

The rest of the blessing followed, the thunder of hooves scattering birds in the trees and unseen creatures in low-lying bushes.

Along the way they paused briefly for a drink from a stream cascading down from the mountains. It took every ounce of

Audrey's will to climb back atop the mare's back. Her thighs ached from hanging on and her butt was surely bruised from bouncing on the mare's broad bony back.

Blake and Franz passed Audrey as they approached the ridge where the northern-most part of the Labyrinth was carved inside. Naiada slipped back and rode by Audrey's side. She explained as they rode that the Labyrinth sprawled east and west, but here it funneled into a singular point with a narrow tunnel system, linking the lower portion to the breeding caves and the Deep Lake plateau nestled within the Black Mountains.

They came to a halt and Blake and Franz slid off their uni's back.

The sun had set beyond the horizon. They had maybe a half hour more of dusky daylight. The peaks of the Black Mountains, snow-dusted and tinged a rosy pink, soared so close Audrey felt like she could reach out and touch them. The temperature had dropped several more degrees and was getting colder by the minute. Frost would most likely greet them in the morning.

Franz poked around a rocky rise, looking for an entrance into the Labyrinth. "I know it's somewhere around here..." He disappeared behind a rock then popped back out. "Found it!"

They breathed a sigh of relief, thankful it had not collapsed in the earthquake.

The mare and the alpha dipped to their knees. Naiada with Moonstone and Audrey with many bruises slid off their backs to the soft woody ground.

Audrey wobbled, her legs stiff and aching. She worked her hands, sore and cramped from clinging to her horned beast.

The blessing stomped around in a circle, anxiously awaiting word from Naiada.

"Franz said the portal is not far," Blake said. "Maybe a mile or two from here. I think the two of us should keep going, pass through before it grows completely dark. We don't have the luxury to wait out the night. We must get Alvarez a message before they fall into Arkis' trap. With the wacky time difference, we can't spend long on

Earth, an hour or two at most. Realistically, we'll be three days, a quick over and back."

Naiada pulled the alpha she rode aside and conferred. Shortly after, he rallied his blessing with a stomp of hoof, melodic whinnies, and flapping of lip. They gathered around him and huddled as a group, heads pressed together in discussion. One of the unis broke from the group and approached Blake.

Naiada said, "The alpha said it would be an honor to help you. Sunny will be your mount. She is the fastest in the blessing and will dutifully wait by the portal for you to return. We will prepare and meet you in the fields west of the breeding caves, a place we call The Ruins. Your mare knows where it is, and so does Franz."

"And if we don't return in three days?"

"We will forge on without you. I anticipate more allies joining us." After recharging Franz's ball of fire, Naiada added, "Please tell my mother I miss her terribly and not to worry. She trained me well."

He nodded and bid Naiada farewell.

Blake pulled Audrey aside. "I've marked a place on your map where you may be able to use your comm to connect with the team in the Winterlands. Follow an old game trail into the mountains. At that elevation you should find a signal. Give them the plan. I will do the same. Hopefully one of us will get the message through in time."

"How can we possibly pull together a response in such little time?"

"We've got the same Merluma time advantage Arkis has. He's had the luxury of lots of it, to plan and to set his traps, while we were on Earth frantically trying to catch up. So rest, stay focused, and wait for my return."

She looked away and nodded. "Sure."

His finger found her chin and raised it, forcing her to look at him. His eyes narrowed. "Please, no unnecessary risks. This is our best chance to get this guy. Can you promise me that?"

Audrey nibbled her lip. "You mean don't do anything stupid. I'll try, but..."

He grabbed her by the shoulders, gazed directly into her eyes like a father laying down the law. "No *buts*. It's a little word spoken carelessly with much danger attached to it. Practice patience, watch your ass, and follow your instincts. They've served you well this far. Naiada is a great asset, *listen* to her. She is wise well beyond her years."

He hugged her, let her go. It felt like suddenly being ripped from a safety tether. She momentarily regressed to her ten-year-old self, scared and alone, when she lost her mother and her father withdrew in grief. Tears threatened to spill.

Blake took notice, regarded her. "Hey," he lifted her chin. "I'm not leaving you."

Her face wadded, then she nodded. "I know."

He gently squeezed her chin. "Stay strong."

"And be patient. Rest. And don't do anything stupid. Got it." She looked toward Franz, bidding Naiada goodbye. "Keep a close eye on Franz, he has a funny way of getting himself into trouble. Got a soft spot for the little guy."

Blake chuckled. "Me too."

They joined Franz and Naiada, who was scratching Sunny behind the ears.

Audrey knelt by Franz, glorying in the heat radiating from the recharged ball of purple fire he held in his hands. "Blake is the world to me, okay?"

He frowned. "Hey, what about me?"

She kissed him on the top of his head. "You take care of yourself too. Watch out for each other and try to avoid shiny temptations."

"Yeah, yeah, ya sound like me missus."

Audrey held up a fist. Franz bumped it. She thought she saw a tear forming in his eye. She wrapped her arms around his tiny body and gave him a mighty hug.

Sunny knelt. Blake mounted first, then pulled Franz up in front of him. Franz slipped the ball of fire into a knotted pocket at his belly that Blake tied in the oversized shirt he wore. Once Franz had grabbed onto the beast's mane, Blake clicked his tongue and kicked his heels. Sunny took off to the south and they disappeared down a steep grassy slope as the last remnants of sunlight dipped below the distant mountains.

Blake rode as if he'd been born to it. Audrey wondered what else she didn't know about him and sincerely hoped they both survived long enough for her to learn more secrets he harbored from his past.

Naiada scratched the alpha's muzzle and pressed her cheek to his. He flicked his head high and stepped back with a whinny. He led his blessing down the steep slope to the field of tender grass to settle for the night.

Audrey, Naiada, and Moonstone ducked into the Labyrinth opening Franz had discovered. They found a dusty chamber near the entrance and away from the main tunnel that linked the top of the Labyrinth to the bottom. The walls and ceiling shimmered from a billion abandoned spider webs. A steady stream of fresh water rushed nearby.

Audrey settled down for a meal-less night on a hard stone surface filled with worry.

Three days.

It was going to be a long and challenging test of her patience waiting for Blake's and Franz's safe return. She gazed over at Naiada, her small body curled up beside her, already fast asleep.

Audrey's heart swelled with a glimmer of hope. At least she wasn't alone.

70

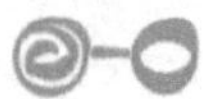

Ramasis' Message

On Isla Salvación, Sinto was jolted awake by his mother's voice, urgently calling for him to come. Something critically important, demanding his attention. She was not in danger, but he should hurry.

He swung his legs from his bunk on *Requiem Sea* II, feet landing solidly on the carpeted floor. It was dark outside. The sun would not rise for several hours.

He donned his Larkian uniform of black shorts and black shirt. He relieved himself and splashed water on his face to rinse the sleep from his eyes, taking a deep drink directly from the faucet. He ran his fingers through his recently trimmed hair, thanks to Rachel.

He scurried down the circular stairway to the gangplank, giving a passing greeting to the guard, a woman the Larkians had recently smuggled out of the Middle East along with several others. She had been well educated before her country imploded and grateful to the Larkians for saving her from a demeaning life under the reign of new leadership.

He hopped on one of many available electric bicycles lined up on the dock. He rode at top speed, past the village, and through the compound to his mother's house.

She was standing in the doorway to greet him.

"What is it?"

"Your father."

"Dead?"

She stepped back so he could enter. "Here."

He slipped past her into the living area. Ramasis lay on the floor clutching himself, moaning and rambling incoherently. He was naked, pale, and appeared half dead. Lorica leaked like sweat from his pores. His body was marred by self-inflicted wounds, his nails overgrown and sharp and stained with his blood. His hair was matted and filthy. Breath, reeking of decay, escaped past his chipped yellow teeth. Arkis' orange nectar had not been kind to him.

Culliford stood guard, ready to act should he lash out. "The island's defenses snared him when he tried to slip through."

His father looked up. "Sinto, my son," he rasped. "Help me. I'm sick, dying, it's hell."

Ianthe came to Sinto's side. The three of them stood over Ramasis, assessing.

"He can barely stand on his own feet. He's weak and delusional," Culliford said.

Sinto pointed. "You can tell his heart's racing." He addressed his mother. "Have you called for Wantemo?"

"Not yet." She looked over to Culliford. "We wanted to discuss our options first, with you."

Sinto said, "See his eyes, pale and colorless. That means his merlux has no spark, his flueox is most likely depleted. It's a miracle he was able to pass through a portal from Merluma and tunnel through the sea to get here." Sinto knelt, pressed his fingers along the side of his father's neck. "Tumors. Arkis' nectar has done its damage. He may soon die."

His father grabbed Sinto's wrist. "No, no, can't die, I must find her," his voice was barely audible.

"Find who?" Sinto asked.

"Naiada."

Sinto grabbed his shoulder and looked deeply into his colorless eyes. "What has happened to her?"

He recoiled and howled as if merely touching him invoked great pain. "Ahhhhh." He started panting and Sinto could hear his heart racing.

"Tell me, what has happened to her?" he asked more urgently.

"She—she—left me." He broke down sobbing. "Trapped me—I think she was talking to someone—right before she—" He stopped to catch his breath.

"Take your time. I need you to remember." Sinto brushed tangled strands of hair from his face.

He looked up at Sinto, pale eyes swimming in tears.

"She locked me in her chamber. Then she—was gone. Left me to rot."

"Who was she talking to? Did you see who it was?"

"Not one, two—blending with the wall—not as good as us—I could see—edges."

Culliford said, "Two of them?"

Sinto looked up to Culliford. "It must have been Audrey and Blake. Francesca's suits when camouflaged have a jerky flicker. It's very obvious to me, up close."

Sinto told them of his experience on Andrew's Island, lying on the top of the ridge, reaching out for Audrey through the Mark. "I'm certain I got a response. I could almost see her... I can't be certain, but I believe she was safe but exhausted, sad but joyful." He lingered on the memory. "I believe she may have found Naiada."

Culliford drew a sharp breath. "Are you sure she was with Blake?"

"Who else could have been with her?" Sinto shook his head. "But I don't know for sure. What we shared were just feelings, passing things I could not completely interpret... but her sadness was not grief, more like how you feel when you observe something that did not need to be, like how I felt when I saw what Arkis had done to the City of Green. I know that doesn't make any sense, but I got the distinct feeling she was not alone. Like she was on a mission with others."

Ramasis interrupted, rambling. "Naiada—angry with me—full grown, a woman now—strong." His eyes wandered over to Ianthe. "Stronger than you. Much more."

Ianthe said. "Did Arkis feed her his poisonous orange nectar?"

"No, no, no—never—I would never—I kept her away from him. I would never let Arkis use her or touch her—I made it my purpose, to protect her." He gasped, closed his eyes, and drew a shaky breath. Then his gaze locked on Ianthe. "He has his other queens. He bred them." He raised a trembling finger, pointing at Ianthe. "Three, from the eggs he stole from you."

Anger flared. Sinto would never forget reliving his mother's memory of Arkis carving up her belly while his father stood by. Not fulfilling his purpose to protect the woman he took as his mate; the woman who bore him a daughter he claimed to love enough to dedicate his life to protecting her from her bastard half-brother. Nor could he forget what Arkis had produced with his mother's eggs.

Sinto bit down the impulse to wrap his hands around his father's neck and finish him, here and now. Sinto seethed against the seed of hate and evil that one small taste of Arkis' orange nectar planted inside of him. Instead he said, "We have seen them. Abominations."

"He has been playing you." Ramasis started to laugh, deep and guttural. Laughter that turned into an unhealthy hacking cough. He rolled to his side and coughed up a splatter of blood on the wood floor. He lay twitching and grinding his teeth.

After a few beats he stilled, panting. "He's planning another trap—"

"We know," Sinto said. "The breeding caves."

His brows rose in shock. "You do?"

"His queens are not as smart as Arkis may believe."

"Ah, hell," he spat, then muttered, "could have saved myself the trip."

"Tell us more."

"He plans to be there, to watch. He likes to watch others bleed."

"Anything else?"

Ramasis' eyes glazed over. "It's where he brews the nectar."

Sinto stood. Ramasis tried to reach for him but his hand failed him. "Please, help me, I know more..." He gasped and wheezed and coughed before continuing, "His queens are weak. The crystal gives them power. Without it they are nothing."

Sinto and Ianthe looked at each other.

Ianthe asked, "What crystal?"

"He found it." Gasping breath. "In the waters—Inception Bay—" Gasp. "Before he took over the City of Green."

Sinto looked to his mother. "Any idea what he's talking about?"

"I have no idea what this crystal may be."

"It sounds like a second stone."

"Second? What stone?" His father's eyes glazed over with confusion, making clear he had *not* been aware of the Salish Stone.

Regardless, Sinto gazed down on his father, seething. All this time his father knew of this other stone or crystal or whatever it may be, and had not shared these important details with his mother. He had been a worthless spy, a truth that his mother should have accepted, especially knowing he had fallen victim to Arkis' nectar. That urge to end him here and now grew stronger but Sinto didn't need his death hanging on his conscience. That he would leave for Arkis. They needed Ramasis alive. But only to learn more of Arkis' advantages and weaknesses.

As much as it pained him, he said, "We should call for Wantemo. Maybe he can help him, at least to ease his discomfort till the inevitable."

"He is a murderer and deserves to die," Culliford said.

"Yes, he is and does." Sinto stared Culliford in the eye. "But so too were you, once. Yet my mother has chosen to forgive you."

Culliford's nostrils flared suddenly, then his face softened. He reached out for Ianthe. "And for that, I am eternally grateful." His gaze cut to Sinto's father. "Unlike him."

Sinto looked down at the broken man who once was his powerful and respected father.

Ianthe decreed, "He may be of some use. After that, let the Council decide his fate. If he survives."

Culliford added, "The Larkian who caught him has been sworn to secrecy. No others can know of his presence on this island. Ramasis is a traitor in our midst. We'll lock him up in the brig on the ship. Wantemo can tend to him there. If there be a devil, may he lay claim to this man's soul, and soon."

PART THREE

71

Arrogant Weakness

IN THE SHADOW OF darkness, Sinto and Wantemo dragged a heavily drugged Ramasis across the black-sand beach and into the shallow waters, his feet carving dual trails in the sand. They each took an arm and swam to *Requiem Sea II*, Ramasis' head lolling.

Culliford was waiting on the platform with Dr. Wickman. They hoisted Ramasis up with a winch and a sling and onto a gurney. They wheeled him through the cargo chamber, down the elevator, and into the bowels of the ship without anyone seeing them.

The brig was a surprisingly large space secured by a thick, sliding steel door. It was open and ready to receive their new prisoner.

Dr. Wickman had set up a makeshift infirmary where Ramasis could be kept alive for however long was necessary to pump him for more information—or until his body failed.

Wantemo and Dr. Wickman took samples—blood, hair, skin, saliva—and scanned his entire torso with a high-tech medical machine they wheeled into the chamber. Critical tests to learn of the effects of continued and long-term use of Arkis' orange nectar. They found many unusual lumps believed to be cancerous tumors. A few were biopsied while Ramasis was unconscious.

Once finished, they left Ramasis in Sinto's care, with Culliford being the last to leave.

Sinto gazed down at the man he once admired and respected. On full display was the tragic outcome of poor choices made in life.

He felt sympathy for what his mother had done to him but could not forgive him for the course of his actions. Had he demonstrated remorse—for killing Audrey's mother, Culliford's crew, Beech, and all the others who fell victim to Arkis and his Orankai—Sinto might have felt differently. But he did not.

Sinto accepted the reason why his father found another woman to share his bed, to love and father another son. His mother's affair with Culliford cut deep. The death of Leela cut deeper. Had his father chosen to leave Ianthe and live the rest of his life with another companion and their newborn son, Sinto would have understood, eventually. But his father chose, on his own accord, to encourage Arkis down his dark path: to destroy everything his mother had accomplished, to break the peace, and to abolish a unified Merahvu.

What his mother and the Circle had accomplished wasn't perfect. Nothing ever was. Nature was full of examples. The Sapien world too. But among the imperfections were swaths of goodness and satisfied people making forward progress. His father failed to realize that polishing imperfection was a hell of a lot easier than wading through the rubble of utter destruction for that elusive gem of peace and balance. Change was inevitable—expected and painful—and required patience as it took root over a long course of time.

It saddened Sinto when he learned neither of his parents had a choice as to their chosen life companion. Their union was forced upon them both by duty and familial expectations—a common story told throughout human history and, not surprisingly, was the thing that tore them apart. And because of it, both made consequentially bad choices. Ramasis lay suffering and near death because of his.

His father's eyes cracked open, glassy and feverish. A moan escaped his lips as the drug Dr. Wickman had administered wore off. His gaze swept around the stark-white chamber, taking in the dim lighting, the scanning equipment, and the gurney on which he lay.

His gaze swept up to Sinto. Redness rimmed his eyes. "My son," he rasped.

Sinto laid his hand on his father's chest. His father reached for it but the chained cuffs around his wrists stopped him.

His eyes danced nervously. "What is this, my prison?"

"You should be thankful you are still alive."

He looked away. "I have been dead for a long time and for that I am not thankful."

"When did it happen? What horrible deed finally killed you?"

A sob slipped from his lips. "My arrogance. I should have let go. I see now with clarity. Why is that?"

"Looking back is easy. It's the looking forward and following the right path that is a challenge. A Sapien named Hervé once said, 'He who will not answer to the rudder, must answer to the rocks.'"

His father closed his eyes. "My rudder was indeed misguided."

"What would you have done differently?"

"I never should have agreed to Join with your mother."

"Did you have a choice?"

He didn't answer right away. "No," he gasped.

"Did she?"

His head swiveled. "No."

"You both were cursed, from the start."

He blinked away tears. "Not cursed. We made you and your sisters. For that it was worth it."

"And what about Arkis?"

He broke down sobbing. Tears streamed from his eyes and spittle leaked from his mouth. He tried to roll to his side but he was constrained by the chains and cuffs binding his wrists and ankles.

He screamed in frustration. "Arkis is my curse!"

"As he is for everyone."

Hearing that from the son he had abandoned for his curse of the other, he became inconsolable. Unsure of what to do, Sinto remained silent and stood by while he suffered. After a while he quieted and slipped into a state of slumber.

Sinto stepped back to leave but stopped when his father mumbled something Sinto couldn't decipher.

Sinto went to his bedside. "What was that?"

"He has a weakness. Arkis," he said. His lips pursed and it took him several tries to form the word and spit it out. "You."

Saying the word took its toll. He blinked and groaned and rattled his chains. "My body is failing. Not much longer shall I be in this world. Please take my hand."

Sinto grasped a hand bound by chains. His grip was weak and nails sharp.

"Arrogance will destroy him—as it has destroyed me." He gasped for air. "He believes he is infallible—will not rest until he breaks you—it consumes him—a great distraction—his weakness—use it... To end him."

His father drew a final breath. His aura blinkered and went out. Then his ravaged body disintegrated to ash.

72

Convergence

SINTO WAS CALLED TO the command center shortly after his father passed. The message was urgent and told him to hurry.

Culliford and his mother were huddled around Alvarez's laptop along with Rachel, the sound too low for Sinto to quite hear. Others from the Larkian Council slipped in shortly after Sinto—Leonard, Francesca, Dr. Wickman—as well as Wantemo.

Alvarez switched what they were watching on his laptop to the large screen mounted on the wall.

Blake's voice suddenly cut through, loud and clear. He was recounting what happened to him and Audrey on Merluma, while a Wekeep sat beside him. Sinto recognized the Wekeep from earlier days spent on Merluma—Franzaboana Bevor Slumpjam Gemtaker Buttmist, an old acquaintance of Wantemo's. In fact, Sinto had enlisted a Wekeep to discretely help him while Audrey was recovering from the deadly wound inflicted by a bluestripe the first time he took her to Merluma.

Franz capitalized the camera, leaning forward and blocking out Blake completely, his nose filling the screen and distorted by the wide-angle lens. Steely gray hair burst from his nostrils. Franz seemed to like the attention he garnered from the crowd on the other side of the screen, butting in and adding his own embellishments to Blake's stories. He grew especially animated yammering on about bats and birdbrains, stealing a prized puzzle, and how much he looked forward to wielding fishsticks with extra sauce and riding in a dohicky.

Sinto slid into a chair next to Rachel.

"What on earth is he talking about?" she asked in a low voice.

Sinto shrugged. "I have no idea. A real character, that one."

"What a hoot! I wanna meet him. He's a—whatcha call it?"

Sinto leaned closer, kept his voice down. "Here you might call them gnomes, but that's an insult. They're called Wekeeps. As their name implies, they tend to take what they like and keep what they find, especially things that are shiny."

"Sounds more like what we call a gremlin," she whispered back.

"One and the same..."

When Blake saw Sinto his eyes lit up. "Sinto! We heard you were injured."

Sinto held up his right hand. The color had returned to normal but not the density of underlying flesh. It looked like an old man's, bony and frail. He made a feeble fist. "My hand, burned rather badly. It will heal, over time."

Blake smiled. "Audrey will be much relieved; she has been worried sick."

"As have we," Sinto said.

Blake whispered something to Franz. Franz rolled his eyes and hopped down from the desk where Blake sat. He hopped up on a thickly cushioned sofa in the background and began munching down handfuls of what appeared to be popcorn from a bowl he held in his lap.

Blake said, "We don't have much time. A full day will pass on Merluma during our conversation. Franz and I promised to get back as soon as possible so I'll keep it brief."

Alvarez said, "The floor is all yours."

"We have Naiada, she is well and very appreciative that we found her. She has proven to be a great asset to our team. Ianthe and Sinto, she misses you both very much. It may come as a shock the next time you see her—she has grown into a healthy and wise young woman during her imprisonment here. She has been blessed with a power that awes.

"Arkis is hiding in the lower chambers of the Labyrinth with three queens..." He winced. "I'm sorry to be the bearer of this news, but you must know, Ianthe, he bred them from your eggs."

Sinto looked at his mother. She nodded and said, "We are aware."

"Anyway, Naiada believes they have been rendered useless after Franz stole their crystal ball. Before that, we witnessed them seeding a false message for Ianthe to pick up. He's setting another trap, this time in the breeding caves."

Sinto said, "That message has been received. My father, he—passed it on shortly before he died. Please let Naiada know he's gone. He managed to make it here to us, but Arkis' nectar finally killed him. He also told me that Arkis plans to be there, personally, at the trap. Apparently, he likes to watch the bloodshed."

Rachel scoffed beside him.

Blake smiled "Good to know, we'll try to give him a dose of it. Naiada has a plan she's been a little mum about. I believe we should trust her. She and Audrey are positioned close to the mountains west of the breeding caves, which are located in the upper section of the Labyrinth. Audrey is positioning herself to raise the team in the Winterlands on her comm to coordinate timing and for the role they will play."

Sinto looked to his mother for her reaction. She shook her head, unaware of what Naiada was planning.

Blake continued, "I must ask another favor. I suggest you do not engage in this fight. Naiada was clear on this. Send no more teams to Merluma."

Alvarez sat forward. "Most of the teams have retreated from the City of Ice. A skeletal crew of Larkians and Merahvu remain, searching for both of you. I will alert Stokes to listen for Audrey's instruction."

Blake nodded. "Perfect. The fewer of us we risk the better. Also tell Stokes to use Arkis' spies to our advantage. Arkis relies mostly on raptors but who knows what else. Let word leak we are acting on his false tip, that we're sending an army to attack the breeding caves from the east. It's what he expects. We'll take care of the rest."

He sighed. "By the time you hear back from us whatever Naiada has planned may be over. Time is slipping fast and Franz and I must return. Lock onto this location. It's a cabin tucked in the forest somewhere in British Columbia. Franz discovered a land portal, which is how we hope to return to Earth, to this very cabin. Wish us luck."

Then the screen went blank.

Sinto's mother burst into tears. The underlying tension, borne since learning of Naiada's capture, released from her face and body. Culliford comforted her and she him, sharing mutual joy after learning their children were alive and safe and together, at least for the moment.

Sinto was surprised by the conflict of emotion he felt. Joy and relief he shared with his mother, along with great frustration and a feeling of helplessness. Audrey and Naiada were carrying a great burden he felt he should be there to share.

His mother laid a hand on his arm, gave a squeeze. "*Trust your sister. You are needed here for a different, equally critical fight.*" She tipped her head toward Wantemo who waved him over.

"Come with me," Wantemo said. "We have something to show you. Ryan and I have made great progress."

Sinto bid farewell to Culliford and his mother.

Rachel was bubbling with curiosity. "Spill what you learn. Ya know where to find me." She gave him a hug then spun on her heel to join Alvarez, tapping away on his keyboard.

In the lab on *Requiem Sea II*, Ryan was suited up and working in the inner lab. He waved, clearly ecstatic to see Sinto. Sinto waved back. Wantemo donned a suit and passed through the double chambers to join Ryan.

Sinto watched through a window as Ryan dropped a pea-sized blob of Orange into a tank of sea water. It floated down to the bottom and wriggled around, exploring its surroundings. Next, he dropped a nurdle of plastic that bobbed on the surface. Orange reacted instantaneously and rose up from the bottom. A tentacle burst from the blob, grabbed it, and sucked it inside. Orange sank below the surface and hovered off the bottom, writhing as it consumed the nurdle. Finally, Ryan released a dropper full of a gelatinous, pale-blue substance into the water. It bobbed, then slowly sank.

He stepped back and prompted Wantemo.

Wantemo removed his glove and dipped a finger into the water. He wagged it—left, right, up, down. The blue substance stretched and moved in reaction to his commands, spreading through the water and around the blob of Orange. Wantemo then pinched his fingers, sealing Orange inside. The bubble sparked and went rigid from Wantemo's lock.

Ryan dropped another plastic nurdle in the tank. Orange reacted, pressing a tentacle against the side of the bubble. The bubble held firm. Orange grew frantic, launching multiple tentacles. The bubble held firm. Orange wound up into a tight ball half its original size and hurled itself against the walls of the bubble confining it. The bubble stretched and sparked but held its enclosed state.

This frantic fight continued.

Wantemo chuckled in delight.

Ryan carefully put away his things. They both slipped through the sterilizing chambers, removing their suits. Then joined Sinto, watching the drama unfold through the window. Orange thrashed but failed to break free from its organic prison.

Ryan yawned. "It will still be at it hours from now. I'm going to grab a bite to eat, then come back."

Wantemo said, "We'll join you."

They marched up the mid-ship stairway to the ship's galley one level up.

The galley was a ghost town and it was up to them to rummage for something to eat in the ship's giant refrigerator. Ryan pulled out sandwich fixings. Sinto grabbed a fresh-baked loaf of bread cooling on one of many stainless-steel racks.

Sinto sliced bread, Wantemo spread mayonnaise, and Ryan layered meat, cheese, pickles, and lettuce. The three of them stood facing each other, gobbling down the heaping sandwiches, listening to the hum of the galley's vast freezer.

Sinto was too worked up to eat but he choked down the sandwich anyway. It had been a day of convergence and swirling emotion. His father was gone. They received news from Blake that was encouraging in the sense that Audrey and Naiada were safe and together, but unsettling as to the mystery of what Naiada had planned. A turning point in their fight against Orange was playing out in the lab. He felt anxious to act and helplessly forced to stand back at the same time.

The sandwich tasted like sawdust in his mouth but yet he ate it, all of it, knowing he should. After an unsatisfying and torturous fifteen minutes, Sinto returned to the lab with Ryan and Wantemo with a full and churning stomach.

The Orange blob lay within the blue-tinged bubble. Alive but much less frisky.

"Hm, needs more time." Ryan sighed. "That stuff's not going anywhere anytime soon. Don't know about you two but I could use a vay-cay-day. It ain't over till the fat lady sings, and we just entered the first Act." He slapped Sinto on the back. "The beach beckons."

Sinto quirked a questioning brow. "What does a fat lady singing have to do with Orange dying?"

Ryan chuckled. "It's a colloquialism, from days past when a well-endowed lady with a strong and powerful voice concluded an opera with a spine-tingling, high-pitched solo. It means we wait and in the end we will be rewarded with the story's anticipated conclusion. In our case, the death of Orange, and I predict with ninety-nine point nine percent certainty it will die, eventually."

And it did, exactly thirty-six hours and fifty-seven minutes later without a spine-tingling performance or much fanfare.

73

Summoning

THE RISING SUN HAD barely lit the sky when Audrey rose to an empty chamber. Alarmed that Naiada was gone, she stumbled outside.

Naiada and Moonstone were already in the lower field working with the unis. Audrey had yet to clear the cobwebs from her head, recalling something Naiada said last night before falling asleep. Something about much to do and so little time. Naiada was relentless. Her definition of rest came from a dictionary in a world not of Earth.

It was fascinating watching her work with the unis. A fierce energy surrounded the blessing and the force in which they moved, muscles rippling and sweat forming on flanks, as they ran through various drills.

The alpha was attentive to Naiada's every command. The lift of a finger, the whip of an arm, a click of tongue. It reminded Audrey of the day she met Wantemo in Tallamure. How he easily controlled an army of giant ants to build houses from the excrement of giant worms for an influx of Healers migrating to tend the recently ill. A feat accomplished with the wag of a finger and a twitch of his lips. This was like that, only Naiada was training them in the ways of war; to attack, to distract, and to drop to a knee for her to easily mount in one swift movement.

Moonstone added to the chaos, flying erratically above, pitching against the wind with his missing tail feathers. He clung to the air, swooping side to side, pulling up and diving down. He was getting much stronger. Audrey wondered if Naiada gave him a boost with her unique abilities.

Audrey could use such a boost about now.

Naiada saw her and waved her over.

Her eyes were on fire, smile bright, breath clouding the air between them. "Was hoping you'd wake soon. Care to try a quick mount?"

Audrey twisted side-to-side, stretching her spine, rolling around her hips. "Maybe in a moment. That floor was relentless."

Moonstone dropped from the sky, landed at her feet, and chirped in greeting.

She scratched him on the neck, where his previous wound had fully healed.

"Did you help with that?" she asked Naiada.

Naiada quirked a smile.

Naiada demonstrated a quick mount. Then it was Audrey's turn. The mare trotted in a wide circle. Audrey readied to grab her mane and swing her leg up and over once the mare came alongside and dipped to a knee.

The first try was comical. When the mare dipped Audrey launched her leg over and slid off the other side, landing on her ass among prickly-stemmed wildflowers.

The blessing whinnied and snorted. Naiada suppressed a chuckle. Moonstone chirped in a way that sounded suspiciously like *ha, ha, ha.*

"Again," Naiada said.

Audrey seethed at Naiada's choice of word, but Audrey repeated that embarrassment two more times.

"Again."

She gritted her teeth and nailed the fourth try. By then Audrey was ready to stop.

"Nice, but you're not done," Naiada said. "You're too mechanical, single-minded. It works but it's prone to failure. Be one with the mare, sense her every move, *flow* with her."

Naiada opened her mouth to say that word once more: *Again*—one that stirred up unpleasant memories from the grueling training her father forced upon her as a child, one that made Audrey seethe and want to scream—but Audrey stopped her with a finger pressed to her lip.

Audrey said, "I know; it's not my first rodeo. I get it: again, and again, and again, until perfected. Just please, do not use that word, *again*. Anything but that."

Naiada studied her for moment, then her brows shot up as if she had stopped time and mysteriously journeyed back to Audrey's past to understand why it disturbed her so. She blinked. "Oh no, *my* mistake." She said nothing more but gestured for Audrey to continue.

Audrey put forth every ounce of will she could muster. The skill was in the read. Less muscle and more finesse. Over and over she practiced—running alongside her mare, grabbing her mane, and gracefully mounting—until she was as breathless and as sweaty as her mare. With each try they bonded, gaining a new appreciation for their partner.

She had no idea how mentally and physically involved riding a uni could be. She gained an all-new respect for cow wranglers, imagining it wasn't much different.

While they rested, they nibbled on roots Naiada had dug up at first light from prickly thistle-like plants growing in the meadow. They were sweet and earthy; a meal packed with protein, fiber, and a heady cocktail of nutrients. Not a meal you'd expect from Leonard but her belly was full and hunger satiated. They dug up several more and wrapped them in grape-like leaves for later, which Audrey stuffed inside her suit's attached pack.

"So, what is the plan?" Audrey asked.

Naiada twirled a lock of her hair—the gesture an echo of Ianthe's own habit when pondering something worrisome or important. "We need allies, many more."

"And I need to find higher ground and try to connect with the teams in the Winterlands."

She smiled. "So do I for a similar purpose." She stood. "We will ride into the mountains with Moonstone as our guide."

Naiada conferred with the alpha in her silent way, palm resting against his flank. He called over two unis from his blessing. They readily approached. A smaller gray one knelt before Audrey, offering its back. A spirited white-speckled roan knelt for Naiada.

Naiada ordered the alpha and his blessing to head south and meet Blake and Franz outside the portal. They took off, leaving a flattened swath of grass and wildflowers in their wake.

Audrey wore her suit, fully charged from the sun and a quick electrical topper from Naiada. Audrey adjusted her goggles and pulled on her hood, her map at the ready should they need it. She trusted Naiada knew her way but felt better for the redundancy.

Moonstone took flight and they were off. They rode camouflaged so as to not risk being observed by one of Arkis' flying scouts or roving Orankai. All they would see was a pair of unis traveling along a well-trodden game trail.

The unis the alpha picked were nimble and strong for good reason. The journey was challenging; threading through the forest and along narrow switchbacks up steep hillsides. They reached the first of many dramatic views after several arduous hours of riding and they stopped to marvel at the spread of wild jungle and forestland where it met the Great Ocean. Audrey immediately recognized it as the place where Sinto first brought her to Merluma.

"We call this part of Merluma Inception." Naiada pointed and drew a circle in the air with her finger. "The ring of reefs and obsidian ridges is all that is left of a great mountain peak. It collapsed into the sea during a great earthshake long ago."

What Naiada described was apparent. Outward bowing reefs sheltered the large cove from the Great Ocean and the steep ridges hemmed in the beach, jungle, and forestlands, forming a perfect circle where a mighty mountain once stood.

When Audrey was here before, she had not fully understood Sinto's intent and attempted to escape, hoping to climb over the western ridge or find a valley through the mountains. It was apparent from their present perspective that she would have failed. Even for someone with climbing equipment or local knowledge it appeared impossible to escape the confines of Inception.

Naiada continued her story. "The mountain that collapsed was rich with magnetic metals, the roots of which burrow deep, and the Merahvu believe that is what connects Merluma to Earth. There is no true north or south pole on Merluma, just the singular magnetic point of Inception. Go straight across the Great Ocean and it will lead you right back to here. We use the lay of what was once tribal claimed lands and Inception to designate direction."

She pointed to the west. "Desertlands of the Seakai." In the distance lay a barren peninsula of pale sandstone and arid mountains beneath a bright, blue sky, forming the Sea of Meura. The direction from which she and Blake came when they first arrived. In the foreground, the Labyrinth sprawled deep within the western ridge, framing one side of Inception.

Naiada pointed south to the glittering blue sea, bowing with the curvature of Merluma. "The Great Ocean is deemed neutral and unclaimed."

She pointed to the mountains behind them. "Beyond the Black Mountains are the Winterlands of the Arctakai: high plains, lightly forested, but mostly barren and glacial. And there—" She pointed east. "Are the Forestlands of the Terrakai." Curving east from the Black Mountains, the thickly treed Forestlands spread like a carpet of coarse green velvet.

And above that coarse carpet of green, a thick plume of black smoke marred the sky.

Audrey asked, "What do you make of that?"

Naiada didn't answer right away. Her eyes narrowed as she studied the sky. "Wildfire…"

"Should we be concerned?"

"Not at the moment." She pondered for a beat longer. "Though it might work to our advantage." Worry furrowed her brow and she drew a deep breath. "We mustn't linger. We've a little further to go." She kicked her heels and her uni took off, Audrey's leaping behind.

Audrey's map showed an ancient trail that Naiada was following. The same one Blake found and marked as her route to an elevated position to raise the teams in the Winterlands on her comm. The air cooled and thinned as they climbed higher. Between barren rock and mountain scruff were pockets of ice and snow.

Naiada dismounted, dropping her camouflage. "You should try to contact your friends from here."

Audrey was relieved for a chance to dismount and stand on her own two feet. She ached from riding but not as much as the day before.

She switched off her camouflage. Her batteries were holding sufficiently with benefit from the sun, fueling a blanket of warmth against her skin in the chilling elevation.

A stiff, frigid wind blew in from the Winterlands and swirled around mountainous peaks. From their vista, they could see clearly in almost every direction. The white glacier covering the Winterlands spread far and wide from the base of the Black Mountains like a wedding dress train.

"Comm on," Audrey said. A squelch, then static emitted from her goggles. She circled their flat perch high above, searching for a signal. Nothing. She checked the map. A lone peak rose between her and where the map indicated the City of Ice was located. She sighed. "No good." Pointing, she said, "That peak is directly between us and the city."

"I know of a better place," said Naiada. "It's not far, but first let's stop for a while." She stepped to the edge of the ridge, gazing down at Inception. "Inception is home to the fae; the Forestlands and Winterlands to many other creatures. This is the perfect location for me to send them all a message." She crinkled her nose and smiled. "I suggest you take the unis and shelter behind those rocks." She pointed behind Audrey.

Audrey clicked her tongue. To her surprise, the unis responded, giving her their full attention. She led them where an upheaval of rock converged, large enough where they could all safely wedge in between, far from Naiada. Moonstone landed at her feet and began scampering around looking for frozen bugs in cracks and crevasses.

Naiada stood still as a statue at the peak of the ridge facing Inception, eyes blazing with purple fire. She raised her hands and face toward the sky. The air crackled and sparked around her. She released a war cry and splayed her fingers.

Threads of electricity burst from her hands. They swirled toward the sky then exploded in every direction. Thousands of them lit up the sky with a cool purple hue. They flew over Audrey's head. The uni's pranced and ducked to dodge them. They launched down the slopes of the ridge to the south and burrowed through the jungles and forests of Inception. They cut through the thickening smoke and across the fields and forests of the Forestlands. They slid down snow-covered slopes and bounced across the glaciers of the Winterlands, turning their glacial-blue hue a deep lavender.

The air Audrey breathed was charged with electricity. Her lungs tingled and face stung, and she caught the sharp whiff of ozone before a gust of wind blew it away. The tangle of purple and white threads extending from Naiada's hands cracked and popped across the sky.

Audrey grabbed the manes of their unis and tried to settle them, their eyes wild and feet restless.

Naiada remained entranced. The threads she birthed connected with the creatures of Merluma, spreading her message far and wide. The air hummed softly as she settled into that state for quite a long while. The unis finally calmed and settled on the ground. Audrey did the same. Moonstone plopped down beside her and began preening his feathers, using extra care with the new ones growing from his tail.

A half hour or more passed before the crackling threads wound their way back to Naiada's fingers. The sky darkened and the potent smell of ozone cleared.

Naiada opened her eyes and lowered her head. She wobbled a little, sucking deep the cool mountain air until fully gaining her balance and restoring the natural glow in her eyes. Then she meandered over to where Audrey, the unis, and Moonstone waited. She sat beside Audrey and released a deep sigh. "It is done."

"What is done?"

Naiada raised a brow. "The ask."

"For help?"

She nodded.

"What kind of help?"

She gave Audrey a grimacing smile and she shrugged. "I honestly don't know. What happens next will depend entirely on them."

Audrey was unsure what to make of Naiada's indifference and uncertainty. She could only hope that whatever message Naiada sent to the creatures of Merluma would spell trouble for Arkis and his Orankai.

Naiada looked over at Audrey's pack. "I'm starving."

"From what I just witnessed, I'd imagine you are more than that." Audrey dug out a couple of thistle roots and handed one to Naiada.

"It is a bit taxing, and—" She took a bite of her thistle root. "This will help, greatly."

Audrey was burning with questions but respected the fact Naiada needed a moment to herself so they nibbled their roots in silence.

Once they finished, Naiada grew more somber; something was clearly bothering her. She finally broke the silence. "The fae are alarmed—frantic no one has reached out to tell them what is happening. They believe they were abandoned by the Merahvu. Their queen, Anya, was a bit testy, but eventually agreed to summon her frolic of fae to spread the word to others about Arkis' planned trap at the breeding caves and to share my request for help."

Naiada grew quiet, a lock of hair twisted around her finger. Audrey watched her expectantly, sensing there was more she wanted to say. Naiada frowned. "It saddens me, what is happening here. I felt Anya's terror, the panic from those that are near the fire. It's... I wish there was more I could do. I've never felt so powerless as I did when I was locked up for all those years." A tear slipped down Naiada's cheek, then another. Then in an unexpected outburst, she slammed her fist against the earth. "Damn, my father! He—he was a part of this, fueling this mess, and now—" A sob slipped past her lips. "I—I sense something horrible has happened, a feeling as if he's gone, dead even. It's hard to explain, but it just is. I sense his absence in both of our worlds as acutely as I feel my rage."

Audrey laid her hand atop Naiada's fingers twining a lock of hair. "I am sorry, truly, if what you sense is true."

She squeezed back, wiping tears from her pock-scarred cheeks with the back of her hand. "If he is dead, I hope it was merciful, not that he deserved it. He made terrible choices, dark and hurtful choices. Imprisoning me against my will, what I discovered he did to my mother—and what he did to yours—that was unmerciful." She sucked down a sob. "But I can't lie, I will miss him terribly. He was a good man once, before my mother made her own bad choices, as did that bastard son of his. They led him to a dark path. After that... everything good about him was smothered by grief and rage and that wicked nectar Arkis brews."

Naiada collapsed into her arms. Audrey held her while she wept, recalling the first time they met. Audrey had sensed a deep-seated anger as she lay weakened and visibly scarred by the toxin she had ingested; one Audrey's father had exposed her to, intentionally. She wondered if Naiada still felt that anger from the trauma she had endured. Add on top of that her forced isolation by her father, the knowing of the terrible things he did. And now, possibly, the reality of his death.

Audrey could sympathize. She too had been robbed, never having the chance to say goodbye to her mother, and no mother to nurture and offer guidance as she grew. She felt that deep-seated thrum of grief that never ended and a void that could never be filled. But she learned to cope and live with the festering wound. It would always be a part of her.

Audrey said, "I know what it's like to feel abandoned. But you're not alone. You have your mother. You have Sinto. And now you have me."

Naiada looked up, her eyes glistening. "For that, I am grateful." She hugged Audrey and when she withdrew, she sat a little taller. Audrey felt warmth bloom in her heart and that void inside grow a little bit smaller.

The moment passed and Audrey offered Naiada another root. She shook her head, ready to get back to their important task at hand. "We must keep moving."

She stood and pointed toward the trail, rounding the peak between them and the City of Ice. It was steep and precarious. "Moonstone, sweep for spies."

Moonstone departed with a hasty flap of wings. Audrey and Naiada mounted their unis and started the slow and difficult climb along a shelf cut into the side of the mountain. The narrow trail appeared to have been there for a millennium, forged by thousands of unis, ruminants, Merahvu, and countless other creatures of Merluma, past and present. Audrey kept her eyes and her uni on the trail. One misstep could lead to a fatal fall.

And once they reached the highest point on the other side of the peak Audrey found a strong signal. But it was Naiada who sent the message using Audrey's comm, summoning for help with detailed instructions on how and where to find them.

74

The Ruins

It was an arduous ride back. Night had fallen and their path was lit by the half-moon, cutting through the forest canopy. Naiada asked Audrey to lead, using her mapping system and technology-enhanced night-vision goggles. It was late by the time they reached the dusty cobweb-ridden cave where they stayed the night before.

At first light they continued their trek to the agreed-upon rendezvous point that Naiada had discussed with Blake. Moonstone took to the sky, scouting for Orankai.

There were no more roots to eat. Audrey was starving. Her ribs and hip bones had grown more defined and her suit fitted looser. She had given up on restful sleep. The anxiety of not knowing what they would be facing in the coming days—where they would find their next meal, if Blake and Franz were able to contact the Larkians, if they would ever return to Earth—all weighed heavily on her mind. These worries gnawed, rendering sleep nearly impossible.

Moonstone saw no spying Scouts or roaming Orankai during his frequent sweeps. It was as if they had vacated Merluma. Naiada assured Audrey that was not true, that much activity was occurring within the Labyrinth, the breeding caves, and the Forestlands where the fires raged. Regardless, they remained alert, and Audrey and Naiada remained camouflaged. Moonstone stayed close, scouting from the skies as they neared the rendezvous point; a place she called The Ruins.

The Ruins were an ancient city built by the original Homo-Sapiens who migrated from Earth. They were north of the Labyrinth, next to the Desertlands, and far from the heavily used entrance near Deep Lake and the connecting tunnels within the Labyrinth to the south.

Naiada pulled her uni beside Audrey's and told the story of The Ruins as they rode. "Early Homo-Sapiens who first arrived on Merluma discovered a perfect Eden—mild climate, fresh water, rich soil, and other species who migrated from Earth around the same time. They found no need to wander as they once had on Earth and settled in a valley at the base of the Black Mountains, where there was an endless supply of fresh water, hillsides of rich soil, and abundant greenery. They formed bricks from sandstone with tools forged from obsidian, which was plentiful from landslides and past eruptions. They terraced hillsides for crops, funneled streams for irrigation, and cut pathways for easy access to surrounding lands...

"But that was before the Great Upheaval. What followed was chaos, death, and desperation. The Black Mountains erupted and Mount Inception collapsed into the sea, forming the bay and lands of the same name. Vegetation shriveled and died and was consumed by wildfire. Sea water trapped beneath layers of Merluma's mantel rose to the surface in a great flood, swallowing whole continents yet to be discovered."

Her gaze grew distant. "Many species perished." She swept her hand through the air. "The seas never retreated. All that was left above sea level was this small bit of land. Over time, the sea flourished, and the few Homo-Sapiens that survived evolved to hunt and travel through the seas. It was after these early evolutionary changes that the remaining humans split into the three distinct tribes, and evolved further. As their numbers increased, they squabbled over these sparse lands. The Forever War followed. Thousands and thousands of years of conflict until peace was reached and the tribes merged into a singular people, the Merahvu."

"What happened to the city?"

"Nature spared the valley but the city was long forgotten and abandoned."

Moonstone dropped from the sky with good news. Nary a Scout or Orankai this side of the breeding caves nor in the valley and lands surrounding The Ruins.

Audrey looked at Naiada and they both smiled. Naiada kicked her heels. Her uni took off in a gallop. Audrey followed. The trail crested a rise where Naiada reined in her uni's mane. They came to a swift stop.

A valley lay below where the remains of a once vast city sprawled along its floor, weaving among fields of wildflower and grasses and up terraced hillsides. Woodlands threaded in between, offering shelter for wildlife and protection from the fierce winds that kicked up across the Desertlands, funneling up from the west. A layer of smoke from the wildfires had settled along the valley floor.

Naiada kicked her heels and her uni took off down the trail that switch-backed down the hillside to the valley below. It ended at the shores of a lake fed by streams flowing from the Black Mountains. Waterfalls streaked the obsidian faces capped with snow.

Audrey dismounted, dropped to her knees, and slaked her thirst. The unis slurped their fill and wandered to the nearest field of wild grasses to graze.

The smoke cast a brownish haze in the sky and was a mild irritation to throat and eyes. Naiada gazed up with concern. "We should be safe here from the fires." She pointed toward the mountains. "It's what's happening to those on the other side that worries me."

That wasn't the only worry Audrey had. Hunger gnawed. It felt as if Audrey's stomach was eating itself. Naiada was in agreement and they set out to satisfy this primal need. She pointed out things that were or were not safe to eat. There were plenty of berries, greens, and even flowers that were easy to find and pick. They both ate greedily.

In their distraction they failed to notice a dark speck approaching in the sky. It was Moonstone who alerted them, bursting into a string of caws and shrill tweets.

They looked up. The dark speck was moving unnaturally fast through the smoke-filled sky, directly toward them. They crouched in the tall grass, helpless to do anything to stop it as it zeroed in and circled. Audrey recognized it immediately. A long-range, winged drone about six feet long. Painted on its dark side was the white Larkian symbol.

Audrey jumped to her feet and switched on her suit's comm. Stokes' voice boomed through the tiny speaker embedded in her goggles. "Audrey, is that you?"

"Yes, and I'm with Naiada!"

The drone circled low and the camera mounted on its nose swiveled to focus on the two of them, waving excitedly.

"Are you well?"

"I would give my left foot for a Leonard meal and a hot shower, but otherwise we're good, and thankful you've found us."

"A Leonard meal I can't promise, but company I can." She could hear the joy and relief in his voice. "We received your message. Tucker, Dyer, and I are en route to meet you. ETA eighteen hours. We'd be sooner but wildfires are forcing us to travel farther west then we had hoped."

"By what means are you traveling?"

He chuckled. "You'll soon see. We picked up some interesting new friends who presented themselves and offered help in a most peculiar way. Quite hair raising at first, but we worked things out."

Audrey noted the hint of a smile curling on Naiada's lips.

Stokes continued, "Blake made contact with Alvarez. We were relieved to learn you were alive. Things have been somber since you disappeared. Arkis set a trap and we blindly stepped into it. We lost good people, both Merahvu and Larkian, and sadly, Burns was one of them. Those bastards are heartless. Stay out of sight and keep your eyes open."

"He's setting up a trap at the breeding caves."

"Blake filled Alvarez in on the details along with information provided by Ianthe. Arkis set the fires in the Forestlands, to smoke us out and funnel us into his trap. Khani and Vesna let slip to his spies that we're falling for it. We'll fill you in more once we arrive."

And with that the drone made one last circle and disappeared in the haze of smoke swirling around the mountains.

Eighteen hours of nothing to do but wait. For Blake and Franz to return. For Stokes and the others to arrive. Audrey and Naiada sat among the wildflowers, pleasantly satiated. The sun warmed their faces.

They settled into silence, exhausted and anxious, fighting to keep their eyes open.

75

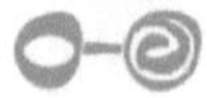

The Gathering

AUDREY AND NAIADA WERE jolted by a growing rumble and distant shrieks of terror, growing louder.

Naiada screamed. "Run!"

They leaped to their feet, ran toward the nearest ruins, and slipped behind a stone wall. The ground rumbled and jostled. Loose stones rattled free and tumbled to their feet. Dust rose ahead of a fast-running river of frantic beasts. A stampede of every imaginable creature descended upon the valley, their eyes wide and fearful. They came running, slithering, rolling, flying, buzzing, and crawling. Herbivores, carnivores, and omnivores ran side by side, oblivious to each other. A massive migration triggered by fear.

Naiada yelled above the din, "Creatures from the Forestlands, running from the fire!"

She jumped into action, calling for them to calm. Some blew through grassy fields and kept running toward the Desertlands at the end of the valley. Many heeded Naiada's call and circled in confused groups among wildflowers and throughout the surrounding woodlands. Bluestripe tigers, bobcats, wolves, and wild dogs eyed the defenseless goat and sheep and darted between moose and elk in a tense standoff. Audrey watched, fearing for

Naiada's life as she wedged herself between the hostile groups. Her eyes blazed with fire. In the bright sunshine, Audrey could barely see the tiny threads that swirled from her hands and wove between collectives of varying creatures.

Audrey heard Naiada's voice and felt her message threading inside her mind as one of those tentacles reached out for her. Naiada set forth a story in images, sound, vibration, and primal feeling; a story that told of a common enemy to all—fire and the Orankai—and what that meant for Merluma and every creature that called it home. Her story ended in a plea for peace and an ask for their help.

There was a notable calm that befell those within the field and those hiding in the forest surrounding it. Once tensions abated, the creatures that had gathered in tense standoffs aimlessly wandered, confused and lost from suddenly being driven from nest, cave, tree, forest, field, and burrow by the fires. Creatures favored tender paws, singed fur, and soot-filled eyes. Naiada's presence calmed the many and soon she was surrounded by a diverse animal kingdom of curious faces seeking her command, an impressive feat for someone so small. Ears twitched, hooves pawed, claws retracted, and the weary plopped down to rest.

Audrey watched from afar with amazement as Naiada deliberated with the animals as the afternoon wore on, keeping the peace and sharing details of her plan with each and every group of them, communicating in various ways in which they understood. Some slithered or sneaked off but most stayed, committed to help reclaim Merluma from Arkis and his Orankai monsters.

Late in the day a frolic of fae arrived in a murmuration of tiny black bodies held aloft with rainbow-colored wings, the buzz and hush of anxious voices preceding them. They dove and darted and circled, wings shedding a shimmering dust. The frolic took residence in the forest. Clouds of bioluminescent light bounced between the trees.

The fae queen, Anya, stayed behind and settled on Naiada's shoulder, chattering incisively with a forceful whispery voice in a foreign language. Naiada nodded, brow furrowed with sympathy and concern, as she listened to Anya's grievances.

When Audrey settled for a moment to rest, she was soon jostled awake by yet another rumble of many hooves approaching; a sounder of wild boar with a dozen or so Wekeep clinging to their backs and led by a trio of young warriors whose faces were streaked with war paint. The trio rode up to Audrey standing on the stone wall. She jumped down to greet them.

A redheaded Wekeep said, "Snookibottom Sweetfeet Pudfall Slimbabe Gnatswater sent us."

The smallest of the three, with stiff wild hair cut in a mohawk, puffed up his chest. "We're 'ere to kick that cad's ass."

"Death to the trolls!" screamed the third.

Audrey told them Franz would be returning soon and showed them where they could make camp among the ruins. She watched as the trio of young warriors slid from the backs of their boars and corralled the rest of the sounder in an open spot in the field near the forest. Then they guided their small army of like kind—hauling bundles of blankets, hatchets, spears, and cooking tools—to the protection of the ruins. Their voices rose and fell as they proceeded to settle in for the coming night.

Blake and Franz rode in as the sun was setting, a fiery red ball floating in a smoky orange sky. They led the blessing of unis Naiada had sent to meet them, plus many more. The original blessing had grown from thirty to over a hundred. Many had supply boxes slung across their backs.

Blake dismounted and ran to Audrey, hugging her so tightly she could barely catch a breath. He kissed her cheek and gave her a bright smile before releasing her. The scent of sweat and animal clung to his hair and suit. His hair was matted and greasy, and his face was tanned with grit. She was sure she looked and smelled the same; like that of a wild animal, living off the land without the benefit of hot water and herbal soap, her last shower and a good brush of her teeth a distant memory.

"Sorry it took so long," he said. "We circled back to pick up the supplies and weapons we buried in the cave." He looked around at all the creatures that had gathered. "But, wow, maybe that wasn't necessary."

Naiada approached, a joyful smile on her face. She stood on tip-toe and planted tender kisses on Blake's forehead, nose, each cheek, then his lips. His brows rose from the traditional greeting the Merahvu reserved for family.

She stepped back, her gaze lingering on his bright blue eyes. "Welcome back."

"Glad to be." Blake gave her a strained smile. "But I have some bad news. Your father—".

Her face fell flat. "He's dead."

Blake looked a little confused. "How did you know?"

She took his hand. "I sensed it. But thank you for telling me so I can accept it as truth."

"Your mother and Sinto were greatly relieved to learn you were with Audrey. They send their love."

Her eyes welled. "And I them."

Franz tugged at Naiada's free hand. "Hey, what 'bout me?"

She laughed and dropped to her knee. She pinched Franz's cheeks, then kissed him the same way she greeted Blake. Franz's head flushed, red as a cherry, beneath a layer of grit.

Naiada beamed as they gazed at Merluma's creatures gathered in the woods and fields below The Ruins.

"What now?" Blake asked.

Naiada said, "We wait. I have done all I can. There are more to come, and soon Arkis will learn who truly rules Merluma."

76

Franz's Secret

THE GROUND WHERE AUDREY slept was hard and cold. Anxiety wound through her core like an electric snake, coiling and flaring in a way that made it impossible to sleep. From the sound of constant rustling, she knew she wasn't alone and wondered if it was Blake. She hadn't had the chance to catch up with him since his return. The only news he had the chance to share was that Sinto had badly burnt his hand, but not how or for what reason.

"Blake," she whispered. "You awake?"

Franz whispered back, "He's sleeping, whatcha want?"

"Nothing, just—um, never mind."

Franz crawled over to where she lie on the hard ground. "Trouble sleepin' eh?"

"I miss Sinto."

He pulled a dim ball of fire out from under the shirt Blake gave him and laid it on the stone floor between them. It cast a soft lavender light across their faces. He propped his head atop a bent elbow. "I can't sleep without me Snooki."

Audrey was overcome with a sudden wave of sadness. The senselessness. Sinto there, her here. Always a conflict. Death and destruction. The innocents caught up in between, especially the young ones. Franz dragged into it and forced to leave his precious Snooki and the wee ones who fondly looked up to both of them.

He wiped a tear from her cheek. "That bad, huh?"

"It feels like everything's falling apart."

"Don't look to me for a speech about hope and all that other sappy babble." He shrugged. "What happens, happens. Change is inevitable, so, I adapt."

"You sound like Sinto."

Franz smiled. "I remember him, Wantemo's protégé, Queen Ianthe's kid."

"One and the same." She thought of little Wendi, the Wekeep who had adopted her. "I couldn't imagine being a parent right now. Did you have wee ones?"

"Snooki and me... nah, we tried, but." He didn't say anything for a long time, but when he spoke his voice was thick. "Broke me Snooki's heart but she made it work, *we* made it work. We're granpapa and grannana to all the wee ones."

She squeezed his hand. "I bet you are the best granpapa and grannana the Wekeep have ever had."

"Yeah, yeah, and life is filled with rainbows and unicorns. Maybe we oughta change the topic before we both start crying."

"We need to get mopey, we need to be sad and cry, so we don't forget the reason why we're here to fight."

He grew somber and serious. "Arkis must die. Someone has to do it. That's what heroes do, heroic things. Heroes fix the world."

"You sound a little like my friend Dr. Wickman. Full of wisdom and advice. What happened to snark and wise cracks?"

"Ah, the snark and wise cracks keeps ya from seeing the smooshie nostalgic who pines for a simple life and regrets never givin' me Snooki the one thing she dearly wanted in this life, a wee one of her own. Only Snooki knows the truth of me." He held up a hand. It was shaking. "I'm not so tough. I'm terrified as hell but don't tell anyone, especially those youngsters with the war paint on their faces. I gots my tough-guy, wise-crackin' rep to keep up."

"Your secret is safe with me." She leaned over and gave him a kiss on the forehead. It was sticky and gritty like hers certainly must be.

He took her hand. They lay facing each other, hands grasped together. "I miss Snooki."

"And I Sinto."

That was how they both finally fell asleep.

And while Audrey and the others, along with the creatures in the forest and the fields slept, every rodent and winged fae guided by Queen Anya left for Deep Lake high up in the mountains beneath the cover of darkness.

77

Larkian Reunion

AUDREY WOKE AT DAWN, stirred from sleep by a thundering ruckus radiating from the fields. Blake jumped to his feet, with Franz and Audrey following suit, rubbing sleep from their eyes as they rounded a stone wall of the ruins.

The unis reared and pranced, menace in their eyes. Tiger, wolf, fox, and weasel paced in the shadow of the trees. Troops of busheetail monkeys screeched, riled up and anxious from their perch in the trees.

A sleuth of giant white bears had arrived. With passengers.

Franz asked. "Who are they?"

Blake smiled. "Friends."

"The bears or the humans?" Franz sounded alarmed.

Naiada strode up next to them. "Both."

Sitting atop a trio of giant white bears were Stokes, Tucker, and Dyer donning their high-tech suits. A couple dozen more of their sleuth were in tow, heavily saddled with large satchels and the drone that circled earlier. The bears eyed the unis, growing antsy. The trio of Larkians expressed alarm and confusion, grappling to hang on and avoid being tossed, trampled, or eaten.

Naiada jumped into action, putting herself between blessing and sleuth in an effort to keep the peace. After several tense moments the unis calmed and the others skirting the forest retreated to the shadows. Busheetails settled. The bears quieted, pawing the ground, eying the lake thirstily.

Stokes slid off his great white bear, then Tucker and Dyer, all looking a little shaken from their bears' sudden change in demeanor and the vast numbers of differing creatures that had gathered in the fields and forests surrounding The Ruins.

Naiada waved for Audrey and the others to join her among the unis and the bears.

Franz's eyes were the size of platters. "I ain't getting anywhere near those beasts! Catch up with ya later." Then he ran off to join the other Wekeeps cowering behind stone walls, including the youngsters with smudged war paint on their faces.

Audrey and Blake approached Naiada and their fellow Larkians cautiously.

"Whew! It's not easy taming the wild!" Naiada looked thoroughly enchanted by the whole affair.

Audrey said to Stokes, "Well this is a surprise, bear wranglers are we now?"

Stokes laughed, deep and bellowing. "Not by choice but it sure beat walking for days through subzero temperatures." He pointed to the sleuth milling around the green field looking out of place. "And we were able to pack along a few surprises for our friend Arkis."

"That was fuckin' amazing!" Tucker added.

"Oh, sure, you say that now." Dyer leaned over and whispered. "He was whining like a baby when Stokes ordered him to mount his bear."

"Shut up, that's not what 'appened. I was whining about gettin' the smallest one." He whipped his attention back to Audrey. "How 'bout you give old Tucker a hug, my little badass Shelia."

Blake said, "Don't fall for it."

Audrey hugged him anyway.

He sniffed, made a face. "Woowee, don'tcha smell sweetly awful, but damn glad you're alive. Thought I was going to have to contest your will to get my badass hat back."

"Oh, about that, didn't you know? I willed it to Stokes, with no means to contest."

Stokes said. "Jokes aside, it's mighty good to be here, and I guess it's because of this lady." He flashed a brilliant white smile toward Naiada.

Naiada tipped her head respectfully and held out a hand. "Naiada, pleased to meet you in person."

Stokes looked at it unsure what to do—bow, kiss knuckle, or both.

Tucker grabbed it, giving Naiada's hand a firm shake. "Tucker, tech wizard and weapon ordinance master at your service."

Naiada laughed. "Please, I am of no higher stature than any of you. You don't serve me. I'm just a girl who luckily sent those bears the right message."

Tucker's gaze swept across her curvy, naked body, adorned by swirled and dotted markings. "Yer more than a girl."

That made Naiada blush and Audrey cringe.

Dyer put a hand on hip, held out his other. He bent slightly as he stood a full head and half taller than Naiada. "I'm Dyer and I fully respect your talents no matter what sort of package they may be wrapped in." He fluttered his lashes and gave her a sly grin. Naiada took his hand and he raised it to his lips and kissed her knuckles.

Stokes rolled his eyes. "Guys, I think we all agree Naiada is quite a nice sight for sore eyes, but enough with the flirting and the jabber. What's the plan?"

"See what we've had to put up with?" Dyer said with a roll of his eyes. "All work, no play. Party pooper."

Naiada ignored Dyer's comment and got right down to business. "Arkis has been distracted by the advance of Khani and Vesna's teams forced to avoid the wildfires the Orankai set in the

Forestlands. They're coming from the south, through Inception which is what he wanted them to do. He believes they are falling for his trap. As far as I can surmise, he is unaware of our presence here at The Ruins or of your passage from the north. He's expecting an attack from the other side."

Stokes cocked a brow. "So, what happens after that?"

"Oh, not after, before." She grinned and pointed to the creatures gathered in the field. "*They* are what will happen, then..." She shrugged. "We'll see."

He looked around at the gathered creatures looking a little confused. "So what are we supposed to do?"

"Ah, we help get things started, then stand aside." She pointed at the satchels slung across the white bear's backs. "What might you have there?"

Tucker grinned. "Lots of little things that go kaboom."

She pondered, then smiled. "Perfect, Mr. Tucker. That's exactly what I meant by *help*."

"Oy, formalities aren't necessary, you may call me Tuck."

That was the first time Audrey heard Tucker refer to himself as Tuck but got the impression he reserved that name only for his lady friends. She wasn't sure Tucker was aware that Sinto's little sister was just a child not long ago, *Earth* time. Audrey was still trying to grasp this grown-up version of Naiada, and his unabashed advances felt grossly inappropriate. She'd been witness to the type of thoughts that swirled in Tucker's head. His mind had two settings: solving incredibly complex problems or seeking his next conquest to conquer in hand-to-hand combat or to pleasure in his bed—sometimes both.

Audrey cleared her throat. "You know who Naiada is, right?"

Dyer slapped Tucker on the chest. "Yeah, back off little man, else Sinto's gonna turn you to toast."

Tucker gave Dyer a look that would kill.

Blake's head swiveled between them in amusement.

Audrey intervened, "Boys, maybe we ought to stay focused on the task at hand."

"Agreed," Stokes said.

Naiada slipped her arm through Tucker's. "Actually, Tuck here seems deadly focused. Have a moment to talk, privately?" She led him away from the group.

Tucker shot the rest of them a grin, the scar running from ear to mouth twisting his upper lip.

"Go figure. He always gets the girls." Dyer said. "It's that damn scar that twists up his lip that gets 'em." Dyer pushed his upper lip up with his finger. "Oh my, does it hurt when I touch it? Shall I kiss it to make it feel better?" He mockingly said in a high-pitched female voice.

"Naiada's smarter than that," Audrey said. "In fact, she's beyond wise and not one to fall for tricks or illusions. She has a talent for pulling threads and weaving them into something efficacious and potent. Somehow she conjured these creatures to gather here and has maintained the peace among them. An impossible feat for an ordinary person."

Dyer gasped. "Oh my! Is she a goddess? Never met one before." He wiped his hands across his chest, dusty from their travels. "And look how I'm dressed."

Audrey chuckled and punched him in the bicep. "I've sure missed your humor, Dyer. She's no goddess; she's merely Sinto's sister and she doesn't care what you look like or how you're dressed, or whether you are at all. I'm truly glad she's on our team, not Arkis'."

They watched Naiada and Tucker smooth a large patch of dirt. They began setting rocks and drawing lines in the dirt with sticks, mapping out a plan. Tucker was in problem-solving mode, brow furrowed in concentration, making gestures with his fingers, pointing at their rudimentary plan then simulating an explosion with his mouth and fingers. Naiada nodded and added her own suggestions.

The four of them observed from afar, feeling a little useless while Tucker and Naiada worked out a battle plan and all the little details involved.

After about an hour, Naiada waved them over.

She pointed to the ground. "We have a plan." At her feet was a crude but effectively clear map of the breeding caves and the chamber where Arkis brews his orange nectar scratched into the patch of smoothed earth. Three large chambers in all. Lines drawn in between depicted tunnels connecting them to each other and the Labyrinth. Xs marked outside entrances. One to the east and another, lesser used one on the west side, and the stairway up to Deep Lake at the top of the mountains. Annotations with arrows and notes and scribbles signified places to use explosives.

Naiada and Tucker stood up, grinning proudly.

Naiada said, "Once Khani and Vesna reach the far entrance..."

Tucker gestured with his fingers and made the sound of an explosion. "Time to riot."

78

The Windup

NAIADA AND TUCKER PRESENTED their detailed plan for attacking the breeding caves to Audrey and the others, including Franz and the trio of Wekeep warriors. After a few tweaks, all agreed the plan was sound. The time to prepare had arrived.

Naiada took to the center of the field and commenced the strangest meeting Audrey and the others had ever witnessed. The air around her was aglow and growing brighter.

Creatures emerged from the forest, from underground, from lake and stream, from field and sky, mesmerized. Creatures of all sizes and forms, prey and predator, peacefully gathered around her. Herds, packs, murders, swarms, prides, charms, troops, and more, settled, giving Naiada their full attention.

The light Naiada emitted expanded until it encapsulated the entirety of the field and every creature within. She moved in fluid silence among them. It was anything but still; in their minds she wove a story—the plan she and Tucker had conceived. Electrical threads radiating from her body swirled among the gathered, connecting one to all. Eyes shifted and bodies twitched as her story unfolded, each and every one imagining the role they would play.

It was a miraculous and beautiful thing that brought tears to Audrey's eyes.

Once it was over, Naiada collected her threads and respectfully bowed to those gathered. Then the creatures returned from whence they came, awaiting the call to action.

Tucker launched the winged drone. The plan was for the drone to remain in the sky for relaying messages to Khani and Vesna's teams staged on the other side of the breeding caves after its opening salvo.

Tucker and Stokes were the first to depart. They led their sleuth of bears, carrying explosives and communication equipment, to the higher grounds located above the breeding caves and the chamber where Arkis brewed his nectar.

Franz and his team rode up to Audrey and Naiada on their wild boars, short legs sticking out from the boars' broad backs and their thick fingers gripping leather reins. Freshly applied red and black war paint graced their faces and bare chests. A dozen more boar with Wekeeps astride stood at attention by Blake's and Dyers' side.

Franz and his trio of Wekeep warriors had been chosen for the most dangerous and critical task of destroying the laboratory where Arkis' brewed his nectar. The remaining Wekeeps were to join Blake and Dyer, assigned to guarding the lab's only exit on the east side.

The three younger warriors—Lucky Nibbledigits, Tipsy Rumdoodle, and Friktit Dirtyass—were pretty hyped up about the idea of blowing things up. They gazed back, eyes wide with restlessness and toothy grins stretched across their paint-striped faces. Audrey was thankful Franz was in charge, but feared the younger ones' hell-raising enthusiasm may compromise the mission and, more concernedly, their safety.

Naiada stepped forward and pressed her hand to Franz's heart. "You know what to do."

Franz patted a large satchel astride his boar's back. "Easy peasy, get in, do our thing, get the hell out."

Naiada nodded. "Make quick work and a faster retreat. Don't linger or pause to watch. Do and get out. Do you understand?"

Franz rolled his eyes to his warriors. "Pfff. I know that, but these guys..."

Naiada quirked a brow toward the young warriors and addressed each one individually. "Lucky, do as Franz says. Tipsy, live for another day. Friktit, bring your friends home, alive. And to each of you, today you will earn another name honoring your heroism." Naiada bowed her head. "Be safe and wise."

Off they rode, legs bouncing, whooping like banshees, clouds of dust rising in their wake.

Blake said, "Have mercy on their souls."

"Mercy, aye, and a lot of luck." Audrey said. "Arkis surely will have that chamber heavily guarded."

The fields and forests were suddenly vacated. Collectives of creatures departed, to where and for what specific purpose, well, Naiada wasn't sure exactly. Only that they were pissed off and determined in their own sort of way and well aware of how the Larkians planned to help them. How they expressed their animal emotions and convictions was anyone's guess, but Naiada was confident it would be expressed to great effect.

"Time to ride!" Naiada said.

They mounted unis with weapons and ammo strapped across backs. Blake and Dyer rode south, toward the east entrance with the remaining Wekeeps and their singular of wild boar. Audrey and Naiada headed north, toward a ridge with a vista of the sparsely forested lands above the trio of chambers to oversee the unfolding attack.

Hordes of creatures gathered in the fringes of nearby forests, waiting patiently for the signal.

By the time Audrey and Naiada reached the upper ridge, Stokes and Tucker were planting explosives far below. Their bodies were black specs among the sleuth of white bears assisting them. Once their task was complete, they mounted their bears and the sleuth headed for the protection of the surrounding forest.

Audrey's comm lit up. Stokes was calling Khani. Khani confirmed their teams were ready to go.

As Tucker rightly said before, time to riot.

The drone swooped low, a bomb strapped to its belly, and released it.

The nose of the bomb dropped, heading straight for the ground above the largest chamber and toward the center of where Tucker and Stokes had planted a giant ring of explosives.

The bomb pierced the ground and disappeared. At first Audrey thought it was a dud. But the silence was shattered with a ground-shaking, muffled blast, then a series of deafening explosions as the outer ring of bombs ignited.

The creatures awaiting Naiada's signal riled and pranced in the trees.

Dust settled, silence descended.

Then the earth collapsed.

79

Game Riot

THE MAIN BREEDING CHAMBER collapsed spectacularly with a loud rumble, the clacking of rock, and thundering of falling trees. From Audrey and Naiada's prominent location, the ground shook violently beneath their feet. A cloud of dust and rubble exploded upward. Rock rained and a sudden gust of wind swirled dust and organic debris across the land.

At first there was nothing but swirling dust and silence. The air cleared, revealing a gaping hole the size of a football stadium with an inviting rubble stairway that stretched from top to bottom, several stories deep.

Carnivorous and angry beasts exploded from the forest, frothing for a fight. They ran, loped, and slithered; bear, wolf, tiger, hyena, monkey, and many others. Hoofed herbivores and smaller beasts followed, disappearing down the gaping hole like a furry river.

Naiada raised her hands. Silk-like threads danced through the air as she forged a multi-pronged connection to the hordes of beasts fighting below, living through them what was happening in real-time. She passed along a barrage of differing sensory perspectives to those experienced and receptive to the Merahvu's way of mind-speak and sharing: to Khani and Vesna's teams staged at the eastern entrance, and to Audrey and Blake, who had mastered that skill.

The scene unfolded in Audrey's mind—an omniscient perspective, as if watching the attack unfold in a movie-like format and from many points of view. Her heart pounded and her mind was filled with expanding imagery of what was happening inside.

The caves had been emptied of the young, the birthing, the weak, and the innocent, and filled with Arkis' most capable and vicious warriors, lying in wait for Khani and Vesna's teams.

Orankai caught below the initial rain of boulder and rock were pancaked and exploded into ash before they had the chance to blink. Those who survived the initial collapse would soon wish they hadn't been so lucky. Their faces expressed shock and disbelief once they realized their foe was not of their own breed but of a wild and unpredictable nature. And that foe was raging mad.

Rivers of rabid beasts poured into the opening from the ground above. Bears ripped heads from bodies. Tigers ripped limbs from torsos. Snakes slithered through bloody openings, spreading their poisonous venom. Monkeys bashed open skulls and dined on eyeballs and brains.

Many creatures were electrocuted; others observed and changed tactics. They emptied Orankai chests of their merlux with razor sharp claws, mighty canines, and sharp hooves. Meat eaters munched down sputtering bits before Orankai could trigger a meager spark.

Audrey lived the battle through Naiada's connection as if she were a vital participant. She flinched from electrical shocks, her mouth filled with the taste of Orankai blood, her nose clogged from inhaling clouds of ash. Rage flared as she become one with the creatures inflicting the horror unfolding on the battlefield below. The smell of death and blood and shit overwhelmed. Her stomach pitched with nausea.

The central chamber became a bloodbath sprinkled with the ash of the dead and the milling of beasts hungering for more. Orankai who tried to fight died suddenly and violently. The cowardly who ran died slowly and painfully, for the beasts easily caught up, ripping and biting flesh and tearing them to pieces while still alive.

Others attempted to hide by camouflaging, but the creatures had other sensory ways to detect them, and they were easily found and devoured.

Others clambered over rubble to the east chamber and into a second party of mayhem.

Fae streamed down the stairway from Deep Lake into the east chamber. They swirled through stalactites reaching for the chamber floor, hallucinatory dust dripping from their wings. Mild-mannered ruminants, moose, and elk ripped at bodies with a blur of sharp hooves. Orankai stoned on the fae's dust laughed as their internal organs and tangles of intestines spilled from their torsos, only to drop to their knees with horrifying realization etched on their faces before exploding into ash.

Those who bucked the odds, with a nose full of fae dust, tried to escape through the narrow stairway that led to Deep Lake. But they never made it to the top, caught in a stream of rodents racing down from above. Rat, nutria, squirrel, and many more devoured their foe one tiny bite at a time. More streamed from the lower tunnels connected to the Labyrinth, cutting off another means of escape. They chased the rest toward the eastern exit.

There they were greeted by Khani and Vesna's teams armed with weapons supplied by the Larkians. Spears found flesh, darts spread poison, bodies were blown to bits. Ash rained on the victorious warriors.

Naiada's sharing vision swept back inside, across rubble and ash and beasts searching for survivors. Audrey stiffened when she caught sight of Arkis, perched on a walkway above, a look of horror and alarm etched on his face. Below, Merluma's creatures slavered for revenge, leaping and attempting to claw up the stone wall. They roared in frustration when he darted down a secret passage too high for them to reach.

Arkis slipped along a passage to the west chamber where his nectar was brewed, rats nipping at his heels and latching onto his legs. He kicked and launched balls of fire. The screams of the dying and the scent of burnt flesh trailed behind him as he raced to the west chamber.

The rats descended on the Orankai guarding the chamber's entrance. Arkis pushed his way through and slipped past the door's seal. The guards swirled in confusion, trying to follow Arkis, but the seal wouldn't budge. Arkis had locked the seal as he passed through, leaving the guards to fend for themselves. The passage filled with furry bodies, burying the guards. Their screams quickly faded and ash plumed. The sealed door bowed as rodents pressed to break through.

Naiada bounced her focus to Franz and his trio of Wekeeps within the west chamber. They sneaked around twitchy and apprehensive guards, strategically planting little bombs. They targeted critical equipment and every access point to the chamber: a tunnel from the lower Labyrinth, the doorway to the outside, a lava tube with a fast-running stream that led directly to the Great Ocean.

The Wekeep had avoided detection by the dozens of guards worriedly milling throughout the chamber. Once their little bombs were placed, Franz did a quick survey. Bombs were set to destroy the equipment used to brew nectar and seal access points to the chamber. He made sure no explosives were set by pots of raw Orange and finished nectar. Naiada was quite clear in her instruction to not let those spill, fearing the Labyrinth's main water source would be contaminated. She had assured Franz that once the chamber was sealed, the pots of Orange and nectar would spoil and rot, organically, over time.

Franz and his Wekeep warriors were interrupted when Arkis stormed into the chamber. He raced down a hidden stairway, rage rolling off him in waves. Franz and his Wekeep team dove for cover, hiding in their Wekeep way, in plain sight, disguised by whatever was around them.

Arkis was livid, arms waving, spittle flying. "Who blew up my cave! And who the fuck sent those creatures! Why are you all standing around, do something!"

The guards flinched, pointing accusingly or melting against walls, anything to avoid Arkis' ire, oblivious to ticking bombs peppered around the chamber.

Arkis spotted Friktit coiled around a pipe and yanked him up by the neck.

"What is this?" Arkis screamed. "A Wekeep pest in *my* laboratory?" His eyes narrowed once he saw the red and black war markings painted on Friktit's face and chest. "A mighty warrior, are you?" Arkis' ground his teeth. "Were you the one who stole my crystal?"

"What crystal?" Friktit squeaked.

"You took it, didn't you?"

"No, no, not me."

"Who then?"

"I don't know, I know of no crystal."

"Let's try something more obvious—your trespass here."

"I—I seek mushrooms—ones that grow in caves—smelled fungi—slipped through a crack—"

"What crack? Where?"

"There." Friktit pointed opposite of where the Wekeep had entered, and away from where Franz, Lucky, and Tipsy hid.

Arkis ordered his guards to find it.

Audrey felt Franz's struggle through Naiada's connection: Save Friktit or take advantage of Friktit's wise distraction? Emotion warred but logic won. There was nothing he could do without exposing them all. He signaled Lucky and Tipsy toward the real crack where they entered and signaled them to make a hasty retreat. They had to stop and hide among the vats of orange nectar when a guard passed by.

Arkis held Friktit high, hands clasping his neck. Friktit squirmed to escape. Arkis' eyes narrowed. "And if you're lying..."

"No crack over here," a guard said.

Arkis' eyes flamed red.

Friktit said, "Sorry—confused—maybe it was over there." He pointed in a different direction.

Arkis squeezed Friktit's neck until his eyes bugged and face bloomed red. He tried to suck air but was unable. Trembling, he pissed down the sleeve of Arkis' red silk shirt.

Arkis looked down at it, appalled. "Why you little shit."

Arkis drop-kicked Friktit across the chamber. Friktit smacked into the stone wall with such force his neck snapped, killing him instantly.

Franz's flood of shock and anger bled through Naiada's connection, setting Audrey's own emotions aflame. She willed Franz not to react.

"Get out of there, there's nothing you can do to save him!"

She didn't know if Franz heard her, but he remained diligent and cool-headed, slithering around a massive vat until he could make eye contact with Lucky and Tipsy who were looking quite terrified and distressed from witnessing their friend die. Franz signaled to them to move, quickly, quietly.

"Where there's one, there are others." Arkis threw up his hands. "Find them!"

Dozens of his finest guards fanned out, rounding the vats just as Franz, Lucky, and Tipsy slithered away, across the floor to the small crack hidden behind a large stalagmite connecting the floor to ceiling. Franz was last to exit, planting the rest of his explosives throughout the crack as he crawled out backwards. He was last to witness Arkis' discovery of all the little black boxes with blinking red lights peppered throughout his laboratory.

Arkis' jaw dropped and utter panic filled his eyes. "Flee!" he screamed.

Guards broke through the western sealed door and spilled into blinding daylight to an awaiting sounder of wild boar, restlessly pawing the earth with their breathy snorts fogging the air.

Dyer and a team of Wekeep stood among the boar, armed with crossbows leveled at the guards' heads. Blake held a remote in his hand. He raised it for them to see, then pressed the red button.

The bomb set at the chamber opening exploded, blowing the guards off their feet. From within the chamber, muffled explosions went off in succession. The crack from which Franz, Lucky, and Tipsy escaped collapsed, Franz barely slipping out in time.

The boars circled the guards.

"What should we do with them?" Blake asked the Wekeeps, milling around.

Franz ran as fast as a Wekeep could and slid to a stop at Blake's feet, gasping for breath. Lucky and Tipsy skidded to a stop at his side.

Lucky screamed, "They let Arkis kill Friktit! They deserve no better."

"I agree!" Franz clicked his tongue to get the boars attention, then he pointed to the guards, and yelled, "Truffle!"

The boars lurched and attacked the stunned guards, frantically digging into their chests seeking their most treasured treat, and upon not finding it, dug into another, and another, and another, until what lay at their feet was blood, guts, and ash.

The sounder stomped on what remained of the guards, squealing in victory.

Franz crumpled at Blake's feet and broke down sobbing.

Naiada lowered her hands and broke off her shared visions. Audrey's mind snapped back to her present reality. The image of glistening blood and gray ash shifted to the bright green grass and the black rock at her feet. The mare beside her shuffled and snorted, having experienced the same disturbing images. A gentle breeze cleansed the stench of death from her nostrils and the bloodcurdling screams from her ears. The violence and death she witnessed was a haunting reminder of the senselessness of war.

Naiada stood by her side, frantically twirling a lock of golden hair. Her gaze was distant and lips were pursed in concentration. Her face folded. "Damn, he got away! Arkis slipped through a lava tube to the Great Ocean before it collapsed!"

She stewed only briefly. While the breeding caves and nectar laboratory had been destroyed, they weren't finished.

The image of Khani and Vesna's teams came to life in Audrey's mind.

Khani's team swept through the Labyrinth, winding down tunnels past abandoned chambers, backtracking and starting anew as they stumbled across rubble blocking their paths. They moved, slowly but determinedly, from the mountains to the sea, freeing slaves and killing Orankai, until at last they found Arkis' abandoned queens, weak and dying and lying in their own excrement within their pitch-black lair. They were not spared and seemed thankful to be put out of their misery.

Vesna's team swept the barren land and caves surrounding Deep Lake, which had been vacated. They dove to the depths of the lake and killed the Scouts guarding the portal. Then they passed through to Lake Superior on Earth, armed with the last of the explosives provided by Tucker.

The City of Green was a cesspool of misery. They freed what innocents and slaves remained, feeble and grateful, having been locked inside by departing Orankai once they deemed the city unlivable.

They rounded up the giant lamprey beasts Arkis had loosed in the Great Lakes and killed each and every one of them.

Afterward, they set explosives along the base of the city's dome and ignited them all at once. The dome imploded in a muffled and devastating blast, destroying the city Arkis had poisoned with his evil and filth.

Then they returned to a liberated Merluma.

80

Braveheart

KHANI AND VESNA SENT Naiada victorious messages from afar, sharing their success clearing the Labyrinth, destroying the City of Green, and ridding Lake Superior of the over-sized, invasive lamprey. They bid farewell and left to give the Larkians news of Arkis' defeat on Merluma.

Audrey and their ragtag team of Larkians planned to return with Franz to share their news with the Wekeep and to mourn and celebrate the life of Friktit.

Naiada released the many creatures who had gathered and helped liberate Merluma, except for a few unis and boars they required for the ride back to the Wekeep's encampment.

The fires still raged from the east but were confined to a single valley that butted up to the base of the Black Mountains with steep rocky faces and little to burn. The smoke had thinned significantly and warm winds from the Desertlands cleared the air of its toxic scent. Naiada predicted the fire would soon flame out.

"We go this way," Lucky told Naiada, pointing to the right once they reached a fork in the trail they were following. "Our home collapsed durin' the earthshake, no one wants to go back. The woodlands are home now."

And with this news, Naiada insisted Lucky and Tipsy lead. Tucker and Dyer fell in line behind them, pumped with adrenaline, and declaring how much respect they had gained for the creatures of the natural world. Stokes was on high alert, scanning the forest and far across vistas watching for danger. Audrey rode beside Franz, who was especially quiet, which suited her just fine. Once or twice she nodded off before jolting herself awake. Naiada and Blake lingered behind, quietly conversing. Every now and then Audrey would hear Leela's name, as well as Sinto's.

Once they dropped down from the higher elevations the air grew warm and more tropical. Audrey and the other Larkians stopped to shed their high-tech suits and roll up the legs and sleeves of their underlayers. She eyed Naiada jealously, wishing she had flaps of skin to cover intimate parts and could be free to run around naked in the moist warm air, without anyone batting an eye.

The ridge soared to the east of them, a fast-running river carving around its base. Palm, fern, mangeleno, and sweet-smelling succulents grew to the trail's edge, and the delightful sound of children playing in the jungle floated on a gentle breeze.

A gaggle of young Wekeeps burst from the woods with war-painted faces and sword-fighting sticks. They ran ahead of Lucky and Tipsy, screaming to the others of their return.

The trail swung around to a clearing, butting up to a large, yawning cave that was once an enclosed chamber in the Labyrinth, the side of which was partially collapsed. A small stream had been diverted from the river and ran through the clearing.

Their unis leaped across the stream where Wekeep were busy building a wood-planked foot bridge for easy crossing. Others gathered and laid stones along its shores.

The sound of wild chopping added to the cacophony of many voices, children screeching, and men barking orders or crying out in pain from a pinched finger. The felling of trees scattered women gathering mushrooms and roots in the woods.

Homes formed of rock, wood, and mortar-like mud were in varying stages of completion, some with Wekeep crawling all over them, other's abandoned and unfinished.

Wekeep randomly moved from one project to another, sometimes colliding and dropping their tools with choice words Audrey didn't recognize but surely weren't meant for wee ones to hear.

The scene was chaotic bordering on complete mayhem.

Franz shrugged. "I know, kind of a mess, but that's how we Wekeep get things done, bits at a time, always had and always will."

To Audrey it seemed the Wekeep might just have a bit of an attention deficit hyperactivity disorder buried in their genes.

Lucky and Tipsy led them to the far edge of the clearing, by the stream where there was ample shade and grass for the unis to graze.

They dismounted.

While Audrey had grown fond of the small gray mare she rode, she was glad to have her feet on firm ground. The gray mare whinnied and shook, starting at her head and shimmying down her spine. The way she gazed back at Audrey it was apparent she was equally relieved to be free of a rider. They shared a tender moment; Audrey scratched an irritating itch behind the mare's ears and the mare nuzzled Audrey's neck with sloppy kisses.

They collected their suits and other supplies strapped to the unis' backs and piled them up out of the way. Then they wandered over to the cave opening.

Here the mayhem stopped. Women bustled in harmony, hanging garlands of fragrant flowers and herbs along the walls, and placing cracked bowls, large clam shells, and carved-out tree husks filled with a bounty of food gathered from the land and sea on tables. Groupings of tree-rounds and large stones had been arranged across a well-swept stone floor.

Snooki saw to it that cups were filled with honey wine and passed around to all. Naiada launched balls of lavender firelight that hovered below the obsidian ceiling, refracting light and adding a celebratory feel.

Naiada called the men from their chores and children from the woods. Franz and Snooki stood beside her while the Wekeep gathered around, settling on their bums and giving them their full attention. Tucker, Dyer, and Blake hovered behind Stokes, whom wee ones were climbing as if he were a great tree. Snooki shooed them off. Chattering excitedly, they pressed their way to the front of the gathering crowd.

Audrey watched Naiada with great pride. She was of good heart and had grown wise beyond her years. Audrey thought of Sinto, wishing he were here to share the joy and pride she felt witnessing his sister organize and lead a mix of extraordinary and diverse resources in the fight for Merluma in her own creative and powerful way. Naiada was a true leader—compassionate, fierce, thoughtful, and caring—and deserved full respect and recognition for all she had accomplished.

The Mark in her arm warmed as she shared these thoughts, not knowing if Sinto would receive them. She imagined him beaming by her side, and believed it might be true.

Naiada called for silence, then addressed the crowd. "Merluma has been liberated from Arkis and his Orankai!"

The Wekeep roared.

"This could not have happened without the creatures of Merluma who are unable to be here. Let us share our gratitude." She held up her hands.

The Wekeep *oohed* and *ahed* when electrical threads burst from her fingers and threaded far and wide, through the woods and over the ridge to Inception, along the banks of the river, to the mountains and beyond. One of them wound its way to Audrey and she listened as Naiada held court with the creatures of Merluma, thanking them for their unfailing dedication. From those gathered outside came snorts, whinnies, caws, and the pounding of hooves.

Naiada then called Lucky and Tipsy forward and they came up to stand before her.

"We could not have stopped Arkis without your bravery and risk to life."

She tapped Lucky's left shoulder, then his right, with two stiffened fingers wielded like a sword. "Lucky Nibbledigits, from this day on you shall be named Lucky Nibbledigits Firecaster."

Next she honored Tipsy. "Tipsy Rumdoodle, from this day forward you shall be named Tipsy Rumdoodle Firestarter."

Franz was staring at his feet.

Naiada place a hand on his shoulder. "Franz?"

He looked up, eyes rimmed red and ready to burst with tears.

He faced her and she tapped both of his shoulders with sword fingers. "Franzaboana Bevor Slumpjam Gemtaker Buttmist, from this day forward you shall be named Franzaboana Bevor Slumpjam Gemtaker Buttmist Truffletrumpeter."

The Wekeeps lurched to their feet whistling and yelling their praise.

Naiada held up her hand and the Wekeep settled and quieted.

She drew a deep breath and struck a somber tone. "We lost someone important today. Friktit Dirtyass selflessly fought for your freedom with bravery and panache. May Friktit never be forgotten."

Franz's eyes welled when he shouted, "May Friktit never be forgotten!"

Naiada nudged Franz forward. The crowd quieted. Franz gathered his composure. Snooki stood by his side, holding his hand.

"I duly grant Friktit Dirtyass to be remembered as Friktit Dirtyass Braveheart."

Tears burst from his eyes. Snooki handed him a square of cloth. He sopped up tears from his cheeks and wadded up the cloth. He whispered something to Naiada. She nodded, then he handed it to her.

She placed the cloth in her palm. It burst into flames, dancing purple and pink and yellow, then it sputtered and disintegrated in a puff of smoke that rose and swirled to the ceiling before dissipating.

Franz raised his cup. "To Friktit!"

All raised their cups. "Friktit!"

Music floated and those with decent, and not so decent, voices sang along. Tongues tripped over lyrics from too much sweet wine. Fae swept in from the woods and danced aloft on iridescent wings. Unis pranced and nuzzled in the clearing. Moonstone and his raptor friends swooped and dived and caw-cawed around Naiada's balls of hovering fire.

Audrey hugged Tucker, Tucker hugged Stokes, Stokes hugged Dyer, Dyer hugged Blake. And around the hugs went. They were sticky and stinky and in great need of a shower but none of them cared.

Honey wine was guzzled, bellies were filled, and they danced like the wild animals they felt and smelled like. And once they had their fill it was time for the Larkians to go.

Little Wendi Wetbottom clung to Audrey's leg. "No go!" she cried.

Audrey picked her up and held the precious girl to her breast. She breathed deep the scent of earth and vitality her tiny body emitted, the sweet, vital scent of Merluma and all the living things it represented. Audrey kissed her goodbye and handed her to her mother, who struggled to console a bawling Wendi Wetbottom.

Blake patted Franz on the head. "I guess this is the end of the road for us."

"Like hell! You, me, *Portal* 2—a standing date once a week—uh, what would that be Earth time?"

"Seven hours, roughly," Audrey said.

"Ah, geez." Franz shrugged. "It is what it is." He turned to Tucker. "You don't suppose ya could leave a few of them little black bombs with me?"

Stokes said, "Not on your life."

"'E's right, that stuff doesn't belong here." Tucker said, drawing a deep breath of the woodland scent. "Got all ya need, why spoil it?"

They gathered their things, which wasn't much. They left the last of their supplies minus the weapons. Franz dragged his feet through the woods the entire way to the portal.

"Sure you gotta go?" he asked once they arrived.

"Afraid so," Audrey said. "We miss our families and loved ones."

The guys hugged Franz farewell, lifting him off his feet which he wasn't quite too happy about.

"Hate to break up the party," Stokes said. "But Arkis is still out there."

Audrey tugged on Naiada's hand. "And Sinto is anxious to see you."

"I'm not going, yet," Naiada said. "I've something I must do, here on Merluma." She turned to Blake. "And I could use your help."

Blake looked around the group. No one objected. "Certainly."

She clicked her tongue. The alpha uni and his mare came running up the trail from the Wekeep settlement.

Naiada said, "Don't worry about us. I'll see that Blake is returned safely." She took Audrey's hand and grinned. "Tell Sinto I look forward to demonstrating my new-found skills. Tell him I love him dearly and I never would have lived to see this day if it wasn't for him." Then she pulled Audrey's face down to meet her, kissed her forehead, nose, each cheek, and then her lips. "See you soon, sister."

"Hey, whata 'bout me?" Franz said.

Naiada knelt and kissed him the same way.

"Yeah, yeah, now skedaddle before I start crying again." His red cheeks were streaked with tears. "Look what ya did to me! I'm a soggy mess!"

Blake play-punched him in the shoulder.

Audrey grinned. "Not a bad look, I'd say."

Blake and Naiada mounted their unis and took off to the north.

Franz led them down a trail that ended at a large crack in the ridge. "Straight through, cabin's on the right, key under the mat. And don't eat all the popcorn, supply's gettin' low."

Audrey knelt and gave him a kiss on the cheek. "Take care of Snooki and Wendi Wetbottom and all the others. I'm going to miss you, Franz."

His face bunched, pinching off a fresh round of tears. Then he composed himself, waving his hands. "I'm sure Sinto's anxiously waiting, so off with ya."

Stokes went first, then Tucker, Audrey, and Dyer, and they slipped from Franz's summery woodlands to the cool misty forests of Canada on planet Earth.

81

Marks Sing Again

SINTO RACED TO PERSONALLY greet Audrey as soon as the Larkians heard news of the victory on Merluma. Audrey and the others were holed up in a cabin in Canada, ready to be picked up.

His tunnel spit him out in the Salish Sea near the shore of South Pender Island, one of many Canadian Gulf Islands visible from across Haro Strait from his favorite perch on Andrew's Island. South Pender Island was sparsely populated and the busy summer months had yet to come.

He had snagged some Sapien clothing before he left, jeans and T-shirt, nothing more. Not exactly suitable for the Pacific Northwest in March but it would be good enough. Alvarez gave him a phone preprogrammed with the cabin's GPS location along with some Canadian currency.

Once on shore he found no easy options for transportation but he'd been told that if he stuck out a thumb, someone would give him a ride. Sure enough, a friendly older woman returning home from the market picked him up.

She apologized profusely for dropping him off at the bottom of a steep drive, saying there was no way her bald tires would make it up the muddy potholed road to the cabin his phone guided him to.

Sinto was more than happy for the ride thus far and thanked her with a crisp Canadian twenty.

He sprinted up the long and winding driveway. By the time he reached a modest and well-maintained log cabin tucked in the woods, he was breathless. Despite it being midday, thick clouds and the dense canopy of evergreens towering above his head made it feel like early nightfall. Soft lights glowed from behind the cabin's closed curtains, warm and welcoming. He wasted no time knocking on the door.

There was a moment of chaos coming from within. The scraping of chairs, slamming of doors, lots of shushing. Then the door swung open. Stokes. He breathed a sigh of relief upon seeing Sinto and invited him inside.

"All clear," he said, tossing the words over his shoulder. "Aren't you a sight for sore eyes. Nice to look up, not down all the time." He chuckled. "Those Wekeep—certainly interesting little people, clever and resourceful."

Sinto went to say something about the Wekeep but his eyes were drawn to the back of the cabin. Audrey emerged from behind a closed door wearing ill-fitting clothes. She gasped when she saw him, then the next thing he knew, she was in his arms.

Their lips clicked together like magnets. Words could not describe the overwhelming emotion that swirled between them. Two parts made whole. Their bodies melded, hearts sang, and lips kneaded with a desperation as if they stopped it would be forever, so they vowed to never stop...

Someone cleared their throat.

Their lips parted and eyes popped open and they both realized they were surrounded.

Dyer said. "I'd suggest you, ya know, get a room, but van's on its way."

Audrey blushed and laughed and tried to pull away, but Sinto held her tight. He'd rather die than let go of her. The others let them be and went about the business of gathering their things.

Audrey cradled his face, ran her hands down his arms, finally coming to rest on the hand he nearly lost. She traced the veins popping along the surface and the prominent frail bones with the tip of her finger. She pressed his hand to her cheek. A tear slipped out. "You are whole."

"As are you." Though she had noticeably changed. Hardened. The worry line cut between her brows was deeper than when he last saw her. The innocence she once held in her eyes before they began this strange and violent journey was gone. Her face was gaunt and her body more sinewy. She was in need of hydration and nourishment.

He looked around at the others. They looked the same, scrubbed and freshly showered but with a thick patina of exhaustion.

"When was the last time you ate?" he asked.

Dyer frowned. "We haven't had a decent meal since we left."

"Unless you call roots and bugs a meal," Tucker added, rolling his eyes.

Sinto suddenly realized the group wasn't complete. "Where's Naiada?"

"She stayed behind, with Blake, said she had something important to do before she left Merluma. She promised they wouldn't be gone for long and would meet us back at Isla Salvación."

Sinto was disappointed, but understood. When Naiada deemed something important he knew there was nothing anyone could do to convince her it could wait.

A van sent by Alvarez arrived shortly after. They tidied up the cabin, putting all back in its rightful place and scrubbing the grime from Merluma from the shower stall. Then they left, using care to leave the key under the mat for Franz.

It was a short drive to Bedwell Harbor where a sleek, black-hulled Larkian yacht waited to take them to Seattle. In Seattle, a private jet waited to fly them to Isla Salvación.

Sinto pulled Audrey aside. "We've somewhere else to go first."

"Where?"

His eyes flicked to the others, then back. "Somewhere we can be alone."

The Mark danced and tingled in their arms. She was quick to understand what he meant and a burst of fire bloomed in his chest and both their hearts pitter-pattered.

Her lips curled. "No more waiting?"

"And no more excuses," he said.

"What about your struggle with the Joining?"

He smiled. "It's not yet time for that. Hard to describe how I know, I just do. And about the other... the Mark agrees it's long overdue and has given us its blessing."

She patted the inside of her upper arm, where something small dimpled the flesh. "So has Dr. Wickman."

82

Dreams Do Come True

Audrey and Sinto bid farewell to the others, then he wrapped them in a lorica cocoon and dove into the water. Fingers tugged at clothes and tongues twined as they sank to the soft bottom.

Gasping, Audrey said, "Here?"

"No, somewhere not far."

Her whole body trembled. "This is really happening?"

He squeezed her. "Yes."

Audrey felt his heart pounding against her chest. The Marks in their arms thrummed in harmonic rhythm as if singing a love song, its whispered lyrics telling them it was time.

Sinto cut a tunnel through the water.

It took less than a minute to reach the shores of Andrew's Island, across the border from Canada to the United States, on the other side of Haro Strait.

They emerged from the sea, arms entangled, stumbling and laughing as they ran along the trail, up the hill to the middle of the island, past an overgrown garden to a hidden hole in vertical rock, and to a camouflaged door that swung open after it recognized Sinto's face.

Sinto lifted Audrey in his arms and carried her through a corridor burrowed in stone and through a carved wooden door. They fell on top of an old sofa, their legs in a tangle.

Audrey looked around the old modestly furnished bunker Francesca once called home. "Where are we?"

"Does it matter?"

She laughed. "No!" She yanked his shirt over his head and pressed her hands to his chest, her whole body trembling. "This is real, not a dream?"

He kissed her. "Share your dream and we'll make it come true."

She did, one where she finally discovers what Sinto's been hiding within his protective genital pouch. Like her dream she wasn't disappointed.

They fumbled around awkwardly, a lovers' first tryst. Her first time ever; whether it was his they never discussed. They giddily laughed and gasped upon discovering new things about each other's bodies. Things they had declared a red line at a time of uncertainty about the Mark and what triggered Sinto's need to complete the Joining.

Audrey ask Sinto if he still had that under control. Sinto asked Audrey if she was confident with the birth control Dr. Wickman had given her. Both assured the other that yes, the Mark was content, and yes, the slow-release birth control implant Dr. Wickman inserted into her arm was firmly in place.

Nothing to stop them now.

Audrey's eager gaze met Sinto's patient one. Heat fluttered from the places where their skin met. Audrey could feel his pulse beneath her touch, as rapid as her own. His eyes were steady, locked on hers. Green and gold swirled around his pulsing pupils. She let the pull of his eyes drag her in, let herself slip into his mind to share this experience even more intimately.

They shared every sensation, every emotion. The brief pain as Sinto eased into her, the following pleasure as they moved together, learning each other's rhythm. Breath danced across skin, fingers tangled in hair. Everything else in the world disappeared, leaving only the two of them, truly and finally together. They moved as one, their motions slow at first, but building as their heat and pleasure did. Their release was simultaneous, linked through body and mind, and they shuddered as the cascade of sensations lit their bodies afire.

They collapsed into each other's arms, trembling and exhausted, Audrey's legs wound around Sinto's hips and bound by crossed ankles.

"I'm never letting go," she announced, squeezing her thighs tighter.

"Never is a long time."

"So be it," she said, nuzzling his neck with her lips.

They lay like that, afraid to move, to spoil the moment, to break their magical connection. And it was like that that they drifted into a satisfied and euphoric slumber.

Audrey woke with Sinto swelling inside her. She felt his insatiable need as acutely as her own. But he put his hands to her prominent hip bones, stilling them.

"I can wait." He pinched the loose skin along her belly. "You need to eat, gain your strength. One can only live on berries and bugs for so long."

"You forgot mushrooms and thistle root."

He rolled off her, got to his feet, extended his good hand, and pulled her to his chest. He wrapped an arm around her waist, grabbed her hand, and gently clasped it with his right. He shuffled his feet and twirled her, moving her toward a bookcase on the far wall in a simple, made-up dance step.

He tipped the spine of an old leather-bound book, and the bookshelf slid out and to the side, revealing a hidden living space encased in thick steel. Lights clicked on.

"Welcome to the vault," he said with wag of brow.

The vault was simply furnished with every known twenty-first century amenity. Audrey poked around while Sinto dug around in a large freezer.

He held up several vacuum-sealed packages. "All that's left is macaroni and cheese and coconut cream cake."

Sinto slipped the macaroni and cheese packets in a bath of warm water—*sous vide*—Sinto explained. While it was warming they slipped into the shower, scrubbing and exploring every inch of each other's bodies, murmuring things they wished to do later.

They ate curled up together on a small sofa with only a blanket draped across their shoulders.

Audrey missed a bite and a spoonful of cheesy macaroni landed on her belly. "Oops."

Sinto licked it up with a grin. "Oops."

They paused, eyes meeting, thinking the same thing. They tossed aside their forks and slipped to the floor, licking the rest of their dinner from each other's bodies, expressing their desires with plops of cheesy macaroni and a one-worded language of "oops."

They got especially creative with the coconut cream cake, warming them both up for round two.

Sinto lowered a bunk from the wall and rolled to his back on a soft bed of silky sheets and a fluffy down comforter.

Audrey rolled on top. "Uff!" she exclaimed. "My inner thighs are killing me from riding unis all across Merluma. Or maybe—" She poked him in the belly. "From something else."

He pulled her down to his chest. "May your inner thighs forever be tender, and other places ceaselessly crave for more." Then he kissed her and satisfied those cravings.

Audrey slept for ten hours straight and when she woke, found Sinto wrapped in a robe and sitting in a chair beside her, sipping on a cup of coffee, gaze cast to the ceiling.

"Hi," she said.

"Hi," he said, turning to face her.

"Whatcha doing?"

He brushed her cheek with his shrunken and weakened hand. "Thinking."

"Thinking about what?"

His eyes sparked. "How much I love macaroni and cheese."

"I think I loved the coconut cream cake a teeny weeny bit more."

He bent and kissed her, sweet and tender. She giggled when he mind-shared his favorite body part from which he licked up his dinner, making both of their faces flame.

She stretched. "I feel like I just passed through a portal, ripped limb from limb. Not in a bad way, a good way. Like after a hard and satisfying workout."

He gave her sheepish grin. "It was rather vigorous that last time."

She propped her head on her hand and rolled her eyes. "And I thought it was from all that sleeping on the ground on Merluma. Which, I might add, I vow to never lie on the ground again, ever. It's not natural to sleep on dirt and rock."

He frowned. "How disappointing. I was going to suggest we do it again from my favorite viewpoint overlooking the Salish Sea."

She sat up. "I might be able to make an exception."

"There's a nice bed of soft moss."

"Moss works. And after that?"

"The beach."

She grinned. "And after that?"

"The sea."

She gasped. "Is that possible?"

He smiled. "Mm-hmm."

She laughed, liking this game. "And after that?"

"You pick."

"Home."

"Can you be more specific?"

"Isla Salvación, the cove where we first met. Our home, yours and mine, once this mess with Orange is over."

"You're my home, no matter where we are in this world, or another." He slipped onto the bed beside her and cradled her in his arms. "Us together, wherever, whenever, forever." He nuzzled her neck. "Mmm, home."

83

Distracted By Love

REALITY SANK IN. WHILE Audrey and Sinto could have stayed in the bunker on Andrew's Island forever, duty and responsibility beckoned.

They dressed in black Larkian-issue clothing they found in the vault, then proceeded to tidy up, giving Audrey a chance to poke around at what else had been hidden or stored there.

Her curiosity piqued when she found a green blanket wrapped around something very heavy tucked beneath the desk. Lying on top was a tri-folded piece of parchment paper secured with a black wax seal. She pulled them both from their hiding spot.

She set the object wrapped in the green blanket on the sofa and sat down beside it, fingering the parchment paper and the outline of the Mark she shared with Sinto that was pressed into the black wax seal. She flipped it over. Her name was neatly printed on the other side.

She held it up. "What is this?"

"A letter I wrote to you. It—it was right before Arkis killed Victoria. I honestly didn't know whether I would ever see you again."

She raised a brow, her finger poised to break the seal. "May I?"

He didn't answer right away. "If you want to," he said finally, sitting down beside her.

The letter said:

My dearest Audrey,

Something moved me to put the words I failed to speak to you upon our last parting to paper. I never should have left you with such bitter feelings.

I should have respected your request for me to stay longer. I was a fool to rush off in haste to strike vengeance against my half-brother, harming the one that I truly care about more than anything in our respective worlds.

Our journey is one fraught with danger and the possibility of failure is quite high. I do not take lightly my commitment to my people, my family, but most importantly, to you.

Should our paths fail to cross again know that with all my heart, mind, and body, I will forever love you, and wish that you find all you deserve and desire in this life and all those that follow.

Should I leave this world before you, know that you are free to love and cherish another knowing that I too am free. Free as stardust circling the universe awaiting the moment we will once again be united in another form in another time in an all-new world.

I believe deep in the essence of all of me that we are meant to be together through a force greater than any *other in the universe. A force that neither of us can truly understand. We must trust that force to right the wrongs that may be inflicted upon us.*

One day we will complete our unfinished purpose. Of that I am certain down to the marrow of my bones.

Yours and solely yours, now and forever, wherever, whenever.

Salamora,
Sinto

When she finished reading it her hands were shaking and a knot in her throat kept her from speaking. She folded it up, pressed it to her heart and rolled into Sinto's embrace.

He held her as tears slipped down her cheeks.

"That is the most beautiful thing anyone has ever said to me." She looked up and gazed into his beautiful and mesmerizing green eyes. "I love you, Sinto. I love you with the whole of me, forever, wherever, or whenever we may find ourselves."

They kissed, reluctantly pulling apart as they both knew their dangerous journey was far from over. Merluma may be safe, but Arkis was still alive and the threat of Orange loomed.

Audrey patted the object in the green blanket. "And what is this?"

"The reason I nearly lost my hand." He reached over her and peeled back the layers of the blanket to reveal the Salish Stone inside.

Audrey ran a finger across its perfectly round surface. A faint amber fire danced inside. Her Mark flared as her eyes swept across its crystal-like surface. She looked over at Sinto questioningly. "What is it for?"

"My mother found it, here in the Salish Sea, after a great earthshake shortly after meeting your father and his crew. It's what enabled her to crack into the Timeless Dimension. It is the reason she can foresee the future. I retrieved it from the rubble left from the collapse of Tallamure. It was stuck on a ledge inside an active geothermal fissure. It's a miracle it was not lost entirely. She was afraid my father had found it and given it to Arkis. She believed it was how he was able to foresee our every move. But I found it and we both agreed it should be hidden in a safe place, far from Arkis' reach." He stood up, wrapped it again in the blanket, and put it back behind the set of drawers where Audrey found it.

Audrey stood and tucked the letter from Sinto into her pants pocket. "Arkis had a crystal that looked like it, only its center was green, not amber; green like your eyes. Naiada said it was what gave his queens their power, that they too cracked the barrier to the Timeless Dimension because of it. Franz stole it after we freed Naiada. Arkis wasn't happy and killed an innocent Wekeep because of it."

Sinto looked anxious, working the fingers of his weak hand. "Where is it now?"

"It rolled away, lost somewhere within the Labyrinth during an earthquake on Merluma. Blake was ready to go back and find it, but Naiada said it would be safer if we left it. That was before we attacked the breeding caves." Audrey took Sinto's hand, stilling his fingers. "Why, what's wrong?"

"I trust if Naiada believed it safe than it is—but..."

"But what?"

"I'm not sure; just a feeling." He shook his head. "Probably nothing. We should go."

They sealed the vault and left the bunker.

Once they were outside and assured the bunker door was sealed and locked, Sinto said, "Before we leave, there's one last thing I need to do."

He led her to a spot in the garden where the ground had been disturbed. He rummaged around collecting rocks and began stacking them until there was a neatly stacked pile; a cairn.

He knelt before it. "This is where Victoria died."

She placed a hand on his shoulder and they gazed at the pile of rock in respectful silence.

An unexpected voice cut through their moment of silence. "Well isn't that sweet! Mourning poor ol' Victoria with a pile of rubble."

They both swung around, Sinto leaping to his feet.

Arkis stood alone, dressed the same as always; a red silk shirt and black leather wrap. They were torn and dirty from his hasty retreat from the battle on Merluma, but there was a defiant and fierce gleam in his glowing orange eyes. A man not yet defeated.

Audrey's blood ran cold with that sudden feeling when you realize you aren't safe or alone, caught off-guard and defenseless. Distracted and complacent.

Suddenly Arkis wasn't standing alone. A pair of guards dropped their camouflage, one taller than the other, standing beside him. She felt Sinto's instant recognition of the guards through the Mark. That icy feeling spread to her bones. Fear deeper than she'd ever felt before. She heard a familiar buzz—a merlux firing—not Sinto's but from someone else, close behind her. She pivoted on her foot, saw a circular loop raised high above Sinto's head.

She didn't think. She reacted. Years of training kicked in. She thrust her arm out to deflect it. Sinto jumped to the side. She felt a jolt of electricity. The band fell to the ground, crackling.

The air shimmered.

Camouflage.

She imagined the outline of a body, zeroed in on where the chest might be, then lunged back and lurched forward, driving her elbow toward it. Her elbow made contact with something solid.

She was jolted by a powerful shock. Quick and painful. Stars blotted her vision. She shook it off and fell back into a guarded position.

Sinto struggled with what looked like air; a second body, camouflage flickering. Electricity crackled between them. A band, like the one she deflected, slipped over his head and tightened, binding his arms to his side.

He roared like a caged lion. The band crackled and sparked and he fell to his knees, gasping.

Audrey targeted the disturbance of air moving toward her with merlux crackling. She focused on the sound and imagined it floating before her. She spun, turning her back to her target, coiled her knee to her chest, then explosively kicked straight back at chest height. Her heel made sudden contact with something solid and electrified.

Sharp pain zinged through her bones from her heel, up her spine, to the top of her head. She stumbled from the shock of it but stayed on her feet.

She learned quickly. If she hit electrified targets with a quick and sudden thrust she could endure the shock.

Whoever she hit fell to the ground in the fetal position, camouflage flickering on and off, mouth gasping for air. She didn't look at their face, nor did she care if it was a male or female. Only one thought filled her mind and she acted. She leaped into the air and landed with one foot to neck, the other to temple. There was no shock. The body crumpled beneath her feet and dissolved into ash.

She whipped around, legs braced, hands raised ready to defend.

Sinto was on his knees. One of Arkis' guards gripped a handful of his hair and yanked his head back. A second guard slapped a sharp knife against his neck.

Audrey was grabbed from behind. A mighty shock made her knees buckle and she fell to the ground. An Orankai woman dropped her camouflage. She wasn't much older than the one Audrey killed to save Ryan a few months back. She must have been fresh from the breeding caves before they were destroyed.

The woman grabbed Audrey's wrists from behind, pulled them back, and slapped a band around them, wrenching them high. Then she wound the other end of the band around Audrey's neck and secured it. Audrey's shoulders screamed in protest. The band cut into her windpipe. She had to tighten the muscles in her neck to ease the pressure and draw a full breath. Greatly compromised, like Sinto, with her wrists and neck hog-tied. She clenched her teeth, cursing herself for letting down her guard.

Arkis came up to her clapping his hands. "What a show! Aren't you a feisty one." He swiveled his gaze back to Sinto. "I can see why you are so enamored by her." He came closer, pressing his face until their noses nearly met. His breath was hot and rancid. She tipped her head back and he came a little closer. She went back a little more. He pressed even closer. Then she head-butted him. His nose cracked and he stumbled back.

"Why you little bitch!" Blood streamed from his nostrils. His guards looked at him for instructions. He waved them back.

She spat. "I thought you liked feisty."

"Oh I do," he said, wiping blood from his lip. He pinched his nose and tipped his head back. "Buying time, I see, for the inevitable."

Sinto twitched. The guard pressed the blade harder against his neck.

"Did Sinto tell you what happened to Victoria?"

"*Don't engage him*," Sinto pushed. "*Stay calm.*"

Arkis signaled for the woman holding her to tighten the band wrapped around her neck until she could barely breathe. He wasn't going to make the same mistake twice.

Arkis came forward a second time. "My my, you certainly have far exceeded my expectations. I must say, Sinto has good taste." He looked back at Sinto. "This one's much better than Victoria, wouldn't you say, brother?" He leaned forward and gave her a big sniff. "Ooh and you smell all *warmed up*. Did Sinto bring the goods? Were you satisfied? Wait until I have a go at you. You'll be screaming for more."

Sinto writhed. His eyes were on fire. The band around his torso crackled. Blood trickled from the tip of the blade pressed to his neck.

"Best not to fight it, brother, else you might burn out before the real fun begins. Hate to have you miss it."

Audrey pushed. *"Wait for him to make a mistake."*

"No one knows we're here. I can't fight this band for long. Already, I feel weak."

"You're not the only one who knows how to fight."

"Bound as you are?"

"I'm working on it..."

"Beware the power of a merlux."

"If I strike fast, the shock is manageable."

"The one holding you is more powerful than the one you killed. If only you can wrangle free."

"Yes! And get weapons in the vau—"

Arkis slapped Audrey's face. "Stop that, else I will cut out your tongues—uh—" He turned to his guards. "How exactly do you cut out a mind-speak tongue?"

One of the guards said, "You crush their skulls."

"Oh my, that might be a bit dramatic." He clicked his tongue. "Though maybe later, maybe—" He winked at Audrey. "After I have her. I want her to tell Sinto all about it." He pinched her chin between his bloody fingers. "Every little gritty detail." He shocked her on that last word. It bit and burned into her skin.

Audrey felt sick to her stomach, racing through every scenario her father had trained her for. In none of it did he provide a lesson for outwitting a human capable of shocking her to death, much less bound the way she was. Sinto was rendered helpless by the band secured around his torso and the knife pressed to his neck.

Outnumbered four to two, that they knew of. There could be more Orankai hiding among the trees, waiting and watching for one of them to make a suicidal move. Maybe they could overpower them, but not with the merlux factor or the fact they were both severely compromised. The more she worked through different possibilities the more panicked she became. The odds were grim.

"Figured it out, huh?" Arkis said to her. "You can't win. I see the frustration in your eyes. You know it too." He tsked. "You know, I'm not the monster you think I am. You need not die." He whipped his gaze toward Sinto. "Only him. He's a traitor. Slipped away once, but twice…" He addressed the guards holding Sinto. "I think not, right Taylee, Suevo?"

They grinned and nodded.

Arkis ran a finger down her chest to her groin, cupped her crotch with his hand. "And maybe I'll leave my guards a little taste once I'm done."

She spit in his face. He wiped it away with a finger, stuck it in his mouth, sucked it clean, and laughed. "So *tasty*." His arms crossed his chest, and he fake-quivered. "I shiver with anticipation."

Then he turned to the woman who had bound her.

"Strip her and hold her to the ground."

84

Déjà Vu Remix

Something exploded inside Sinto. The image of Victoria bound and spread on the ground while Arkis' body doubles cut her mercilessly was fresh in his mind. He struggled against the band sucking down his reserves and the knife sawing into his neck.

Audrey's voice threaded in his mind. *"We can't win. Maybe he will have mercy."*

Sinto pushed the last image of Victoria he held in memory to Audrey. He knew she got it by the terror that flashed in her eyes.

"Arkis knows no mercy. String him along, stay alive. We must find a way to beat him."

The Orankai woman holding Audrey shoved her to the ground. She landed hard on her side. Through the Mark, he felt the pain shoot through her shoulder from the contortion of how she was bound, hands wrenched back and hog-tied to her neck.

The woman used her finger to burn through Audrey's clothes and tore them away. She lay in nothing but her underwear and bra.

Sinto had never felt such rage. Rage beyond witnessing Victoria's violent death. Rage beyond what he felt in the City of Green. Rage beyond what Arkis' orange nectar ignited. Rage coiled around his merlux, sparking and sputtering weakly from the life-sucking band wrapped around his chest. He closed his eyes, unable to bear what was about to happen.

His eyelids were forced open by Suevo. "Oh no, pretty boy, you get to watch."

Arkis drew a knife from a sheath tied around his leg. It was jagged and sharp and something you would use to skin a bear. He dragged the tip down Audrey's cheek, drawing a thin line of blood. Her eyes were wild and breathing erratic.

"*Play to his ego.*"

Her demeanor shifted. "Wait, not like this."

Arkis raised a brow. "Oh really?"

"How can I pleasure you, bound like this?"

Arkis grinned. "I could imagine many ways, love."

"At least let me breathe. Free my hands so I can touch you. I'm a helpless Sapien, shock me if I try to escape."

Arkis gazed down at her, contemplating.

She gave him a coy smile.

Arkis flipped Sinto a wicked look. "You hear that, brother? She wants me." Arkis returned his attention to Audrey. He pierced her with his fiery orange gaze and tapped the tip of the knife on her left breast. "But I'm not stupid. Bound you stay. Now, where was I…"

What happened next came as a shock. Not from the band wrapped around his chest or another's merlux. A bolt of lightning and hurling spear came out of nowhere.

The knife pressed to Sinto's neck slipped when Suevo's head exploded. Taylee's grip eased. He fell to a knee, the spear buried in his chest. He burst into ash. The parasitic band around Sinto's chest sputtered. Its spark died. Lifeless, like its master.

Sinto jumped to his feet, arms bound, merlux firing, and ran headlong into Arkis, poised over Audrey with the tip of his knife aimed at her heart.

The knife slipped from Arkis' fingers and clanked against the rocks Sinto had gathered for Victoria's memorial. They tumbled, scattering the pile, with Sinto landing atop Arkis. He scrambled to escape but Sinto pinned him to the ground, chest to chest. Sinto splayed his legs with his toes planted deep in the earth. Arkis flailed his arms, slapping Sinto's face, punching Sinto's head.

Bolts of lightning and a volley of spears were launched in a fury, whisking through air from the direction of the bunker. Orankai emerged from the trees. Their camouflaged bodies exploded into ash. His mind faltered from the sudden and violent frenzy.

Who could it be?

Arkis squirmed, laughing hysterically, nose crooked and bleeding from Audrey's timely head-butt. He was slippery as a snake and hard to grasp. Sinto feared losing his advantage and pushed against the band trapping his arms. The band was tightly wound and unforgiving. Arkis writhed out from beneath him and crab-walked away, gasping for breath and was stopped by a rotting tree stump.

Suddenly, Sinto's arms were freed. He looked up.

Audrey held Arkis' knife. She grinned. "Miss me?"

He grinned back. "Always."

Together they lunged for Arkis and wrestled him to his stomach. Audrey jolted and grunted from Arkis' electrical shocks, her teeth gritted in determination. Sinto held Arkis' arms behind his back. Audrey wrapped the band she cut from Sinto's torso around Arkis' wrists and looped it around his neck. She gave it an extra jerk, tightening it until his eyes bulged and every breath was a struggle. She secured it with a constrictor knot.

Audrey said, "You like feisty? You got it, asshole!" She stood up and kicked him in the head three times. His eyes bugged then winked out. Then she kicked him in the ribs for good measure, not once, but three solid strikes, the last producing a resounding crack of bone.

Arkis lay unconscious, body bruised and bleeding, but alive.

Audrey crouched, staying low and away from the volley of spears finding camouflaged bodies. She spun around, gaze assessing the situation.

Sinto ducked, then crouched beside her, reeling from the sudden explosion of chaos. "Who are they?"

"Not sure, but they can't hold them all off alone!" She pointed. "Look!"

Lying on the ground were several crossbows, and a pair of them seemed to hover in the air, firing automatically. Sinto and Audrey kept low and ran to join whoever was firing.

Sinto stripped off his clothes and camouflaged. Audrey was the only human visible, launching spears at shimmering air, her near-naked body rippling with taut muscle and sheer determination.

"Good to see you, brother," a familiar voice said. "I came with my new friend, Blake. Now who's saving whom?"

Naiada!

She briefly dropped her facial camouflage to give Sinto a bright smile while firing the crossbow as if it were a weapon she frequently used. He was shocked at how much she had changed since he last saw her. Skin dark like their father's, but a face like their mother's, and matured.

Blake's disembodied voice said, "Slowly retreat, toward the bunker door. Draw them closer until they're concentrated in the confines of the garden."

The four of them formed a semi-circle, firing at invisible targets in controlled sweeps at chest, knee, and head heights. Ash rained and clogged Sinto's nostrils. Arkis' unconscious body was buried by the remains of his dead monsters.

Naiada fired directly at those who slipped through, acutely sensing the advances none of them could see. More kept coming.

Once they reached the crack concealing the bunker door, Blake said, "Get inside, I'll set the charges."

"Charges?" Audrey pressed her face to the lock and the door clicked open. "Wait. What about Arkis? What if he gets away, again?"

Blake's voice drifted from several feet away. "I'll make sure that doesn't happen, trust me. Get inside, all of you."

Naiada said, "I'm staying, to help you."

Blake said, "No, you are not."

He must have pushed her. She fell into Sinto and Sinto fell into Audrey, and together they tumbled inside and down the short flight of stairs. The door clicked shut.

Sinto and Naiada dropped their camouflage.

Naiada lurched for the door. Sinto held her back. "No, he mustn't!" she screamed.

"Mustn't what?" Audrey asked.

Then the ground rumbled as several bombs exploded. A series of explosions that lasted several minutes until all Sinto could hear was a high-pitched ring and the thrum of his battered eardrums.

85

What To Do With Monster

AUDREY OPENED THE BUNKER door; smoke wafted inside. They poked their heads out. The air was heavy with dust and ash. Combined with the settling smoke, it was unbreathable. Sinto grabbed towels from inside the bunker to cover their faces, then they cautiously stepped outside. Sinto went first, then Audrey and Naiada, armed with crossbows.

It looked like a war zone after the last bomb was dropped. Things slowly came into focus as the dust settled.

Body parts littered what was left of the garden, Orankai from what they could tell. Bodies ripped apart before their minds triggered the impulse to burst into ash.

A sickening feeling lodged in the pit of Audrey's stomach as they wandered through the destruction, picking through bloody remains.

Oh, Blake, no...

She couldn't imagine the possibility he was gone. Surely they would find him, alive, a lopsided grin spreading across his face. He couldn't possibly be dead...

The bombs had been keenly targeted, not for complete destruction of their surroundings but targeted specifically to strike warm bodies. Smart bombs launched and detonated by thermal detection. Blake had mentioned them once during one of their planning discussions. Splintered trees stood beside those still whole. Patches of flowers stood proud within the garden, deep holes ripped in the earth beside them.

Ash and unidentifiable body parts were strewn everywhere.

Arkis lay where they had left him, buried beneath the ash of his army, bound and still alive, and wheezing. A splinter of wood had lodged in his chest.

"Leave him, for now," Sinto said.

So that's what they did; left him to wallow in a puddle of his own blood and the carnage of his shredded followers while they continued their search for Blake.

They called Blake's name, cognizant of possible Orankai survivors. They found nothing but ash and shredded flesh, flung throughout the trees and scattered across the forest floor.

Reluctantly, they searched for a black suit or a mop of dark hair. They found neither.

They ran a second sweep, working outward from the bunker door, around the garden, and into the nearby forest. They scanned the ground, treetops, around bushes. Nothing. No trace of him, only death. Once they completed their sweep, Audrey and Sinto circled back to Arkis, who had regained consciousness.

"I'm going to keep searching." Naiada said, and climbed the rocky ridge above the bunker.

Audrey stood above Arkis lying awkwardly on his back, hands pinned behind him, neck straining against the band tied around his neck.

She lurched. "You son of bitch! You killed him!"

Sinto grabbed her around the waist, held her back. "We don't know that for certain. Blake may still be alive."

Arkis tried to say something, choked, and coughed up blood. Blood stained his teeth. "Why do you hate me so, brother?"

"I never hated you, not before. I can't say the same now."

"Father loved you more than me. I didn't ask to be the bastard. You were the *perfect* son." He tried to spit, but what came out was bloody dribble.

"Who you are is of your own making. I never claimed to be perfect. You dwelled in a fabricated reality. Look what it did to you."

"You made me the villain."

"You made yourself that way! I had nothing to do with it."

"I was cursed the day I was born. Arkis, the bastard. The others never said anything, but they knew something was different about me. And my mother, oh how she coddled me. She thought I was weak. It made me sick. Did I ever tell you what happened to her?"

Sinto shook his head.

He chuckled. "I killed her." A trickle of blood leaked past his lips. "Killed her, slow and methodically. No one knew, not even our father.

"Like you I experimented with nature. I called it *Mother Shade*, my gift to her on my thirteenth birthday. You see, she couldn't sleep, constantly worried your mother would find out she was Ramasis' lover and I her bastard son and that she would retaliate against us. She was weak and I hated her for it."

He gasped, drew a gurgling breath. "*Mother Shade* was a special tea I created to help her sleep, until it stopped her heart. I told her it was what she was, my shade. She thought I meant my protector, a loving gesture, shading me from the truth of who I was and could never be—an equal to my brother."

He laughed, which turned into a bout of much gasping. "I did it as a joke. I wanted to make her sick. It was her own weakness that killed her. She hid who I truly was from everyone, even you, brother. Oh, the irony. I shaded her in the end."

"You are one sick fuck," Audrey said through gritted teeth.

She wanted to crush his sick brain to mush. It would be easy with a well-calculated stomp of her foot—her heel at full force to the intersection between his eyes and the bridge of his nose. The skull was weakest there. It was the first of many strikes to kill that her father taught her. The first strike would collapse the facial structure. A second would drive bone into the brain. The third would—

Sinto jerked her back. "*Patience, my love.*"

It angered Audrey that Sinto gave a stage to this madman. It was time to end this. Here, now, and not delicately. He squeezed tighter. "*Not yet.*"

Arkis kept rambling, "I gave the Terrakai what they yearned for; independence and the power to punish those who suppressed them. Ianthe, the Circle, and everyone who enabled them—you, the Seakai, the Arctakai, and in the end, that Larkian slime."

His eyes blinkered and breath faltered, but he continued. "The Sapiens are our *enemy*. Your mother and her Circle embraced them. *You* embraced them—" His gaze found Audrey's eyes. "And fucked them, and let them fuck you, and who knows what else. The Terrakai wanted revenge, demanded *Orankai.*"

He choked and spit out a wad of congealed blood. "You are a fool, Sinto. It matters not whether I live or die. Orange cannot be stopped. The Orankai cannot be stopped. I did that, brother. Spread my seed far and wide. There are millions of us, bred for a single purpose. Rid Earth and Merluma of their oppressors. It is I who give the Sapiens what they idolize, what they believe their gods have planned: the end of days, the rapture, the horrors they are obsessed by. It is I who should be rewarded, idolized, for making their beliefs come true."

"You're delusional," Audrey hissed. "We don't idolize those things, and we certainly don't idolize the likes of you."

Sinto said. "If there is a devil, then you are he. I was blind. You were broken from the start."

Audrey paced. "What shall we do with him?"

Sinto gazed down at his bastard half-brother, aged well beyond his twenty-plus years, his cursed nectar accelerating cellular degeneration, rotting his mind and ravaging his body.

Sinto shared with Audrey what must be done. Arkis tried as a traitor. Merahvu justice for such an act was swift and the punishment harsh and conclusive: Undoing. Physically, it was painless, mentally not so much. Sinto explained they were granted the right of judge and jury, for which there would be no rebuttal from his mother or the Circle. Arkis' crimes were felt by all and were indefensible.

Sinto said out loud, "We end him, the Merahvu way."

Arkis gasped. "Brother, have you no mercy?"

"And what do you believe mercy to be?"

Arkis cracked a wicked smile. "Quick, painless, maybe a little nookie-nookie before, a last tryst with a feisty Sapien. It's the least you could do for a dying brother, don't you think?"

The son of bitch was serious, and his plea ignited a rage she had held deep inside; for his cavalier treatment of women, for killing an innocent Wekeep and all the others who would not bow to his sick plan, and for having the balls to think he would ever have the chance to touch her.

She responded to his snide question with a swift kick to his ribs, emphasizing each word. "Not. Happening. You. Righteous. Fuck."

Ribs cracked and his mouth gaped as he fought to stay conscious.

Sinto tsked. "Hmm, I might have to agree." Then he knelt and grabbed Arkis' by the head. "Besides, I have something much more interesting in mind for you—to use Audrey's colorful words—you righteous fuck."

86

Undoing

Sinto forced Arkis' eyes open with his thumbs and gazed fiercely into his eyes. Then he sucked Arkis' mind from his body. Arkis gasped and went limp, his sightless gaze fixed on the sky.

Sinto stumbled back, jolted from the sudden invasion of such evil inside his mind, and was quick to lock Arkis away within a deep recess; a survival technique he learned from his past trials of sharing with those he knew or did not—his mother, Korvasi, Ramasis, and his sister. He didn't cherish the thought of Arkis' poison inside his mind. He crushed Arkis' thoughts and muted his voice.

Though he made one exception: A window to the outside world so Arkis could witness his death.

Audrey stood over his body. His black-ringed eyes gazed mindlessly to the sky. She looked up. "That's it, he's dead?"

"Not yet." Then Sinto pointed to his own head.

She gasped. "He's in your *head*?"

"To witness his Undoing."

Sinto bent and picked up the jagged knife Arkis had intended to use on Audrey. The thought of what Arkis had planned to do with it made him reluctant to touch it.

"You should do it." He handed the knife to Audrey. "Arkis must watch his body die. The conscious mind cannot survive without one. He lives as long as I am willing to hold him in my mind, which won't be for long as it is a heavy burden."

Audrey looked down at Arkis' body, breathing and alive, empty eyes gazing, and void of the consciousness that Sinto held in his mind. She drew a deep breath, looked up.

"You say he's watching?"

He nodded. "That's the point, and he deserves it; his crimes are not questionable. He would have killed you as he killed Victoria. He deserves the same."

"But—I,"

He gave her hand a squeeze. "Do it for all the innocents he murdered, raped, and tortured. Do it for justice."

Audrey's eyes filled with steely determination. She knelt over Arkis' body. She tapped the blade of the knife against her thigh. She closed her eyes and breathed, deep and steady. She opened them, put down the knife, then wrapped her hands around the large splinter of wood stuck in his chest and yanked it out. Blood and green flueox leaked from the open wound. He didn't scream or complain, for he had no mind to work his mouth. His heart beat and his lungs drew breath—autonomous functions controlled by the primitive brain, requiring no conscious thought.

The whisk of many wings drew Audrey's attention. She looked up. Turkey vultures drawn to the scent of fresh meat strewn around the garden and the forest.

She smiled at Sinto and pointed up to the vultures. Then she rolled Arkis' body to the side and cut his binds, freeing his hands. She rolled him to his back and splayed his arms. Used the knife to cut off his red silk shirt and black leather wrap. Then she splayed his legs. He lay naked, as vulnerable and helpless as a starfish beached on a reef.

She picked up the knife and slashed him repeatedly. Across cheek, chest, leg, arm, belly. Shallow and non-life threatening.

He would be screaming, if he could, though they were merely a fraction of the violations he inflicted on Victoria. Blood oozed and tainted the air with the smell of salty copper.

Her gaze fell to his genital sack. The blade wavered above and her breath quivered; Sinto was aware of what she was thinking through the Mark. He gave no direction. It was her choice as to the punishment that fit the crime.

She put down the knife and peeled Arkis' genital sack open, exposing him.

Audrey came to Sinto's side and clasped his hand. Together they watched the turkey vultures swoop down and land beside Arkis' body.

They took his eyes first, then his genitals. Arkis' screaming began as they devoured one testicle at a time, saving the flaccid flesh of his penis for last. Then they ripped at his torso and feasted on his organs. It did not take long for his heart to stop beating.

The body did not explode into ash after it passed, for it no longer had Arkis' mind to make it do so.

And once the vultures sufficiently ravaged what was left of him, Sinto flushed his mind of Arkis' vile consciousness.

The being called Arkis was gone, Undone, forever. A mind untethered, never to return to flesh, not even as dust to seed the next circle of life. An evil forever snuffed.

87

Found

THE PICKED-OVER REMAINS OF Arkis' body lay at Audrey and Sinto's feet.

Naiada called down from a rocky perch above. "I found him."

They scrambled up the rocky slope where Naiada knelt beside Blake, splayed on his back. The towel she had used to mask her face was neatly folded across his eyes. Half his head was singed and most of his hair was gone. His face was deeply scratched. Blood trickled from his ears. His mouth worked, as if trying to clear them.

He breathed freely through his nose and was conscious and aware. His body appeared untouched, though the pallor of his skin was worrying.

Naiada said, "He's alive." She ran her hands along his chest. "Heart strong, a couple of cracked ribs, but his body is whole, except for—" She looked down at his face.

Audrey knelt and took his hand. "Talk to me," she said to Blake.

His head shifted as if looking around. He squeezed back but didn't say anything.

"He can't hear you, his ears—" She tenderly cupped one of them. "The explosion, it—I fear both are irrevocably damaged."

Audrey reached for the towel covering his eyes.

"No," Naiada said, drawing Audrey's hand back. "His eyes, they're..." The look in her eyes said it all.

Don't look, it's not pretty.

"I'm calling for help." Sinto climbed down from the rocky perch and disappeared below.

Audrey clasped Blake's hand in both of hers.

His voice threaded through her mind. *"Audrey, is that you? I'm sorry, I miscalculated, nearly blew myself up."* He laughed, then stopped with a confused look on his face. *"I can't see or hear anything."*

Tears burst from Audrey's eyes. *"Best you can't. It's a bloody mess and the ruckus of crunching and cawing by the vultures is unbearable."* A sobbing laugh slipped through her lips. *"You got them, Blake, all of them. We got Arkis too. He's gone, finally."*

"Not sure why Naiada won't let me get up. Got a headache and my chest hurts, but I feel alive. I just can't see or hear. How do I look otherwise?"

Her gaze swept across his head. *"No one will be braiding your hair anytime soon."*

He chuckled, nervously. *"Ha, hair's overrated. I was thinking of trying bald anyway. Honestly, how bad is it?"*

"A few singed strands, couple of scratches, nothing really." She glanced up at Naiada, feeling guilty for lying. *"Maybe you should rest. Help's on the way, with much to clean up thanks to you."*

88

The Other

SINTO CAME BACK WITH a blanket for Blake and clothes for Audrey, who was cold and shivering, wearing only a bra and underwear. They covered Blake and Audrey slipped on the clothes, ever grateful.

Audrey stayed by Blake's side while Sinto and Naiada stepped away for a private moment.

Sinto gazed at his sister, grappling with the dramatic changes from the last time he saw her. Now a grown woman, though the pitted scars on her cheeks remained. Otherwise, she had the same face as their mother's. Especially her eyes, crackling with power and a smoldering soft lavender.

He said, "I thought I would never see you again."

"What, no faith in your little sister?"

He laughed. "I didn't mean because of you—what matters is you're safe and alive and free from Arkis and Father."

A wave of sadness rippled across Naiada's face. "Blake told me he's dead."

"Ravaged by Arkis' nectar and the guilt that ate his soul. I'm sorry you weren't able to see him before he passed."

"I saw him plenty. He died long ago," she said bitterly, tears welling.

Sinto hugged her. One thing had not changed. Her height. The top of her head barely reached his chest. He buried his face into the crown of her head. "I find it difficult accepting this new version of you."

She pulled back and laughed. "You can no longer call me your little sister!"

"You lost your childhood."

She grew somber. "For that, I struggle to forgive Father. I spent the last several years—several miserable *years*—locked up in a chamber in the Labyrinth with nothing but pots of measly paints. I would have gone insane without them and my ability to pierce the Timeless Dimension. I was able to see some of what was happening here, but the picture was incomplete without Mother's guidance. She taught me just enough before Father kidnapped me, but not everything. There was much I had to figure out on my own. I am fortunate to have been gifted with her power of foresight, as well as some of what we both inherited from our father."

Sinto cocked a brow. "Such as?"

She grinned. "The power to shock."

"Aye, what you demonstrated today was quite impressive. Lightning bolts! And so many at one time! Remind me to never find myself on the receiving end of your fireworks, or else my heart might stop for good."

"I would never want to stop your heart, brother." She glanced over to Audrey, gently smoothing what was left of Blake's hair away from his face. "You've much to live for."

"I do, and will."

She pinched his cheek. "Don't suppose you would want to share exactly what you two were doing here last night?"

Sinto smirked. "Not on your life."

"Your aura has taken on a peculiar glow and I can tell by the look on your face it must have been something pretty spectacular."

"It was and it's none of your business."

"Hmm, I was hoping to learn more of what I can look forward to, and soon, I suppose, now that I'm all grown up."

He pinched her cheek back. "Some things are best kept secret and are far more fun to discover on your own."

She laughed. "Usually your secrets can't hide from me but I notice you've grown particularly good at guarding your mind."

"Call it a form of survival."

They shared a good laugh at how much they both had changed. They shared tears from the horrors they lived through since they were together in Tallamure. It felt like a decade ago. For Naiada that was mostly true.

Sinto wondered. "By the way, how did you and Blake end up here? If you had not shown up when you did…"

"A thought that makes me shudder," Naiada said. "We came here for two reasons, actually. I had a strong feeling something terrible was going to happen to both of you. I saw this place in my visions but had no idea where it was. Blake recognized it when I shared it with him. We came straight away."

"And the other?"

"Oh, actually, the other reason is quite important, and one we must deal with immediately."

He could hear the pounding of a helicopter's rotors approaching—the Larkian rescue he had called for Blake.

"Come, we must hurry before they arrive." She scurried down the rocky rise, Sinto following, to the crack near the bunker door. Hidden under a pile of branches and leaves was a round object wrapped in a dried-out broad leaf secured by pliable vines. She picked it up and handed it to him. It was of a familiar size and weight.

Sinto pulled off the vines and peeled back the leaf. He gasped when the Mark in his arm came to life.

"The crystal Arkis' queens used to enter the Timeless Dimension. Because of this, Arkis was able to learn everything you and the Larkians were doing. Then he would send Scouts to spy and confirm. It was his advantage. After Blake and Audrey found me in the Labyrinth, Franz sneaked away and stole it, only to lose it during an earthshake. After we defeated the Orankai, Blake and I went back to retrieve it."

The crystal was exactly like the Salish Stone but with a green center, faintly aglow. It was exactly as Audrey had described it. It was the glowing orb that he, along with his mother, had observed as Arkis' queens tapped into the Timeless Dimension.

The helicopter circled and began to drop lower where Blake lay above the bunker.

"Blake suggested we hide it here, a safe haven for many Larkian treasures."

"A sound suggestion. Go, help them with Blake; I'll put it with the other."

She spun around. "Wait, what other?"

"I'll tell you once we get the chance. Now go."

He hid it in the same place as the Salish Stone, then locked up the shelter and raced back to join Audrey and Naiada at Blake's side.

A large metal basket dropped down from the hovering helicopter that was whipping the tops of fir trees. Two men slipped down ropes after it. They introduced themselves as Smith and Jones.

Smith and Jones carefully and meticulously transferred Blake to a board and strapped him down by chin, chest, hips, and legs so he couldn't move if he tried.

"In case his spine is compromised," Smith said.

Audrey, Sinto, and Naiada watched, shell-shocked, as Blake was drawn into the belly of the mechanical bird aboard the metal basket.

Jones gave Sinto and Audrey a message. "Alvarez wanted me to tell you that Wantemo and Dr. Wickman will tend to Blake in Seattle. He needs you and Audrey back on Isla Salvación right away."

The basket came down to pick up Smith and Jones. Naiada insisted she go too. She and Sinto exchanged a quick hug and the traditional kiss. She clambered aboard the basket, waving as she rose into the air.

Sinto and Audrey watched as the black helicopter disappeared to the south. The air stilled and grew silent but for the caw of turkey vultures and the crunch of cartilage and gristle.

89

Race With Time

SINTO AND AUDREY RETURNED to Isla Salvación via the sea, weary and restless.

The situation on Earth had grown dire. What Arkis started now reeled out of control. While many Orankai were killed on Merluma, many more—the Larkians speculated hundreds of thousands—had already migrated to Earth.

And it was on Earth that the Orankai continued their relentless and stealthy attack against the Sapiens; like a hydra, cutting off the head meant nothing, as many others emerged to take over. The situation had worsened without their leader. Monsters beget monsters, and those monsters' goal was to obliterate Sapiens.

Stories from news feeds across the globe grew wilder. Reports of the seemingly healthy and young dying by sudden heart failure were becoming common. Others told of a new drug that gave one great strength and confidence. It was free if you knew where to get it, and it became quite popular.

Arkis and his Orankai had successfully brought many Sapiens under this new mind-controlling drug by staying one step ahead of the authorities; and when the authorities got too close to discovering them, they brought them into the fold by infecting them.

New conspiracies popped up daily and old ones were renewed. Alien invasions and demonic possession. Portals opening to hell and other dark worlds. Monsters eating children while they slept in their beds. Others speculated a secret society was working to rid Earth of the poor and the meek. The formation of new tribes and cults exploded. Deaths by homicide and suicide ticked up exponentially. The recent boom in artificial intelligence, misinformation, and social media fueled the hysteria.

Governments of western nations were getting twitchy, speculating about a new face of warfare and terrorism. But the attacks were random, spread far and wide, and impossible to easily target. They couldn't identify from which country or terrorist factions the attacks were ordered or originated.

With the Orankai deeply integrated into Sapien societies, there was nothing the Merahvu and the Larkians could do but to hit them hard at their source of control and power: Orange. And it was growing faster than ever—fed a steady diet of plastic, thanks to the stepped-up efforts by the Larkians to corral it by giving it more—a short-term solution that would soon backfire.

So far, the Larkians had been able to concentrate Orange where it originated; dead center between the Hawaiian Islands and the coast of California. On Isla Salvación, the Orange team had been caught in a catch-22 situation. It was a race as to which would grow faster: Orange or the lorica-inspired biological substance they were farming to contain it. But time ran out, so they delivered what they had to waiting ships, which had recently departed for their next battlefield in the Pacific.

That night Sinto and Audrey's lovemaking was physically subdued but emotionally desperate. Everything they fought for seemed to be falling apart and it felt as if they were swimming in a sea of mud. But they were alive and had each other. They vowed to fight until the bitter end, when the Orankai and Orange were defeated or death claimed them both.

The next morning, they rode in silence in the UTV from their south-end house to the command center.

Rachel greeted them once they arrived. Dark circles framed her eyes. Everyone looked defeated, even Alvarez, who never displayed emotion. Audrey's father was especially clingy after hearing of their close call with Arkis on Andrew's Island. Audrey extricated herself from his embrace and greeted Ianthe with the traditional greeting kisses. Ianthe's gaze was distant and worrisome.

Wantemo slipped in, having just arrived from Seattle, surprising both Sinto and Audrey.

She asked, "How's Blake?"

He grimaced. "We were unable to save his eyes, or his hearing, and he may never be able to grow a full head of hair. Otherwise, he's lucky to be alive. I gave him a boost, and his ribs should mend rather quickly. Naiada has not left his side and is keeping his spirits high."

Sinto was curious about this new and strange relationship his sister had developed with Blake. Mostly he was relieved she was distracted and far from the fight.

Alvarez called for order. Those in attendance took a seat or wall to lean against. That included Khani, Vesna, Isden, and the Larkian Council—minus Blake and Dr. Wickman—as well as Audrey and Sinto, Culliford and Ianthe, and, of course, Wantemo. Rachel was ever-present by Alvarez's side.

Francesca's research ship was steaming at full speed toward Orange's last known location. Traveling alongside were two Larkian-owned research ships and five others, hired under contract with strict non-disclosures, and captained and crewed by people Francesca had worked with before. These ships carried precious vats of cargo, the biological substance rapidly cultivated to contain Orange.

Stokes led the flotilla in *Requiem Sea II* with a full team of Xiphias pilots, including Tucker and Dyer. Ryan was also aboard and at the ready in the lab. Three other sister ships from Seattle were en route to meet them, each fully crewed and loaded with Xiphiases and mid-sized submarines capable of extreme deep dives to assist in the delicate operation.

Francesca, Stokes, and Ryan participated in the conference virtually, gazing back from screens mounted on the wall, faces tense and solemn.

Alvarez rose from his seat and addressed the room. "Now would be a good time to review the plan." He turned toward the screens with the virtual participants. "Francesca, you start."

She said, "My team delivers and deploys the biological source for containment." She smirked. "My crew likens it to vats of spit, and fondly call it *brig slime*."

Ryan raised a hand. Alvarez nodded for him to speak. "We're running hourly tests to ensure its integrity and health. So far, it's holding as expected."

Wantemo waved a hand and stood up. "Once this—*brig slime*—is deployed into the waters, Sinto and I will mold it into a biological sphere around Orange."

Audrey was not the only one gazing back at Wantemo questioningly.

Sinto stood. "Perhaps I should explain."

Wantemo gestured for Sinto to go on and sat.

"This *brig slime* Francesca and her crew are transporting is just that, a biological slimy substance that looks and feels like spit. To render it useful for our purpose it must be—to use a technological term many of you are familiar with—*programmed*. Wantemo and I will program it to wrap around Orange with a secure lock. Essentially forming a biologically locked sphere, or as Francesca calls it, a *biobrig*. In order for this to work, Orange must rise from the ocean floor to shallower waters in a concentrated ball."

Stokes added, "Francesca and I have worked out a plan for dropping bundles of condensed plastic from above with an assist from a trio of submarines armed with plastic torpedoes to help shape it."

Culliford asked, "Do we anticipate resistance?"

Alvarez tapped the table with his fingers. "From Orange, no. From the Orankai, absolutely. We firmly believe they are ever-present at the site, harvesting."

Sinto leaned forward. "If we can lure Orange to rise up without much fanfare, we hope not to disrupt them. They should be accustomed to its erratic movement. If all goes smoothly, we'll wrap them up along with Orange."

Culliford raised a hand. "And if they refuse?"

"Our teams will be at the ready," Khani boomed.

Stokes added, "And we plan to deploy our full complement of Xiphiases should they resist and attack." He paused when he saw Audrey through the link. "But because of recent unfortunate circumstances, we're short of pilots." He quirked a sharp brow.

"Count me in," Audrey replied.

That made Stokes smile, and Sinto and her father flinch.

The plan sounded simple but everyone knew it was anything but.

Since time was of the essence, Audrey and Sinto kept their goodbyes short. Sinto's mother and Culliford were visibly distraught, and before either could object, they left.

Rachel was the most upset and feeling useless. Sinto reminded her she had an important role providing assistance to Alvarez. Ongoing updates and communications would be critical for the teams once they arrived at their destination. No one could predict what they may encounter.

Sinto and Audrey wasted no time and departed with Wantemo on their heels.

Wantemo and Sinto cut tunnels in the sea. Sinto tucked Audrey in the safety of his arms as they flew through the Pacific to meet the Larkian fleet, halfway to their destination.

Khani, Vesna, and Isden followed with their warrior teams.

90

Practice Makes Perfect

DOZENS OF VORTEXES CUT through the Pacific. Khani's, Vesna's, and Isden's teams burst from the surface, landing on the decks of the Larkian vessels churning across the Pacific. Sinto, Audrey, and Wantemo landed on the aft deck of *Masquerade Ball.*

Francesca ran from the bridge to greet them and wrapped Audrey in a bear hug. "May the gods bless us! First Merluma, then that business with Arkis on Andi's island—I thought you were gone for good." Francesca pulled back with her hands still grasped around Audrey's shoulders. "You're like a damn cat. What's that leave you, seven more lives?"

Audrey laughed. "Actually, six, if you count the time I reefed a friend's boat running from Stokes, who was chasing Sinto and me down in a helicopter. I would have drowned if it wasn't for Sinto."

Sinto cleared his throat. "Actually, you *did* drown. I believe it was Stokes and Dr. Wickman who revived you."

Audrey rolled her eyes and tsked. "So many close calls, I forget."

"Why the hell was Stokes chasing you?" Francesca asked.

"A long story that might take a full bottle of rum to tell."

"Sounds like a date."

Wantemo piped up with a grin. "May I join too?"

"Absolutely!" Francesca let go of Audrey's shoulders and cocked her head. "I heard you did a number on Arkis."

"Trained to kill is one thing, doing it is another."

"Don't I know it; there are too many dead bodies in my past to count," Francesca said.

"Technically, I didn't kill him. The vultures did, but I did my part to make him too irresistible to pass up. In the end, he got what he deserved: to watch himself being devoured one mouthful at a time. Sinto was the one who ultimately freed this world of his evil essence."

Sinto said. "My only regret was not doing it sooner."

Francesca swept her gaze across the vast expanse of the Pacific, where eight other ships were merely specks rising in and out of view on a heaving sea, steaming in the same direction.

Francesca clapped her hands. "I suppose we ought to get to work."

Before departing Isla Salvación, it was agreed that Sinto and Wantemo would personally run continual tests with samples of brig slime under Ryan's watchful eye. Since it was a live substance, it was critical to ensure its health and integrity during transport and up to the point Sinto and Wantemo employed it to contain Orange.

Francesca led them into the bowels of her ship where large bladders filled every available space. They filled the laboratory, unused crew cabins—even the galley's large pantries. Audrey was surprised when she swung open the door to the self-contained greenhouse that occupied a third of the ship. Bladders were wedged among bushes and trees and blooming flowers.

Francesca had set up several twenty-gallon fish tanks for Sinto and Wantemo to use for their tests. Space was tight and they had to shimmy sideways to slip past the slime bladders to get to one of the tanks.

Wantemo broke the seal on one of the bladders. Sinto scooped out a small sample with the cup of his hand and Wantemo immediately resealed the opening.

Audrey wrinkled her nose. "Ew, it looks more like snot than spit."

Wantemo smiled. "I assure you, it is neither."

Sinto dipped his hand in the tank of water. The sample of brig slime slithered away and slowly began to sink.

Wantemo stuck his finger in the water. His eyes brightened with electricity pumping through his veins. He flicked his finger. The brig slime stopped sinking. He twitched his lip and wagged his finger. The brig slime stretched and curved, and appeared to be tying itself into a knot. When he pulled his finger from the water, it settled to the bottom in the knotted state Wantemo left it.

Francesca plucked a chestnut from a tree and handed it to Wantemo. He dropped it in. Gaze fiery and finger wagging, Wantemo's lip twitched and the sample unwound, stretching and swirling and winding its way around the nut bobbing just below the surface.

"That's it? Looks easy," Francesca said.

"It is, with something inanimate. Let's try again with something more challenging."

He stuck his finger in the tank and released the nut from the biobrig he had formed. The sample of brig slime slithered to the bottom of the tank.

Wantemo looked around Francesca's lab, then snatched a small fish from the pond. "Sinto, find a worm." Sinto did, tangled in the roots of a fully mature onion growing among other vegetables. It wriggled in the cupped palm of his hand.

Wantemo dropped the fish in the water. "First, let's see how we do under a little more pressure."

He repeated the steps as before, only this time there was lot more wagging and twitching to wrangle the brig slime around a darting fish. Wantemo released it and took the worm from Sinto.

"Let's try again, but this time we'll lure it with the worm, then lock it inside." He looked to Sinto. "We should do this together."

Wantemo and Sinto each stuck a finger in the water.

"Feel its vitality," Wantemo said. "Now for the bait." He dropped the worm into the water; it writhed in shock.

They flicked their fingers, twitched their lips, furrowed their brows. Mirrored gestures and expressions as they manipulated the sample with linked minds. The sample stretched like a net and scooped up the worm, forming a bubble twice the size of the fish. The fish circled the bubble, wary of the slimy substance between it and its meal. After probing a couple of times, it slipped inside and sucked up the worm.

"Now for the lock," Wantemo said, eyes blazing.

Sinto and Wantemo each pinched their fingers, trapping the fish inside. It grew frantic, swimming in circles and bouncing off the sides until it was near total exhaustion. Then they released their fingers and the fish burst from the bubble.

Wantemo said. "We should test each and every bladder to be sure of full viability."

Francesca's brows shot up. "That's a lot of testing."

"Call Ryan, let him know we're ready to get to it."

"And this little trick is going to work with all of it, thousands and thousands of gallons, all at once?" Francesca asked.

"It is not the quantity that poses a challenge, but distraction from our task. As you can see, it takes a great deal of concentration from the two of us working together." Wantemo said. "Once Orange is properly positioned, we should be able to contain it quite easily—that is, if we aren't battling opposition."

"And if you are?"

"Sinto and I will find out rather quickly if it's as easy to accomplish under duress."

Audrey grinned. "That's where my team comes in."

91

Ground Zero

SINTO TRANSFERRED AUDREY TO the *Requiem Sea II* via the sea after bidding Francesca farewell. Doing otherwise would have required halting the ships and impacting their schedule. But with Sinto's help it was easy and caused no disruption. They both regretted him having to leave her, but he did, returning to Francesca's ship to work with Ryan.

Sinto stumbled into Audrey's cabin early the next morning, mentally exhausted but physically wired and anxious. He told her of a grim discovery. One batch of brig slime was unresponsive, having died during transport. So Ryan returned to the lab on *Requiem Sea II* in the middle of the night to figure out why, while Sinto and Wantemo proceeded to test each and every bladder. Luckily, no other failures were found. Regardless, they were thirty-six hours from their destination and the discovery confounded and alarmed the three of them. Every bladder had been tested prior to departing Isla Salvación and found to be healthy and vital. Why one failed was a mystery.

There was a desperation to Sinto's physical need, and after a brief and frantic copulation, he fell fast asleep without kissing her goodnight. Afterward, she dressed and quietly slipped out to get a workout in the gym.

There she found Tucker and Dyer and several other crew mates she came to fondly respect after their last adventure when they discovered the true horrors of Orange and were attacked by Orankai. Seems Sinto wasn't the only one anxious about their arrival and the likely encounter with rogue Orankai. Without Arkis as their leader, it was anyone's guess as to what to expect.

"Oy! Déjà vu," Tucker said. "Shall we try another challenge? You, me. Here, now. I want that hat back."

"Not on your life. I'm retired from all that."

Dyer shook his head. "Oh no, that's not how it works. The loser may challenge the winner any time they want."

"Is that so?"

"Yep," Tucker grinned, lip tugging awkwardly from his facial scar.

"Maybe you ought to save all that pent-up aggression for the Orankai."

"Buzzkill!" Dyer said, then he sighed and elbowed Tucker in the ribs. "She's right, you know."

She stepped onto the gimbaled gym floor covered with a firm black matting. She worked every major joint in her body, warmed up with a series of sun salutations, then plucked a fifteen-pound clubbell off the wall.

Someone turned up the music. The thump and whine of loud and grinding punk matched the aggressive mood swirling in the gym.

Dyer and Tucker joined her, each working through a different series of movements. She ripped off a series of open and closed mills, swinging the clubbell until her lats and shoulders burned. Then she hit the mat with a combination of squats and lunges, planks and burpees, till her core screamed and legs felt wobbly. After forty-five minutes she was dripping with sweat and ready to kick some Orankai ass.

After a quick shower, she padded her way to the lab where Ryan was analyzing the failed batch of brig slime. The buzz she earned from her workout faded fast.

"It just died for no particular reason; it seems it simply reached its natural end," he said. "Wantemo's not too happy—in fact, he seemed very concerned. Looks like we've got a shorter window of survival than we thought."

News traveled fast among the crew, and Stokes ordered the throttles of every ship pushed to their stops to shave off a few extra hours to their destination. With Sinto and Wantemo's discovery, every hour counted. Bucking weather, Stokes estimated another full day until arrival.

Sinto lived in the labs along with Wantemo and Ryan and other scientists called to assist. There was a great deal of hand-wringing and brainstorming about how to extend the life of an organic substance they barely understood.

Audrey participated in training simulations and finding more ways to push Xiphias technology during battle.

Dyer and his team continued to reinforce the more vulnerable parts of the Xiphias' exteriors against an Orankai mob attack like the one Blake found himself victim to on Merluma.

Tucker tinkered with the weapon systems, adding an AI-assisted "smart target" system to distinguish between friendly Merahvu and not-so-friendly Orankai targets using the dChips each of them had embedded in their arms.

Khani, Vesna, and Isden worked with their teams plotting attack and defensive maneuvers to draw an attack away from Sinto and Wantemo should one occur during their most critical stage of containing Orange within the biobrig.

Alvarez and Rachel sent more dire reports from Isla Salvación of a world under siege by an invisible enemy. The Orankai's reach had spread beyond the Pacific Rim to Pacific nations in the southern hemisphere, inland areas of the United States, and across the remaining world like wildfire. The numbers of deaths were staggering.

Audrey and Sinto were like ships passing during the night, sharing only a brief hello and a quick peck on the lips.

They arrived at ground zero shortly before dawn under a dark sky. They wasted no time.

Submersibles were launched to survey the ocean floor and map out the battlefield based on the size, shape, and location of Orange.

Francesca's ships circled and began dropping concentrated bundles of plastic.

Sinto and Wantemo transferred to Francesca's ship. Other Merahvu teams went to the others, readying the bladders for dispersal.

Audrey gathered with the other Xiphias pilots in the cargo chamber on *Requiem Sea II*, watching images beamed up from the submersibles scanning the depths.

The submersibles beamed images of a reef of glowing Orange to every screen throughout every ship. Orankai scooped up Orange, transferring what they collected to bellies of giant translucent jellyfish, like worker bees gathering flower nectar. The addition of jellyfish was a new wrinkle to their plan. Audrey wondered how many more surprises may be lurking.

The reality of the situation hit Audrey hard and suddenly. No one had discussed the possibility of failure. They had no plan B. Looking around at the others, she realized she wasn't the only one having these thoughts.

"Maybe we ought to plan on what to do if—" She looked to Tucker.

"Oy, the only other what-if plan is that we drag 'em all to hell along with ourselves. Don'tcha worry, I got that one taken care of."

It was said. Plan B was a suicide mission, kamikaze for them all. A very large unspoken one, residing in the belly of a ship ready to detonate, thanks to Tucker. No one argued. You could hear a pin drop as they watched the scene unfolding on the ocean floor.

92

Biobrig

THE BRIG SLIME SURVIVED the journey, much to Sinto's relief. Only the one bladder was lost, which wouldn't make a difference in the entirety of what he and Wantemo had planned.

Once arriving at the Pacific gyre, Sinto and Wantemo dove in. Khani, Vesna, Isden and their warrior teams followed. Bladders of brig slime were dropped into the sea, linked together by steel cables. The warrior teams dispersed as planned, with bladders in tow.

Francesca directed her ships to form a tight circle. The brig slime teams formed a second, much wider one just below the surface.

Sinto and Wantemo patiently waited as Francesca's ships dropped the plastic bait to lure Orange up from the bottom.

A pinpoint of orange light emerged from the darkness; a bioluminescent tentacle, reaching for its prize. A writhing finger of Orange looped around a bundle of plastic and yanked it to the depths with surprising strength and speed. Bait taken. Darkness returned.

Sinto's heart pounded with anticipation.

Multiple tentacles emerged from the depths, drawn to the plastic bundles raining like giant hailstones. Below the tentacles, a floor of Orange rose from the deep.

The brig slime teams widened their circle of linked bladders as the immensity of Orange became apparent. Bladders were separated as necessary as the circle widened. Wantemo was on the opposite side of the circle and Sinto quickly lost sight of him, communicating telepathically as they were forced to spread further and further apart.

Orange was an ever-changing monstrosity. What began as controlled positioning turned chaotic. Linked bladders strained against the steel cables as each team towing them raced to reach the outer fringes of the rising blob of Orange. Sinto was paired with Isden's team, Wantemo with Khani's. Vesna and her team rounded out the third flank.

A steady feed of plastic bundles descended. Orange snagged every one. It ran hot, heating the surrounding water to well over a hundred degrees, bordering on the point of discomfort. Sinto's lorica thinned and he wondered how much the heat would impact the vitality and resilience of the fully formed biobrig. They had thought of that, and had tested it under heat, but anything over one-hundred-forty degrees would be a problem.

Wantemo sensed Sinto's unease from the other side of the writhing blob spread between them. He nudged Sinto's mind, "*Stay focused.*"

Wantemo's terse message did little to calm the icy dread pumping through his veins.

Isden swam alongside Sinto, his face reflecting the sickly orange light and eyes wide as saucers as he took in the immensity of what nature had spawned from Sapien-made plastics. A monster of their own creation, ready to consume a technologically advanced world.

Sinto gazed up at the school of Xiphias fighters, circling above like a pack of hungry tuna readying to feed on a swirling ball of herring. Audrey was in one of the Xiphias rigs. The Mark in his arm buzzed with anxiousness and a deep determination to end the monsters Arkis had spawned, emotions equally shared between the two of them. But a deeper emotion swirled inside him: dread. One chink to her Xiphias' armor and it would implode. The thought of her ripped to shreds gnawed at his heart. Her life, along with the others, hung in the hastily made enhancements Dyer and his crew implemented, should they encounter Orankai.

His thoughts must have leaked. Wantemo's voice threaded through his mind, "*Your mind strays... clear it of all but one purpose. If you and I fail we will* all *die.*"

Orange rose greedily, devouring the endless supply of plastic bundles that floated down from the surface as a concentrated trickle. As anticipated, the flat nebulous blob of Orange gathered into a concentrated mass, balling up into a misshapen sphere hovering a few hundred feet beneath the surface. An army of hundreds followed. Orankai rose, along with dozens of giant jellyfish with bellies swollen with Orange, all circling the blob like a planet with many moons.

They watched, camouflaged, with lorica masking their heat signature, as Orankai passed by, busying themselves with their harvesting as if the rising mass was something that frequently occurred, and apparently oblivious to their presence and the armed enemies circling above.

Wantemo gave the signal.

Sinto swam down and positioned himself beside Wantemo, hovering below the balling mass of Orange. Merahvu warriors took a post at each of the bladders. The call was made and the bladders were released, spilling their slimy cargo into the open sea.

Sinto and Wantemo linked minds and reached for the slimy organic substance. Together they melded with its biological structure.

Sinto was tickled by how easily the brig slime responded to their bidding. They began by gathering it beneath the mass of Orange like a flat sheet, then coaxed it to rise up and wrap around the mass of Orange, the hovering jellyfish, and the Orankai darting alongside—blind to the invisible barrier slipping by. Brig slime stretched and stretched until it rounded the top. With the pinch of Sinto and Wantemo's fingers, they zipped up the seam where the edges met, entrapping everything inside.

Merahvu warriors dove down and latched onto the surface of the completed biobrig, feeding it an initiating electrical charge. Once set, they scurried back. Then Sinto set the lock.

Inside the biobrig, Orange tentacles reached for the last few bundles of plastic sinking from above. The tentacles met resistance, recoiling from a powerful shock. The Orankai inside began to take notice that something was amiss. There was a moment of confusion, followed by the realization something was horribly wrong. They saw armed submarines circling above. The Orankai grew frantic, flinging themselves against the invisible barrier. But instead of bouncing off, they got stuck, and the electrically charged surface drew on their electrical reserves like the parasitic bands Arkis' guards once used on their captives.

Sinto was astounded at how easily the gamble worked. It felt strange; an anti-climactic end to an inconceivably complex foe. After the frantic rush for a solution and the last-minute panic that bio slime would fail, the tractability of the Orankai and how easily Orange was manipulated and trapped seemed surreal.

Screams of terror erupted from within the biobrig. Orange grew frantic with its new predicament and sought out other things to attack. It pushed aside the jellyfish and went straight for the Orankai. Tentacles wrapped around bodies and dragged them to its center. Orankai frantically thrashed to escape its greedy grip. Heads, arms, and legs popped to the surface before being pulled under, as if drowning in Orange.

Sinto was overcome by a sudden sense of disbelief as he watched Orange tear apart the Orankai and then the last of the jellyfish; a final battle won. Merluma was free and Arkis and Orange had been defeated.

Wantemo swam over to join Sinto and together they surveyed the biobrig's hold. The screams from within subsided till all that was left was a shriveled, misshapen ball of Orange.

Ryan and Wantemo didn't believe it would take long for Orange to starve and die. They estimated anywhere from as little as one day or up to a week.

Sinto and Wantemo checked the biobrig's lock one last time. It was sound and at no risk of breaking. Xiphiases circled on the surface waiting their turn to be plucked from the sea.

It was over, so they thought, and neither of them anticipated what happened next.

93

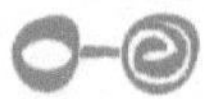

Kamikaze

AUDREY FELT THEM BEFORE they arrived—a gentle vibration, then a deafening buzz—reverberating through the hull of her Xiphias. They came as a swarm from far and wide, thousands and more, descending thick, fast, and angry, like hornets ripped from their nest. They didn't bother to camouflage. They didn't need to hide, because there were so many of them.

Arkis was gone but what he left behind was the mob he created, connected by hive-mind, primal and mindless, and seeking revenge from those who had cut off an essential life substance. Orange to them was like water to everyone else. Orange was the only thing left to keep them alive.

They far outnumbered the Merahvu warriors and Xiphias pilots milling around in a post-victory buzz, ready to board the ships.

Tucker's voice burst through her comm, "What the f—"

Then—

Complete and utter mayhem.

Audrey's Xiphias jolted violently. Swarmed by dozens of Orankai latching onto every possible extremity sticking out from Xiphias' outer structure. Angry faces pressed against the transparent dome above her head—male, female, young and old. Electricity rippled across Xiphias' outer wall and her batteries sucked up every bit before reversing the flow and blasting it outward in a single powerful burst. Dyer had added that automatic relief value during their trip across the Pacific.

Her Xiphias was suddenly clear. Dazed bodies littered the water surrounding her, and some burst into ash.

Audrey kicked her Xiphias into gear. There was a brief pause, then a shudder, then she began to spin like an out-of-control top. A mangled body cartwheeled away from her rear props and burst to ash. She wrangled control of the spin, then engaged the bill. It sprang from the nose like a sword drawn from its sheath, with jagged teeth glinting and hungry for flesh. She thrust and parried, slicing heads and appendages from bodies until she was surrounded by a cloud of blood and ash.

She raced for another Xiphias under attack, firing rounds of spears and poisoned darts front and rear. Bodies disintegrated; others bounced and reeled when she slammed into them.

The Mark in her arm crackled; Sinto was under attack too, fighting for his life, somewhere below and under great duress.

She instinctively pulled back on the throttle. *Big mistake!* A fresh batch of manic Orankai caught up and attacked. A ferocious back and forth of electrical current passed between metal and flesh. Audrey was jolted within her harness with each electrical punch. Sweat trickled from her brow and stung her eyes. Gasping for air, she fought back. The harder she punched back, the more agitated and aggressive the Orankai became.

The comms were alive with the calamity unfolding around her. They were drowning in hostile bodies. Screams rang out from other Xiphias pilots rendered helpless as their subs were stripped of prop and bill and the mob dragged them to the deep, beyond the depth limit Xiphias could safely endure. Screams were silenced as they imploded.

Tucker reeled off tactics and profanities.

Stokes and Francesca barked orders and told of unrelenting attacks to the ships on the surface above, of hand-to-hand combat unfolding on their decks.

Bombs rained from ships above. Concussions from their explosions battered the undersea combatants, killing some Orankai but stunning others only temporarily.

Another round of Orankai spotted her. Sinto's voice screamed in her mind, "*Run!*"

Audrey spun in wild circles, launching a constant volley of every weapon she had in her arsenal, killing many until she had no more ammunition.

And yet, they kept coming.

She ran for the surface, then felt a sudden jerk as her movement shuddered to a halt before starting to descend again. Orankai clung to her props. She punched with electricity. They punched back, rendering her defenseless. From below, a volley of spears sailed past, striking Orankai. They slithered away and she was able to burst free.

She spun to see who had helped her. Dyer. Angry Orankai rose from the depths and attacked him. They ripped away his pod drives and toroidal props. His bill was snapped free. The ease at which they striped his Xiphias was terrifying. Audrey punched every button hoping that maybe she missed a spare round of ammo. Depleted. All she had was her bill. She revved forward, back, twisted left, right, stabbing her bill toward bodies swarming around Dyer.

They sensed weakness and pounced on Dyer, ignoring her completely. His Xiphias was smothered. They dragged him to the deep.

She screamed for help, but no one responded. Everyone was fighting impossible numbers. She watched helplessly as the mob slithered and smothered and dragged more disabled Xiphiases to the deep.

Tears and sweat spilled down her cheeks. Dyer was but a speck and fading fast in the dark depths.

Dyer's voice faltered through her comm. "Tell Tucker he's a jerk—that I love him. Tell Ryan he's—he's the bomb. Tell Sinto he's lucky—that he deserves you—I regret you and I never—we would have been a hell of a team..."

"No!" She screamed. "You tell them! We are a team! Just—hold on—we're coming for you!"

Sinto fought for his life, tail swinging, merlux firing, yet the mob held onto him, determined to tear him apart limb from limb. He caught a brief glimpse of Audrey's Xiphias above covered by layers of Orankai scrambling across its surface, slavering for her death. Frustration and dread bloomed. He had never felt so helpless in his life.

A partially dismantled Xiphias slipped by, its occupant screaming. A mob of Orankai dragged it to the deep. It did not return.

A second disabled Xiphias slipped by. Sinto turned in time to glimpse Dyer through the transparent dome, his face fixed in a grimace.

Sinto tugged and burst free from the mob and swam to the dark depths. He grabbed a fin of what remained of Dyer's Xiphias. He pulled with all his might, tail whipping. The fin slipped from his grasp. He dove after it, landing on the transparent dome. Dyer gazed back shaking his head, tears streamed down his cheeks.

Dyer mouthed, *Love you, brother.*

Sinto was jerked back by the tail.

Dyer slipped deeper. Inside the red-lit interior he unclipped his harness, sat back with his hands braced against the console, and accepted the inevitable.

Dyer's Xiphias faded into the darkness as a pair of Orankai grabbed Sinto by the arms, yanking them in opposite directions, attempting to rip them from the sockets. He whipped his tail wildly, aiming for their heads, stunning them enough to break free.

He dove once again but was struck by the reverberation of crumpling metal. Dyer's Xiphias imploding.

The mob that had dragged Dyer down rose from the darkness and came after Sinto.

A third Xiphias was dragged down. He was unable to see who was inside.

Please not her...

Sinto fought to shake off the mob, stealing glances toward the surface where Orankai crawled across every remaining Xiphias, all slashing with razor sharp bills and firing volleys of explosive-tipped spears.

Bombs detonated. Shock waves rippled and jostled Orankai. Yet it was not enough to deter them.

Orankai kept coming.

Sinto sensed Audrey. She was alive and still fighting. Relief and anger fueled him. He used every means to break free from the mob—teeth to jugular, fingers to eye sockets, head to head, until his nose was bloodied. He wound his legs around necks, squeezing until they snapped. His tail whipped, cracking heads and snapping bones. He fired his merlux and released wallop after wallop of concentrated electrical fire until, finally, he overpowered the mob and broke free but with his reserves severely depleted.

He cut a short tunnel through the sea and dove in to escape the mob organizing for a second attack. Wantemo was fast behind him, then Isden and a small but determined contingent of Merahvu warriors who managed to escape.

From the fringe of the fight Sinto and the others witnessed the horror unfolding, stunned and speechless by the sheer numbers and ferocity of their enemy.

The biobrig containing Orange hovered sixty feet below the surface. Xiphiases circled to protect it from attack and engaged in close combat, bills whipping. Torpedoes, spears, and poison-filled darts found flesh. Blood and ash clouded the water.

Orankai streamed from far-off shores. The sheer numbers displaced the waters of the surrounding sea.

Bombs splashed down from Larkian ships with muffled explosions, dangerously close to the biobrig and taking their toll on nearby Orankai, giving Xiphias pilots a brief reprieve to regroup.

Oil seeped from the *Masquerade Ball* and darkened the surface, blotting out blades of light piercing the ocean from the new day's sun.

Sinto and Wantemo linked minds and reinforced the lock on the biobrig.

A corner of the fight stilled for a beat, as if hive-minds were calculating a shift in strategy. A group of Orankai peeled away, drawn to the biobrig with Orange trapped inside. They swarmed like hornets protecting a nest. They prodded. They hurled their bodies against its surface.

Sinto sensed a dramatic sea change about to happen as the entire mob's focus shifted, with the biobrig their new foe and the Orange inside their new target. The surface of the biobrig rippled, compressed, and stretched with each hurling blow. Threads of electrical current crawled along its surface, testing its defenses.

"*Will it hold?*" Sinto asked.

Wantemo replied, his thoughts heavy with despair. "*Looks doubtful.*"

There was a loud explosion above. *Masquerade Ball* heeled over and began sinking, stern first.

Sinto grew anxious. "*We must do something!*"

"*They are angry, we took away what they find most dear.*"

"*Obviously!*"

"*Perhaps we let them have it.*"

"*Releasing Orange will only make them stronger—*" Then the idea struck and he turned to Wantemo. "*Unless we open a small doorway, invite them inside.*"

"*They'll rip it wide open. We won't be able to control it from here.*"

"*I wasn't thinking of opening it from here.*"

Before Wantemo could stop him, Sinto cut a tunnel toward the biobrig, leaving Wantemo and the others in a cloud of fizzy bubbles.

Audrey jerked her Xiphias hard to port as the aft end of a sinking ship shifted and dropped, nearly taking her down. Through the transparent dome she caught sight of the ship's name; the *Masquerade Ball*, sinking quickly. Audrey popped to the surface.

Orankai crawled along the surface of the ship with Francesca and her crew trapped inside. Audrey opened the comm and called the ship, "Get out!"

Francesca answered in a frantic voice, "They'll rip us to shreds! We'll take our chances with the sea!"

"Tell me what to do!"

"Run! Save yourself!"

"No, we fight to the end, as agreed."

She flipped her comm channel. "Tucker, where are you?"

"A little busy here!" He was gasping from effort. In the background, she could hear the whine of prop and the drum of bodies attacking his Xiphias. "These fuckers keep coming!"

Exasperated, she reluctantly said it. "Is this where we switch to Plan B, as in the big *kaboom*?"

He didn't answer. Francesca did.

"Girl, what you suggest will release an ecological disaster and—" She sighed. "End us all."

"And those monsters!" Audrey said.

The tenor of Francesca's voice struck deep, a mother telling a child what to do. One where the child had best do it. "I said—*run!*"

Audrey swiped sweat from her eyes and did just that. She gritted her teeth and ran. "Take care of yourself, Francesca. I expect to see that brilliant smile again, and we're going to perfect your ship's greenhouse farm, together."

As she ran the Orankai retreated, slipping away from the last of the Xiphias fleet and toward the biobrig hovering close to the surface. Audrey searched for Sinto through the Mark, sensed him, alive and whole, and then she felt the crushing weight of his heavy heart; a decision made, a fate accepted.

Something bad was about to happen.

She turned around, went back, and dove.

Sinto wrestled a pathway through a sea of writhing bodies clinging to the biobrig. They ignored him, their minds focused toward a single purpose. He drew water through his gills, thick with the exhalations of so many others. He slithered between bodies, a crush of humanity, until finally his hands made contact with the surface. His fingers slipped through the slimy skin and he yanked, opening a large seam.

Orange reacted instantly. Tentacles reached out from its center, probing the weakened wall of its prison and seeking what was beyond. One found him, wrapped around his arm, and yanked him inside. The invitation he sought. Orankai followed in a relentless stream of bodies, bursting into the biobrig like a geyser letting off steam.

Audrey navigated her Xiphias to where Wantemo and the last of the Merahvu teams hovered, visibly shaken, gaping at the biobrig. Sinto was not among them. Isden looked over at Audrey, eyes connecting through her transparent doom. He pointed at the biobrig. Something indeed was happening. The biobrig was growing and the number of Orankai outside of it was shrinking. Orankai were diving inside through a rip in the biobrig's side.

The reality struck like a knife entering her chest. She gasped. Isden nodded, confirming her fear.

She slammed into gear only to be held back by Wantemo and the others. She screamed, fighting the controls, but they held fast until her hands shook so violently she could no longer grip the stick.

The Mark in her arm crackled and pulsed erratically.

Sinto was inside the biobrig, fighting, dying...

Sinto kicked, wagged, punched, and bit his way free from the tentacle yanking him down to the heart of Orange. Once free, he was a fish swimming up a stream, battered by frantic bodies diving inside the biobrig through the rip he created.

His body was on fire. The heat rising from Orange was unbearable, growing hotter with each new body it drew inside. His gills gasped for oxygen, thin and nearly non-existent. His heart threatened to burst from the physical effort and stress.

He kicked and crawled and punched until the fingers of his good hand found a tiny thread of brig slime fluttering from the seam he had split open. He squeezed tight, pulling himself up as high as possible, and reached up with his weakened hand, fingers teasingly close to the opening. He stretched and wagged his fingers, but the edge of the seam fluttered hopelessly out of his reach.

His body began to fail. His vision winked. His heart skipped. This was how he ended. He could hear Audrey's screams through the Mark, which was also straining under the stress. He fought to stay conscious, using what was left to form a final message of *salamora*—

He was yanked up by the arm. Isden straddled the seam on the outside, with Sinto's arm clasped in his hands. Orankai slithered through Isden's legs to get inside. He kicked them away and yanked Sinto from the heat and the carnage within to the shockingly cold sea outside.

A tentacle rose up and grabbed Isden by the leg, another by the waist, a third by the neck. It dragged him inside, into the mayhem, then down its gullet.

Sinto watched in horror, shocked by the suddenness of it. Isden was gone and there was nothing he could do to save him but to honor his sacrifice and finish what he had started. Sinto clung to the outside of the biobrig replenishing his breath as the last of the Orankai dove inside, driven by madness and the monster of addiction.

The heat of Orange and its tentacles of destruction plundered the bodies of its own creation. And after the last Orankai dove inside, Sinto sealed the seam, locked the door, and hid the key deep in his mind where no one could ever find it, not even himself.

94

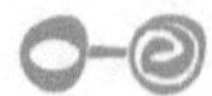

Celebration

THE BIOBRIG HELD. ORANGE eventually shriveled and died.

Reports from around the globe were still grim but with green shoots of encouragement. Wantemo and Dr. Wickman concluded that the addictive nature of Orange was less debilitating to Sapiens than to Merahvu. The effects of Arkis' wrath echoed but slowly tapered.

News feeds were filled with stories of grief for the millions lost and hope for those recovering from the bewildering array of unexplained deaths, random violence, suicides, and explosion of unfounded conspiracy theories that most of the Sapien world never clearly understood. The why of which the Larkians vowed to keep secret.

Audrey and Sinto stayed on the *Requiem Sea II* to monitor the decline and eventual death of Orange, a process that took five days. Yet joy was elusive. It was a time to mourn. Their hearts felt raw. It was too soon to celebrate, if ever. They were both numb from the harsh reality of all that had passed since they were reunited.

Audrey stood with her back to Sinto's chest, watching the ship's trailing wake fade to the northeast. White clouds peppered the sky, whose shadows painted a mosaic of varying shades of blue across a bumpy ocean. The ship's wings captured the warm breeze, powering them home toward Isla Salvación.

She nestled her face against Sinto's neck and he wound his arms tighter. "I should be happy. Why do I feel so sick inside?"

"Perhaps the senselessness of it all. Misguided intention, greed, the seduction of complete power... that's war. No one ever wins. Perhaps one day humanity will figure that out."

"I thought the Merahvu had it all figured out."

Sinto laughed. "We're the same, you and I, with the same human flaws."

"What if those flaws could be fixed?"

"Flaws innate in the very essence of who we are? That would take a miracle. Which, I might add, we just received and should be grateful for."

She sighed. "It's not a crime to wish for something more."

"Like what?"

"More empathy, for one... and the ability to see past our biases, resentments, and those innate cravings to attack one another when we don't get what we want; to reacquaint ourselves with the miracle of the natural world and embrace those things we don't understand; to not be afraid of the unknown but to accept it for what it is. Watching the creatures of Merluma fight to save Merluma—tiger fighting beside elk—that was truly inspiring, living beings working together to save a world they depend on. Afterward, they peacefully went their separate ways."

"And probably resumed eating each other."

She looked back to capture his gaze. "That's a bit morbid, don't you think?"

"It's the way it is—all creatures are part of the food web, part of the circle of life. Including us. One day you and I will be stardust, feeding a future universe, breeding a new form of life."

"I suppose..."

Audrey turned around to face him. "I agree we're the same but…" She slipped a finger inside his shirt and rubbed that place where his fluke was tucked tight along his shoulder. "Not entirely."

He kissed her, soft and tender. "Entirely enough, but for you I would give up my tail."

She slipped her fingers through his, fingering the soft translucent webbing. "And this?"

"Yup."

She pressed her hand to his chest where his merlux hummed and heart beat steady and strong. "And this?"

"Hmm, perhaps I would argue to keep that." He slipped an electrified finger beneath her shirt and circled her belly button, leaving a tingling wake. He teasingly slipped it beneath the top of her jeans, a gesture that set her smoldering. "Would you agree?"

She laughed, sliding her fingers along the transparent ridges of his gills along the side of his neck. His eyes sparked and beckoned for more.

She said, "Most certainly. That, and your magnificent markings. Those I would definitely keep."

His lips brushed hers. "Perhaps I should disrobe so you can do a more thorough inspection, just to be sure."

"Yes, perhaps you should, just to be sure."

~ ~ ~

The next day, the *Requiem Sea II* steamed into the harbor of Isla Salvación. The normally vacant slips were packed full of ships. Sadly, the *Masquerade Ball* was not one of them. Francesca's favored ship had lost its fight to stay afloat and sank. During the sudden retreat of the Orankai they were able to escape in their tender and were picked up by another ship.

The sound of music and laughter floated from shore. The island was alive with an air of celebration.

Audrey and Sinto disembarked, along with Ryan, Tucker, Wantemo, and Stokes, who had captained the ship back to home port along with what remained of the crew. They were a somber bunch reeling from the loss of their Larkian and Merahvu brothers and sisters.

Ianthe and Audrey's father were waiting on the dock to greet them. Alvarez and Rachel raced from the compound once they safely docked.

Mako and Poe arrived with leis of sweetly fragrant pua kenikeni flower. They were presented in a traditional Hawaiian welcome, followed by a hug and a kiss. It was a sweet and kind gesture that warmed Audrey's soul.

"Blake's waiting with Naiada for both of you at the south-side house," her father said.

After hugs and welcome-home greetings, Audrey and Sinto jumped in a UTV and raced to the house to join their siblings, still numbed by what had passed.

Naiada greeted them at the door. Sinto picked her up and spun her around, planting kisses on forehead, cheeks, and nose, Naiada giggling with glee. Audrey slipped past and found Blake on the lanai, sitting on the sofa, staring blindly at the sea. He smiled when she sat down beside him.

"Hi, sister." He grabbed her hand and kissed her knuckles, reached up and traced the lines of her face. "Funny how losing the sense to see and hear enhances another. I could *smell* you coming."

His voice sounded a little uneven and Audrey was unsure of the best way to respond, with him no longer able to see or hear after the incident on Andrew's Island. His eyes held a fixed gaze; both were glass, she had learned, and replicated to look exactly the same as those they had replaced. The cuts on his face had faded significantly, and the skin on his head that had been badly burned was freshly pink, with the rest shaved clean. He looked different, but was quite handsome bald.

She wrinkled her nose. "*I hope in a good way!*" she replied in mind-speak.

He continued to speak out loud. "Oh yes, sweet and spicy, like peaches and cinnamon—at least that's how Sinto describes it." His brow furrowed. "I hear things got rough."

A tear slipped down her cheek. "*We lost a third of our Xiphias pilots and many Merahvu warriors. Isden struck the final blow. Sacrificed himself to save Sinto, who secured the biobrig in the end after leading the Orankai to their death. And Dyer—*". She couldn't say it, much less think it, without giving pause. "*Dyer, he—he came to defend me—then they attacked him—I tried to fight them off—he's gone, I failed him.*"

Blake reached out and she leaned into his arms. "He's gone because monsters took him, not because of you. I'm sorry I wasn't there to help."

Her throat was thick with grief and she was thankful for mind-speak. "*I'm sorry you can no longer hear and see.*"

"Please, no pity. A whole new world has opened up for me. I can see and hear and much more than before."

She leaned back. "*How do you mean?*"

Sinto and Naiada emerged from the back door and sat down across from them.

Naiada piped up. "Through me."

Audrey and Sinto looked at each other puzzled.

Naiada leaned forward and set her hands on Blake's knees. "Do you want to tell them or shall I?"

Blake's lips slipped into a lopsided smile. "Naiada and I are *espoused.*"

Sinto raised a brow. "As in mated?"

Naiada said, "Not exactly. I vowed to be Blake's life companion, so what I see and hear and experience he equally experiences, through me, and vise-versa. We haven't worked out that other part of what being espoused may mean." Her pock-marked cheeks flushed. "Yet."

Blake turned his face toward Audrey, his perfect glass eyes capturing hers.

Audrey said, "So you can see and hear me now?"

"With Naiada by my side, as clearly as before."

"Is this what you want?" Sinto asked Naiada.

She nodded. "Blake sacrificed himself to save us, and he helped to free me, with Audrey, on Merluma. I am eternally grateful. Besides, we have so many interests in common! I've taught him to paint and he's taught me origami."

"And how to sail," Blake added.

"Right! And how to cook and how to beat Franz at *Portal 2*!"

"Naiada has taken me through many worlds in the Timeless Dimension."

She squeezed his knee. "And we dove together in the sea."

"Aye, we did," he said with a wry smile.

Naiada's eyes glowed with joy and infatuation. "And I look forward to learning so much more."

After sampling one of Naiada's kitchen creations, which was indeed surprisingly tasty, Audrey and Sinto left them on the lanai and took a long stroll on the beach. They walked hand in hand, toes splashing in waves licking the shore.

"Speaking of life companions..." Audrey said. "What about us, and... you know, the big commitment."

"Joining?"

"Mm-hmm."

"I see no rush at the moment."

"No angst on your part?"

"Oh, that. That's always there, like a swift current, tugging on my consciousness."

"But?"

"Like Naiada said, it's something to look forward to, our *yet*."

"So not *yet*."

He stopped walking, cradled her face and nuzzled her nose with his before kissing her. "Correct, not yet." His lips traced her neck. "But."

She giggled. "But what?"

They had rounded a rocky point to the beach where they first met as children and often sheltered in the shade of the curved palm tree—under which they were now standing—reading Audrey's favorite books together.

Sinto smiled and cast his gaze to the calm waters in the cove. "Remember when you once asked me if it was possible to make love in the sea?"

"I do."

"Would you like to find out?"

It was Audrey who pulled Sinto into the water.

After a long swim, Sinto pulled her under to demonstrate exactly how it was possible to make love in the sea without her drowning. Afterward, they returned to the house flushed and giddy to get ready for that night's planned celebration at the compound.

A note on the counter from Naiada said they would meet them there, having gone to visit their parents. Audrey and Sinto were grateful to be alone a little while longer, regardless of how much they loved their siblings. After so many forced separations since they were reunited last fall, they savored every moment to be alone.

The dining hall at the compound had been decorated for the night's celebration. Strings of lights looped from rafters and bouquets of flowers burst from pots spread around the room, their fragrant scent interlaced with the savory scent of the feast Leonard and Poe had prepared. Fans lazily swirled, moving the tropical air drifting inside through wide-open sliders.

Audrey and Sinto sat at a large round table with Blake and Naiada, Alvarez and Rachel, Stokes and a lovely Polynesian woman Mako recently introduced him to, and Ryan with the new love of his life. A woman recently recruited, along with others—saved, she often said—from the Middle East. She was part of Ryan's team that developed the biobrig slime and was highly educated in the sciences and grateful for the opportunity to apply her knowledge and skills as a Larkian. Her vivid green eyes and smoldering features glowed with equal infatuation toward Ryan.

At the table next to them, Ianthe and Audrey's father were seated with Tucker, Francesca, and Dr. Wickman and a quiet woman from Seattle he had met in university circles and had known for a long time. And, of course, Leonard, accompanied by a voluptuous shop owner from the village, both of whom were already well liquored-up and joyously sharing tales, some much taller than others.

Khani's voice boomed from the next table over in spirited conversation with Vesna and those who remained from their warrior teams. A lone chair stood vacant in Isden's honor, as did one at Ianthe and Culliford's table, next to Tucker, in honor of Dyer's sacrifice.

Champagne poured from an endless supply of bottles. Mako and Poe, who organized the event, jumped up and joined a local band playing Hawaiian-themed songs, with Poe performing the traditional hula and Mako strumming the guitar.

Much to Audrey's chagrin, Poe insisted she join her. It had been years since she practiced hula. Audrey's heart ached with longing as she recalled days past, learning the subtle movements of the traditional Hawaiian dance from her mother.

After a few stumbles, she found her rhythm in the soft steps and water-like flow of arm and fingers and sway of hips. In that moment of quiet movement and reflection, Audrey realized some things were never meant to be forgotten. Endearing memories of those most loved should be polished and put on display, like the movements she mirrored and once admired while watching her mother.

She swept her gaze across the faces filling the room and locked onto a familiar pair of glacial blue eyes, glistening and swelling with pride. She thought her heart might burst when her father nodded his seal of approval. A simple gesture she had pined for but never received, until now, after countless years of confrontation and challenges.

After an enthusiastic round of applause and several embarrassing calls for more, Audrey bowed out and jumped off the stage to join Sinto, who was grinning ear to ear.

Tucker slipped from his seat and knelt beside her. "Now that was *badass*. I could never top that. You've earned that hat, more than once. It's yours, forever." He knuckled her head and gave her a kiss on the cheek, then stood and gave Sinto a solid pat on the shoulder. "You're a lucky man, Sinto."

Soon the tempo shifted; acoustic was switched to electric and a new set of musicians took the stage and ripped into some seriously loud and rocking music. They danced and hugged and partied until the wee hours of the morning. With the help of pulsing music, the company of friends, and delightful libations, the horrors from the past months melted away.

Tomorrow a new day would dawn and life would begin anew.

But as much as Audrey might wish that to be true, a kernel of unease lingered. A sense of something left undone. A something that simmered, impatiently, waiting to be fixed. And based on the tremor she felt through the Mark, she knew Sinto felt it too.

95

The Joining

SINTO WAS AWAKENED BY a sudden jolt and violent shaking. Glass shattered and the bed on which he lay with Audrey rumbled across the floor and slammed into the wall, knocking them both to the floor.

A bookshelf toppled, blocking the inner door. Naiada screamed from the other bedroom. Sinto and Audrey stumbled across tempered glass pebbles from the shattered sliding door and onto a bucking lanai.

Inside the house, Naiada was helping Blake navigate from the sofa in the living room to the back door. Sinto grabbed Naiada, then Blake, and they stumbled off the lanai and crossed to the beach. They fell to hands and knees as the ground beneath them shuddered continuously.

Audrey clung to a sheet wrapped around her naked body, mouth agape in disbelief. Blake clung to Naiada's hand, glassy gaze sweeping the sky. He wore nothing but a pair of boxers. Both Sinto and Naiada were in their natural form, as they were accustomed to sleeping that way.

Palms whipped and the bay danced with frantic confused waves under the new day's dawn, glowing faintly from the east.

They watched as the small house Audrey grew up in swayed and squeaked. A corner buckled, then a wall. Cracks and pops erupted as the Earth rumbled, a minute became five, and still the ground shook. They watched in horror as the roof buckled and the house collapsed.

A scream formed in Audrey's mouth but came out as a gurgle. Sinto felt her grief as the house where she was born and that held her most precious memories was reduced to rubble.

Sirens blared in the distance. A solid stream of Larkian ships raced from the harbor and into the open sea.

Sinto whispered, "Tsunami. We must warn the others."

Naiada placed her hand to his chest. "They know. We need to seek higher ground."

The shaking finally subsided and they ran to the carport. The roof had fallen atop the larger UTV, but the other was free and clear. Audrey jumped into the driver's seat, Blake with Naiada on his lap in the passenger side. Sinto remained standing.

Audrey gave him a pleading look. "What are you doing? There's room in the back."

"The tsunami. I can stop it, or at least mute its full impact to the island. Go on ahead, I'll find you."

She hopped out. "No, I'm staying with you, now and forever, no matter what."

Sinto opened his mouth to argue but by the determined way Audrey was gazing back he knew nothing he said would change her mind.

Naiada hopped out. She grabbed Sinto's hand and pulled him aside. She shared a persistent vision she had experienced many times. Something he knew all along, but had suppressed, afraid of the truth of it. A reality that could no longer be ignored. No words were passed. There was no need. Naiada nodded, confirming this undeniable fact.

He embraced his sister, for what might be the last time. "*Salamora*, forever. Wherever, whenever."

Audrey picked up on the vibe bleeding through the Mark. Tears welled in her eyes as she hugged Blake goodbye. "Be safe, brother. Wherever, whenever."

He squeezed her hand. "You too, sister. *Salamora.* Now go. Finish what should have been done long ago."

Sinto grabbed Audrey's hand as Naiada and Blake drove away and disappeared around the bend of the road. Audrey found the flower-print dress she wore the night before, cast haplessly aside after Sinto had dragged her down to the sand in a passionate joining of bodies before they went inside to retire. She dropped the sheet from her body and slipped the dress on.

Together they crossed exposed sand, rock, and reef until they finally reached the edge of the retreating water. Sinto looked at her, deeply troubled. He shook his head. "There is nothing we can do to stop it. No one can. Yesterday you asked the question of when would be the right time to complete the Joining, our *yet.* That time is now, but it's not meant to happen here." He gazed at the water, strangely calm and slowly slipping away from the shore, gathering somewhere out at sea.

Sinto encapsulated them with a gelatinous cocoon and soon they were flying through the sea.

It didn't take long before they emerged next to the reef that grew from the bones of an old sunken sailing ship, exposed by the unnatural ebb of the Salish Sea.

Naiada had told him that nowhere on Earth had been spared the earthshake or receding ocean waters. To where the waters receded, she was uncertain. She was just as uncertain whether the water would return at all.

Smoke rose from fires on the mainland and across the surrounding islands. Earth was burning, the air thick with it.

Sinto led Audrey through a forest memorized by heart, climbing over fallen trees and leaping over fresh cracks in the ground. The bunker door was cracked open, the frame skewed.

"Wait here," Sinto told Audrey. Then he slipped through the door and into the darkness, stumbling over debris cast to the ground by the trembling earth. He returned with both stones cradled in his arms, one wrapped in the green blanket, the other in a broad leaf with vines securing it.

He led her up the ridge to that place where he once called to her on Merluma and Francesca had mourned the loss of her lover, Andi.

He set the blanket on a bed of moss and unfolded it. He tore the leaf off the other one and lay the stones beside each other. Earth stones, cast from the bowels of Earth and Merluma, each glowing faintly. One amber, one green. The one his mother had found in the Salish Sea, and the other that Arkis had found in the waters of Inception.

They were jolted by a loud explosion. Mount Baker, forty-five miles to the east, erupted, spewing ash and boulders into the sky, pummeling nearby communities. The entire North Cascades rumbled, awakening the dormant and not-so-dormant volcanoes up and down the Cascade chain stretching from Canada to Oregon. Earth was tearing itself apart. Naiada confirmed his fear before they left and shared a reoccurring vision. A truth he had suspected but ignored.

The end of their respective worlds was nigh.

He motioned for Audrey to kneel across from him with the stones in between. He gazed into her eyes, their hearts pounding in synchronized rhythm.

He grasped her hands and said, "These stones represent us, our worlds—Earth and Merluma, Sapien and Merahvu. Long ago Earth attempted to spawn a replica of itself but something went wrong. A seed meant to travel far across the universe and birth a new Earth in a duplicate solar system never made it. That seed got stuck, here, in the Salish Sea and cracked open, forming Merluma, Earth's unnaturally conjoined twin. It was always a matter of time before the imbalance would tear them apart and disrupt the part of the galaxy of which Earth and Merluma are a part, destroying all within the solar system and beyond."

"The wobble Blake told me about."

"Yes."

"So this is the end."

He cast a watery gaze toward a wall of ash blowing in their direction. They had very little time until it would consume them completely. "So it would seem."

She drew a shaky breath. "How utterly unfair."

"For us, for everyone. But Naiada told me she didn't believe it needed to be so." He gazed down to the stones. "These stones hold the truth as to how to fix it."

"And what is that truth?" Her voice quivered. "How can we possibly fix *this*?"

He shook his head. "She didn't know exactly, just that we must try."

"Try, how?"

"She believes by Joining."

"Why now? Why not before all the angst and meaningless death we've gone through?"

"She believes that everything that has passed before was in preparation for the right moment. Something about righting the balance, about which she was quite adamant. Before now was too soon. Everything we have accomplished in this conflict has struck the right balance... that moment is now."

Audrey gazed down at the stones whose centers were swirling like electrified smoke, amber and green, like earth and water.

"It's like déjà vu," she whispered.

Sinto quirked a brow.

"The night I Marked you at Club Ballo and the Mark presented itself. Hovering above us, the orbs you said represented each of us. Memories and experiences in our life and the lives of our ancestors passed down through us, everything that represented the essence of ourselves. Our souls. Look at the stones, don't they look strangely reminiscent of that?"

She was right, they did look like the orbs presented that night. He looked up, a tiny bit hopeful that, indeed, Joining was the solution. "Yes."

Her eyes brightened. "What if they're not stones, but *seeds*, like the one that got stuck and formed Merluma?"

He gazed at a wall of ash racing toward them. "Then we should free them."

He took her hands and set one on each stone, then he did the same, twining their pinky fingers.

Her eyes met his. A wave of sorrow and grief for their dying worlds passed between them, followed by a blanket of love and peace, warm and sweet and engulfing, knowing they would end, together. Their hearts quivered with the terror and uncertainty of what it meant to die. Tears slipped from Audrey's eyes, mirrored by Sinto's own.

She gulped and said, "Flow as water."

"Swift as wind..." echoed Sinto.

They leaned forward, breath shared, and together they whispered, "Fierce as fire."

Then their lips melted together in a final kiss.

The Marks in their arms burst into flame with a rush of sparkling ash. The seeds beneath their hands cracked open, releasing a blinding explosion of energy and light that cut through the galaxy.

Audrey and Sinto orbit a fiery sun in a star-studded sky, their ethereal selves gazing back at the broken pieces of Earth and Merluma. Rock and dust spark and swirl, folding in on itself in an endless crush of destruction, forming a single, dense black thing from which nothing can escape.

It grows tinier and tinier and tinier until it is merely a pin-prick of darkness, hovering.

Waiting.

Then comes a question in resonating voices from the depth of the darkness, voices Sinto has come to know as that of the Earth Stones.

Which threads shall we weave?

Audrey finds the question odd, but Sinto understands the Stones' terse unique language and explains it to Audrey, as once his mother explained it to him.

Audrey and Sinto briefly confer and answer the Stones, together in spirit.

Balance. Compassion. Harmony.

Is that all? *the Stones ask.*

No, *Audrey replies,* More humor and less... violence.

And *friendly* competition, *Sinto adds.*

Then it shall be, *the Stones reply.*

Time stills, but only briefly, then the dense black thing swells once more, filling their vision.

It grows and grows and grows—painted with swaths of blue and green, white and brown—and engulfs the stardust that is Audrey and Sinto. In a final spasm, the brilliant orb turns inside out and releases Everything trapped inside its core to populate this new world. Things inanimate, things alive, things remade—all that existed before, but nothing quite like it was.

EPILOGUE

World Remade

IN A FIELD OF wildflowers under a bright blue sky, Audrey and Sinto dozed on a blanket. Lying cheek to cheek with their bodies spread in opposite directions, Audrey stirred to a lazy awakening.

A large black bird with a crown of red feathers swooped, casting its long shadow across where they rested. Its eyes flickered white and blue and it chirped in greeting as it flew by.

Audrey took notice, wondering how oddly familiar the bird seemed. A sense of déjà vu filled her mind—of the bird gazing at her with those strange eyes on a white-sand beach, a copper chain with a single green stone clasped around its neck. Her nostrils suddenly filled with the briny scent of the sea and she could clearly hear the clack of palm fronds as if suddenly transported to a faraway land.

A soft voice threaded through her mind, "*Merluma...*"

She gasped at the oddity of it.

Sinto stirred and asked, "What is it?"

But the elusive memory slipped away as suddenly as it had presented itself, as did the word she thought she heard.

A memory much more top of mind was of their recent lovemaking, from which her heart still thundered and body tingled.

How she felt in the final throws, a sensation she had never felt before, of every cell in her body being turned inside out, of the universe exploding and being reborn, before opening her eyes to a clear blue sky and the scent of the earth blooming around them. She felt different and renewed.

She wondered if Sinto felt the same tingling sensation that reverberated through her body like ripples in a pond, bouncing back and forth, shore to shore, to infinity. He turned to face her and by the way his lips curled she knew he felt it too, just as vividly. They lay a bit longer, gazing deeply into each other's glowing eyes, lost in the afterglow of their lovemaking.

The bird cawed and broke the connection.

Audrey blinked, noting the low angle of the sun in the sky. "Oh no, what time is it? We must get going."

Sinto rolled his body around to lie by her side, "Audrey, you didn't answer my question."

Audrey sat up and pinched his chin between her knuckles. "It was nothing, really. We must go. Ianthe will never forgive us for being late!"

Sinto pulled her atop him, his merlux buzzing in his chest. "She can wait."

They shared a passionate kiss.

Reluctantly, she broke it off. "Very tempting, but so can you, my love. Twice is enough for now; we'll save thrice for later." She playfully nipped his lip then rolled to her feet.

Sinto watched as she gathered their clothes, her bronze skin still buzzing from a surge of electricity flowing through her veins. Sinto had a way of sparking her merlux by simply looking at her.

Heat bloomed on her cheeks. "We shouldn't take such risks, out here, in the open."

He rolled to his side, head propped by bent arm. "What, that the Unis might roam by to see how us humans do it?"

"You know how horny that alpha Uni is. He doesn't need any more incentive. I'd hate to be trampled underfoot by him chasing down his mare unaware of what lay at his feet. But no, not for that reason."

She pulled her dress over her head, stopping briefly to finger the tropical floral pattern printed on it. It too, like the bird, invoked a distant memory. Of her wearing this same dress while rushing through the sea to an island, of their hands pressed to fiery stones, the two of them sharing a desperate last kiss... Just a tickle of a memory, there, then gone.

She shook off the sensation and continued, "What if someone saw us. Oh, the scuttlebutt!" She spread her arms wide. "Mayor Sinto taking his Scientific Councilor among the wildflowers—rather vigorously I might add—for all the world to see!"

Sinto chuckled. "Might earn me more votes in the next election. Better yet, give me a boost for my future run for Governor of the Salish realm."

She tossed him his pants. They bounced off him and plopped to the ground, where he lay teasingly naked. "You are impossible! Think of me and the humiliation of facing my protégés."

He stood, ringed her waist with his hands, and hitched her hips to his. "I confess. I could not help myself. What better way to end a romantic picnic." He crinkled his nose. "Besides, the crackers were stale and the cheese stinky and blue with mold."

She laughed. "The cheese was the finest the Wekeeps have to offer. It's supposed to be stinky and blue with mold, and it was thin-sliced salt-bread, not crackers. You certainly liked their honey wine. Slurped it down like a fish!"

"Me, a fish?" He peered over his shoulder to his bare and quite spectacular backside. "See, not a fish. I have no tail."

"And if you did?" She traced her fingers across his unique markings, embossed swirls and dots, peppered across his bare shoulders and down his spine to his buttocks. Sinto did the same to her, circling the edges of a rose-shaped petal at the base of her neck.

"I suppose that would make me a Merman and I would have to steal you away to my secret lair at the bottom of the sea."

"And then what?"

He nuzzled her lips. "I'd have my way with you, again and again."

"And after that?"

He sighed. "I suppose having chosen you as my mate I'd have to take you to meet my mother, Queen of the Mer Kingdom."

"So in this fantasy, you are a prince? That's quite a story! That would mean—"Audrey paused as a detailed and very real vision swirled through her mind. Of her and a tailed version of Sinto swimming through an underwater city beneath a magnificent dome with a mock sun shining down on coral-shaped buildings with strawberries and fragrant roses growing in between. A grand tower shimmered with gold, silver, and copper in the distance.

Sinto shook her. "Hey, are you okay?"

Audrey blinked and shook her head. "Sorry. Just a little lightheaded. Probably from too much wine."

Sinto grinned and ground his hips against hers. "Or maybe from something else."

She blushed, handed him his pants, and began braiding her thick dark hair. "I will admit, you do have quite the imagination and extraordinary stamina."

His eyes sparked. "Because of you."

They rolled up the blanket, gathered their unfinished picnic and empty wine bottle, and strolled, arms linked, to the polished obsidian lot where they parked their hover-rover, designed and gifted to them byAudrey's brother Blake.

Sinto secured their things inside a small storage compartment beneath the seat.

His eyes flashed with electrical energy when he pressed his finger to the surface of the crystal-like stone that powered the rover. It came to life with a soft green glow, the same color as Sinto's eyes. He swung his leg over and settled in the seat. Audrey slipped in behind him and wound her arms around his waist, squeezing her thighs to his. It felt like coming home.

Sinto spun around to gaze into her eyes. "Do we really have to go? I'd rather stay here in the country; the city can be... so busy."

"We talked about this already. Of course you have to go. It's Naiada's coronation. The entire world will be watching! Friends we haven't seen in a long time will be there! Ryan, Rachel and Salvo, Tucker, your mentor Wantemo, Francesca, Leonard, and Dr. Wickman. And don't forget, Franz and Snooki and their Wekeep clan. Our families have been planning this for months and your mother would be especially upset if the Mayor of Tallamure—Naiada's brother!—missed it. Don't forget, you promised to walk her down the aisle."

He rolled his eyes. "Merely a formality; she's been in charge longer than anyone would know." He paused. "Shouldn't Blake be the one to walk her down the aisle?"

"They're merely pledged, and in the case of an unwed queen, it falls to her closest family member to honor her in that way." She poked him in the back. "That means you."

She picked a crushed flower stuck in a golden lock of his hair. "You'll need to clean up first." She slapped his backside. "So make haste."

He grinned. "In that case, hold on."

They hooked their feet on elevated pegs and the rover took off like a jet, hovering inches above a road of polished obsidian embedded with the magnomeasium that enriched these lands and gave the rover its loft.

They passed open fields of grain and grazing goats, then the rich woodlands where the Wekeep farmed and settled. A fast-running river snaked alongside the road as it poured down from distant snow-capped mountains toTallamure, the capital city of the Salish realm.

The city emerged in the distance, a vital community with dwellings smothered in green foliage. Sea glitter lighted the Salish

Sea at city's edge, and further still, an archipelago of islands where the seafaring Larkian moored their sleek sailing vessels and called the islands their home.

Audrey pressed her cheek to Sinto's back, savoring the wind whipping through her hair. Strange, dreamlike images floated through her mind. Feelings and snippets of what felt like another life, a much harder one than this, filled with frustration and regrets. She let her eyes slide shut and let the strange vision drift away with the wind, grateful for Sinto as their future together spread before them.

She couldn't imagine wanting anything different from what she had, what they all had, right now. Each other. Family. Safety. A world in balance. And the profound settling of heart and mind that only love and peace can bring.

A Bit of History and Acknowledgments

I HAD NO IDEA where Audrey's and Sinto's journey would lead when I wrote the first draft of *Flow As Water* in 2009 (originally titled "Emissary"). I was a writer who didn't know what I was doing, blindly scribbling words into scenes as I imagined them, coming in brief random flashes while running, or pulling weeds in the garden, or mindlessly driving to the store for groceries. And from these ideas more words flowed. I was on a journey to what I hoped would be an exciting and worthy conclusion.

I didn't know it at the time, but many writers call this "writing into the dark." A method that can be thrilling but also frustrating when it leads you into an impossible corner. But writing this way has its rewards. The gold lies in the hills of gray matter. It's a special kind of gold, alive and fleeting. It can't be mined. It is illusive, only revealing itself when you least expect it while in a creative mind-flow state.

By entering this darkness of mind, I found joy and sorrow, tears and laughter. I forged onward until I had my first novel. I went to writer conferences, shopped it around to agents and editors. Got interest, submitted my manuscript, and received many rejections. Rewrites followed. I knew I was onto something. But. When I set out to write book two, I lost the thread of the story. My characters became strangers to me. It took some soul searching, but I realized they weren't the problem. The problem was me. So I set this project aside when I realized I lacked the writing skills I needed to truly express Audrey's and Sinto's story. So I got to work. I took writing classes, I experimented with my writing (nothing I'd care to publish), I researched (I LOVE science), I read and read some more, and I studied the masters—the *bestsellers*. And followed the journey of risk-taking independently published "Indie" authors.

Fast forward to 2021, a time when the world was still sifting through the disruption of Covid. A great time to write, right? Not for me. I had honed my writing skills. I was ready! But I was lost, my head-space was distracted, perhaps the same as many others, wondering about the future. My future. Enter my rock. It happened serendipitously. A simple phone call. Me spilling my frustration. I got the nudge, was reminded what I was capable of. And like Rachel giving Sinto advice, I was told: "Get your shit together." But it wasn't Rachel giving me this advice, or who made me face the thing holding me back—courage—it was my sister, Lynn Nansen-Dale.

And with that courage came trust. Trust in myself; to let the story flow in gushes or dribbles, to be surprised, to find joy (and horror) in what ultimately poured from my fingers. That first draft provided a framework. Then my characters revealed their true identity. New ones surfaced. And the Earth Stones Trilogy was born.

Lynn has been my rock throughout this journey. Always patient. She helped me work through those impossible corners. She listened to my rants. She fixed my words. She drew maps and symbols. She converted my words into beautiful books, electronic and printed. She advised on the covers, the blurbs, and I'm certain there will be more she'll be involved in long after I write this acknowledgment. Lynn, you are my gold nugget.

And Lynn and I wouldn't be here if it wasn't for our parents: Ralph and Phyllis Nansen, who helped plant gold in my mind. A rocket engineer and opera singer, dragging along their three kids between Seattle and New Orleans; between houses remodeled and schools whose names remain fleeting. The dirt was ever fresh under our feet, jostling any fears of complacency. They endured hardships and built the boat that set them to sea; then lived their dream of sailing the world. Words alone cannot express the magnitude of my appreciation for the examples they set, for the support they offered as I ventured into the world as an adult. So hear my *Salamora*, wrapped in love and tears. I love you and miss you greatly, Mom and Dad, and regret I was not able to finish the Earth Stones story in time for you both to read it.

Many other people helped with the Earth Stones Trilogy. My first beta readers to my most current. My ARC team. My technical advisers. My family and friends.

Dana Cram, thank you for the beautiful artwork on the covers. You continue to amaze me with your artistic talent!

Stephanie Cariker, my communications consultant, who continues to spread her magic in helping me promote my stories to the outside world.

A special thank you, my dear readers, for choosing to take this wild and crazy journey alongside Audrey and Sinto.

And lastly, my husband, Doug, who is ever present in my life, and in my characters. Doug is more than just a gold nugget. He's the entire mine.

With the conclusion of the Earth Stones Trilogy, my headspace has calmed. Audrey and Sinto are at peace and we have parted on favorable terms, with an emotion-filled *Salamora*. And within the void, new voices have risen. And I am having a blast writing their story.

Stay tuned and informed of future releases, featuring these new voices at lisacram.com.

May I ask you for a favor?

Reviews serve a dual purpose: to help readers find new authors, and independent authors, such as myself, connect to a community of new readers. I would be forever grateful if you could leave an honest review, if possible, wherever you acquired this book and/or on goodreads.com.

You can learn more of what I'm up to at my website: www.lisacram.com. Subscribe for important announcements and upcoming releases.

May you always find words to bring you joy, entertainment and wisdom!

Lisa

About the Author

Raised on a Louisiana bayou and the evergreen-cloaked shores of Puget Sound, Lisa Cram spent most of her life on the water, fantasizing about what lay beneath. The Earth Stones Trilogy is her debut as a writer. When not writing, you might find her reading, immersed in the outdoors, swinging a golf club, or her steel mace to raucous music. She divides her time between the Pacific Northwest and the California desert with her musician husband.

For news on upcoming releases from Lisa, visit lisacram.com